SUSAN JOHNSON

"Her romances have strong, intelligent heroines, hard, iron-willed men, plenty of sexual tension and sensuality and lots of accurate history. Anyone who can put all that in a book is one of the best!"
—*Romantic Times*

"No one . . . can write such rousing love stories while bringing in so much accurate historical detail. Of course, no one can write such rousing love stories, period."—*Rendezvous*

"Susan Johnson writes an extremely gripping story. . . . With her knowledge of the period and her exquisite sensual scenes, she is an exceptional writer."—*Affaire de Coeur*

"Susan Johnson's descriptive talents are legendary and well-deserved."—*Heartland Critiques*

"Fascinating . . . The author's style is a pleasure to read."—*Los Angeles Herald Examiner*

Susan Johnson

TEMPORARY MISTRESS

BANTAM BOOKS
New York   Toronto   London
Sydney   Auckland

TEMPORARY MISTRESS
A Bantam Book / November 2000

All rights reserved.
Copyright © 2000 by Susan Johnson.
Cover art copyright © 2000 by Alan Ayers.

No part of this book may be reproduced or transmitted in any form or by
any means, electronic or mechanical, including photocopying, recording,
or by any information storage and retrieval system, without permission in
writing from the publisher. For information address: Bantam Books.

ISBN 0-553-58253-4

Published simultaneously in the United States and Canada

Bantam Books are published by Bantam Books, a division of Random
House, Inc. Its trademark, consisting of the words "Bantam Books"
and the portrayal of a rooster, is Registered in U.S. Patent and Trademark Office and in other countries. Marca Registrada. Bantam Books,
1540 Broadway, New York, New York 10036.

PRINTED IN THE UNITED STATES OF AMERICA
OPM   10 9 8 7 6 5 4 3 2 1

Dear Reader,

Temporary Mistress came to life as a fleeting image in my mind. In a shadowed room with candles flickering and malice heavy in the air, an elderly lawyer is reading a will. A young woman is weeping, her grandfather having died only recently. But her relatives are untouched by sorrow, for their niece and cousin is delegated sole heir of a fortune they wish for themselves, and bitterly resentful, they regard her with hatred.

That was the first time I saw Isabella Leslie and I could tell she was going to need some help.

At the same time, Dermott Ramsay, Earl of Bathurst, is gambling in London's finest brothel, unaware of Isabella or her problems and indifferent, in any event, to all but the pursuit of pleasure.

An unlikely pair to ever meet.

Except for the hand of fate and the feeling I had that they'd enjoy getting acquainted.

I hope you enjoy the course of their friendship too.

Best wishes,

Susan Johnson

1

April 1802

THE STEADY DRIZZLE had turned to a downpour ten minutes earlier and the lady clinging to Dermott Ramsay on the high-lurching seat of his racing phaeton was not only thoroughly drenched but furious. Which meant he'd have to set her down at the next inn, practically ensuring Hilton a win in their race to London. Damn Olivia anyway. He'd not wanted to bring her along, but she'd coaxed with such enticing fervor as they lay naked in her absent husband's bed that morning, he'd found his better judgment overruled by lust.

Again.

Damn.

He squinted into the driving rain, the road barely visible through the deluge, but his Thoroughbreds were running strongly despite the rough going, and if his racing phaeton didn't snap an axle, by the grace of God and some damned fine driving he *would* have won the race.

"Ram!" the countess screamed, her nails biting through the fine wool of his coat as the carriage hit a pothole and tilted crazily. "Put me down this instant!"

For a fleeting moment he was tempted to do just that, but he was a gentleman for all his faults and couldn't indulge his wishes and leave her in the middle of the muddy road. He raised his voice enough to be heard against the storm. "I'll set you down at The Swan in Chaldon."

"It's too far!"

While he agreed, it wasn't as though he had another option. Forcing himself to a politesse he was far from feeling with his chance of winning virtually destroyed, he shouted, "Just ten minutes more and you'll be dry!"

"I should never have let you talk me into coming along! Look at my bonnet and gown!" she cried. "And the state of my . . ." Her voice died away, the glance he shot her way chill enough to silence even the overweening vanity of London's most celebrated beauty.

The rest of the wet, miserable journey to Chaldon passed in silence.

Bringing his matched pair to a plunging stop outside the entrance to The Swan, the Earl of Bathurst tossed his reins to an ostler and leaped to the ground. He was around to the countess's side in a few racing strides, his arms lifted to catch her. Carrying her inside, he bespoke a room, set her down, paid the innkeeper a generous sum over and above the required amount to assure his companion would have every comfort, and bowed to the lady who had cost him not only the race but a ten-thousand-guinea wager. "I'll send my carriage for you in the morning." Without waiting for a reply, he strode back outside.

Hilton had passed him, of course. He'd been close on his heels since Red Hill. Dermott didn't need the ostler's report to know he'd been bested. Softly cursing, he tossed the man a guinea, vaulted back onto the phaeton seat, and snatched up the reins.

It wasn't as though he'd not been behind in a race before, he thought, taking heart from the instant response of his powerful grays. Their will to win matched his, and his Thoroughbreds and custom-made phaeton had garnered more than their share of racing wagers in the past few years. "Come on, sweethearts," he crooned, leaning forward on the high-perched seat, knowing they recognized not only his voice but his urgency. "Let's see if we can catch them."

Their ears pricked forward, then twitched as though signaling their acknowledgment, and their strides lengthened.

A half hour later, Hilton's phaeton rose out of the gray mist, the outline faint in the distance. Dermott's nostrils flared as though catching the scented hint of victory. He'd raised his grays from foals and knew them as well as he knew his own family. Better, his mother would complain on occasion. "Here we go now, darlings," he murmured, letting the reins slide through his gloved fingers, giving his racers their heads.

It was a slow, laborious undertaking with Hilton's horses renowned for their speed. But Dermott's team slowly gained ground, and when they were within passing range, Hilton did what any driver who wanted to win would do. He moved squarely into the center of the road.

Boldness was required now, perhaps a rash tempting of providence as well with the possibility of an approaching carriage ever present. Not to mention the threat of a hidden pothole lying in wait to snap a horse's leg, or the critical question of passing space. But long celebrated for his audacity, the young Earl of Bathurst had been recklessly testing the limits of self-destruction for over a decade.

He began easing his grays to the left, the surface quagmire looking a modicum better on that side.

Hilton moved left as well.

The earl countered by directing his team to the right.

After a quick glance over his shoulder, the Duke of Hilton immediately blocked Dermott's attempt to pass on the right, and a continuing shift from left to right and back again ensued for the next several miles—at tearing speeds. Dermott watched Hilton's Yorkshire chestnuts for signs of fatigue, aware of Hilton's rough hands, his habit of hauling on the reins playing havoc with his horses' mouths and confidence. He could see Hilton's team jostle against each other several times, their momentary distress evident. And then suddenly Dermott saw his chance, the shoulder of the road ahead widening for perhaps a hundred yards. With boldness he swung his team over, forcing them into the meager space.

At times like this, nerve alone prevailed. Either Hilton or Dermott would have to give way. Dermott's grays valiantly obeyed his command, plunging forward as if they had the open downs before them instead of an impossibly narrow passage.

When the duke realized Dermott's intent, he held his ground, although his gloved hands nervously tightened on the reins and his mouth narrowed into a grim line.

"Get out of the way!" Exhilaration resonated in Dermott's cry, and a madcap triumph that overlooked all but the thrill of winning. The grays responded with a surge of power, mud flying from their pounding hooves, their courage and heart surmounting the foul weather and wicked footing.

The phaeton wheels inched closer and closer as Dermott began drawing even with the duke, disaster only a hairbreadth away now, the possibility of slipping sideways in the treacherous mire not only real but likely. It was a moment when a prudent man might contemplate whether such a race was worth one's life.

A second passed, two, then three, the racing horses neck and neck, the phaeton wheels slicing through the soft roadbed, the drivers so close, they could have touched whips.

The vehicles careened over the crest of a hill and the dangerous, infamous Danner curve suddenly loomed.

Death faced them head-on.

Hilton hauled on his reins.

Dermott smiled and shot past.

An hour later the earl dropped into a sprawl at one of the gaming tables in Molly Crocker's opulent brothel, said "Hilton just lost ten thousand on our race from Crawley," and accepted the congratulations of his friends. He was soaked to the skin, his dark hair falling in damp, windswept curls to the limp linen of his shirt collar, his powerful body blatantly obvious beneath his wet, clinging clothing, his broad smile evidence of his high good spirits.

"So Hilton owes you ten thousand," a young man drawled.

"He does indeed." Dermott's grin was infectious. "He pulled off."

Another man looked up from perusing his cards. "He never did have your nerve."

Dermott shrugged. "Danner Curve changed his mind."

"You could have been killed!" one of the lovely ladies surrounding the gaming table cried out. The earl was a great favorite at Molly's, and the dangers of that section of road were well known.

"Now, why would I take a chance on being killed with you to come back to, darling Kate," Dermott replied with a smile. Catching a servant's eye, he signaled for a drink.

"Hilton's going to want a rematch." Everyone knew of the rivalry between the two men.

"As long as he pays, I'm willing."

"He don't like to pay."

"Too bad." Dermott had a habit of seducing the ladies Hilton fancied, although their dislike of each other had begun long before at Eton. "His papa left him plenty."

Kate had moved to Dermott's side. "You're going to be wanting a bath." Her voice had taken on a huskiness and, leaning over, she brushed his cheek with a kiss.

Lazily lifting his arm, Dermott gently cupped the back of her head and, turning his face, kissed her back. "Give me a half hour, darling, to drink some of Molly's fine brandy," he murmured a moment later, his breath warm against her mouth.

"I'll be waiting," she purred, sliding from his grasp,

standing upright in a stirring of cerise silk muslin that set off her pale skin and dark hair to perfection.

"Pleasant thought," Dermott murmured, lifting his glass to her. "I won't be late."

"She doesn't even see anyone else," a young noble complained after Kate walked away. "Deuced selfish of you, Bathurst, to keep her for yourself."

Dermott raised his palms in disclaimer. "Acquit me, Kilgore. I'm not concerned with exclusivity."

"You should tell her, then," the young man grumbled.

"I think my feelings on that subject are clear."

"Hear, hear, Kilgore," one of the men interposed. "Not a person in the ton don't know Dermott's not in the market for permanence. And Kate makes up her own mind whom she favors. Now, I've got a damned good hand here, so stop your grousing and deal us another card or two. Are you in or out, Bathurst?"

"In, of course." Dermott grinned. "At least for half an hour."

The small candlelit study was filled with the relatives of the man who had recently died upstairs. They sat on the few available chairs, and those not fortunate enough to have arrived early were left to stand. Like so many sharp-beaked scavengers and harpies, their beady gazes were riveted on the man seated behind a massive desk slowly reading from a document.

Only one person in the group of eight showed any evidence of sorrow. Isabella Leslie stood in a corner, softly sobbing, a handkerchief to her eyes. Her grandfather had been her entire life, the center of her world, the most kind and indulgent friend and parent.

And now he was gone and she was alone.

His illness had been long and lingering. She'd thought she'd had time to say her good-byes, to reconcile herself to life without him. But the immensity of her sadness was threatening to overwhelm her. She scarcely heard the lawyer's words as he read her grandfather's will. Until a stark and utter silence struck her senses and she looked up to see every eye in the room trained on her.

"Your grandfather left you sole heir, my dear," old Mr. Lampert quietly said.

"As if she didn't know," her aunt snapped. "He could have had the decency to leave us small portions at least, the dotty old coot."

"Mr. Leslie's wishes were quite plain," the lawyer replied, "and his mind was clear. He spoke to me only yesterday, reminding me of my duty to Isabella."

"For a tidy sum, I don't doubt, you'll see to her care," her uncle growled.

"My fees were paid long ago by Mr. Leslie. Isabella owes me nothing."

"Then we won't require your presence any longer, Lampert," Isabella's eldest cousin curtly said, his corpulent body quivering with rage. "Get out."

"Harold!" Isabella softly exclaimed, shocked at the discourtesy.

"Get out, Lampert, or I'll throw you out," her cousin barked, ignoring Isabella's outcry. He moved with ominous intent toward the frail, elderly man who after casting a distraught glance at Isabella scrambled from his chair and backed toward the door. Greatly outnumbered, physically threatened, he stammered, "Forgive me, Miss Leslie," and escaped the room.

"Wretched little man," her uncle muttered, walking to the desk and picking up the pages of the will in his beefy hand. Crumbling them into a ball, he tossed them into the fireplace flames. "So much for Uncle George's will." Turning to his wife, he held out his hand. "Give me the marriage license." As she unfastened her reticule, he nodded in the direction of the clergyman who had conferred last rites on George Leslie. "Keep the ceremony short, if you please. I've wasted enough time cooling my heels in this house, waiting for that old codger to die. Harold, get over here."

Isabella's heart had begun beating furiously as she listened to her uncle give orders, and the sly glances she was receiving from her relatives did nothing to soothe her fears. She knew how they felt about her, and while she'd not expected congratulations from them for her inheritance, she'd not considered them dangerous. "If you'll excuse me," she quietly said, wishing to remove herself from the ominous situation, "it's been a fatiguing week." She began walking toward the door.

"Stay where you are," her uncle murmured, his tone acid with dislike. "We're not done with you yet."

"You can't order me about." She kept her voice firm with effort. Suddenly in the midst of enemies, her heart was beating furiously.

"Now, that's where you're wrong, my dear."

The menace in his voice wrapped around her like icy

fingers, the wicked gleam in his eye mirrored in the others watching her. "Uncle Herbert, consider—this is my home now, I'm of legal age, as you're well aware, and you have no control over my life."

"As soon as you're married to Harold, he'll have control of your life. As God intended when he made women subservient to men."

"Married!" She turned ashen for only a moment before her cheeks flushed a blazing red. "You must be mad! My cousin Harold suits me not at all"—her voice rose as she surveyed the fleshy, overdressed man who fancied himself a dandy—"and if I *should* chose to marry, your son certainly wouldn't be a candidate."

"She's saying our Harold isn't good enough for her! Herbert, how dare she, when everyone knows her mother—well, it can't be mentioned, of course, in polite company. Now, you just listen to me, my high-flown missy," Abigail Leslie cried, shaking her thin finger at Isabella, "you should be *honored* Harold is willing to take you as his wife. He could have any number of wellborn ladies."

"Then he should marry them!" Isabella always bristled at allusions to her mother's unconventional background, as if sailing a ship around the world detracted from one's quarterings. Her mother had bluer blood than any of these bourgeois bankers.

"Mr. Leslie, sir, you said the young lady was amenable to the hasty marriage." The minister abruptly rose from his chair, an expression of consternation on his face.

At the interruption, Isabella quickly glanced around the room, looking for a ready exit should her uncle truly intend to force this farcical marriage. The doorway to the hall was blocked by numerous stolid bodies—Harold's fat form among them. But the windows facing the street opened on a small balcony only a few feet above the sidewalk. Her cousins Amelia and Caroline, seated before the windows, weren't likely to be formidable obstacles. Only capable of squealing or giggling, neither would raise a finger to stop her, and with their rotund bodies balanced precariously on Grandpapa's small Renaissance hassocks, she could easily bowl them over.

"Shut your mouth, Dudley." Herbert Leslie pushed the minister back into his chair. "Save your speeches for the ceremony." He snapped his fingers. "Harold, get your bride and bring her here." Swinging around, he pointed a finger at Isabella. "And if you know what's good for you, you'll do as you're told."

"You don't really think I'm going to allow myself to be married off to Harold, do you?" she hotly inquired.

"I'll gag and tie you if necessary."

"Such a marriage would never stand in court."

"We have sufficient witnesses to testify to your willingness," her uncle silkily said. "And we're all going to see that you're properly wedded and bedded this night." He surveyed the various relatives with a fierce gaze, as though reminding them of their duty. "You'll be married right and tight," he went on, smiling at her with a well-pleased complacency, "and the money will be kept in the family, as is only proper."

All the tears and sorrow she'd been experiencing only moments before were burned away by a rage so towering, she silently swore she'd see them all in hell before she married fat Harold. She was already running before her uncle had finished speaking, and the Misses Amelia and Caroline were dumped on the floor a second later with two hard shoves. Racing between the tumbled hassocks and flailing arms and legs, she jerked the drapes aside, wrenched the window open, and leaped through it onto the balcony. The cold rain struck her like a blow, but there wasn't time to completely register the wet and chill. Throwing a leg over the wrought iron railing, she pulled herself up and over and dropped to the walk below in a splash of muddy water. Her silk gown was already drenched, her stained skirts catching on her legs as she ran full out down the street.

The shouts and cries behind her only added to her speed, and when she reached the corner, she careened right, hoping to gain shadowed refuge in the tall oaks of St. James's Square. Moments later, panting, she slumped against the wet bark, trying to draw in much-needed air to her lungs.

Her gaze was trained on the corner.

If they turned left, she was safe.

Harold was first under the streetlamp in the intersection, followed shortly by his portly relatives—father, uncle, and two cousins. They apparently couldn't agree on a course, their raised voices echoing down the street, indecision in their milling forms. Then Harold seemed to point directly at her, although he couldn't possibly see her in the murky darkness of her surroundings.

Nevertheless, terror washed over her and, turning, she ran down King Street without waiting for further confirmation of their possible route.

Unable to avoid the light on the next corner, her saffron gown glowed in the night like a beacon as she sped past.

Immediately a hue and cry rose behind her, and she knew she'd been sighted.

A half block later, she turned again, then again in another block, hoping to evade her pursuers in the narrow lanes, and when she spied the flaming torches illuminating a fine-porticoed entrance, she raced down the wet cobblestones and banged on the blue door with both fists.

The portal abruptly opened before her, and she stumbled into an elegant foyer lit by a Venetian chandelier of such vast proportions, she wondered if she'd entered some hidden palace. Quickly surveying her surroundings, she took note of gleaming white marble and elaborate gilding, elegant paintings and plush carpets, and a majordomo so enormous and tall, she had to tip her head upward to see his face.

"May I be of some help?"

His calmness seemed to descend on her, and she could almost feel a lessening of her fear. "Forgive me for . . . barging in, but . . . someone was pursuing me." Her heart was pounding, her words broken by gasps. Taking a deep breath, she struggled to compose herself, hoping he wouldn't consider her some demented female and put her out in the street again. "If I might see . . . your master or mistress, I could explain. . . ."

"Of course. Please, let me show you into the small drawing room." With a wave of his hand he indicated a highly polished door. "I'll have some towels brought to you," he politely went on as though soaking-wet women being chased in the night wasn't out of the ordinary. Opening the door, he ushered her into a candlelit room decorated with painted panels of colorful birds and foliage and quietly closed the door behind her.

The towels arrived quickly in the arms of a servant girl, and by the time the majordomo returned, Isabella was marginally dry. Her pale hair tumbled onto her shoulders in damp ringlets, and her gown, while soiled at the hemline, had been sponged to a semblance of presentable.

Dermott's game lasted slightly longer than a half hour because he was on a winning streak and even Kate's splendid charms couldn't compete with the run of luck he was having. But a servant came to fetch him as the half hour stretched to an hour and, folding his hand, Dermott rose from the table with a bow. "Until tomorrow, gentlemen. I expect I'll see most of your faces here again once you wake from your hangovers."

"We aren't all impervious to drink like you."

Dermott offered them a tight smile. "India does that to you—if it doesn't kill you. . . ."

"Or make you a nabob."

"Among other things."

He spoke so low, most at the table couldn't hear him, but his tone was such that no one asked for clarification. And he was already walking toward the door anyway, tall and commanding even in his disheveled state.

He entered the foyer from the gaming room just as Isabella stepped through the drawing room door. Mercer offered him a blank gaze and without comment showed the young woman up the stairway to the main floor.

Transfixed, Dermott watched her ascent, the lady's beauty uncommonly rare. Pale-haired and rosy-cheeked with eyes the color of gentian, she had the look of a meadow sprite, particularly with her flowing damp tresses and wettish gown. She moved too with an ethereal lightness, her slender form seeming to flow up the stairs without effort on violet-slippered feet. He caught a scent of her fragrance as she passed, and the perfume drifted around him, evoking memories of cascading roses and summer nights.

He spoke Mercer's name as they reached the top of the staircase, but the majordomo didn't reply.

And then they were gone.

2

*

ISABELLA WAS SHOWN into the presence of a middle-aged lady and left on the threshold of a sitting room softly lit by two torcheres.

"Do come in. I'm Mrs. Crocker." Molly Crocker gazed at the young woman in the doorway with a practiced eye—the bedraggled but expensive gown, her fine amethyst and pearl jewelry, the beauty of her face and form. And she wondered why a lady of fashion was being pursued in the night.

"Please accept my apologies . . . for intruding so precipitously," Isabella murmured as she moved forward. "But I saw your light outside—"

"No need to apologize, my dear. Mercer tells me you're in some danger. Come sit down by the fire and join me for tea. You look chilled to the bone."

"Thank you for your kindness." Sitting opposite the well-dressed mistress of the house, Isabella stretched her hands toward the fire and luxuriated briefly in the welcome warmth. Abruptly recalling her manners, she turned from the fire. "Forgive me, my name is Isabella Leslie."

Molly looked up from pouring a cup of tea. "Delighted to meet you, my dear. Would you like a wrap against the chill?"

"No thank you. I'll soon be warm with this glowing fire."

"Sugar? Milk? Lemon?"

"Milk and sugar, please." Isabella softly sighed. "How grateful I am to have found a safe haven."

"You must tell me what I can do to help." Molly offered the cup of tea and nudged a plate of tea cakes across the small marquetry table, nearer her guest.

"I'm afraid I don't know *what* to do. Everything happened so quickly." Isabella took a deep draft of tea, as though needing sustenance before going on. "You see, my grandfather died just hours ago," she explained, "and without warning, my relatives tried to force me into a loathsome marriage to my cousin."

"I'm so sorry. How awful for you."

Shaking away the sadness that overwhelmed her at mention of her grandfather, Isabella wiped at the wetness that had risen in her eyes. "Thank you." Her voice was unsteady. "Even though he'd been ill for some time, the finality of losing him is—"

"Devastating, I'm sure," Molly murmured.

Isabella nodded and blinked away her tears. "And then to have my relatives so cruelly ignore his death . . ." she whispered. "Can you imagine anyone so unfeeling?"

"There must have been a great deal of money involved."

Isabella's brows arched upward. "How did you know?"

"I've seen much of the world, my dear. Heiresses are ready prey for the unscrupulous."

A flare of indignation illuminated Isabella's eyes. "I have no intention of becoming anyone's prey. I refused to marry my cousin." Her fingers clenched on the tea saucer. "When my uncle threatened to tie and gag me for the ceremony, I bolted." She grimaced. "And was indeed hunted, wasn't I?"

"It was fortunate you turned down our lane."

"Your light gleamed like a beacon in the night."

"And Mercer hasn't reported any unwelcome visitors, so your relatives must have lost the scent."

"Thank God."

While Molly admired the young lady's indomitable spirit, courage alone wouldn't ensure her independence. "Have you someone you'd like us to send for, or a friend you'd care to go to tonight? Another relative perhaps who would offer you refuge. My carriage is at your disposal."

Isabella's expression turned grave, and she shook her head. "Grandpapa and I lived a quiet life. And my few relatives have all entered into the conspiracy against me."

"What of a legal advocate outside your family?"

"I'm afraid Mr. Lampert, Grandpapa's lawyer, is quite unable to help me. He was thoroughly intimidated tonight when my uncle threatened him." She set her cup down and nervously twisted her fingers. "I doubt he can afford me protection."

"Perhaps another barrister of more resolve could warn off your relatives."

"I'm not so sure Uncle Herbert would comply regardless the warning given. When he threatened to tie and gag me in order to consummate the marriage, I understood how pitiless his intent. So while a legal advocate could theoretically protect me, in truth he would also have to serve as bodyguard to be effective."

"Perhaps that's what you need. A bodyguard."

Isabella's fine nose wrinkled in a grimace. "How dreadful life would be if it came to that. I'd hate to be under constant surveillance."

"Better, perhaps, than marriage to—"

"Fat Harold." Her smile was fleetingly impish. "Forgive me, but he's really frightfully fat and he fancies himself a dandy as well. I couldn't imagine being married to him even if he were likable—which he isn't in the least." She sighed again. "I wish Grandpapa were still alive. Having his money is turning out to be terrifying."

"You could give it to your relatives."

"They're all hateful. I'd as soon give the money away on the street as hand it over to them. Besides, Grandpapa's charities have to be funded, especially his home for retired sailors, which takes enormous work to keep going, what with Mr. Gandy and Mrs. Thomas scrapping every day over the smallest administrative details. I'm sorry." Her fingers fluttered across her mouth like those of a child caught speaking out of turn. "As though the particulars of my life are of interest to you."

Molly gazed at the lush young woman who had appeared on her doorstep in a fashion those less pragmatic than she might have construed as miraculous. "I may have a solution to your problem." Ever the businesswoman, she recognized advantage in the unusual circumstances.

Isabella immediately leaned forward, her expression

brightening. "Would you really? I've been unable to think of a means of extricating myself from this disaster. If I return home, my uncle will coerce me into that hateful marriage. Even if I find other quarters, he's sure to track me down. The courts, while just, I'm sure, can't protect me every minute, and Uncle Herbert wants Grandpapa's money so badly, he's not likely to leave me in peace."

"What I'm about to propose might curtail his interest in you as a marriage partner for"—Molly's mouth quirked faintly—"fat Harold."

"His son."

Molly nodded. "I suspected as much." Her gaze took on a sudden sharpness. "I don't mean to alarm you, but would your relatives inherit should you die?"

"No. Grandpapa's will is very clear. If I die without children, his fortune goes to his charities."

"So you must marry your cousin in order for them to benefit."

"Which I have no intention of doing," Isabella firmly declared.

"I understand." Molly's glance briefly swept the room. "Do you have any idea where you are?"

Isabella gazed about, taking in the fashionably decorated chamber, the opulence of the furnishings, her hostess clothed in elegant dishabille. "In a house in St. James's. Other than that, I'm at a loss."

"This is London's finest brothel, and I own it."

Color flared high on Isabella's cheeks. Even in the candlelight her flush was unmistakable. "Oh, dear," she said in the merest whisper, her eyes wide, shock numbing her mind.

"You're completely safe."

It took her a moment to answer, and her voice was still wispy. "Really?"

"Of course, you're free to go if you wish."

A sudden silence fell.

Isabella had little choice in places to go.

"Or if you find yourself in need of help," Molly said, her voice temperate, "you might consider my proposal. It's nothing more than a suggestion—with no coercion intended or implied. Your independence won't be compromised."

Another silence ensued while Isabella experienced the full impact of the old adage Out of the frying pan into the fire. Chewing on her lower lip, she tried to dredge up other options to the dangers her relatives posed. But no easy means of salvation came to mind, no Good Samaritan dwelt in the background of her life waiting to respond to her pleas. She was entirely alone. The enormity of her solitude tightened her stomach with dread. But a pithy sense of survival had served her well since her youth, when she'd lost both her parents, and lifting her chin, she met Molly's gaze. "Tell me. I'm listening."

"Your relatives must marry you off to one of them to insure they gain your money."

"It seems to be their plan." Isabella's voice was low.

"Without you, the money goes elsewhere."

"So Grandpapa's will maintains. Although they might try to alter it."

"Wills are filed with the court. It would be difficult to challenge it or your grandfather's soundness of mind without convincing proof. Now, if you were ruined or disgraced, would they still wish you to be their bride?"

"I'm not sure disgrace matters to them so long as they can seize Grandpapa's fortune."

"If you were *publicly* ruined, would that put another face on their plans?"

Isabella smiled despite her apprehensions, beginning to understand the gist of Mrs. Crocker's proposal, understanding deliverance might be within reach after all. "It would have to be exceedingly public. I'm not sure disgrace alone would be sufficient."

"Say you were not only morally disgraced but pregnant? I could see that such a tidbit was placed in the gossip columns. Would you be persona non grata then?"

"Pregnant?" Isabella whispered. "I couldn't."

"In theory only, my dear. You needn't fear."

With her heart racing because she was anticipating the answer, she quietly asked, "What exactly would be required of me?"

"In return for the temporary security of my house and a ruined reputation conspicuous enough to deter your relatives' plans, I would ask you to agree to a limited role as a courtesan."

"A courtesan!" She'd thought—good God! She didn't know what she'd thought—but a courtesan! Impossible, for a thousand reasons that had to do with sense and rationality and her dear grandfather's memory. "I couldn't . . . really, I couldn't."

"It would involve a very limited role, my dear. And if you wish, your relatives could be informed of your denouement quietly, with a warning of public exposure only should they threaten you. It could be handled very delicately. Few need know beyond a very limited circle—all of whom could be relied on for their silence."

"Couldn't we—I mean, couldn't we just say that—"

"With so much wealth at stake, your uncle might require evidence of your altered state."

Isabella's spine went stiff. "Surely, you can't mean that!"

"You heard of the Westmore scandal last season, where Lady Jane's fiancé insisted on a doctor's examination before marriage. In his case, he was questioning her virginity. Your uncle might question your avowal of ruin, and should he press the issue in court, he could have you examined."

Suddenly the flashing images of a dozen black-robed judges staring down at her with undisguised lechery along with stout Harold, hideously nude, waiting for her in the marriage bed, caused bile to rise in her throat. Forcing back the urge to vomit, she swallowed hard and drew in a steadying breath. "Considering the alternative, your proposal begins to take on a degree of merit. I know my relatives are utterly ruthless. I would have been married tonight against my wishes and the minister's protest if I hadn't run away." She took another deep breath, exhaled, and gazing squarely at Mrs. Crocker, asked the damning question. "What would I have to do to implement your plan. Please be frank."

"You'd have to sleep with one of my clients."

"Sleep?"

"Make love to one of my clients."

"And what would you get out of this?" She knew of

course; she simply wished to gauge the candor of her hostess.

"Money, of course. The price for a virgin is dear."

"What makes you think I'm a virgin?"

Molly could have been blunt and told her the truth—that her innocence practically glowed like a nimbus above her head. But diplomatic in the delicate negotiations, she said instead, "Let's just assume you are. And whatever the personal price of your experience here, it would be considerably less than being married to your cousin for the rest of your life. The liaison I'm suggesting would be of a finite duration."

"How finite?" She felt as though she were bargaining for the future of the universe. Or her universe at least.

"We could discuss it with the client."

Isabella's voice turned brisk. "A night, a week, a fortnight? Tell me, what is the usual commitment?"

"No more than a fortnight. Probably more likely a day or so."

"A day or so . . ." The price of her freedom suddenly looked more affordable. She cared little for her virginity if losing it meant thwarting her relatives' plans. Not that they'd care whether she was a virgin or not if they could get their hands on her fortune. But the pregnancy suggested by Mrs. Crocker was ingenious. If she was ruined, ostensibly pregnant *and* publicly exposed—or threatened with the possibility—they'd be forced to give up any thought of Harold marrying her. Their position in society was already insecure with the stench of trade in their backgrounds. It would be untenable should the scandal surrounding her sojourn in Mrs. Crocker's house become known. Particularly with Amelia and Caroline in the market for husbands.

"My options are limited, aren't they?"

Molly tipped her head in acknowledgment. Lifting the plate of cakes, she offered it to Isabella. "Should you agree, your independence would be assured."

"Is that chocolate?" Isabella pointed at a diamond-shaped petit four glazed with pink icing.

"Chocolate with raspberry crème filling."

She smiled and picked up the small cake. "This is ever so bizarre, Mrs. Crocker."

"But of benefit to us both."

Isabella took a bite of the cake and shut her eyes against the sublime taste. When she opened her eyes a moment later, she indelicately spoke through a mouthful of chocolate and raspberry. "I'd be rid of them once and for all, wouldn't I?"

"I'd bet a large sum on that eventuality."

"A pleasant thought." Isabella gazed into the dancing flames for a contemplative moment, and when she turned back to Mrs. Crocker, a new determination shone in her eyes. "Very well, I'll do it."

"You're sure?"

"Considering the alternative . . ." Isabella softly drawled.

Molly smiled. "A wise choice."

And so the bargain was made.

Dermott's head rested against the rim of the marble tub, the steam rising around him, a pleasant sense of lassitude permeating his senses. He'd been up for days, thanks to Olivia's sexual demands, the race had taken its toll on his energy levels, and after a half dozen brandies downstairs, the warm water was putting him to sleep.

"You're not allowed." Kate's voice was playful and very close.

His long, dark lashes slowly lifted. Her lithe, curvaceous form, and then her smiling face, met his gaze. "Am I on call?" he teasingly inquired.

"Consider, darling, I haven't seen you for a week." Stepping into the tub large enough to accommodate two comfortably, she eased herself down until she was straddling his thighs. "And you have to stay awake long enough to allow me my pleasure."

"Have to?" One brow rose in sardonic query.

"*Have* to, darling. I'm ravenous for you. And if I weren't so polite, I would have jumped you immediately you entered the room."

"So you should be commended for restraint."

"You should reward me handsomely for my restraint." She grasped his penis and squeezed gently.

"What did you have in mind?" he murmured softly, suddenly fully awake.

"Something large and stiff and capable of—um . . . darling, is it only that I haven't seen this for a week, or is he really larger than usual tonight?"

"We could better tell," Dermott replied in a throaty growl, "if you'd let him measure the limits of that sweet pussy of yours."

"You're not too tired? You don't mind?"

"Have I ever?"

She feigned a moment of contemplation and then grinned. "Not since you turned fifteen, rumor has it."

"Fourteen, thanks to Harvey Nicols's very attractive mother, who liked to seduce her son's school chums."

"She still has an eye for the men, gossip attests."

"She's distinctly a woman of passion. Like you, darling Kate. Now, come here and I'll show you how much I missed you."

While Dermott and Kate renewed their friendship, Isabella was shown into a pretty bedchamber in Molly's apartments. Two servant girls bustled about, bringing in bathwater and towels, scented soaps, and a tray of food that smelled delicious.

Isabella stood in the center of the room while her bath was arranged, feeling as though she were watching a stage play. As though the sprigged-muslin curtains and bedding, the crème-colored French furniture, the crystal chandeliers, were beautiful props, and the only reason she could smell the scented beeswax candles with such vividness was that she had a front row seat. The servant girls bobbed and bowed to her but didn't speak, and only when the last bucket of hot water was poured into the painted porcelain tub did a voice break into her reverie.

"Would you like a maid to help you with your bath?"

Molly had come in at the last, carrying a robe, and when Isabella spun around at the sound of her voice, it took her a moment to merge the apparent fantasy with stark reality. "Thank you, but I'd prefer to be alone."

"I thought as much, so I had our chef make you a tray

you can enjoy by the fire later. I thought this would warm you after your bath," she added, handing over a delicate cashmere robe.

"I appreciate your"—Isabella lifted her hand in a sweeping gesture—"kindness and—"

"You're welcome to change your mind at any time." Molly recognized Isabella's hesitation.

"You're extremely benevolent."

"Just sensible. My ladies are here by choice. I wouldn't have it any other way. Although many are here for reasons that bear a resemblance in one form or another to your situation. Their options, too, were limited; they often are for women in this man's world." Her voice took on an amiable briskness. "Now, make yourself as comfortable as you may tonight, and we'll talk some more in the morning. Nothing is cast in stone. Perhaps you'll think of someone who will serve as advocate for you, and all your despicable relatives can go hang themselves," she finished with a smile.

"Wouldn't that be wonderful," Isabella replied, buoyed by her benefactor's optimism. "I shall rack my brain tonight."

"Don't forget to eat, now. Guillaume pouts when his food comes back to the kitchen untasted."

"You needn't worry on that count." Isabella's smile held a genuine warmth, her mood much improved by Mrs. Crocker's candor. "I'm famished."

"I'll see you at breakfast, then."

The door softly closed a moment later, and Isabella found herself alone.

In London's finest brothel.

And if someone would have told her a day before that she would be so placed tonight, she would have thought them mad.

As Mrs. Crocker noted, she still had time to consider alternatives. But the savory aroma of her supper was causing her to salivate, and even if she hadn't been damp and dirty from her flight through the rain, the hot, scented bath would have been potent lure. She had the entire night to consider solutions to her dilemma. Just then both her supper and bath were getting cold.

Short moments later, she was seated in the luxurious warmth of the bath, the supper tray balanced on the rim of the tub, her mouth full of dover sole that was as near to heaven as culinary art allowed. Guillaume needn't worry about his food coming back untasted. She intended to eat every morsel and perhaps lick the plate as well. She'd eaten very little in the days past with her grandfather's life slipping away, and for the first time she'd become aware of her hunger.

Not until the last fragment of the lemon genoise was gone did she look up with a satisfied sigh and set the tray on the floor. A half bottle of very good champagne had come with the meal, and whether it was the food or wine or the soothing warmth of the bath, she felt lulled and appeased.

After a time, she dried herself, and wrapping the luxurious white cashmere robe around her, rested on a chaise conveniently placed near the fire. Her grandfather's long illness had taken its toll on her stamina. She'd not slept through the night for almost a month. And within minutes, she'd fallen asleep.

Molly quietly came in to check on her some hours later and covered Isabella with a blanket where she lay. The firelight gilded her pale skin and golden hair, the white robe clothed her in softness, the picture of innocence so breathtaking, even Greuze couldn't have improved on it.

3

❧

THE SUN WAS SHINING brightly through the lace-and-muslin curtains when Isabella woke with a start.

Her grandfather's funeral!

She sat bolt upright, threw off the blanket, and leaped to her feet. Running to the bellpull, she yanked on it and then nervously paced until a servant responded.

"I must see Mrs. Crocker at once. Which room is hers?"

Agitation rang through her voice, and the maid, wide-eyed and nervous, pointed through the open portal across the sitting room toward a closed door. "She be havin' breakfast, miss."

"Thank you," Isabella briskly replied, already moving in the indicated direction. Reaching the door, she knocked firmly and without waiting for an answer, turned the latch and walked into the room.

She came to an abrupt standstill and flushed to a bright shade of pink. A shockingly handsome man, bare-foot and shirtless, was seated across from Mrs. Crocker, having breakfast.

Good God, Dermott thought, his gaze on the woman

he'd glimpsed the previous night. She was even more beautiful at close range. And barely clothed, he pleasantly noted. His body instantly responded to the opulent vision, the lady's sumptuous breasts, narrow waist, the soft curve of her hips, and slender legs conspicuous beneath the fragile fabric of her robe.

"Come in, my dear," Molly invited Isabella. "Join us for breakfast."

"No thank you—that is—I need"—she tried not to look at his half-naked body—"I mean, I'd like to talk to you immediately."

"Let me excuse myself." Dermott began to rise.

"No need." Molly waved him back down. "I'll come to your room," she said, smiling at Isabella, who had taken startling note of the muscles rippling across the man's shoulders when he moved. Coming to her feet, Mrs. Crocker spoke to her companion affectionately. "You eat. I know how you need food in the morning." With a smile for the earl, she ushered Isabella out of the room, followed her into her bedchamber, and shut the door. "Now, tell me what I can do for you."

The few moments it had taken to reach her room had given Isabella time to compose herself—Mrs. Crocker's breakfast companion had nothing to do with her. "I came to tell you I *must* see to the arrangements for my grandfather's funeral," she explained. "I don't know how I could have forgotten last night!"

"It's completely understandable with your life in jeopardy. Surely you're not thinking of attending his funeral?" Mrs. Crocker quickly interjected. "You'd be whisked away and married off, with certainty."

"I know." Isabella's nervousness was apparent. "But I must see that the arrangements are *en train*. Or at least contact Mr. Lampert so he can handle things in my stead. Although," she said in a near whisper, "how can I not be there to put my grandfather to rest?"

"Once the danger is past, you can pay your respects. If anyone would allow you that latitude, I'm sure your grandfather would. Let me send a servant to Mr. Lampert with a note from you."

"Anonymously," Isabella's said, her trepidation plain.

"Of course."

"I'm sorry." She looked embarrassed. "How rude of me after all you've done."

"No need to apologize, my dear. I well understand society's strictures. Mr. Lampert will be contacted with the utmost discretion. Now, write your instructions to him while I see that some breakfast is brought up for you. Or, if you wish, you're more than welcome to join Bathurst and me."

Isabella colored. "I couldn't."

"Then one of the maids will bring your breakfast to you here," Molly affably replied. "And whenever your letter is ready, I'll see that it's sent. With luck," she cordially added, "you'll be delivered from your relatives' malice in short order."

"I pray you're right, Mrs. Crocker." Heartfelt emotion accompanied the simple phrase.

"Where did she come from?" Dermott's query greeted Molly's return.

"I'm not sure. Pursued and terrified, she stumbled on us by accident last night. Apparently, she was being forced into a repugnant marriage." Molly took her seat at the table.

"That takes a certain boldness. To run into the night."

"Or rank terror. She's quite without connections, and those she has are after her fortune." Molly poured herself a fresh cup of tea.

"A fortune and no partisans? She might as well put a target on her back."

"So she quickly came to understand last night. Her grandfather wasn't an hour dead when they hurried her before a minister."

"Ah, the lure of easy money."

"You're one of few who can so casually disallow the phenomenon."

"I paid for my fortune with my blood, Molly. There's nothing casual about my wealth."

"Or mine."

He dipped his head in acknowledgment. "We've both overcome obstacles, have we not?" His eyes went blank for a moment, and he reached for the porter he was drinking with his breakfast.

"We can't change our fathers' inhumanity or the buffeting of fate."

"Only try to forget it," he murmured, a harsh bitterness in his tone. Lifting the mug to his mouth, he drained it, set it down on the table, and smiling at Molly with a practiced nonchalance, said, "Surely we have better things to discuss on a bright sunny morning like this, with the smell of spring in the air."

"I believe we were talking of my newest houseguest."

"Much better. She's very delicious."

"Yes, is she not." Molly picked up a strawberry tart.

"And?" One dark brow rose in query.

"Her status is still in question."

"That sounds interesting. Might she be available?"

"She might."

"You're being very coy, Molly. Unlike you."

"While your habitual urges haven't deserted you."

"Let's hope they haven't. I'm only twenty-nine. Now, tell me the percentages on 'might.' "

Molly explained the possible bargain made the previous night between herself and Isabella while she nibbled on the pastry. "Do you know of the Leslies—either her grandfather or the relatives who intend her harm?" she asked. "The name means nothing to me."

Dermott shook his head. "They don't run in my circles, but then," he noted with a grin, "my friends are decidedly scandalous. Not an arriviste banker in the lot."

Only the Prince of Wales and his set, Molly silently noted. Dermott moved in the highest society. "Regardless Isabella's background, her innocence is real. So I'm not sure about percentages or the extent of my profit motive. Perhaps I may choose to be benevolent."

"Not necessarily a kindness to her," he pointed out. "In terms of her future, she may prefer less innocence and ultimately more freedom. And don't infer selfish motives on my part. Rather, I'm reminding you how the world views an untouched, undefended heiress. She's fair game for every rogue, and you know it."

"So what am I to do?"

"Wait for her decision. It's not for you to decide."

"And should she ultimately agree to my offer? What do I do then?"

His smile was warm and boyish and full of charm. "You let me outbid the other contenders."

"I don't want her hurt."

"Have I ever harmed a woman in any way?"

"No," she grudgingly replied, knowing full well Dermott's speciality was more in the nature of offering them the ultimate pleasures.

"And are the women I know ever unhappy?"

"You're much too vain." But her smile was affectionate. She'd known Dermott before he left for India and she'd helped him forget his painful memories on his return. "I'll think about it."

"Let me bid last. That's all I ask."

"It may not come to that."

"*If* it does, I'd be happy to help make you richer."

"The nabob speaking."

He shrugged, not about to argue. "I saw her last night, you know, when she first came in. She disturbed my sleep, and that doesn't happen as a rule. I hope she decides to stay for a time."

"Since you're so interested, I might ask a favor of you."

"Ask away." Feeling decidedly content with the possibilities in his favor, he set to eating again, his appetite commensurate with his youth and level of physical activity.

"This note that's to be delivered to her lawyer. I might use your man rather than mine. To put anyone who might be watching off the scent."

"Be my guest." He reached for another slice of ham.

"No one will dare to interfere with you."

"True." He didn't argue his reputation for violence. Nor his record for surviving more duels than anyone in England. Glancing up from his plate, he cast her a quizzical look. "She really intrigues me. Tell me why?"

"She's very beautiful."

He resumed cutting his ham. "It's not just that."

"Maybe the scent of innocence provokes you."

His gaze came up again and his dark eyes were strangely cool. "I don't like innocence."

"Then she's the exception, unless you want to be second."

He shook his head very gently. "Not a chance." His mouth twitched into a grin. "It almost makes one believe in—"

"Bewitchment?"

He laughed. "I was going to say avarice."

"Greed in conjunction with a woman isn't unusual."

"It is for me." He abruptly pushed his chair away from the table as though the thought were objectionable. "I'll be downstairs until Tattersall's opens," he crisply said, standing. "My man will be available for your errands." And turning, he walked away.

Molly watched him leave the room and wondered what had come over the most profligate rake in London. Too little sleep, she pragmatically thought, or simply the male fear of emotion. Bathurst was particularly insensitive to finer feeling since his return from India. He lived on the edge, betting on anything, needing to win, always outbidding the competition for objects he desired. No need to look for philanthropic sentiments concerning his interest in Miss Leslie. Shaking the crumbs from her skirt, she rose from her chair and went to see if Isabella was finished with her letter.

"I'm ready," Isabella said, sealing the letter with a bit of wax as Mrs. Crocker entered the room. "There wasn't much to say. Lampert has had instructions for Grandpapa's funeral for years now. Grandpapa was like that. He preferred making his own arrangements. I simply told Lampert I'd be out of town for some time and should he need to get in touch with me, he could send a note to the bookseller on Albemarle Street. Mr. Martin won't mind. He's known me all my life." Standing, she turned and moved toward Mrs. Crocker with the letter.

"Very sensible, my dear. We'll see that your Mr. Martin is contacted should any messages be sent there. Let me take this to a servant, and if you wish, when I return we can find something to amuse you, to divert you from the awfulness of events. Certainly, you're in need of some gowns."

"Perhaps mine could just be cleaned."

"Of course. In the meantime, make yourself comfortable while I see that your letter is on its way. Did you notice the novels on the shelf near the window?"

She hadn't, and after Mrs. Crocker left the room, Isabella examined the selection of books. Astonished, she surveyed not only the latest novels but an array of works in Latin, Greek, and French. One would hardly expect to see such erudition in a brothel, however elegant. Who read these? she wondered. Taking out a copy of Christine de Pisan's *The Book of the City of the Ladies,* she thought it strange reading for the ladies—or men, for that matter—who inhabited this house. Taking note of Madame de Sévigné's letters next—one of her favorites—she slipped out the small morocco-bound volume. Her gaze swept the shelves in fascination—one after another of books she loved was available in this cozy, sun-filled room. The sensation of fantasy returned to her, as though she'd stepped into a magical refuge filled with comforts, safety, and simple pleasures.

But the door opening to admit her hostess reminded her that in addition to the pleasures that seemed fantastical were other improprieties she need consider.

"Ah, you've found some you like." Mrs. Crocker carried in a breakfast tray.

"They're all quite wonderful. Are they yours?"

"Reading is my greatest pleasure. Come, sit and have something to eat." Placing the tray on a bureau top, Molly lifted off several dishes, a teapot, and cups and arranged them on a small table. "Guillaume sent up some warm pastries with an omelet. I hope you like marzipan tarts and strawberries."

"Have you somehow tapped into my mind, Mrs. Crocker?" Isabella queried with a smile. "Not only are the books superb, along with the room, but marzipan has been my favorite since childhood."

"Perfect. Along with chantilly cream, I hope." Sitting, she waved Isabella over and began pouring tea for them. "Your note is on its way. The lawyer should have it in his hands within the half hour."

"Thank you again." Isabella set the two books she held on the table and pulled up a green faux bamboo chair of the latest fashion. "Since I'm not able to attend the funeral, I hope I may soon visit Grandpapa's burial site. He wished to be placed in a vault he had constructed at our country home."

"I'm sure your troubles with your relatives will be brief."

"Particularly if I go through with our arrangement." Her gaze slid away from Mrs. Crocker.

"Would you like me to try to find you a barrister willing to offer a stronger challenge to your uncle et al? I know how difficult a choice this is."

Sighing, Isabella traced the pattern on the silver teaspoon with the pad of her finger. "I'm afraid any warning would only postpone my relatives' dastardly plans. And unless, as you pointed out last night, they are publicly shamed out of the idea of marrying me into their family, they will continue to harass me."

"You might move to the country."

"I think I'd be even more afraid. The solitude—" She made a small moue. "I've probably read too many popular novels, but I can imagine them locking me into the attic and leaving me there once they have my money. Who would even know?"

Who, indeed, Molly thought, when the young lady was without friends. "I'll be perfectly frank. When I spoke with you last night, I planned, as you know, to make a profit on our bargain. But I find myself increasingly uncomfortable doing so."

"It was a bargain I well understood, Mrs. Crocker. I'm

not a child, nor do I delude myself on the need for this extremity."

"I understand—and I agree with the need. But I shan't take any money. I was once in a similar predicament—albeit not one that involved wealth such as yours. But I was a young woman without friends, subjected, no, forced into a grossly obscene relationship. It took me many years to rise above the shame. There are those who would say I have not yet done so, but I did what I had to for survival. Which explains my requirement that the ladies who live here do so willingly. Forgive me." She smiled faintly. "I didn't intend to digress into circumstances of no concern to you."

"On the contrary, your story is very pertinent to mine. How old were you when—"

"Sixteen," Molly quietly replied, the cruel memories never completely suppressed.

"How awful for you." Isabella took a deep breath and sat up a little straighter. "Certainly at twenty-two I can be as resolute." She smiled faintly. "It's not as though my virginity is of any use to me. In fact, it's a liability, is it not? As to my reputation in society, I have never set foot in society. So any reputation is my relatives' concern, not mine." Her smile broadened at the thought of their discomfort and her voice took on a measure of composure. "When one considers this in practical terms, the situation becomes much less emotional."

"One can't disregard emotion completely," Molly cautioned. "I speak from experience."

"Nevertheless, I feel much better now." Isabella fluttered her hands over the tabletop. "As though a huge burden of indecision has vanished. I think I shall have a marzipan tart with a large dollop of chantilly cream to start, and consider myself fortunate not to be married to Harold this morning."

Molly couldn't help but smile at her good cheer. "Perhaps it's all a matter of perspective after all."

"Indeed it is. Consider I have escaped a dreadful fate and am now quite comfortable in this pleasant room with lovely books and marzipan tarts. And if Grandpapa were alive instead of dead, I would have the best of all possible worlds."

Her expression had sobered, as it always did when she spoke of her grandfather. "You said he had been ill for some time," Molly kindly noted. "Perhaps he was ready to leave the world."

"Except for saying good-bye to me, he was. From the very beginning when his heart began to fail, he'd never feared death. He'd had a good life, he always said, and was long overdue. But I miss him dreadfully."

"Of course you do. Were you with him long?"

"Since I was four. Mama died at sea, and when Papa and I came home to England, he missed her so dreadfully, Grandpapa said he felt as though Papa was just waiting to die. That first winter, when he fell ill with a fever, he didn't have the will to survive. Grandpapa and I were together ever since. Do you have family?"

Molly shook her head. "Only my girls here. And Bathurst in a way. He doesn't have much family—a mother who's retreated from the world." Often literally, she thought, but knew better than to breach Dermott's privacy.

The beautiful man at breakfast had been Bathurst. "Does he live here with you?"

Molly chuckled. "On occasion. He's a great favorite with everyone."

"I can see why. He's astonishingly handsome."

"The Ramsay good looks. They've been a curse to some generations, although he carries them well. With uncommon modesty actually. I'm not sure he's aware of his beauty."

"Surely he must be. He fairly takes one's breath away." Isabella suddenly blushed. "I can't imagine what you must think of me. I didn't intend to be so forward, but he's quite stunning."

"He strikes every woman that way. You're not the first," Molly noted. "And I don't know if that's consolation or cause for envy. Would you like him?"

Isabella's color heightened, and a fleeting shock crossed her features. "You mean—"

"Would you like Bathurst to relieve you of your virginity?" Molly spoke bluntly because she didn't want any ambiguity about what was in store.

"When you put it like that, I don't know—I mean . . . I didn't actually think of choosing someone for—" Isabella broke off, clearly embarrassed.

"He's more than willing. You kept him awake last night, he said."

"I did?" Her pulse rate spiked, and she wondered what had come over her that mention of his interest could excite her so.

"He saw you on the stairs and was struck by your beauty."

"Surely not."

Was she so truly innocent that she didn't realize the dazzling extent of her beauty? Had she been so sheltered from the world? "Absolutely, in truth. And he's willing to pay handsomely for the privilege of your company."

"For my virginity, you mean." Talk of money suddenly chilled her.

"Actually no. He has no truck with virgins."

Isabella glanced at Mrs. Crocker quizzically. "Am I missing something?"

Recalling Dermott's uncertainties at breakfast, a half-smile curved Molly's mouth. "Coincidently, he said as much. He desires you *despite* your virginity."

"What is normally perceived an asset is not an asset at all, it seems."

"He would agree."

"Is it a problem?"

"Probably not. If you want him."

The directness of her reply gave Isabella pause. "I've never thought of a man . . . that way, I mean . . . in terms of actually . . ." Her voice trailed away, the sheer magnitude of what she was about to do so audacious, she had no measure for such rashness in her life.

Molly's tone was mild, although she was astonished at such chasteness in a woman of twenty-two. "Had you no contact with other young people?"

Isabella shook her head.

"At your age?" She couldn't quite conceal her surprise. "What did you do with your time?"

"I mostly helped Grandpapa with his business. He was in merchant shipping. That's how my father originally met my mother. At our transport depot in New Guinea. And then in our leisure time Grandpapa and I were involved in a cartographers' society." Her even white teeth flashed in a grin. "Servants to business, some would say. But I enjoyed it immensely."

"There were no young men in the society or shipping company?"

"Not really. Everyone had been with the company for years. As for the society, they were all friends of Grandpapa's. It was his undertaking in all respects. He financed it. We have a superb library open by appointment in Grosvenor Square. Once I'm free to move about again, I'd be happy to show it to you. The displays are quite beautiful and the collection of rare maps is probably the best in England."

"Bathurst will be intrigued."

"By the maps?"

In her discussion of the cartographers' society, she'd become animated. It was clear to see she was a great devotee. "By you *and* the maps. He lived in India for five years, traveling widely in Asia and the Pacific as well. He's not the usual idle young nobleman."

"I doubt anyone would describe him as 'usual,' who had once seen him."

Molly found the young woman who had appeared on her doorstep last night more and more engaging as they talked, and the smallest germ of an idea began to form in her mind. Bathurst was interested. Miss Leslie was interested even if she didn't realize it completely. And both were essentially alone in the world.

Perhaps . . . Molly mused, and although a goodly

amount of cynicism accompanied her romantical conjecture, she might indulge in a bit of matchmaking. It would be amusing if nothing else, and what had she to do with her life if not amuse herself? She had all the money she needed. She even had considerable influence should she choose to wield it. Her clients came from the highest reaches of society and government, and she knew all their secrets.

But occasionally the sameness of life beset her. For purely selfish reasons, she'd been pleased when Bathurst had returned to England. He amused her mightily. So why not do them both a favor and amuse herself in the bargain? "I have an idea," she said.

"Like your last night's idea?" Isabella offered her a playful glance, thoughts of the handsome Bathurst in conjunction with their plan curiously pleasurable.

"A variation on the theme. And if you don't like it, I guarantee, Bathurst will."

Having finished her tart while they'd talked, Isabella reached for the plate holding her omelet. "While you tell me, as you surely will from the pleased look on your face, I'll eat my omelet and wish all my relatives to the devil."

"That's the spirit."

"I intend to stay focused," Isabella sportively declared, slicing into the herbed eggs. "And I don't mean on my breakfast."

"Revenge is sweet, I assure you."

Her fork poised near her mouth, Isabella asked, "Did you have your revenge?"

"With interest," Molly replied.

"Tell me." Isabella ate the bite of egg.

"Some other time." Miss Leslie was still too wholesome and naive to hear the details of her vengeance on the father who had sold her for a pittance to a brutal man. "Right now I'm thinking of an enchanting way for you to indulge yourself and bewitch Dermott at the same time."

"His name's Dermott? Not *the* Dermott—the Prince of Wales's close friend?" Suddenly all the names came together—Bathurst, Ramsay, and the infamous Dermott, who accompanied the Prince in all his revels.

Molly nodded. "The same."

"Even in my sheltered world I've heard of the profligate Dermott. His excesses are the stuff of legends in the scandal sheets."

"The scandal sheets fail to take notice of the other facets of his life. Dermott was left to salvage the estate and care for his mother when his father died drunk in the bed of one of his light o'loves."

"I do remember that," Isabella softly murmured. "Grandpapa's bank held some of the mortgages on the property. He is the same Bathurst who came back a nabob—"

"Three years ago."

"And paid off all his creditors. Grandpapa was impressed with him. He said it wasn't easy to make a fortune in India like it might have been a generation ago. He admired the earl's acumen."

"Courage, more like. Dermott was fighting on the northern frontiers and in the process saved the life of a Sikh prince. For which he was well rewarded. They mine rubies in the prince's domains." Molly didn't mention that Dermott was rewarded as well with the prince's sister's hand in marriage, nor that it was a love match. Or that he'd barely maintained his sanity when his wife and their baby son had been killed in one of the internecine border raids.

"And now he spends his time and money in debauch. I doubt I could bewitch so licentious a man—nor, perhaps, would I care to. . . ." The equivocation in her tone mirrored her uncertainties, for beneath her disdain for his salacious pursuits she found herself strangely drawn to him.

"The scandal sheets reveal only that which appeals to their readers. Dermott's more than a member of the Prince's fast set. But good deeds don't sell with the same relish as delicious gossip. He takes care of his mother and estates with benevolence, and while he wouldn't wish me to reveal his personal affairs, let me only say he is living under a great burden of sadness."

"And excess is a means of forgetting."

"Not unique certainly, but understandable."

"And I would be another transient moment of forget-fulness."

"Surely, your need is as transient."

"Touché," Isabella quietly replied. "I have no reason to take offense, when I would be using him as much as he me."

"A mutual need, pleasurably accomplished. Without encumbrances."

"How reasonable it all seems." Isabella leaned back in her chair. "Tell me of this enchantment you offer me."

"You have agreed to be a courtesan—for some limited time frame."

Isabella nodded.

"If you would care to be schooled in that role, not only would *you* be more comfortable, but Dermott would be exceeding grateful, I assure you."

"Particularly since he dislikes virgins."

"That's not to say he wouldn't be capable of giving you pleasure. His reputation for pleasing women is well known. But in the interests of offering as well as receiving pleasure, you may wish to be less of a novice."

"I think I would."

Molly was surprised at her ready acquiescence. "No need for convincing arguments?"

"I dislike a passive role on principle. If I intend to go through with this—agreement, I should like a modicum of control."

"You surprise me."

"I may be an innocent in terms of lovemaking, but I'm not by nature a shrinking violet," Isabella declared. "I lived in a man's world most of my life, while my mother's example was anything but that of a conventional female. In fact, I lack many of the traditional attributes normal to a young lady. I know nothing of flirting, nor of polite conversation. Grandpapa liked to talk of subjects with substance, he used to say. We never discussed anything of fashion."

"And yet your gown was in the height of fashion."

Isabella smiled. "Because I like pretty things and Grandpapa indulged my wishes."

"I'd say Madame Duclaisse had a hand in the design of your gown."

"How astute. She's quite my favorite."

"So you're not all bookish and business after all."

"I've been fortunate in my life, but I also understood there was a larger world that I could only read of and never know. I would dream, on occasion, of exotic locales and adventure. Everyone does, I'm sure."

"Not everyone. There are those in society who are content with the round of parties and amusements and never think beyond that circumscribed world."

"I should be bored within a week if there were only parties to fill my days."

"I think Dermott, too, has found life confining in England."

"And yet he stays?"

"He stays for his mother."

"A dutiful son. I wouldn't have thought so of a rake."

"He may lead the way in scandal, but he's considerably more complicated."

"I shall scandalize you and myself in the bargain when I say—what appeals to me when I think of him isn't his complexity but his great beauty and reputation for vice. Perhaps I've lived too long in seclusion. Perhaps my aunts are right after all when they compare me to my free-spirited mother. Although the terms they use to describe her aren't so pretty."

"How did she come to sail?"

"She stowed away on her uncle's ship when she was fifteen and found herself on a voyage to Trinidad. It was the end of any opportunity for a suitable marriage and the beginning of a life of adventure. She never regretted it, according to my grandfather."

"Your life has been unconventional as well."

"As has yours. Will you write your memoirs someday?"

"And terrify every man of influence in the country? I'll leave that to others. I've plenty of money."[1]

"As do I—perhaps," Isabella murmured, "should all go well. Now, tell me," she added, "of these pleasures," suddenly curious to hear more of the enchanting arts suggested by Molly. An extraordinary door had opened into her sheltered life, and the beautiful, much-desired Dermott Ramsay waited for her on the other side. "Is he really the most-sought-after man in England?"

"Women pursue him mercilessly. He hides here frequently."

Her clear blue eyes widened. "Is he really that good?"

"He's really that good."

Isabella smiled. "So I should be honored."

"You won't be disappointed. Or so my ladies tell me."

"Do they share him?"

"You're full of questions."

"I want to know everything. I want to know what he does and how he does it, what I should or shouldn't do. I want to know how to make him want me."

"He already does."

"But more than he has before. I like to be the very best at whatever I do."

The innocent Miss Leslie continued to astonish her. Emerging before her eyes was a plain-speaking, educated young lady with both unconventional antecedents and an upbringing that would do justice to a man of parts. And an interest in the challenge of captivating Dermott's interest. "Then we must see that you're the very best seductress Bathurst has ever had the good fortune to meet."

"Grandpapa always said I was a quick study."

Miss Leslie was approaching her new education with an enchanting candor. Molly concealed her amazement with effort. "You're sure now." She felt as though a last caveat should be offered.

"Absolutely." Dermott Ramsay filled her senses, her thoughts, her imagination, and she could no more vanquish those images than she could stop breathing. "I'm very sure."

"It's Dermott, isn't it?" Molly had seen that look before.

"I've never felt like this before. Increasingly awash with feeling. I wonder if this is what my mother felt when she stowed away. My heart is beating quite rapidly." Isabella placed her palm over her heart and inhaled slowly.

Molly chuckled. "At least it's not beating with fear like last night."

"Oh, no, not at all. Believe me, the thought of lying beside Dermott Ramsay is much superior, even celestial compared to the alternative of lying beside Harold Leslie." Shuddering, she made a face.

"In a more perfect world you wouldn't have been forced to make the choice."

"But since I am," she said, "I chose pleasure, thank you very much."

"Life is unfair to women." Molly's voice held a degree of anger.

"I don't choose to despair my predicament. Rather, I look forward to securing my fortune and freedom by indulging in illicit pleasures with the notorious earl." Isabella grinned. "You see, I am quite untroubled."

Molly found it ironic that a young woman harried by the world should be consoling her. She gave her high marks for courage. "If at any time you wish to discontinue this . . . education, you need but say the word."

"But I'm quite sure now I want him. And I've never really wanted anything with such . . . partiality," she finished softly.

"He's not for sale," Molly warned. "Nor is he tractable." Miss Leslie suddenly sounded like a spoiled young lady who had been overindulged, who wanted what she wanted.

"I know. Perhaps that's what makes this entire endeavor so enticing."

4

IN THE LATE FORENOON, the Leslies were assembled in the small chapel where the service for George Leslie was about to commence.

"I tell you, she won't miss her grandfather's funeral," Harold whispered, his gaze on the doorway.

"I hope you're right," his father muttered, casting another glance at the entrance. "Or we're going to have to search the entire city for her."

"She has no friends, no money, and Lampert's frightened enough not to give her assistance. And if he should find his courage, we've plenty of men watching his office and home."

"Then it's just a matter of time. Who else can she turn to? She has to come to him eventually."

The minister began reading from the funeral text, his voice carrying out over the small group.

"It looks as though she's not coming," Harold grumbled, taking out his watch from the tightly stretched pocket of his striped vest and surveying the painted face. "I hope this doesn't take too long. I've a race meet at two."

"My milliner is coming to the house at one," his

mother whispered across her husband's rotund form. "And she's considerably more important than this useless funeral."

Herbert waved his ringed hand at the minister, indicating he speed up the proceedings. Herbert had a card game he didn't wish to miss.

And so George Leslie was hurriedly sent from this world with little fanfare and less sorrow.

Mr. Lampert watched the brief ceremony with a grim expression, and when he left the chapel, he went to neither his office nor his home. He walked to a bookstore on Albemarle Street and took inordinately long to purchase one book.

It was a waste of time to follow him, Herbert's man reported that evening.

The old man had spent the entire day in a tavern, drinking one pot of ale and reading.

Out of courtesy, Molly had seen that Isabella was alone when the letter from Mr. Lampert was delivered.

Isabella's hands were shaking as she broke the seal and opened the single page.

I'm being watched, he wrote, *so don't send a message directly to me. Your grandfather was buried this morning and is being conveyed to the vault at Tavora House. Mr. Martin has money for you should you need it but take care approaching the shop. I'm not sure how many spies your uncle has in the city. I wish I could do more.* And he'd signed his name with a shaky hand.

Isabella immediately wrote a reply, telling Mr. Lampert

not to worry about her. She needed neither help nor money at the moment. And when the time was appropriate, she would explain her circumstances.

She tried to read again afterward, but her mind was consumed with having missed her grandfather's funeral, and the book lay unread in her lap. She should have been with him as he was put to rest, she thought; it would have been the last service she could offer him. And regret of what might have been lowered her spirits. But reminders of her despicable relatives evoked a simmering anger as well, and she took a degree of pleasure in planning revenge.

Her uncharitable impulses offered a kind of respite, however meager, to her sadness while the troubling uncertainties of her future brought further disarray to a mind already in turmoil. She might be able to maintain an air of resolve concerning her circumstances in the company of Mrs. Crocker, but once alone, she wasn't sure she possessed the courage to actually see it through.

Regardless Bathurst's appeal.

Regardless he was probably her best option.

Regardless he seemed to want her.

And she him.

Such outlandish possibilities shocked her when she allowed herself to consider them, as did the strange and curious desires evoked by the beautiful young earl. But contemplation of Bathurst also generated intoxicating, thrilling tremors deep inside her, and she clasped her hands together tightly on the book lying in her lap to still her trembling emotions.

How should she deal with her feverish response, she wondered, and her only companion in life unconsciously came to mind. Silently, she spoke to her grandfather, the simple act of communicating offering her solace. As she explained her feelings, it seemed as though he were with her again, as though she weren't so alone. She even found herself describing the handsome young earl as though her grandfather might enjoy a description as much as she.

She smiled at the ludicrousness of her imaginary conversation. But a comforting ease overcame her as she offered the bits and pieces of her tremulous thoughts—until a knock on the door interrupted her reflections and a second later Mrs. Crocker bustled into the room, followed by several maids laden with colorful gowns and accessories.

"We brought some things to cheer you up," she briskly said, indicating the items be placed on the bed. "Have you written a reply to your lawyer yet? Dermott's man is downstairs."

"I'll get it." Rising from her chair, Isabella walked to the small table where her note lay and handed it to a maid.

"The earl's man is a precaution, should anyone be watching," Molly explained.

"Thank you for your caution and your company as well. I find myself too alone with my thoughts."

"Exactly why you need a diversion. I had Madame Duclaisse send over some frocks to amuse us."

"I shall pay you, of course."

"At your leisure, my dear. Come now," she said, sitting down, "which would you like to try on first?"

Isabella selected a morning gown, her immediate need that of replacing her robe. The pale blue gauze was embroidered with a wide row of floral designs at the hem, but the simple lines were otherwise unadorned.

Not unfamiliar with servants, although she'd preferred living without a lady's maid, Isabella allowed the girls to help her dress. Mrs. Crocker had thoughtfully provided a chemise of the finest lawn, and after quickly discarding her robe and having the chemise slipped over her head, Isabella tried on the blue day dress.

"You have an eye for size." Isabella twirled before a cheval glass, the belled skirt billowing out around her.

"It was easy. You're the same size as Kate . . . one of the ladies here," she added in explanation. "The blue is excellent with your eyes."

"It is rather nice."

"Try on some of the slippers. There's some matching ones in several sizes."

A perfect fit was selected from the array, and she could have entertained royalty in her elegant gown. "I must say, a pretty dress always does wonders for one's disposition."

"My feeling exactly. Do try the apple-green silk next. The cashmere shawl is a delicious contrast."

"I don't plan on stepping out just yet," Isabella playfully noted, although the delectable fabric was alluring. Napoleon had introduced cashmere shawls to Europe after his Egyptian campaign only a few years past, and they were the height of fashion. And very dear.

"For when you do, then. I kept two of them for myself." Mrs. Crocker waved to have the green silk brought over. "Humor me. That color is going to be adorable with your coloring."

Before long, a half dozen dresses had been tried on and the room had the air of a dressmaker's salon, piles of colorful silks and gauzes scattered about the room, shoes and shawls and bonnets adding to the flower-garden effect. Mrs. Crocker had had a bottle of iced champagne brought in to add to the festivities. After having put on a rose-colored silk afternoon dress awash with ruffles they'd both agreed were overdone, Isabella and Molly were giggling over the ostentatious confection and casting on eye on the next possibility in their private fashion show.

"You're a trifle young for black lace, but try that one on anyway."

"It has the air of seduction."

"The point, I'm sure. Let's see it—just for fun."

Dermott had spent the morning at Tattersall's adding to his racing stable and had taken lunch at Brooks's afterward. He'd gone home for a time, intent on discussing some business affairs with his secretary and steward. But he found himself unable to concentrate on the ledgers and correspondence, and his employees exchanged speculative glances after he said "Would you repeat that" for the tenth time. They politely repeated their statement, only to find the earl indifferent to the crop figures he normally followed with great enthusiasm. After returning from India, he'd had the means to see to enormous improvements at Alworth. And until that day, he'd taken a detailed interest in each rick of hay and bushel of wheat, every head of cattle and sheep his acres produced.

"If you'd prefer discussing the crop projections some other time," Shelby, his secretary, suggested.

A small silence fell.

The young man was about to repeat himself, when the

earl pushed away from the desk and stood. "Some other day would be preferable," he said, glancing at the clock on the mantel.

Both men came to their feet.

Another awkward silence filled the large study. The earl seemed not to take notice of them, his dark eyes shadowed by his lowered lashes, his mouth pursed.

The steward cleared his throat and Dermott's lashes lifted. "Thank you very much." His smile was distant. "We'll do this another day."

He remained standing for several moments after the door closed on his employees, his large frame immobile, even his breathing difficult to perceive in the stillness of his pose. "I shouldn't go," he murmured into the hushed room.

He raised his hands to his fashionably windswept hair and raked his fingers through the heavy waves. Softly swearing, he held his head between his palms for a transient moment and then, exhaling, dropped his hands. "How the hell can it matter," he muttered, and strode toward the door.

But he resisted still, and once arriving at Molly's, he strolled into the card room and joined a game. He lost, and the rarity of the occurrence caused him to give in to his impulses. Excusing himself to the wide-eyed group of men who speculated once he'd gone that he was surely ill to have overlooked a straight flush, the earl took the stairs to the main floor in a run and walked into Molly's apartments without knocking.

He heard the giggling from the bedchamber immediately on entering the sitting room, recognizing the women's voices. He knew Molly's as well as his own. The other trilling tone was the reason he was there.

Against his better judgment.

Against every principle of disinterest he'd nurtured since his return to England.

He should have knocked, but bad tempered at his need, impelled by desires he'd tried to resist all day, he invaded the women's room like a man intent on plunder.

Molly said, "Hello, Dermott," her voice remarkably calm, her gaze knowing.

And the young woman who had dominated his thoughts since the night before whispered, "Oh, no!" in the merest of breaths.

"Join us in some champagne," Molly invited the earl.

He looked at her as though he'd not heard, his gaze immediately swinging back to Isabella, standing in the middle of the Aubusson carpet, her eyes wide with shock. She was dressed or, more aptly, undressed in black lace over flesh-colored silk mousseline, and he restrained himself from moving forward, picking her up, and throwing her on the bed.

"Do you like the dress?" Molly asked.

He forced himself to respond. "Yes," he said. His nostrils flared as he drew in a calming breath. "Very much."

"Isabella wasn't sure it suited her."

"It does." Like sorcery suits an enchantress, he thought, not sure he cared to stay in the same room with a woman who could make him forget everything but lust.

"There, you see?" Molly smiled at Isabella and then,

turning to Dermott, who'd not advanced past the threshold, she asked, "Would you like to see another gown on Isabella?"

"No." Male and female voices, instant and soft, spoke in unison.

"Very well." Molly waved the servants out and crooked a finger at Dermott. "Come in and join us." She patted a chair beside hers. "I hadn't expected you so early. Did you have good luck at Tattersall's this morning?"

The commonness of her question set the tone, and Dermott brought his errant senses to heel. "Very good luck," he replied, moving toward her. "I found two yearlings with promise and Harkin's roan was on the block."

"So you helped ease Harkin's gambling debts?"

"I may have paid them off," the earl noted, taking the chair beside Molly and sliding into a sprawl. "That roan is a damned fine racer."

"Do join us, Isabella." Molly pushed a delicate fauteuil forward.

There was no way to refuse and not look like a child, so Isabella tamped her feverish emotions with supreme effort and walked across the pale carpet.

He watched her from under his lashes.

Skittishly aware of his gaze, Isabella approached them with a wildly beating heart and pinked cheeks.

She fairly glowed, the provocative juxtaposition of trembling innocence and flamboyant sensuality intense, her ripe body displayed in all its splendor beneath the sheer black lace, her downcast gaze chaste as a virgin's.

Which thought momentarily disconcerted him, but anyone with a body like Venus herself couldn't be completely chaste, he decided. As if reason were a requirement with the state of his erection. He shifted marginally to ease the tightness of his trousers.

His movement, however slight, drew Isabella's gaze, and her breath caught in her throat. He was blatantly aroused, the black knit fabric of his trousers tightly stretched. And for the first time in her life, she felt a heated shimmer deep within the core of her body, the feeling so exquisite, she came to a halt.

He smiled as if he understood.

She smiled back because she couldn't stop herself.

And Molly thought it best to slow the pace. She wished her young guest to acquire some of the expertise necessary to entice more than Dermott's fleeting lust. "You must tell Dermott of your cartography society," Molly declared. "Miss Leslie owns an uncommon library of rare maps," she added, turning to Dermott. "Pour us all some champagne, and you can compare your visions of the world."

His vision at the moment had to do with a finite view of the paradise between Miss Leslie's legs, but he could see that Molly was intent on putting pause to their heated encounter, and no one ever bested Molly in a confrontation. "Really?" he said, reaching for the bottle in the bucket of ice. "Not the library in Grosvenor Square?"

"You know of it?" A new concentration overtook the fever of arousal, and Isabella took her seat with them.

"I've been there only twice. I didn't realize you were that Leslie, nor that the banker who held my mortgages was your—"

"Grandfather," Isabella quickly supplied. "My goodness!" She felt as though she knew him suddenly, his recollection of their connection enough to make him not so much a stranger who took her breath away but a family friend—who took her breath away, she reflected with an inner smile.

"Isabella will be staying with us for a few days," Molly noted, offering the information as though they'd not discussed her previously over breakfast.

"Lucky for us." Dermott leaned over with a glass of champagne for Isabella, careful not to touch her fingers. Regardless Molly's presence, he couldn't guarantee his docility.

The scent of him wafted over her as he leaned close, and heady with the fragrance of maleness and fresh citron, Isabella took the glass from him and proceeded to drink a good deal of it in one swallow.

Her agitation was appealing. Of course, what about her wasn't appealing, he mused, concentrating with effort on what Molly was saying as she offered him a plate of petit fours.

"She was thinking of perhaps acquiring some additional skills while she's with us," Molly declared, putting the plate down at his refusal.

Suddenly his attention was fixed, his gaze intense. "Additional . . ." he murmured, his glance swinging over to take in the disconcerted Miss Leslie.

"Isabella requires safeguards . . . protection from an unwanted marriage."

"I see." His dark gaze held Isabella's.

"Something in the way of a denouement."

"Ah . . ." His voice was like velvet.

Mesmerized, charmed, warmed by the sultry heat of

his regard, Isabella felt as though he might indeed be her white knight in this outlandish predicament. "I have relatives who wish my fortune," she murmured, half breathless under his spell.

"I could call them out." A strange obligation overcame him, as though he should offer her something for what he was about to receive.

"You would kill them surely." Nervously, she shook her head. "They aren't men skilled with weapons."

"Does it matter when they victimize you so cruelly?"

"I wouldn't wish their blood on my hands." The whole world knew of his expertise.

He didn't answer for a moment. "As you wish."

"Isabella wishes to discourage their avarice in a less fatal way," Mrs. Crocker interposed. "With your cooperation."

"At your service, mademoiselle." His voice was soft, low, oddly touched with compassion. Quickly setting his glass down, he slid up from his lounging pose, impatient with such sentiment.

"This is extremely awkward." Isabella twisted the stem of the goblet in her fingers and would have looked completely artless save for her voluptuous breasts about to burst from her low décolletage.

Awkward indeed, he thought, not sure he was capable of taking what she was offering with such guileless naivete. Equally sure he couldn't long resist her bounteous pulchritude. "Please," he gently said. "I believe I know what you're about to say, and there's no need. I willing accede to your wishes, whatever they may be. You decide what and where and let me know."

She looked up from the goblet in her hands and exhaled in relief. "You're most kind, sir."

"I'm most fortunate, Miss Leslie," he replied softly.

"Perhaps in a fortnight, Dermott," Molly submitted.

Isabella blushed while the earl wondered how he could last that long. But infinitely polite, he gracefully bowed his head. "I await your pleasure, ladies."

Dermott left Molly's shortly after, and waving his driver off, walked away at a pace that indicated his deep frustration. He passed through Green Park, continuing through Hyde Park to Kensington Gardens, completely immune to his surroundings, the uncommon degree of lust Miss Leslie evoked not only torturous but disturbing, his thoughts in tumult. A considerable time later, he found himself on the banks of the Thames, the sun setting over the river in a spectacularly brilliant crimson, and startled, he looked around as though waking from a dream.

Understanding a degree of sanity and good judgment was called for, he found a hackney cab, gave directions for his London house, and studiously avoided thinking of the blond jezebel in the black lace gown. Intent on supplanting images of the delectable Miss Leslie with more available females, he arrived home, quickly bathed and dressed, and set out for an evening at Carlton House, where the Prince of Wales's set could always be counted on for unbridled revelry.

Dinner was informal, with the usual male coterie of the Prince's engaged in outdrinking each other. Mrs. Fitzherbert was in Brighton, so the few women present were of questionable social status, a fact Dermott welcomed in his present churlish state.[2] As the evening progressed, the guests moved into the music room, where they were joined by ladies who were there to entertain them with their musical abilities along with other more titillating delights. And by midnight a general state of inebriated carouse was well under way. While the Prince of Wales swore his devotion to Mrs. Fitzherbert, he was easily dissuaded from the path of faithfulness if she was absent, and tonight a dancer from the corps de ballet was piquing his interest. She not only danced but sang extremely well, charming the Prince, who delighted in music of all kinds and singing in particular.

The party had just finished a rousing second chorus of a drinking song when the Prince cast a glance at Dermott, who alone was without female company, and cheerfully called out, "No cunt tonight, Dermott? Should I send for the doctor?"

"I'm on a rest cure."

"Venus's revenge got you?"

Dermott shook his head as he lay sprawled on a silk-covered chaise with peculiar crocodile feet. "I've found religion," he drawled, his voice rich with liquor.

"Oh, ho! And maybe I've a notion to take back my wife," the Prince hooted.[3] "Although it might be a tad crowded in bed with all her lovers."

A roar of drunken laughter greeted his statement.

"Ain't like you, Bathurst, that's all." Beau Brummell spoke into the lessening guffaws and chuckles in the same fastidious tone with which he dressed, his cool-eyed gaze keen despite a night of drinking.[4]

"But then, variety is the spice of life," Dermott murmured, his dark eyes clear and challenging. "Any argument there?"

"Acquit me, Bathurst," Brummell casually disclaimed. "You know how I dislike intense physical activity early in the morning, not to mention the risk of bloodying my linen."

The sudden silence that had fallen at Dermott's quiet query evaporated in a communal sigh of relief.

"There, there," the Prince interjected. "What we all need is another bottle." Snapping his fingers brought a number of footmen on the run, and the noisy carouse resumed.

But everyone took note of Dermott's departure shortly after, although no one dared question his motive when he rose from his chaise and exited the room.

"He's blue-deviled," the Marquis of Jervis remarked as the door closed on the earl's back.

"Must be a woman."

"Not with Bathurst. He don't care for any of 'em enough."

"Did he losh a race today?"

"No races today, Wiggy," a young baronet interjected. "You're too drunk to remember."

"Naw drunk," the Duke of Marshfield's heir slurred.

"Maybe he's bored," Brummell noted, his sobriety conspicuous in the sea of drunkenness.

"Never saw Bathurst bored with cunt before."

A general nodding of heads greeted the remark.

"A pony says he's hors de combat." A young man winked.

"Never happened before. I'll raise you a pony against it."

The state of Dermott's health continued in heated debate until the betting included most everyone in the room, for or against, a coin toss deciding who would talk to his doctor in the morning. No one considered asking Bathurst personally.

Not in his current ill temper.

When the earl found himself at Molly's several hours later, wet from the rain falling outside and more sober than he would have liked, Kate was waiting. She welcomed him with a smile despite the late hour, and he followed her to bed, trying not to let his moodiness show. He performed well because he always did and because he didn't wish her to suffer for his own black humor, and once he'd pleasured her and found his own relief, he fell asleep like a man dead to the world.

She wasn't without insight, and she sat up afterward and watched him in the candlelight, wondering what demons were driving him. She knew of the death of his wife and son; was tonight some anniversary? But it had happened years before, and even Molly said he was over it as much as anyone can ever be over such a devastating loss. With female intuition she wondered whether the young lady taking up residence in Molly's quarters might more likely figure in his moodiness. Call it a hunch or a bit of gossip revealed by one of the maids, but if she were a betting woman, she'd say Dermott's newest fancy was contributing to his ill humor. And if she were anything but a sensible young woman who understood earls didn't marry courtesans, she might allow herself to mourn the imminent loss of his company.

But she was eminently pragmatic; she was also very near her financial goals, thanks to Dermott's generosity, and soon she would put period to her life here and return to her young daughter in the country with enough money to live the life of a genteel widow.

Dermott was dear to her. She lightly stroked the gleaming black of his hair spread on the pillow and leaned over to gently kiss his cheek.

He woke at her touch, gathered her in his arms, mumbled something affectionate, and fell back to sleep.

She would miss him, she thought, lying in his warm embrace. He was the kindest of men.

5

ISABELLA'S EDUCATION BEGAN the following morning.
A bath was brought in after her breakfast, and she was
bathed and dried in so leisurely and sensuous a manner,
she felt as though she were adrift in a dream. And while
she was supposed to pay attention to all manner of tech-
nique mentioned by Molly, her concentration was fixed,
rather, on exquisite sensation. After her bath, she was escorted to a narrow daybed, where she lay down for the
next lesson in a tyro courtesan's life. Warm jasmine-
scented oil was trickled over her skin, each heated drop
like tingling bewitchment as it struck her. With the gentle
stroking massage on her flesh artfully heating her senses,
her attention wandered once again, Molly's voice explaining the mysteries of amour fading away, the slow, tantalizing hands roving her body too delectable to deny. She
found herself substituting her favorite lush fantasy for the
sound of Molly's voice, experiencing instead the soul-
stirring feel of Bathurst's strong hands gliding over her
softly—squeezing, rubbing, drifting in a slow, luxurious
rhythm downward until, breath held, she felt her cleft

eased open and the sensation of warmth melt into her pulsing tissue.

The intense, spiking pleasure snapped her eyes wide.

"Always see that you are sweet scented everywhere," Molly calmly remarked.

"I see," Isabella murmured, half breathless.

"Bathurst is particular."

His name alone caused a new surge of heat to curl inside her, the perfumed flesh between her legs throbbing anew. "I'll remember," she whispered, remembering as well how Bathurst had looked aroused. How she'd trembled at the sight of his rigid length and size. "Is he here?"

"It doesn't matter."

Half rising, she rested on her forearms. "Is he with someone?"

"He's always with someone." Molly spoke plainly. There was no point in deceiving the young woman.

"Then I shall have to pay more attention, shan't I," Isabella said, lying down again, "if I wish to engage his interest."

"Is that what you wish?" This young girl was refreshing—neither alarmed nor confused.

Isabella smiled. "I do most fervently." Images of Dermott's stark beauty had saturated her dreams, not only just moments earlier but through the night past, and she found herself wanting him with a fevered indiscretion that overlooked all but her urgent desires. Desires she'd not known existed a mere day before. "I almost feel as though I should thank Uncle Herbert and Harold for their villainy in driving me here."

"Such uncomplicated thinking will serve you well."

"Exactly. I'll have my fortune *and* some very fine memories once I leave. Am I not fortunate?"

"Your frankness is disarming."

"You must teach me *everything*," Isabella said with an expansive wave of her arm, "and I shall see that Bathurst has a memorable time."

Molly's brow quirked. "Is this a contest?"

"Do you mind if it is?"

Molly laughed. "He's well ahead of you."

"But not of you, I expect."

"Perhaps . . . although I offer no guarantees. I've not spent time in India."

"There are Hindu love books. I know there are because a captain brought some back once and Grandpapa quickly put them away. Let's have Mr. Martin find them for us."

Her excitement was a delight. "You wish to send Bathurst over the moon?"

"I wish to arouse him to the most sublime colossal pitch." Isabella's downy brows lifted faintly. "Am I terribly wicked?"

"Wonderfully wicked, I'd say. Why don't I see to some books?"

The first frontispiece they looked at portrayed a handsome young footman, partially undressed, servicing a pretty lady in her boudoir. The caption beneath the picture brought a smile to Isabella's lips: *Being in service requires dedication, obedience, and a willingness to learn.* "The lady seems to be enjoying herself. Although I doubt all employees are so handsome."

.

"They are if your husband allows," Molly sardonically replied. "This book is rumored to have been written by several noblewomen of the highest rank."

"Then ladies are allowed their vices as well? I never realized . . ."

"Their vices require a deal more discretion, but, yes, there are ladies who enjoy themselves with equal gusto. For instance, take note of the next illustrations."

In a sequence of five etchings, the tale of a shopping expedition in Bond Street was depicted. The young shop men were dazzlingly handsome and well formed, and from the looks of the various illustrations, bent on offering any particular service a lady desired.

"I always thought the shop men were delightfully handsome, but I never realized *why* they were so good-looking. Is everyone but me aware of their sexual availability?"

"Those who are interested are aware. However, discretion is ever the watchword."

"My education has been sadly lacking," Isabella playfully bemoaned. "Heavens," she exclaimed, gazing at the next illustration, "don't tell me every handsome groom I see in Hyde Park is making love to his mistress."

"I would say, generally," Molly explained, "if one sees a good-looking groom and a lady who takes undue interest in her equine skills, a high degree of suspicion is called for."

"My life has been dreadfully dull. All I ever did was sell shipments brought to London on our vessels."

"Keep in mind, all the pleasures you see depicted are

generally reserved for married women. Virginity is still the gold standard for a suitable marriage."

"Well, since I have no immediate plans for marriage and have yet to see a man who would even interest me in that regard—"

Molly's eyebrows rose.

"Surely not. I know what you're thinking, but Bathurst would no more marry me than he would cook your dinner. So I shall be ever so grateful to you for showing me— well, what I've been missing. And allowing me an education in certain pleasures that may interest me in the future—whether I'm married or not."

"You have a fearless air, my dear."

"And why should I not? Would it help in my present situation to be fearful? Would I better survive if I were? I think not. My relatives showed me most viciously what would have become of me if I were docile." She shrugged. "So I shan't be if ever I was anyway," she added, smiling. "Grandpapa spoiled me considerably."

"Not necessarily a liability in your case," Molly noted. "You seem to know what you want."

"I find myself quite enamored of these feelings that heat my body. Once tasted, as they say . . . I rather look forward to continuing the pleasure."

Isabella was kept busy most of the day with various lessons that would make her more comfortable in the boudoir—how to dress and sit . . . or lie, how to serve food should a man require it, how to offer him a bath should the occasion arise, what exactly were the degrees of acquiescence most necessary to a woman intent on pleasing a client. Her instructors were all pretty women no older than she who directed her schooling with a casualness and humor she found entertaining.

They had orders not to speak personally of themselves, so she learned little of their background and reasons for occupying Molly's house, but none seemed disturbed to be there and all were enthusiastic about her coming liaison with Bathurst.

"Does everyone know?" Isabella asked when the subject was broached yet again.

"Only a few. We who are helping," a woman named Bess replied. "Molly is strict about that. For your own privacy, she says. But you're really going to like Bathurst. There isn't a woman alive who doesn't."

"So I've heard. Why is he so highly regarded? Beyond his startling good looks, of course."

"He likes women. It shows in everything he does—lucky you. Although he and Kate are pretty exclusive now." She shrugged. "So he's been out of circulation for the rest of us. But he wasn't always. Now, look, let me show you what he particularly likes."

By evening, Isabella was nervously pacing the room. It was all well and good to treat lovemaking like some kind of business of skill and expertise, but she wasn't completely emotionless, nor were her senses. And by the time her round of studies had concluded that day, she was acutely aware of her body's responses to amorous suggestion. She'd been feeling blissfully heated for hours, her skin felt as though the merest touch would suffocate her, images of Bathurst were prevalent in her mind, and the thought of seeing his strong body unclothed when at last they met in bed was so titillating to her senses, she feared she would forget all she'd learned and collapse in a puddle at his feet.

On edge, restless, she felt an irrepressible need to escape her room, or better yet, the house, although she knew it was impossible. Another half hour passed, her agitation heightening, inchoate desires bombarding her senses. Perhaps she could at least do her pacing in the corridor or breathe some fresh air on the small balcony at the end of the hall. Following her impulse, she quit her room, strode through the empty sitting room, and walked out into the hallway. Molly's personal apartments were separate from the business of the house, and quiet.

She heard his voice first and then his laugh, and she was drawn to the sound as though he were the magnet of her desires. And then she heard the low, throaty female voice, and somehow shocked when she should have known better in a house of pleasure, she halted in her tracks.

It would be discourteous to eavesdrop; she should return to her room. But even as she acknowledged the most fitting conduct, she was moving toward the low sounds of conversation.

The door at the end of the hall was ajar. Stopping just short of it, she leaned forward and peered inside.

A luxurious candlelit room lay before her gaze. A more luxurious room than hers, one designed for lovemaking, with soft chairs and plush carpets and an overlarge bed on which a beautiful nude woman lay.

Bathurst was pouring himself a drink from a small

liquor table. He wore riding breeches, as though he'd just come in from the country, and his boots had been kicked off near the door. A chamois coat and linen shirt were draped over a chair back, his stockings tossed beneath it. She took note of each item of clothing as though it mattered where he'd discarded it, as if she might discern the degree of his desire for the dark-haired woman if she catalogued the location of the garments. And she experienced an uncharitable pleasure in the fact that he stood across the room from the bed.

"Do come here, Dermott," the pretty brunette murmured, her voice seductive, her voluptuous form elegantly disposed on the crimson silk coverlet.

"Soon." Lifting his glass to his mouth, he tossed it down and turned back to the well-stocked table.

"You said that a half hour ago."

"I have a thirst after talking business with Shelby since morning." He gently smiled. "Be patient, darling."

"You're restless tonight."

"I'm not restless." He added another inch to his glass, topping it off. "I just feel like drinking." Turning back to her, he raised his glass in salute.

"Should I read to you while you drink? I've a new novel."

"Later," he politely murmured, moving toward a chair near the fire. Dropping into it, he slid into a lounging sprawl, tipped the glass to his mouth, and swallowed half the brandy like a man intent on getting drunk.

"Did Shelby annoy you?"

He shook his head. "He's too damned polite to annoy anyone. Remarkable," he added with a half-smile, "considering his heritage. That whole damned family is demented. He must be a by-blow."

"Should I go to sleep?" She spoke with a pouting moue, her voice velvety and low.

He gazed at her through narrowed eyes. "Have I ever disappointed you?"

She smiled. "You're a damned beautiful sight, Bathurst, that's all. I crave your body."

The firelight gilded his bronzed form, the heavy muscles of his chest and shoulders prominent, his long, powerful legs, strong arms, and hands arresting to the eye. His face was more handsome than God should allow—the perfectly modeled bone structure, fine, straight nose, sensual mouth, his dark, heavily lashed eyes so seductive, a single look could lure a woman to destruction. And not to be discounted among his lavish attributes was his distinguished arousal conspicuous even under black breeches in dim light.

"Another half bottle and you'll have what you crave."

"Promises, promises," she playfully replied, rolling off the bed in a lithe, smooth movement. "Maybe I'll indulge myself another way," she purred, moving toward him.

"Be my guest," he offered, leaning over to reach for the brandy bottle. "I'm completely at your disposal."

"Not completely—yet . . ." she murmured, dropping to her knees and sliding between his outstretched legs. She touched the top button of his breeches, sliding her finger over the engraved silver. "But soon," she whispered, slipping the first button free.

"You have a charming way about you," he softly said, half smiling in the firelight.

"And you have what I want." Another button came free and yet a third.

"Now, this is so much better than the dull farm reports that filled my day." He gazed down at her and faintly winked.

"While I've been waiting for *this* all day," she whispered, opening the last button and reaching inside his open breeches to draw out his erection.

He drew in a sharp breath at the touch of her hand.

Isabella did as well at the sight of him.

He was magnificent—immense, towering, flagrantly rigid.

Isabella put her hand over her mouth to curtail her exclamation of astonishment. Her body throbbed with added intensity, the heat rising to her face bringing a sheen to her forehead, and she wondered how it would feel to lie with him, to absorb the enormity of what she saw.

She could scarcely breathe as the woman slid her fingers down his great length, the upthrust head of his arousal stretching, gleaming in the firelight, its size visibly enlarging.

Draining his glass of brandy, Dermott set it aside, leaned his head back, and shut his eyes at the moment Kate's mouth touched him.

He should refuse, he transiently thought, aware of why he was so restless, of why he hadn't wanted to join Kate in bed. But her mouth was drawing him in and he wasn't chaste or incorruptible, especially of late. Suppressing the disturbing images of Molly's newest pet and his own mysterious obsession, he gave in to dissolute pleasure. To a man intent on forgetting, living for the moment was a familiar concept, and he allowed himself to sink into a sea of self-indulgence.

The woman's head seemed to move in slow motion, Isabella noted, her mouth lingering at the crest of the ascent for protracted moments, then sliding down the entire length with silken fluidity. How could she possibly breathe at that point, Isabella wondered, both aroused and furious at the sight, jealousy a nebulous demon in her mind.

Dermott's low, soft moan gave evidence of his gratification, and Isabella's displeasure escalated. How could he engage in sex with this woman when he'd said he wanted her?

But she knew the answer even as she asked the question.

Because a woman was a woman was a woman for the Earl of Bathurst—the exemplary standard and model for casual sex. She would do well to remember that brutal fact. But reality, however brutal, couldn't nullify her heated response, nor her wanting him like any woman who set eyes on him, and seething with resentment, she spun away.

"Where have you been?" Molly was in the sitting room when Isabella returned.

"Enjoying a firsthand view of Bathurst and a woman," she snapped, swiftly moving toward her bedchamber, her cheeks hot with indignation.

"Oh, dear." Setting down her pen, Molly pushed aside the ledger she was working on. "Can I help?"

"No!" Immediately regretting her sharp reply, Isabella

came to a stop and forced a polite smile. "I'd just like to be alone, if you don't mind."

"No, of course not."

Turning away, Isabella swiftly proceeded to her room, slamming the door behind her as though such pettiness would allay her anger. And pettiness it was, she ruefully admitted a short time later when her temper had cooled. What possible hold did she have on Bathurst? What possible reason would he have to preserve his virtue for her? It was laughable. He was the most irresistible man in London, and not because of his charming ways at the whist table. Although knowing him, he probably had entertained a lady or two on the card tables as well. She was able to smile then, imagining the scene, and ever practical, before long she had reconciled reality with ridiculous girlish wishes.

That done, she undressed, put on her nightrail, and climbed into bed with a book, but it was impossible to read with the lurid images fresh in her mind. She sighed, frustrated, torn between anger, need, and practicality, her emotions in turmoil. He was even more beautiful unclothed, she recalled, his powerful body perfection. No wonder women craved him. She shut her eyes against the surge of desire that coursed through her. Strange, how ardent longing could overcome minor matters like a libertine's reputation, his lack of constancy, the bizarre oddity of what they were about to do. Stranger yet that she envied his bed partner tonight when moments ago, she'd been cursing her existence. Imagining another scene with herself beside him, she fell asleep, smiling and dreaming romantic dreams.

* * *

Later, Molly came into Isabella's room, turned down the lamps, and took away the book that had fallen from her hand. Standing at the bedside for a moment, she gazed at the fresh young beauty who had stumbled into her home. Was she doing the right thing? she wondered. Or would Bathurst hurt her in the end? Should she find Isabella a lawyer with clout? Would such a man be able to protect her from all the predators? And at base, was her scheme too outré both for Isabella and her own sense of justice? No simple answers came to mind, only uncertainty and doubt as she pondered the dilemma of this young heiress facing a brutal world.

Perhaps by morning, Molly thought, some solution would clarify her unsettled thoughts. Certainly, she would talk to Isabella once more to see that she understood completely. Too many of her own emotions were associated with the young woman's plight, too many long-ago wounds that never quite healed distorted her ability to deal rationally with the situation.

But ultimately it wasn't her decision, she knew. There was comfort at least in that.

Isabella would make her own choice.

With a sigh, she quietly closed the door behind her.

Dermott stayed with Kate as long as politeness required, allowing her the pleasure she craved, indulging her senses, skillfully operating on instinct if not emotion. But she seemed not to notice, or if she did, she knew better than to take issue. Either way, he left feeling guilty—a ridiculous sentiment to be experiencing under the circumstances, his friends would attest. But ridiculous or not, he wasn't a happy man when he stalked into Molly's sitting room, glanced at the closed door to Isabella's bedchamber to check that she wouldn't hear him, and said in a low, decisive voice. "I'll be back in a week. Get her ready. But I mean to have her when I return, ready or not."

Molly pushed her chair away from the small desk. "I won't have her forced."

"I don't foresee a problem."

"Unfortunately, she saw you tonight."

"Saw me?" His expression darkened. "What the hell's wrong with you?"

"I had nothing to do with it. You left your door open."

"Jesus . . ." He glanced at the clock on the mantel. "How long was she there?"

"Not long. I was gone from the sitting room for only a short time."

"Thank God for that, I suppose."

"I'm not exactly sure what she saw, but she was angry when she returned."

He softly swore.

"Just a word of advice. She's a willful young lady." Her gaze over her reading spectacles was direct. "Consider, you might be taking on more than you wish."

"I don't intend to take on anything. We all understand only a finite amount of time is involved."

"And yet you seem curiously compelled." She took off her spectacles and placed them on the desk. "Hardly a common feeling for you."

"Maybe it's the spring weather," he sardonically drawled.

"Or maybe it's something you won't be able to control as easily as all your other casual alliances."

"Let's not make too much of this arrangement. It's sex we're talking about. She understands, I understand, you understand. Just have her ready for me in one week, and I'll reward you handsomely."

"I don't want money."

His hand on the door latch slipped away, and his gaze took on a new keenness. "You really mean it? You're feeling that charitable?"

"She strikes my fancy. I don't want to profit by her misfortunes."

"You realize what you could get for her virginity."

"Who better than me," she calmly replied. "Should I put her out for auction?"

"No!"

"So sure?"

"Don't toy with me, Molly. She's mine." Gripping the latch once again, he pulled the door ajar. "One week," he gently said, and opening the door completely, he let himself out.

6

❧

DERMOTT RAISED a considerable number of eyebrows the following week as he participated in the punishing schedule of spring planting. From morning to night, he worked alongside the plowmen, setting so wicked a pace, his tenants wondered if he'd gone daft from his weeks of carouse in London. And when he should have been tired at night, he couldn't sleep, so he drank himself into oblivion instead. But even then he couldn't suppress the images of a young, innocent woman with eyes like deep blue summer skies and a face so fair he was reminded of goodness and unclouded days.

He scoffed at his absurd folly. Only a fool put stock in flimflam daydreams. But suddenly there was promise in the air, when his world had been shades of gray for a very long time. And fool or not, he crossed off the days, impatient for the week to end.

The day before he was to leave for London, he went to spend the evening with his mother. She lived, by choice, in a small manor house on his estate, her memories of the main house too painful. He always made it a point to visit his mother each day when he was home from London, but he felt a need for her company tonight as well.

He didn't know why.

But he brought her a bouquet of her favorite ruffled tulips and a special pear from the gardener, who knew her partiality for the fruit.

He waved away the servants when he entered the house and quietly entered her sitting room. Coming up behind her as she sat by the fire, he kissed her cheek, and sweeping his arms around her, presented her with his gifts.

Swiveling around, she gave him a glowing smile. "I smelled your cologne, darling, so you couldn't really sneak up on me. But I adore surprises. You came to see me again tonight." Taking his gifts from him, she lay the tulips in her lap and admired the perfect ripe pear. "Timms is such a dear. He always remembers me."

"He's forcing some new kind of pear for you as well," Dermott said, taking a seat across from her. "I think he said they were from Persia."

"Didn't we go there once?"

"You're thinking of your father."

"We weren't with him?"

Dermott's grandfather had died before he was born, his years of travel preceding his mother's childhood as well. "He told you stories. That's what you're remembering."

"You're sure."

"Maybe I'm not completely sure," he said kindly. "Tell me what you recall."

"I remember the ruins of Darius' palace and the bazaars with all their beautiful colors and smells and the beautiful terraces at Nakshi Rustam."

His mother had retreated into the past the last years of her marriage, and even when his father had died, she'd not recovered completely from the misery of her marriage. He understood it was safer for her to live in her own universe. "That palace should be one of the wonders of the world. It's spectacular, isn't it?"

"Especially at sunrise." She smiled. "I always liked it best at sunrise. You have a Thoroughbred named Sunrise, don't you? And your darling grays. How are they doing?"

She always knew him as her son regardless her tangled thoughts. And she would speak to him of his present events as though he alone was allowed to hold a contemporary place in her fractured reality.

"The grays are getting sleek in the pasture and Sunrise won at Doncaster last month."

"Did you win a tidy sum?"

"Enough to buy you some new diamonds if you wish."

"Now, why would I wish diamonds? I have all I want. You buy diamonds for some pretty young thing who turns your head. You haven't married yet, have you?"

When he'd returned to England, he'd told his mother of the death of his wife and son, but she had no concept of India, and it would never stay in her memory. Unlike Persia, the land she'd heard so much about as a child. "I'm not married, *Maman*."

"Do you have a special lady in your life?" Her voice was playful, her blue eyes bright with curiosity.

"Maybe I do." The words shocked him even as uttered them.

"Tell me about her. Bring her to see me. You know how I'd love anyone you love."

"I don't think it's come to that yet, *Maman*. But she fascinates me."

"Then she will fascinate me as well. Does she ride?"

As a young lady, his mother's passion had been riding to hounds.

"I'm not sure. She's from the City."

"The City? My goodness. Then she must be very rich."

"She is, I think."

"Well, we don't need her money now, do we, darling. So you can love her for herself. That's quite a nice idea. Unlike marriages of convenience." Her expression suddenly changed, the joy vanishing from her eyes.

"She has blue eyes like you, *Maman*," Dermott quickly interposed. "And the most beautiful golden hair, like a fairy sprite. I thought her that the first time I saw her."

His mother's expression immediately brightened. "A fairy sprite? Oh, I adore fairies. Does she look like Queen Titania in *Midsummer Night's Dream*?"

"Better."

She clapped her hands. "Then you're a very lucky man. Better than Titania *and* a fairy. Do hurry and bring her to me."

"I'll have to ask her."

"Yes, you certainly will. Tell her you have the best racing stable in Gloucestershire and she'll be sure to come. Even girls from the City like horses."

His mother assumed everyone loved horses. "I'll tell her, *Maman*."

The thought stayed with him on his journey back to London, when he'd never before considered asking a woman to his country home. There was no explanation, although he tried mightily to make sense of his wish to bring Miss Leslie home to meet his mother. Maybe she reminded him of youthful hope or of happier times when he was young. Maybe there was no explanation for his longing. Like the riddles of the universe.

His feelings wouldn't sensibly fall into some judicious clarity no matter how he rationalized, but it had been so long since he'd acknowledged any feeling other than transient pleasure that he wasn't sure he'd recognize real emotion anyway. But of one thing he was sure. He didn't wish to spend his first night with Miss Leslie in a brothel. No matter the act he was about to commit was businesslike and sexual. It was also more.

It was the first time since Damayanti died that he'd looked forward to a lady's company. He quickly warned himself not to have too high expectations, not to set too great a store on a young woman who was willing to coolly dispense with her virginity in order to safeguard her fortune. Perhaps a good lawyer would have worked for her as well.

She could turn out to be cold and calculating. Although that persona didn't seem to fit the blushing young lady he'd met at Molly's. Not that women weren't capable of the most deceitful theatrics. That he knew from personal experience.

Time would tell, he noted practically. And if sated lust was the only consequence of his liaison with Miss Leslie, he couldn't in good conscience expect more. But he sent a note to Molly on his arrival in London. Miss Leslie was requested to present herself at Bathurst House at seven.

Molly concealed her surprise when she conveyed the contents of Dermott's request to Isabella. "Apparently, he'll feel more comfortable at his own home," she stated, when she and Isabella both knew Dermott spent more time at Molly's than he did at Bathurst House.

"Very well," Isabella politely replied, her degree of nervousness already intense when the agreed-on date finally arrived. The last week had been a frantic round of activities. Her body felt as though it had been washed and massaged and perfumed with such an eye to detail, she could have been presented to the sultan of sultans without disgrace.

Molly stood in the doorway of Isabella's room, Dermott's note in her hand. "I don't think I can teach you anything more."

"You've been very kind, really." Isabella shut the book she'd been trying to read for the past hour.

"Bathurst will send his carriage at half past six."

"I'll be ready." She stood as though matching activity to words.

"We sound as though you're about to mount the guillotine."

Isabella forced a smile, her nerves on edge. "Hardly. Tonight will, in fact, insure me a peaceful life."

"I remind myself of that when I'm in doubt."

"Please," Isabella enjoined, moving toward her hostess, "don't feel responsible for what I'm about to do." Taking one of her hands in hers, she gently squeezed it. "I'm of age and relatively sound mind," she added with a smile. "I'm quite capable of taking responsibility for my actions."

"Nevertheless, I shall warn Bathurst to treat you well or incur my wrath."

"That won't be necessary if all the stories the ladies have been telling me are true. He apparently is the kindest, most amorous and gentle of lovers."

"Hmpf," Molly grumbled, drawing Isabella into her arms. "Take care, my sweet," she murmured. "He may be kind and sweet, but for all that, he's still a man, and I'm not so sure any of them can be trusted." Patting Isabella's back lightly, she stepped away and smiled at the young girl who had captured her affection. "And despite all the damnable training this week, you do what *you* want; the devil with what he wants." Much as she loved Bathurst, he was a seasoned player in the world of amour. He could take care of himself. This young mite needed all the help she could get.

"Yes, ma'am," Isabella playfully replied, dropping a polite curtsy to her protector. "I shall be the soul of selfishness."

"Good for you," Molly said gruffly. "Now I'll have Mercer send up a nice half bottle of wine for you to steady your nerves. And I'll help you dress."

7

HE WAS NEVER NERVOUS. It was impossible he could be nervous. Good God, where was his valet when he needed him? This neckcloth was impossibly wrong. "Charles!" he shouted. "Dammit, what were you thinking when you tied this thing!"

"Sorry, my lord," Charles apologized, coming back into the dressing room at a run, six fresh neckcloths draped over his arm. "I'm sure the next one will be tied to your satisfaction."

But it wasn't, of course, because nothing at the moment was completely satisfying, and when Dermott was finally dressed to an acceptable degree of correctness, Charles disappeared downstairs to regale the servants with a detailed account of the earl's toilette, down to his three changes of evening coat and the crushing of the offending neckcloths under his heel.

"She must be somethin' real special," a footman said. "He ain't never had no—"

"Hasn't ever," the housekeeper corrected him.

"Ain't never," the footman repeated, wrinkling his nose at the housekeeper, who considered herself the superior person below stairs, "had no light o'love to Bathurst House. And what with the cook cooking for hours now and the wine steward ordered to serve only the very best—"

"And the flowers," the upstairs maid declared with feeling. "I've never seen so many flowers."

"I'd say she's a Venus for sure," another footman maintained. "Or like that Helen of Troy, whose face launched a thousand ships, they say."

"Well, we'll soon see, will we not," the butler, Pomeroy, intoned in his haughty basso. Rising to his feet, he surveyed his staff with a piercing gaze. "Places, everyone," he ordered. "She's due to arrive in fifteen minutes." After a meticulous straightening of his shirt cuffs, he turned from the table and moved to the stairs that would bring him into position in the entrance hall.

Dermott stood at the window of the north drawing room, his third glass of brandy in his hand, his gaze on the street below, feeling as though he were going into battle. His pulse was racing, his nerves were on alert, and the tension in his shoulders strained the superfine fabric to a degree that would be unsuitable to his tailor. Draining the glass of liquor, he felt the heat flow down his throat with a kind of relief, as though at least one familiar sensation struck his brain when all else was chaos. The clock chimed the hour, and he glanced at the bronzed winged victory with a timepiece between her feet. Where the hell was Miss Leslie? It was seven.

Had she changed her mind? Had Molly changed it for

her? Had he thrown his entire establishment into turmoil for nothing? The scent of lilies suddenly overcame him, and glancing about the room, he saw a great number of very large arrangements—like a funeral, he thought. "Shelby!" he bellowed.

His secretary came around the corner so instantly, he must have been standing outside the door. "Have the maids take some of these damnable flowers away," Dermott barked. "They smell."

"Yes, sir. Would you like to greet your guest in some other room? The scent may linger even if the vases are removed."

At Shelby's propitiating tone, Dermott realized how rude he'd been. "Forgive me, Shelby," he apologized. "You can see how out of practice I've become at paying court to a lady. And no, this room is fine. Here, you take one of these," he said, handing his secretary a large vase of flowers, "and I'll take another, and that will be sufficient to make this room look less like—"

"A funeral?"

"Exactly."

The two men were at the top of the staircase about to descend to the entrance hall and dispose of their vases when the front door opened and Isabella stepped into the grand marble entrance hall.

Dermott swore at the bad timing.

She looked up.

The butler looked up as well and, wide-eyed, surveyed his employer with a large vase of lilies in his hand.

"Are those for me?" Isabella sweetly inquired.

Dermott grinned. "If you want 'em. Although I warn you, they smell," he said, moving down the stairs.

"I'd be surprised if they didn't. Don't you like lilies?"

"Not this many." Reaching the bottom of the stairs, he offered them to her with a bow. "For your pleasure, my lady."

"One of many tonight, I presume." Her warm gaze met his over the lilies.

"Your wish is my command," he murmured.

"What a charming concept. I do look forward to the evening."

"As do I, Miss Leslie." He handed the vase to Pomeroy and reached for the ties on her cloak, a possessive gesture, symbolic perhaps of the fact he was the taker and she the takee. Standing very close as he untied the velvet ribbon, he said so low the words were for her alone, "I've waited a long time."

"I pray you won't be disappointed." But her tone was playful rather than conciliatory, and his gaze came up from the tangled knot.

"No chance of that," he whispered. And slipping the bow open, he slowly undraped the cloak from her shoulders as though he were unwrapping a personal gift.

The young footmen audibly gasped, but none received a reproach from their superiors, for all eyes were trained on the young lady. Isabella's white lace gown was so sheer, the shadow of her body was only partially concealed, the risqué décolletage more in the nature of a tenuous support for the plump mounds of her breasts, the entire garment held in place with two small silver shoulder bows, the imminent threat of gravity adding a delicious element of suspense to the ensemble.

"My compliments, Miss Leslie," Dermott murmured. "You have taken all our breaths away."

"As do you, my lord. You quite turn my head." He looked large and powerful dressed in perfectly tailored black superfine, his tall, rangy form shown to advantage, his linen, crisp and white, gleaming in the candlelight, the diamond at his throat so large, it could have come only from India.

"Might I offer you"—the heat fairly crackled in the air—"a glass of champagne?"

"That would be very nice," she purred, "for now. . . ."

He acknowledged the delectable purr with an appreciative smile and offered his arm. "Miss Leslie."

"My lord Bathurst." Dipping a small curtsy, she placed her hand on his strong wrist and they both felt the heated jolt.

Inhaling deeply, Dermott wondered how in the world he was going to repress his carnal urges when his hard-on was embarrassing him in front of his staff and the little minx was deliberately leaning into him so her breasts were almost spilling out of her gown. Dinner, he thought. "Dinner," he said to Pomeroy. "We'll have dinner now."

"Now, my lord?" The schedule had been specific. Champagne and brandy first, then dinner at nine.

"Now."

"Yes, my lord." Pomeroy moved forward to escort them to the dining room, knowing the chef was going to tear his hair out with dinner pushed up two hours. On the other hand, he reflected, the earl and his lady seemed oblivious of all but each other. There was a good possibility they wouldn't notice what they were eating.

The dining room positively gleamed, Isabella thought as they entered the large chamber—the polished cherry-wood walls, the massive silver plate on the sideboard and table, the crystal goblets marching in a row beside the two services set on the polished mahogany table, the gilt frames on the paintings adorning the walls, the twin chandeliers of Russian crystal that dripped from the high coffered ceiling. She felt as though she'd entered a shining Aladdin's cave.

"Do you always eat in such splendor?" she asked, slightly in awe of such magnificence.

It took him a moment to answer because he rarely ate at home, and when he did, he generally shared a tray with Shelby in his study. "Actually no." In fact, he couldn't remember when last he'd eaten in this room. "Would you rather have dinner somewhere else?"

In bed with you, she thought, still trembling from his touch, but it wouldn't do to be so forward. Bess had said men never liked women to give orders. "This is very nice. Really."

"Would you like a glass of champagne?" he asked because he badly needed a drink.

"Oh, I would very much. Thank you."

With a nod, he indicated Pomeroy serve them. "The room seems warm, or I'd suggest we sit by the fire, although you're probably not warm," he added with a smile, surveying her scantily dressed form.

"Actually I am . . . dreadfully warm, I mean—the room is indeed warm. . . ."

Her stammering innocence was charming. "So we'll sit away from the fire."

"Yes, please, I'd like that."

Suddenly she seemed very young, very different from the seductive minx in the entrance hall, and he felt an odd disquiet. "How old are you?"

"Twenty-two."

His sigh of relief brought a smile to her face.

"I didn't realize age mattered."

"It's bad enough—just set the tray down, Pomeroy, we'll serve ourselves." As the butler walked away, Dermott said, "It's bad enough you're a virgin; I'm not, however, about to bed some adolescent child." A grin broke across his face. "Although you definitely don't have the look of a child, Miss Leslie. And I mean it in the most complimentary way." He handed Isabella a stemmed goblet of champagne.

"Molly thought you'd like the gown," Isabella said, a half-smile lifting the corners of her mouth. "Do I look sufficiently seductive?"

"In that dress? Completely, wholly, exuberantly. And white—interesting," he murmured over the rim of his glass.

"A metaphor, I believe." Her blue eyes sparkled. "Molly's idea again."

"She sets the stage well."

"I am also well trained, sir," she sportively noted. "Although not to your standards perhaps. Your reputation is formidable."

He slid lower in his chair, his gaze taking on a faintly disgruntled expression at the reminder of their disparate lives. "I wish you weren't a virgin."

"I could relinquish my virginity to someone else first if you like."

"No," he snapped.

"You could watch," she suggested, innuendo in her tone.

"Not likely," he growled.

"Or we could get this over as quickly as possible."

"You have a sense of humor, Miss Leslie."

"I watched *you* one night."

He glared at her. "Damned Molly should have kept you in your room."

"Don't blame her. I was quite alone, and what better teacher than you, after all. Although you were selfish. I'm not sure the lady enjoyed herself."

He relaxed marginally. Obviously, she hadn't stayed long. He was grateful for that. "I'll try not to be selfish with you."

"Molly says I'm allowed to be as selfish as I wish because you can take care of yourself."

"Meaning?" he asked, grinning.

"Meaning you are an accomplished libertine."

"I can't argue with you there."

"Why?"

"Why?"

"Why do you do it?"

What a startling question. "Why not?"

"You engage in debauch without thinking?"

He shrugged. "Mostly."

"*I've* thought quite a deal about tonight."

"In your case, I have too. Don't look so surprised. I

don't as a rule"—he smiled—"engage in debauch with virgins. So you see, tonight is different."

"How different?"

One dark brow rose, amusement in his eyes. "Is this a catechism?"

"Do you know?" She wanted her question answered.

"As a matter of fact, I don't. I don't have the vaguest notion why you fascinate me."

"I fascinate you?"

He shrugged again. "It seems so."

"Because of this?" She swept her hand over her gown.

"Definitely a factor," he said with a boyish grin.

"I confess your good looks are a most potent lure for me."

"Then we can both be accused of being shallow," he sportively affirmed. Although he knew better. He'd slept with scores of great beauties and never felt what he felt right now.

"Do you actually want to eat?"

His heart missed a beat. "You decide," he carefully replied.

"I'd rather not eat—right now. I'm too excited."

He set his glass down, slid upright in his chair, and gazed at her with a look that was faintly quizzical and wholly carnal. "What would you like to do instead?"

She bit her lip, debating how to ask, and then in a rush said, "May I see your bedroom?"

His pulse rate leaped, but he schooled his expression to a well-bred courtesy. "Certainly," he said, coming to his feet.

"If you don't think me too forward. Bess warned me that men don't—"

"It's not a problem." Offering her his hand, he drew her up from the chair.

"I wish I could be calm. I'm so nervous."

Her hand was small and warm in his, and it took effort to maintain his composure. "Should I bring a bottle of champagne with us?" He smiled. "For your nerves."

"Maybe you should, although I already had some wine at Molly's before I left—to calm myself . . . and I'm not sure when I'll get tipsy."

"You may get tipsy if you like," he genially offered, picking up the bottle from the iced container. "I've always found the world looks considerably better after a bottle or so."

As they stepped into the hall, Pomeroy materialized from the shadows.

"Postpone dinner," Dermott instructed. "I'll ring when we're ready."

"Very good, sir." The chef was going to burst into tears.

"I wonder if I might be a *little* hungry," Isabella apologetically said; the smells of dinner were wafting up the dumbwaiter in the hall.

"Something light?" Dermott suggested.

"That would be wonderful. I think I smell chicken."

"A little of everything," Dermott ordered.

"Now, sir?"

Dermott looked at Isabella, then back at Pomeroy. "Now," he said.

"I do apologize," Isabella remarked as they began ascending the stairs.

"No need. Pomeroy will take care of it. That's what he does."

"Our household was rather small—compared to yours. And not so formal. I confess, I'm quite intimidated."

"By Pomeroy? Don't give it another thought. If you're hungry, you can eat. It's as simple as that. What else do they have to do? Hell, I'm hardly ever home."

"Don't you like your home?"

He glanced around the cavernous staircase and entrance hall, a multitude of ancestors staring down on them from the walls, the cupola fifty feet above them. "I suppose I do. Never thought about it."

"And yet you're never home."

"Too quiet."

"You require stimulation?"

He laughed. "You might say that, darling. Come, this way." Tugging on her hand, he led her down the corridor toward a huge painting of a man in Elizabethan dress with a hunting dog.

He'd called her darling. The word strummed through her brain, warming her senses even while she told herself to discount charming words from charming men.

He stopped before two massive carved doors just short of the huge painting, and tucking the champagne bottle under his arm, opened them. "Welcome to my wing, Miss Leslie," he said, ushering her into an enormous drawing room.

"This can't be your bedroom."

He nodded toward another set of double doors. "It's in there. The earls of Bathurst apparently used this room for—" He grinned, interrupting himself. "I haven't the foggiest idea. Come, I'll show you my bedroom. It's built on a slightly more intimate scale."

Only slightly, she realized as he opened the doors into the bedroom. The idea of intimacy must have been in terms of royal levees. The bed was mounted on a dais, crowned with a gilt coronet draped in crimson brocade. Enormous gilt chairs covered in a similar brocade were placed along the walls, as though courtiers had watched their master sleep. Windows ten feet high were draped in swags and tassels and more of the crimson brocade. A large desk sat in the middle of a Persian carpet off to one side. Obviously a working desk, papers were strewn over its surface. The ceiling must have been twenty feet high, the mural adorning it that of a bacchanal.

"Do you actually sleep here?"

"Cozy, isn't it?"

"For two hundred people maybe."

"Let me show you my dressing room." Taking her hand again, he led her across the carpet custom-woven for the dimensions of the room and opened a normal-sized door into a normal-sized room.

His stamp was revealed on every detail of the room, from the riding boots on a stand at the end of the bed to his watch fobs tossed on a tray atop his bureau to the portrait of him as a child tucked away in a corner of the room. The bed was small, made for a single person, and covered in a blue Indian cotton. There was a desk here as well, more cluttered than the one in the imposing bedroom outside. And books. Everywhere. On shelves, on chairs, stacked in piles on the floor.

"Forgive the mess," he apologized. "I don't let the staff move my things. If they clean up too much, I never can find anything."

"You read."

He smiled. "Is that all right?"

"Forgive me. I was surprised, that's all. May I look?"

"Certainly." He offered her entree with a small bow and then took himself to a liquor table, where he set down the bottle of champagne, poured himself a brandy, spilled an inch or two of champagne into a glass for her, and sat down to observe her tour of his room.

"Fielding," she said with a smile, holding out a small volume to him. "I love him."

"He observes the realities with a charming sense of the absurd."

"Yes, does he not? And Richardson. You like him too?"

"When I wish to pass the time. He has less humor and his heroines often meet disastrous ends." He shrugged.

She picked up another book. "I love Gibbon too."

"You are enamored of reading, then," he said with a smile, taking pleasure in watching her excitement.

"Oh, yes, very much. It was my access to a world I'd never know otherwise."

"You lived with your grandfather, Molly said."

"Yes, we had a cozy life but not an exciting one. Business and books, books and business. I'm sure you'd find it very boring."

"I contend with my share of business as well, although my secretary, Shelby—I forgot to introduce you downstairs." His smile reappeared. "You turned my head completely and my manners went calling."

"I love when I turn your head."

"Like you love books."

She turned around to face him, her eyes wide. "Not in the least, my lord Bathurst. In a completely tumultuous, tremulous way that defies description."

"I know."

"You do?"

"It's most odd."

"But lovely," she softly intoned, "like a cozy fire on a cold night . . ."

"Not exactly." There was nothing cozy about the lust drumming through his brain. "Molly's told you what to expect tonight, hasn't she?"

"For an entire week, my lord. Oh, dear, have I kept you waiting with all my talk of books?"

"You needn't call me my lord. And you haven't kept me waiting," he politely lied, discounting his week-long wait at Alworth with cavalier disregard.

"I suppose you'd rather do something else than listen to me prattle on about books, but I confess, I'm not exactly sure how to—begin. It's all well and good," she nervously noted, "to be schooled in seduction, but when one actually is onstage, as it were . . ."

"Come, sit and have your champagne. We'll decide how to begin later."

"Yes, sir."

"Please, my name is Dermott."

"Yes, sir"—she fluttered her hands—"I mean Dermott."

He'd not had a lover say Yes, sir to him before, and while Miss Leslie might be experiencing a degree of trepidation, he wasn't exactly on familiar ground either. "Drink some champagne," he noted, handing her the glass, "and tell me about your map library."

His deliberate effort to put her at her ease was successful, and within moments she was conversing in a completely natural way. He asked questions, she answered, and before long, he was refilling her glass and she was leaning back comfortably in her chair and smiling at him in a deliciously sweet way. It unnerved him transiently, sweetness having never been a trait that attracted him, but she was exceedingly sensual as well—Molly's choice of gown the merest wisp of fabric.

"So you see, if Magellan had had better maps, he might have survived."

"Would you like to see those in my library?"

"Now?"

"We've plenty of time." He had no intention of making love to a trembling virgin. In fact, on more than one occasion since meeting Miss Leslie, he'd tried to talk himself out of making love to her at all.

Taking their drinks with them, Dermott guided Isabella to a secret door concealed in the masonry of the fireplace surround, and holding her hand, preceded her down a narrow, curving staircase that opened into the library below. His maps were arranged in large, shallow drawers, and after Isabella had exclaimed over the rarest of his collection, he showed her the maps of India he was updating.

"I could help you," she excitedly said, lightly touching some mountain elevations he'd added to a section of northern India. "I've some very good inks that will last forever—well," she added with a small grimace, "when I return home, I'll be able to give them to you. Grandpapa had them specially mixed in Paris."

Although she had no way of knowing, taking out the maps of India had been a watershed he'd not been able to cross since returning to England. Gazing down at her head bent low over the table, her golden hair shining in the lamplight, he felt an affection he'd not experienced since he'd lost his family. How could this slight young woman so touch his feelings when none of the scores of women he'd made love to since his return had so much as engaged his interest?

He moved away, not wishing to feel what he felt when the only woman he'd ever loved was dead. Replenishing his glass, he walked to the windows overlooking the terrace and stared out into the starry night.

"I've bored you again," Isabella remarked, putting the maps away, the small sound of the drawer sliding shut forcing him to speak.

"I'm tired, I think."

"I've said something wrong," she said, coming up to him. "I apologize."

"It's nothing you said. Molly tells me I'm moody."

"Then I shall entertain you," she declared brightly.

"Surely, you're not thinking of singing." A smile creased his face.

"I don't see a piano in sight."

"Luckily."

"You don't like female entertainments?"

"Not of the cultural kind."

"Ah . . . perhaps, then, I should show you how these bows open." She reached up to her shoulders.

"Not yet." Quickly placing his hands over hers, he arrested her action, not sure he was ready, not sure an artless virgin could fill the void in his black mood.

"Yes, sir . . . er—Dermott," she softly corrected, the warmth of his hands on her shoulders, the weight of them, his closeness, making her tremble, her wanting him no longer casual, if it ever had been, no longer a practical decision, but deep, specific, and defenseless. "When?"

Never, he should say, her virginity a vast deterrent, his own troubled memories disquieting.

"I want you . . . ever so much," she whispered, gazing up at him with wistful blue eyes, taking a half step forward so her body brushed his.

"This could be a mistake." Irresolute, skittish, he hesitated.

"You promised," she pleaded.

The innocent longing in her eyes, the lush feel of her body against his, weakened his already equivocal resolve, his body automatically responding to her nearness, his erection rising between them.

"You *do* want me," she breathed, moving her hips against his rigid length. "I can tell. . . ."

She was temptation incarnate, the look, the feel of her, and gripping her shoulders, he reluctantly pulled her closer. Her sweet scent filled his senses, her soft breasts pressed into his chest whetted his appetite for more, her hips brushing against his throbbing erection fed his lustful cravings.

She slid her hands from beneath his and, reaching up,

placed them on his shoulders. "I'm going to kiss you now, my lord," she murmured as though she had a schedule to keep. And when she rose on tiptoe to reach his mouth, it was impossible to resist. His hands drifted lower, sliding down her back, cupping her bottom, and pulling her hard against his body. He growled softly, "You'd better be sure." His voice took on a faint drollery. "Then at least one of us will be."

"I'm sure." Her eyes were clear blue, untouched by doubt, her mouth only inches away.

Wanting to be kissed.

He dropped his head slowly, as though she were dangerous.

"Kiss me," she whispered, tightening her grip on his shoulders, drawing closer.

And he impetuously obliged, covering her mouth in a restless hotspur kiss that didn't charm or take heed of her innocence but fed his own rash urgency after a week of waiting—a greedy, incautious kiss that ravished and roused and tantalized.

She sighed into his mouth, unafraid, audacious in her wanting, reveling in his need. Melting against him, she ate at his mouth, tasted him deeply, as though he were hers to savor and relish and he was the reason she'd waited so long for her first kiss.

It was half a lifetime away from Dermott's first kiss, and heated or not, flame hot or blazing, it wasn't enough.

He wanted more. When he shouldn't, when she might regret what she was doing, when he didn't want the burden of her guilt.

Chafing with indecision, he abruptly pushed her away.

Shocked, trembling, she gazed at him.

"I can't do this."

"You agreed!" Flushed, overwrought with desire, she cried, "You can't refuse!"

He was standing very still. "I can do anything I want."

"You're rude!" she exclaimed. "To do this to me . . . to make me feel this way and then—"

He took a deep breath. "Sorry, I changed my mind."

"Well, change it back," she heatedly retorted, "because I'm deeply frustrated and you invited me here tonight!"

"I'll send you back."

"I won't go!"

They stood mere inches apart, hot-blooded, resentful.

Furious at his indifference to her plight, at his indifference to her, quivering with indignation, she vehemently said, "How dare you back out now, when I need you!"

Her breasts trembled above the precarious neckline of her gown in the most bewitching way, Dermott noted, and whether her indignation registered or the provocative tremor of her exquisite breasts most captured his interest, he suddenly smiled. "You're intent on this?"

"Of course I am. Look at me!" She threw open her arms and he looked at the sumptuous, barely dressed female before him, demanding to be fucked.

He inhaled briefly, counted to about two and a half with the lush sexual gift being offered him, and said, "Fine. I give up."

"Well, thank you," she murmured sarcastically, "for your kind concession."

One dark brow lifted. "Do you want to do this or don't you?"

Her nostrils flared. "Damn you."

"Damn us both, probably, before we're through with this bizarre agreement. Let's go." And walking away, he strode toward the hidden door.

She caught up to him as he opened it.

"I'll go first if you don't mind." His voice was polite, cool. There was no way he could follow her tantalizing bottom up the stairs and act with any semblance of decency. On the other hand, he brutally noted, she was there to have her virginity taken from her, and no one had signed any contracts defining the details. He could overlook gentlemanly behavior if he wished and assuage his burning lust in any way he chose. In fact, she had just demanded as much, he reflected, taking the stairs in a run.

But there was no time left for further musing with her following hot on his heels. As they exited the concealed doorway into the bedroom, she grabbed at his arm, not sure he wasn't running away. "Don't you dare change your mind," she breathlessly proclaimed. Reaching over, she deliberately ran her palm over the stretched fabric of his breeches, feeling the entire length of his erection. "Because I want that."

Perhaps passion always won out over reason, he decided, particularly with the determined Miss Leslie. She was pretty plain about what she wanted.

And when she looked up at him and said "Well?" he jettisoned any remaining scruple, swept her up into his arms, and murmured, "Let's see how much you know."

"The way I'm feeling right now"—her voice was exhilarated—"having won," she added, kissing his cheek as he carried her into his private room, "I'd be more than willing to do anything you wish."

"Very tempting, Miss Leslie. Although I might argue who won," he replied with a faint smile, her soft weight in his arms inciting pleasantly covetous feelings.

"Promise you won't tease me anymore," she breathed as he lay her on his narrow bed, "because I can't wait . . . even though I should, even though I shouldn't be *making* you do this."

She didn't realize he was the last man in the world who could be coerced into sex; he turned down dozens of women every week. "You're not making me do anything," he murmured, gently touching her flushed cheek. "No one can." Standing, he swiftly took off his coat and neckcloth and pulled his shirt over his head, his need matching hers now that he'd allowed himself to disregard honor and scruple.

Tugging open the bows on her shoulders, Isabella slid her gown off in a swift wriggle, throwing it on the floor like an heiress might. Her chemise was an insignificant scrap of tulle she lifted over her head, and then, seated in the middle of his bachelor bed, she pulled out her hairpins, tossed them away, and opening her arms wide, smiled at him. "Hurry, *hurry*!"

"This *is* hurrying, darling," Dermott said with a grin, tossing his stockings away and reaching for the buttons on his breeches. She was ridiculously pink and plump where she should be plump, and lithe where she should be lithe; her golden hair was tumbled on her shoulders and she fairly glowed with eagerness.

He slid the buttons free, slipped his breeches down his legs, and stepped out of them to the sound of a rapturous, delighted "Ohhhhh!"

"Come closer," she breathlessly said. "I want to touch it." Leaning forward, she fluttered her fingers in anticipation.

Moving toward the bed, he smiled at such enthusiasm. Although his own zeal was hardly less. When he stood before her, enthralled, she touched him delicately, slid her fingers down his length and then up again, intent, studying the object of her attention with a fierce concentration. "I've never seen any at close range," she softly said, gently stroking the very crest of his penis.

"One can be grateful," he murmured waggishly.

She squeezed the swollen head, and his amusement was superseded by riveting sensation. He moaned deep in his throat, faintly arched his back, and looking down, he saw her smile and knew she was pleased with her accomplishment. "Molly said I could do that. And this . . ." she said proudly, grasping his erection with her small hand, her fingers barely closing the circle, but she squeezed again as her hand moved downward.

"That'll be enough," Dermott said on a suffocated breath, easing her fingers open. "I've been waiting for you too long to settle for this."

"I'm so glad we're done waiting—finally!" she exclaimed, falling back on the indigo-blue coverlet and lifting her arms to him. "Come make love to me."

He didn't need an invitation; he needed a large measure of restraint or he'd ruin the first time for this eager young lady. Sitting down beside her, he resisted her tugging hands, taking them in his and placing them at her sides. "I don't want this to hurt."

"It won't," she lavishly disclaimed, reaching for him again.

He didn't know much more than she on the subject, but he understood losing one's virginity could be painful. "One step at a time, darling," he cautioned, pushing her hands away, easing her thighs open. "Let's take this slowly." Slipping a finger between the sleek moist lips of her labia, he gently stroked her pulsing flesh.

She arched her hips against the delicious sensation. "Ummmm . . ."

So far so good. He felt like he was fourteen again, although Harvey Nicols's mother had hardly been a novice. He eased his fingers in another short distance.

"More . . . more . . ."

He obliged, massaging her liquid interior with practiced skill, slowly sliding deeper and deeper, touching, stroking, until he met the barrier he was slated to destroy.

Isabella was no longer capable of recalling any of the lessons she'd been taught. Eyes shut, she was lost in sensation, floating in a blissful, heated paradise centered between her legs. The trembling, delicious ache heightened by slow degrees; a fevered longing filled her brain. All she wanted was more heated bliss, and she moved her hips in a slow undulation, reaching for the ravishing pleasure, lifting up into the exquisite, inciting touch of his fingers.

Experienced at bringing women to a frenzied hysteria, Dermott watched the flush of arousal color her skin, observed the panting gasps as he slowly penetrated and withdrew, took note of the increasingly frantic arching of her hips. She was a hot-blooded little minx, as if he didn't know, and she was almost there.

Leaning over, he kissed her, inhaling her fevered gasps while he gently stroked her pulsing flesh, wanting her with an unbridled violence he knew he couldn't act on. But words were safe, piquant stimulation for her, delicious anticipation for them both. "I'm going to make love to you soon," he murmured against her mouth. "You'll feel me deep inside you, all the way inside . . . until you're filled so full, you'll squirm to get away. But I won't let you go, I'll—"

As he spoke, the coiling heat inside her burned higher with each salacious word. "I'll make love to you until you can't move, until I can't move, and then we'll rest and start all over again. Because I intend to keep you under me or over me or around me—"

Her climax burst over her, and she screamed at the wild, pulsing beauty, at the unadulterated rapture, the exquisite intoxication lasting and lasting and lasting, until finally she lay replete, eyes shut, a half-smile on her lips.

"Satisfied?" His voice was softly teasing as he sat beside her.

"Ummmm . . ." Her eyes slowly opened and her smile broadened. "You are *definitely* good."

"We try." His grin was captivating.

"You really *aren't* selfish," she murmured, reaching up to touch his muscled chest.

"Usually not."

"I see why you're so much in demand."

"The concept of mutual pleasure is more—gratifying."

She stretched like a young sultana. "*More* gratifying?"

she breathed, one brow raised in delicious query. "We'll definitely have to work on that."

He smiled. "My thoughts exactly."

"I don't know though," she hesitantly murmured. "Can I do that again?"

He nodded. "No problem."

Her eyes glowed. "You're sure?"

"Positive."

She smiled faintly. "I think Molly failed to mention a whole lot."

"I'll show you what you missed."

"Because you're not satisfied yet."

"Partly."

"And I'm the other part?" she playfully noted, arching her back in a theatrical, preening pose.

"Absolutely," he said, enjoying the view.

"Am I allowed to say no?"

"You're allowed anything. But I guarantee, you'll like it."

"And I'll feel that delicious, tingly, end-of-the-world thing all over again?"

He nodded again. "All of it."

"How can you be so sure?"

Years of fucking, he thought, but, circumspect, he said, "I just know."

"Because of all the ladies."

"Because of that," he admitted.

"What number am I?"

Was she resentful or curious? He couldn't tell with her brows drawn together like that. "I don't count."

"I think I might. Keep a diary or list. Like Casanova."

"Casanova didn't have a list. He remembered because he liked all those women."

"Do you like them too? Do you like me?"

Her frankness always surprised him. The ladies he knew were more artful. "I like you very much."

"I *know* I adore you . . . for what you did just now. I've never felt that wonderful before, not even when Grandpapa and I came upon that map of Galileo's."

"I'm honored." He gracefully bowed his head, amused at the comparison.

"All of a sudden I'm ever so hungry," she abruptly confessed. "Are you hungry?"

His hunger had nothing to do with food. "I am if you are," he politely replied.

"Would you mind if we ate first?"

It took a great deal of restraint to say "No, of course I don't mind. I'll ring for Pomeroy."

"You're an absolute darling," she murmured, lightly touching his arm.

Yes, he was. Because he wanted to fuck the delectable Miss Leslie until he fucked himself to death. Nothing he couldn't put off until after supper.

8

DERMOTT HAD NO MORE than rung for Pomeroy than he was knocking at the dressing room door.

"Was he listening at the door?" Isabella's eyes went wide.

"No," Dermott said, stepping into his breeches, although the thought had crossed his mind; it was at least five minutes from the kitchen. He tossed Isabella a dressing gown from a nearby chair. "Put this on and I'll let him in."

Scrambling from the bed, she slid the robe on, tied it around her waist, then rolled the sleeves up half a dozen times and still looked drowned in the large garment. Lifting the fabric that dragged on the carpet, she searched for a suitable spot to receive a stranger. "Should I sit there?" She pointed to a chair near the fireplace. "Or should I stand? Or better yet, I'll hide in the armoire." She wasn't completely teasing.

Dermott swung around, his hands on the buttons to his breeches. "You could be standing naked in the center of the room and Pomeroy wouldn't bat an eyelash—nor should he." He gave her a reassuring smile. "So do what you like—so long as you stay within reach," he added with a roguish lift of his eyebrows.

"With you as incentive to stay," Isabella lightly replied, her gaze slowly surveying his splendid form, "I shall overlook any momentary embarrassment."

He winked. "Smart girl." And with a small deferential bow to her, he turned to the door and called out, "Come in."

Pomeroy looked neither right nor left when he entered the room, his gaze scrupulously on his employer. Isabella could have been absent for all the notice he took of her. "You rang, sir?"

"Miss Leslie is ready to sup."

"Very good, sir. Here, sir?" The butler's demeanor gave away nothing of the chaos below stairs, where the chef had thrown a tantrum and stalked off when the food that had been ordered hadn't been sent for immediately. He hoped the lady wasn't particular about her menu, because several of the dishes were now cold and ruined and the sous-chefs were frantically trying to deal with the crisis.

"Yes, here." Dermott began clearing the books and papers off a table.

"Immediately, sir?" It seemed a pertinent question considering the irregular scheduling of events.

"Yes, yes, of course, immediately." Dermott looked at him as though he were dense.

"Very good, sir." With a bow, he left.

"Is he always so grand?" Isabella asked, comparing him to her servants, who were more apt to tell her what to do than to take orders, since they'd raised her from a child.

Dermott looked up from his cleaning. "I suppose so. I hadn't noticed."

"Has he been with you long?"

"Always. My mother had him first."

"Does your mother live in London?" Obviously, she didn't live *here* or he wouldn't have had her over, she speculated.

"She lives at Alworth." At her blank look, he added, "My country home."

"She doesn't like the City?"

He shook his head. "Come, sit down. I've cleared off enough space, I think. Do you have any favorite foods?"

Obviously, he didn't care to speak of his mother, although she supposed it was highly irregular to discuss your mother with a paramour. "Right now," she politely said, responding to his bland question, "I'm ready to eat just about anything, I'm so hungry."

He half turned from his stacking of books.

"What?" The conjecture in his gaze baffled her.

A small smile curved his mouth. "I misunderstood. Please, sit down. I'm almost finished."

"You're not afraid of domestic duties. How delightful in a man of your notorious repute." She sat on a heavily carved chair with a cane seat and back, of Indian manufacture she suspected.

"When one campaigns in the hinterlands, servants are at a premium."

"Did you enjoy India? Molly said you'd spent some years there."

"I enjoyed some of it." His voice had changed, and setting the remaining books down, he walked to the liquor table. "Would you like a glass of wine or some brandy? It's my personal favorite to blur the harsh edges."

"I said something wrong again." His expression had altered, as it had in the library. "Molly will be quite frustrated with me," she went on, feeling a need to fill the silence. "I was supposed to speak in the most bland way. Please, forgive me."

He smiled, but the easy charm was absent. "It's not your fault. Brandy or wine?"

She understood the Earl of Bathurst had his share of demons; Molly had said as much. "Brandy, please." She was as capable as he of politesse. In future, she would raise no personal subjects.

He drank down one glass before refilling his and bringing hers to the table. "Tell me why you didn't consider a lawyer to curtail your relatives' greed," he said, sitting down opposite her.

Apparently, *he* was allowed personal questions, she reflected, but enamored of his company, infatuated with the sight and scent and taste of him—a not uncommon response to the earl—she obligingly replied. "My relatives would have never given up their pursuit of my fortune. Since that required marriage to me, I didn't feel any lawyer could physically protect me from them. Not twenty-four hours a day."

"And you don't regret your plan?"

"I haven't accomplished my plan yet. And please, don't start being honorable again. If it bothers you, consider this my problem alone. You are but a vehicle for its achievement."

He couldn't help but smile.

Gratified, she went on in a teasing tone. "So you see, I am blatantly using you."

"An interesting concept."

"Are you reassured, my lord? I wish nothing more than your lovely penis."

He laughed. "And I'd be a damned fool to refuse."

"I believe most of your gender would agree."

"Damned if they wouldn't. I suppose I have my reputation to uphold."

"Would you not be condemned, my lord," she playfully said, "if word got out that you refused a lady?"

He didn't answer.

"You do . . . you *have*," she said, understanding his silence. "My goodness, what do you say to an importuning female?

"Something pleasant."

"I shan't let you do that to me."

He couldn't help but chuckle. "So I've noticed."

"Nothing you could say would be pleasant enough. I hope you understand."

"Am I obliged to make love to you?" he teased.

"Of course, absolutely. A promise is a promise."

"Then, I see I must," he softly said, the look of her in his oversized dressing gown, her golden hair in tousled ringlets on her shoulders, her cheeks still pinked from her orgasm—a sight even a monk couldn't resist. And monkish he was not.

"All this talk of making love"—she drew in a deep breath—"is quite intoxicating. I was wondering if perhaps"—her gaze came up and held his for a heated moment—"we could postpone supper for a time."

"I'd like that." How provocative she was, like a sultry houri asking for the favor of his arousal. Reaching across the small table, he eased open the front of his robe, exposing her large, pale breasts. "Why don't we start with these for a first course instead," he murmured, his voice touched with a provocative warmth. "Come closer, set these on the table. . . ." He gently tugged on her nipples, pulling her nearer until she was leaning forward over the tabletop, her plump breasts resting on the polished mahogany.

"I don't know how long I can wait," she whispered, the insistent throbbing deep inside her sending ripples through her vagina, her sensual receptors on total recall, wanting another orgasm.

"You *have* to wait." He touched the tips of her nipples, gently stroking them until they were taut and hard. "If you want me to make love to you." His hands drifted over the fullness of her breasts, sliding over the flaring curves, easing downward until he cupped the ripe fullness in his palms. "Maybe we'll let Pomeroy see you. Do you think he'd like your large breasts?"

"No!" she breathed, but the shameful thought burned through her brain, coursed downward between her legs in a liquid warmth. A soft, needy whimper escaped her lips.

"It sounds as though you'd like that," he whispered, lifting the twin mounds higher. "He saw you in the entrance hall. Your dress didn't conceal much. You didn't mind then. . . ."

"You wouldn't—" Her mouth was half open, her breathing erratic.

He shrugged. "Other men might like to see these . . . and the rest of you. . . ." Easing his hands down, he carefully placed her breasts back on the tabletop, sliding his fingers down her deep cleavage, forcing the mounded flesh wider.

"Please, don't . . . say that."

"What would you do for me if I kept Pomeroy out?"

"Anything . . ."

Taking her nipples between his thumbs and forefingers, he gently squeezed them. "Anything?"

"Yes, yes . . ." She was slippery wet with desire, her need for him overwhelming all else. "I'll do anything."

"May I whip you?" It was a test query only; he wasn't a devotee.

Her eyes grew large for a moment. "Would you make love to me?"

"Afterward."

She took a small breath and nodded.

"You're very hot, Miss Leslie, aren't you?"

She didn't answer.

"Don't be shy. I can see you squirming. You're wet and hot and wanting my cock inside you, aren't you?"

She nodded.

"Tell me."

"I want—"

"This cock." He unbuttoned his breeches and drew out his erection. "Say it, Miss Leslie, if you want me to put this inside you and make you come again."

She shut her eyes and softly said, "I want your . . . cock . . . inside me."

"Now open your eyes and look at me when you say that."

"Please—I want your—cock . . . inside me." The heat in her voice matched the heat in her eyes.

"I don't suppose you've said that before."

She shook her head.

"No more than you've ever felt a prick inside you."

She nodded, her eyes downcast.

"You're very quiet when you're aroused, Miss Leslie. I do believe I've found a way to muzzle your tongue."

Her gaze came up, the heat in her eyes fueled by more than passion, such spurious mockery galling. "How insolent you are, my lord. It almost makes one inclined to show you exactly what I can do with my tongue. Perhaps *I'll* take the initiative," she remarked, beginning to undo the tie on her robe. "What do you think of that?"

"I was only teasing, darling."

"I'm not." Rarely docile, she'd already exhausted her quota in the previous few exchanges with the earl. Rising from her chair, she walked the few steps to stand directly before him. Slipping his robe from her shoulders, she let it slide to the floor. "Look now, my lord, and if you're very good, I may let you touch me." She slid two fingertips down the cleft of her mons. "Would you like to feel this with your cock," she murmured, gently massaging her sleek, heated passage. "I'm not sure how far I'll let you go. Maybe I'll let you in only partway." She shrugged minutely and her breasts quivered. "Or if you're very good, I'll let you put that cock of yours all the way inside me. Do you think you'd like the feel of that?"

"You're pushing the wrong man." His voice was flat.

"And you the wrong woman," she sweetly replied.

"So you're going to fuck *me*?" The words, however softly put, held a distinct challenge.

She glanced down at his lap. "It looks like you're ready.

All I have to do," she said, moving a step forward and beginning to lower herself over his thighs, "is see if this lovely penis wants what I want."

His hands closed around her waist, and lunging up, he lifted her bodily, carrying her effortlessly at arm's length. Striding to the bed, fire in his eyes, he tossed her down and growled, "Don't move."

"I have no intention of moving, my lord," she purred, looking up at him with a correspondingly theatrical gaze. "Do come join me."

His breeches were tossed aside in seconds, and he smoothly lowered himself between her legs with the finesse of considerable practice. "Now then, Miss Leslie, I believe I'll be going in all the way."

Her lashes lifted marginally. "If I let you."

He softly snorted. "No question of that."

"Well, then?" Her blue gaze was insolent, perhaps triumphant.

And he immediately took issue with her victress look. "Perhaps I'll make you wait after all."

"Dermott!" she wailed, suddenly throwing her arms around him. "For pity's sake! You win, you win . . . you'll always win. Now, just make love to me before I die. . . ."

The tension left his shoulders as he lay braced above her, and his flashing grin warmed her heart. "You beautiful, hot little puss," he whispered, bending his head to brush her mouth with a kiss.

"*Hot,* darling, is the operative word. If you don't mind."

"Hell no," he cordially answered, cheerful once again, his joy out of all proportion to the simple act of intercourse. "I don't mind at all." Because of who it was, he thought, because this tantalizing beauty touched some hidden source of pleasure within him. Easing himself forward, he forced her thighs wider with the pressure of his hips. "Relax now," he murmured.

"I am," she breathed, clinging to him, letting her thighs fall open, her pulsing interior wet with desire.

But he was scrupulously cautious as he advanced forward, easing his erection into her sleek warmth by very slow degrees, watching her face for any indication of pain. She squeaked in the merest breath of sound when he struck the barrier of her hymenal tissue, and he paused, not sure himself the degree of brutality required.

"Dermott . . ." Her soft cry was urgent, feverish.

Feeling like some plundering barbarian, he took a deep breath.

"I need you. . . ."

She was gently writhing beneath him as he hesitated, his erection clasped tightly in her heated passage, the friction intense on the very crest of his penis.

"Dermott!" she cried.

He suddenly plunged forward, his momentum propelled by the full force of his lower body, the resisting tissue swiftly pierced, rent, his erection smashing through, driving in so deeply, he was fully submerged before she screamed.

"I'm sorry," he whispered, utterly motionless inside her, feeling the worst of brutes, the echoes of her cry ringing in his ears. "I'm sorry. . . ."

Her nails cutting into the flesh of his shoulders loosened. He felt her take a deep breath, saw the color return to her face. And then her eyes opened.

"That's the worst of it, I think." Regret colored his voice.

Her smile gave him heart. "And now I'm an heiress again," she whispered. One brow rose in teasing query. "Are you going to do anything else for me, my lord?"

He softly chuckled. "I'm ready if you're ready."

"Try."

His talents for finesse were put to the test, but then, he'd passed that test a thousand times before, his expertise in the boudoir both a gift and a skill. He moved by infinitesimal degrees, prudent and deliberate at first, until her arms eased their grip, until the rhythm of her breathing altered to a more natural state, until he felt the liquid heat of her desire flow around him. Until at last she arched up into his downstroke.

"Better?" he whispered, his breath warm on her cheek.

"Very, very good, my lord," she murmured, her hands sliding down his back, resting at the base of his spine. "Exceptionally good . . ." she purred, her palms pressing down hard to hold him in place for a lush second more, the sweet ache spiraling outward, the intensity of sensation filling her brain. "I'm going to keep you here forever."

He found the thought appealing at the moment, his own desires beginning to peak, the only question that of timing. He took the briefest moment to insert a sponge to prevent conception, something she'd learned at Molly's as well. And then gently entering her again, he carefully watched her face as he moved within her, listened to her breathing, matched the increasing urgency of her rhythm, repressing his own eagerness—waiting for her.

And some moments later, she clutched at him, whimpering, and understanding the merits of opportune harmony, and he drove in, buried himself deep inside her, held himself hard against her womb. As she cried out and melted in orgasmic delirium, he too climaxed, flooding her, filling her, experiencing a primordial ecstasy so deep and pure and thrilling, it seemed as though they were meant to mate by some grand design of the universe.

"Don't plan on sleeping tonight," Isabella whispered a moment later, intoxication still stirring deliciously in the core of her body. "I'm going to need you as stud."

"Your devoted servant," he urbanely replied, wondering if they'd been touched by some mystical karma and this woman who'd stumbled into Molly's one rainy night was the Circe of his soul.

"Ahem . . ." The voice was Pomeroy's from the other side of the door.

Isabella went rigid in his arms. "Go away!" Dermott shouted.

"Away, sir?" A very real indication of tears echoed through the door.

"Does he cry often?" Isabella inquired, surprised a man of such hauteur succumbed to emotion.

"Never to my recollection. Don't go away," Dermott murmured, kissing her lightly. Gently withdrawing, he wiped himself on the sheet and was shocked to see blood. "Jesus," he muttered, turning to her, having forgotten. "I'm really sorry. You're going to need some hot water." Jumping from the bed, he shouted, "Wait, Pomeroy!"

Quickly throwing on a dressing gown, he strode to the door and threw it open just as Isabella hid herself under the coverlet.

"We need hot water. And I'll take the food too," he said,

glancing at the numerous footmen holding trays, all of whom must have heard Isabella's screams, for they looked either sheepish or entertained. "I'll take the trays in myself," he quickly said. "Just leave them."

"How much hot water, sir?" Pomeroy's face was expressionless.

"A bath, I think."

"Now, sir?" His master's wishes were difficult to read.

"Yes, now." Dermott glanced at all the food. "I suppose the chef is in a temper."

"He has taken to his bed, my lord, with a bottle of brandy. My apologies if the food isn't up to the usual standards. The sous-chefs have done their best."

"Thank them for me, Pomeroy. Things are a bit—er—irregular tonight."

A moment of strained silence ensued.

"You may give all the servants a bonus," Dermott abruptly said. "Talk to Shelby in the morning."

"Very good, sir."

"And once we have the bath, we won't require any more service tonight."

"Yes, sir."

"Is that clear?"

"Perfectly."

Dermott nodded. "Good." Picking up a tray, he walked back into the dressing room and shut the door.

"A bonus no less," one of the footmen gleefully remarked. "It sure be worth it when the master fucks a beauty like her. He be in a right fine humor afterward."

"Who wouldn't be?" another flunky noted. "She be as fine a piece as I ever saw—and scarce dressed at all, with her boobies near to fallin' out."

A third man pronounced with relish, "I hear tell she were trained at Molly Crocker's by the very best and she be able to do most anything at all that a man do want."

"The kitchen maid at that there brothel where the master spends so much time," another said, adding his tidbit to the stew of gossip, "told her cousin at the Duke of Portland's, who told her cousin Meg downstairs that that beauty we all saw with hardly no clothes on be herself a great heiress."

"That will be enough of such ridiculous gossip," Pomeroy ordered. "An heiress indeed. A female dressed in such a fashion is far from an heiress. Now, I want everyone downstairs immediately, or you won't see a shilling of that bonus. The master doesn't wish to be disturbed—you heard him. And if a word gets out about his visitor tonight," he warned, "I'll sack you all."

Everyone nodded respectfully, but everyone also knew the story would be about town by breakfast the next day, the tittle-tattle of society's indiscretions the lifeblood of daily conversation. From the breakfast rooms of dukes to the penny sheets sold on the street to the common man, gossip was adored, dissected, embellished, and passed on. And the Earl of Bathurst did more than his share to fuel the salacious flames of scandal.

9

❧

"I SOMETIMES THINK I have too damned many servants," Dermott grumbled, walking toward the bed. "You can come out, darling," he added, glancing at the shape under the coverlet. "They're all gone."

Isabella's blond curls first appeared, then her flushed face, and last her creamy shoulders. "You *do* have too many servants," she agreed, the coverlet clutched to her chest, wary still of visitors. "I suppose they heard everything."

"No, not at all," he lied. "I told them I'd bring in the trays myself. So you needn't see anyone. I'll bring in bathwater as well. I have a pool and steam room downstairs along the lines of the Roman ones at Bath, but I don't suppose you wish to go down there."

She looked alarmed. "And have everyone see me?"

He nodded. "I thought not. You should probably stay in bed . . . with—that is, until you feel better . . . and can bathe. I'll bring the trays to you."

She sat up and he placed the first tray on her lap. "I suppose . . . it hurts," he gently said, looking apologetic. "I feel like hell about—well, about what I did."

"I'm not very sore . . . really," she appeased. He looked so uncomfortable. "You were very kind."

He grimaced, feeling awkward in his role of despoiler. "I don't know how . . . there are men who have a proclivity for virgins. I've never understood it."

"In this case, you did me a real service. Don't feel guilty."

"Lie down and I'll take the sponge out. Thanks to Molly, I've a good supply." And as she lay down, he slipped his fingers inside and drew out the sponge, tossing it onto the bloodied sheet he'd pulled from the bed. "Should I have the housekeeper find some salve or balm?"

"I'd be terribly embarrassed," she answered, reaching for the hand he held out for her, easing into a seated position.

"You might need it."

"Let's wait until after the bath. Do stop apologizing though. I'm very pleased, not only that the deed is accomplished but that there was so much pleasure in it. You are very talented, my lord," she teased.

That he knew, but he was pleased she was in such good humor. "I'll get the rest of the food."

"Then join me, darling. You must be hungry, too, after all your work." Her grin was infectious.

He was smiling as he walked from the room, the word *darling* having a particularly intoxicating sound when she uttered it. He began re-counting his drinks, wondering if he was that drunk or just that happy.

Isabella *knew* she was happy. But then, every woman he made love to felt that way, she suspected. A shame he was so unavailable.

Knowing better than to dwell on the unattainable though, she lifted the silver covers from the plates before her and took note of a luscious array of tiny shellfish on a bed of aromatic chutney, a compote of tropical fruit obviously greenhouse grown, and scallop-shaped buttered toast. Picking up a steaming shrimp with her fingers, she dipped it into the chutney and popped it into her mouth. Reality was quite pleasant enough without further contemplation of the earl's inconstancy. The mingled flavors were delectable on her tongue, she was about to be fed with a degree of luxury that matched the splendor of Bathurst House, the delicious heat of her recent orgasm was still shimmering through her senses, and in short order the beautiful Dermott Ramsay would return to entertain her.

If this wasn't paradise, it was verifiably close.

Bearing a second tray, the earl reentered the room. "You like the food."

Her warm gaze met his. "I could be smiling for other reasons."

"I'm reassured, then."

"That you haven't lost your touch?"

"That whatever pain I caused you has diminished."

"Rest assured, I'm feeling no pain, my lord. *Au contraire.*" She waved a hand over her tray. "Your sous-chefs are outstanding."

He set the tray down on a small table, then lifted the table nearer the bed so she could easily reach the food. "I hope you're hungry. There are three more trays."

"Then I hope you like plump women."

He looked at her propped up against his pillows, pink

and flushed from lovemaking, her nudity only half covered by the disarray of bedclothes. "I like you any way at all."

"How charming you are. I almost feel as though you mean it."

"I do."

A small silence fell while the earl speculated on his novel honesty and Isabella wondered if she could allow herself to believe so graceful a rogue.

He glanced away first, uncomfortable with such frankness when his liaisons of late had studiously avoided sincerity. "I'd better get the remaining food."

"Of course."

Her cool murmur brought his gaze back. "What?"

"Nothing."

"You're angry."

"No." She had no right to take offense. They both had agreed to what they'd agreed.

"You're not angry?"

"I'm not angry."

"I'm glad you're here."

She inhaled faintly and smiled. "Me too."

"Friends?" Strangely, it mattered.

"Of course." Her voice was different now, warm, not cool, pleased.

He felt relieved, when he hadn't cared about much for a very long time. "Good." Grinning, he dipped her a small bow.

"I'm glad we had this talk," she teased, lifting a scallop of buttered toast from the tray.

He laughed. "You're a demanding woman."

She flung the toast at him.

He caught it midair, his reflexes superb. "If you want to fight *that* way, darling," he murmured, "I'd be happy to accommodate you. . . ."

"I warn you, I'm very strong. . . ."

"Really." He slipped the morsel of toast into his mouth.

"I unload freight in our warehouses."

He chewed briefly and then swallowed. "Do you now."

"You won't find it easy to wrestle me down."

"But a pleasure, I warrant . . ."

"After I eat and bathe, I may allow you to try."

His smile warmed his eyes. "How nice."

"You needn't sound so smug. I've arm-wrestled some of my grandfather's sailors and won."

"I see."

"They were powerful men, I assure you."

"I'm sure they were."

"You're beginning to annoy me, Bathurst."

He dipped his head infinitesimally. "When I'm trying my utmost to be agreeable."

She snorted softly. "Men aren't always strongest."

He'd fought guerrilla troops for months on end in the foothills of the Himalayas, and while he agreed with her in principle, they were far from evenly matched. "I understand," he pleasantly said.

"Go and get the damned food."

"Yes, ma'am."

"I'll deal with you later."

Bending low, he ran his fingertip over her lush lower lip. "I can hardly wait."

But the food took center stage once it was all brought

in and arranged within reach, the splendid assortment beautiful to the eye, delectable to the palate, and delicious. Dermott sat opposite her while she lounged on the bed, and they ate for some time in a companionable silence broken only by agreeable comments on the food or Dermott's selection of wines.

"You have a remarkable appetite," Isabella observed after Dermott had demolished two plates of steak with oyster sauce and an entire bottle of claret.

He glanced up. "I forgot to eat today. Anticipation, I suppose." His smile was cordial. "Were you able to eat?"

"Actually, no. So you don't do this every day either?"

"Not every day. Not ever."

"I'm the first?" she flirtatiously inquired, knowing full well she wasn't the first in anything with the prodigal earl.

"The first to share my bed in Bathurst House. You see how enamored I am."

"I am wonderful, am I not?" she playfully agreed, spreading her arms wide.

"No argument there." He lifted his wineglass to her in salute.

The sound of a door closing, followed by footsteps and the splashing of water, interrupted their solitude.

"Sounds like your bath." Dermott nodded toward a small door in the corner of the room. Pushing away from the table, he stood. "I'll check on their progress."

The hum of conversation resonated through the door for a time, as did continuing footfalls and the sound of water being poured. Until a final thud of a door closing was followed by Dermott's reappearance. "Would you like me to carry you?" he asked, moving toward the bed.

She smiled at him. "I'm not an invalid."

He frowned briefly. "I wasn't cut out to be a despoiler of maidens."

"Soon I shall be a consummate courtesan and you need no longer castigate yourself."

"We'll see about that," he gruffly replied, the thought of her as a consummate courtesan no less deplorable.

"*We* won't, darling." Throwing the coverlet aside, she slid her legs over the side of the bed. "I'm quite capable of making my own decisions."

"We'll see." His voice was low, scarcely audible, an odd possessiveness overcoming him.

Her brows rose.

He smiled and offered her his hand. "I said, you're right, of course."

"And don't forget it, my darling Bathurst. What I've just done was specifically intended to maintain my independence. I'm not likely to relinquish it to someone else."

"Yes, ma'am," he dulcetly replied, drawing her to her feet.

"You're much too glib."

He grinned. "A failing, I'm told. I shall endeavor to improve."

She stuck out her tongue. "Insolent rogue."

"A bath might soothe your temper, my lady." He was blatantly unctuous.

"But not your insolence."

"A shamelessly intractable trait, I believe." He spoke with unabashed cheekiness. "Perhaps you could school me in manners."

"I doubt you'd comply."

"If the reward was sufficient, my lady, I might be persuaded."

"A sexual reward, no doubt."

"Unless you find poetry as intriguing as I."

She laughed at his outrageous mummery. "You'd settle for poetry?"

"If the conditions were ideal, of course."

"Meaning?"

"After your bath, I'll tell you."

"Now *I'm* intrigued, Bathurst."

"On that common note, my dear, might I suggest you take advantage of the bath while the water's still warm."

He sat well away from her while she bathed, resisting the impulse to ravage her bounteous charms with an unaccustomed self-denial maintained with only the greatest effort. If he were a gentleman, he'd refrain from making love to her again tonight, he reflected, and allow her to recover from her denouement. But he wasn't capable of such chivalry when she was so alluring. In fact, he was hard pressed to remain in his chair.

He drank to distract himself, although he questioned the suitability of further numbing his already tenuous self-control. She bathed with a serene disregard for his presence, as though they'd done this countless times before, and he wondered if she realized how uneasily he was balancing base impulse and good judgment.

"You're quiet," she murmured, tracing her palm over the surface of the water, causing light ripples to wash over the mounds of her half-submerged breasts.

His grip on his brandy glass tightened. "I'm practicing self-restraint; it takes all my concentration."

"How sweet, but you could join me if you wish."

"I'm trying not to."

"What if I were to specifically invite you?"

"I still wouldn't."

"Because?"

"I might hurt you."

"This heated water is making me feel very sexy." She slid up higher so her large breasts floated on the surface of the water. "I think I'm going to be *needing* you very soon."

"You're making this damned difficult."

"I feel perfectly fine—without a twinge of discomfort." Lifting one leg from the water, she balanced her calf on the side of the copper tub and smiled at him.

"It's not going to take very much to change my mind," he growled softly.

"Would something like this help?" Raising her other leg, she rested it on the tub rim, her provocative pose bringing his erection to full alert.

He set his glass down and reached for the tie on his dressing gown.

"Oh, good . . . I have your attention."

"And something more in about a second," he murmured, stripping his robe off as he rose from the chair.

"My God, Bathurst, you're a beautiful sight," she whispered, a rush of desire flaring through her senses. He was tall, bronzed, broad-shouldered, honed to the finest pitch of physical fitness, and blessed with the most magnificent erection. "Do come closer," she breathed, knowing what untold bliss he could offer.

A moment later, he stood at the foot of the tub, no less overcome by desire. "Wet or dry?"

"In the interests of enlightenment," she purred, lifting her arms to him.

He'd stepped into the water before she was finished speaking, and sinking to his knees between her out-stretched legs, he slid his hands under her bottom. "I've been in a ravaging mood since I first saw you." He lifted her gently until her pulsing cleft met the hard length of his penis. "Like some plundering barbarian. I can't guarantee finesse."

"I'm not interested in finesse."

"It wouldn't matter if you were," he said on a suffo-cated breath, forcing his rigid erection downward, easing it into the sleek entrance to her vagina, moving forward by slow degrees so she could feel what he was feeling, so he could forget about good judgment and chivalry. So he could take what he so desperately wanted.

She gasped as he filled her, stretched her, lifting her mouth to his, wanting to feel him everywhere, wanting to completely absorb him and experience the unearthly de-lights he so skillfully dispensed.

The heat of their bodies, their desire, rose by vaulting degrees, as though they had to no more than touch and a feverish passion stung them to the quick.

"Don't stop," she breathed, his penetration inflaming her senses.

He knew better, but he whispered, "Never . . ." and glided in a fraction more, sensitive to the limits of sensa-tion, less reckless than she.

"I want to die of pleasure. . . ."

"A thousand times," he murmured, wanting her as much, submerged almost to the deepest extremity.

"Oh, God . . ."

He held himself motionless against the very mouth of her womb while the world dissolved, heated ecstasy overwhelming mind and body, every trembling nerve incited to rapture pitch.

"You can't leave me."

He heard her through a thundering lust so unrestrained and lecherous, he could honestly answer "I won't" even as he began to withdraw.

"No, no, no!" She clutched at his back, trying to maintain the ravishing pleasure.

"Hush," he commanded, breaking her hold. "I'm coming back." And when he'd reached the limits of his withdrawal stroke, he plunged in once again and felt her soft sigh of gratification as he buried himself to the hilt.

Riveting sensation jolted their bodies, thrilled through their senses, burned away all but rapacious need, and they moved in the heated water in an agitated flux and flow that sent waves of water onto the carpet. Unmindful, driven by a frenzy of torrid desire, they wildly took and gave, greedy, impatient, consumed by a carnal hunger that burned away all but feeling, and when their orgasmic culmination exploded over them, they were both left breathless.

"My undying . . . thanks," she whispered, lying prostrate, her head thrown back.

"The pleasure . . . was . . . mine," he gasped, his forehead resting on the rim of the tub.

"I'm . . . going . . . to be . . . wanting more. . . ."

He turned his head and met her voluptuous gaze. "Wet or dry?" he softly drawled.

"Whatever you want."

What he wanted might alarm her, he thought, the possibility of fucking himself to death mildly alarming to himself as well. "I'll make a list," he whispered, a faint smile playing across his mouth.

"And I'll accommodate you."

"Sight unseen?"

She moved her hips in the smallest of undulations. "As long as I have this inside me, I'll accommodate you any way you wish."

"An inspiring offer."

"I can feel your inspiration already." He'd grown rigid again, and the exquisite sensation brought a smile to her lips. "How lucky I am."

A consummate gambler, he understood the laws of chance and he knew full well the ultimate degree of luck involved in their meeting. "We both are," he softly said.

10

HE CARRIED HER from the bath sometime later, wrapped her in one of his robes, slipped on a dressing gown as well, and led her through the imposing crimson-bedecked bedchamber to another dressing room so large, she stood in the doorway, rapt.

"Is this your Roman bath?" The walls and floor were of green-veined marble, the high-domed ceiling a colorful mosaic depiction of fauna and flora, the light from numerous wall sconces reflected in dozens of gilt-framed mirrors lining the walls.

He shook his head. "That's on the ground floor. My great-grandfather apparently saw this room in a villa in Naples and brought back twenty Italian craftsmen to replicate it for him. I thought you might like to use the facilities."

"Thank you." Her blush deepened the pink on her cheeks.

"I could leave if you wish."

"If you would . . . although I suppose at this point—" A flaring bit of scarlet rouged her cheeks. "I mean, after what transpired . . ."

"I'll wait outside," he gently said. "The water closet is through those doors." Pointing at a trompe l'oeil woodland scene, he added, "Just push on the clump of primrose."

She stood for a moment after the door closed on him, in awe of the magnificence. Nothing in her past compared with the degree of luxury evident in Bathurst House. Although Dermott seemed not to notice—his small dressing apartment was almost ordinary in its plainness. A clock suddenly struck, and glancing around, she saw a tall case clock set between a freestanding marble tub and a silk-covered chaise. A large family could live comfortably in this chamber, she thought, smiling faintly, the warmth from the fireplace adding to the creature comforts of the room. Vases of flowers perfumed the air as well, and she wondered if one ever became blasé about such splendor.

Not that she would have the opportunity to find out, she decided with the practicality she'd learned at her grandfather's knee. And on that pragmatic note, she moved toward the hidden doors and gently touched the primroses.

The doors swung open soundlessly on well-oiled hinges and another chamber decorated in marble met her gaze. Pink marble this time, with a water closet in the guise of a throne and a sink with faucets that implied Bathurst House was supplied with running water. She wished she had someone to describe these luxuries to, and incongruously, considering her reasons for being there, she wished her grandfather were available to listen.

Dermott was seated near the large boulle desk when she reentered the bedchamber, refreshed as well after using the simpler accommodations in his dressing room. Lounging in an outsized chair, he held a brandy glass in his hand. "Did you manage to make all the faucets work?"

"Yes, thank you. How beautiful, and ingenious as well. Grandpapa would have enjoyed seeing your plumbing."[5]

He smiled. "And I would have liked to see your grandfather again. He raised a very unusual woman." He rose as she approached and offered her a chair beside him.

"Do you think I'm unusual?" Sitting, she thought how gracious he was to charm after as well as before.

"Without doubt. Champagne? I had some more brought up." Which required waking the servants he'd dismissed.

"Yes, thank you." She took the proffered glass. "Unusual because of this—arrangement, you mean?"

He momentarily pursed his lips. "A consideration perhaps, but no—I think your lack of affectation most appeals."

"My lack of social graces, you mean," she noted with a smile.

"Hardly. You could grace Almack's with the best of them. I suppose I dislike coy women, and you are not that. What you are, darling, is the fascinating focus of my desires—in a most disturbing way. And there, I've said enough. I despise conversations about feelings."

"As do all men, in my experience."

"*Your* experience?" He cocked one dark brow.

"In my grandfather's business. If one ever broached a subject that even veered in the direction of how one felt— say about a shipwreck, for instance, or a spoiled cargo, or the plight of laborers on the plantations that supplied much of the cargo—they would invariably say 'And so life goes,' as though it were possible to avoid an emotional reaction. Even Grandpapa, darling that he was, rarely mentioned his love for me other than to say, 'You're my sun and moon, Izzy'—he called me that from childhood—'now tell me what you want and you may have it.'"

Dermott grinned. "A spoiled young lady—which accounts for your sexual demands. Not that I'm complaining."

"Nor I, Lord Bathurst. You've lived up to your reputation splendidly."

"We're not done yet."

"I should hope not."

His lazy smile was overtly sensual. "Wanton minx."

"Indeed." She winked at him over the rim of her glass. "And I never had the least idea."

"I should be grateful to your disreputable relatives."

"In a way I am. Because of you, of course."

His gaze went shuttered, wary of female flattery after years of avoiding entrapment.

Her trill of laughter drifted to the bacchantes overhead. "Do they all want to leg-shackle you?"

"Enough to make one cautious."

"I know better. No need for alarm. But I'm glad you were the first," she softly added.

And perhaps the last, a rash, impulsive voice inside his head avowed. Which voice was instantly quashed by those brute impulses that had sustained him in recent years. "Thank you." He didn't know what else to say. He had no intention of becoming involved.

"You're very welcome. And when you're sufficiently rested, I was wondering—if you didn't think me too forward—"

His gaze came up, and he waited with interest.

"Whether we could have some of that chocolate dessert that we left on the tray in your dressing room."

He laughed. "I fear I'm losing my touch."

"Not in the least. In fact, I was trying to think of a way we could—do them both."

"Since I'm not particularly interested in chocolate dessert, perhaps something could be arranged," he murmured. "Although I have the perfect wine for your chocolate. Come," he said, rising and offering his hand.

He led her first to the dressing room, where he picked up the dessert plate she wished, and then, drawing her along, traveled through the large bedroom and drawing room, down the hall and staircase. Turning to his right, he ignored the hall porter dozing in his chair and walked down a lengthy corridor to a small door set oddly in a corner. "Watch your step now." Opening the door, he slowly led her down a narrow staircase, a coolness immediately apparent as they descended, and at the bottom of the stairs he opened a door into a well-lit wine cellar.

Obviously, he spent some time there, for a small anteroom entirely of brick was furnished with an elegant table and four upholstered chairs, a bow-fronted console, and a cupboard gleaming with glassware. Waving her into a chair, he set the dessert plate on the table, rummaged in a drawer for some flatware, produced an ornate fork and knife along with an embroidered napkin, and placing them beside the plate, bowed with an impudent grin. "If Mademoiselle will allow me a minute more, I can assure her a pleasant interlude."

"But of course," she playfully replied with a cheeky grin of her own. "So far I'm most impressed with your qualifications. All the gossip is quite accurate, my lord."

"As for you . . ." His voice was like velvet. "You've more than lived up to expectations."

"Perhaps you should thank Molly's tutelage."

He gently shook his head. "You're just a hot little puss."

"Then we're well matched." Her brows rose faintly. "And I mean it in the most specifically sexual way."

His smile would have dazzled from a furlong away. "We'll have to explore that sexual specificity."

"I was hoping you wouldn't mind, although," she gently added, glancing at his robe jutting outward rather than falling in silken folds to the floor, "it looks as though I need't worry."

"The only thing you need worry about is stopping me. I seem to be obsessed tonight."

"Not so unusual, according to rumor. Haven't you set all the sexual records of late?" The girls at Molly's had delighted in telling her.

"Not that I know of." He never had sex for records, only for pleasure.

"So modest, Bathurst."

"Dermott."

"Dermott." For the briefest moment it felt as though his name on her tongue gave her claim to him. She savored the fleeting impression for an unrealistic second before coming to her senses.

Bending low, he brushed her mouth with a kiss, touched by that same dizzy sensation. "I'll be right back," he murmured against her lips, because his propensity for sexual adventuring was well established in contrast to his lesser-used sensibilities and he easily reverted to type. "And then I'll make you come."

Leaning back in the soft chair, Isabella luxuriated in pleasurable anticipation, giving thanks as well to the benevolent hand of fate that offered her such a delectable means of securing her inheritance. What good fortune that she'd run down that particular lane and caught sight of Molly's blue door. What glorious luck that Dermott had been there—had seen her . . . and wanted her. And instead of being chained forever to her hideous cousin, she was here tonight—blissfully enchanted.

When Dermott returned a moment later with a dusty wine bottle, she looked up. "Have you ever considered yourself in the role of savior? Because you definitely are for me."

He had been for hundreds of women but not exactly in the manner she was implying. "I'm pleased to be of service," he murmured with a well-bred smile. "But acquit me of such philanthropy. I'm self-indulgent in the extreme. And to that point, let me get this bottle open. You'll like it with your chocolate." He roguishly winked. "I'll like it with your chocolate." Lifting a towel from a rack on the wall, he wiped the bottle clean and deftly opened it, the strength in his wrists as he twisted the cork free sending a little frisson down Isabella's spine. He was utterly exquisite, tall, powerful, more beautiful than even Michelangelo's *David*, which had always been her ultimate measure for male beauty. He was perfection. In every way, she reflected, recalling his ravishing sexual expertise and the rapturous pleasure he bestowed. Lost in her reverie, she glanced up when his hands closed on her waist.

"Your dessert's ready for you," he whispered, lifting her from the chair, holding her with effortless strength as he took her place. Arranging her comfortably on his lap, he brushed a blond curl from her temple. "Would you like me to feed you?"

"Do I have a choice?"

She spoke in a flirtatious contralto that made him conscious, however briefly, of the possibility of miracles. "Not at the moment," he softly enjoined. "Open your mouth."

She did with such languor, his erection surged, and her gentian eyes held his for a highly seductive moment as he placed the forkful of chocolate torte into her mouth. She gently sighed as the flavors tantalized her taste buds and Dermott's erection pressed into her bottom.

"I think I'll fatten you up with chocolate," he whispered. "And keep you filled with cock as well."

"You must read minds," she breathed, licking a fragment of chocolate from her plump bottom lip. "I do adore chocolate and you," she murmured, shifting gently, rubbing against his arousal.

"Then we'll have to accommodate you."

"And you?" Her smile was lush with suggestion.

He grinned. "I'm there . . . except for the chocolate." Setting the fork aside, he lifted her slightly and turned her so she was facing him, straddling his thighs. "Up," he softly ordered, lightly touching her bottom, and as she rested her hands on his shoulders and raised herself on her knees, he pulled open the skirt of her robe and his. "Now then . . ." His voice was velvety. "How much do you want it?"

She smiled into his dark eyes. "About as much as you."

His soft chuckle vibrated under her palms.

"No sense in waiting, then," he whispered, guiding his erection into place. And before he had time to adjust himself, she slid downward, more impatient in her tyro state.

"There now," she whispered, her mouth only inches from his, her eyes shadowed in the candlelight. "That's a very good fit."

He thrust upward fractionally, impaling her that last distance more, and they both sighed in unison. "Tailor made," he murmured when next he caught his breath.

"You'll have to come and see me sometime—later when I'm back home," she breathed, undulating gently so she felt him on every sleek bit of tissue. "So I can feel this . . ."

He had no intention of sending her back anytime soon. "Maybe I'll keep you."

"And add me to your legions of lovers? I don't think so."

"Maybe I'm not asking." Grasping her around the waist, he raised her until she was balanced on the crest of his erection.

"Don't . . ." She squirmed, trying to lower herself, bereft of the ravishing pleasure.

"What do you say to my keeping you?" He resisted her struggles, holding her aloft without exertion, the powerful muscles in his arms flexing under her weight.

"You're cruel," she protested, her mouth set in a pouty moue.

"Just selfish. Answer me and you can have it."

"Yes, yes, yes . . . whatever you want."

"You don't mean it."

"I do at the moment."

"Not good enough, darling."

She shut her eyes against the aching urgency, and when she opened them again, she gazed at him with smoldering ire. "I'm going to send you to the Sandwich Islands on one of my ships and leave you there if you don't—"

"I never respond to orders." He was smiling.

"Oh, very well, have your way. I capitulate."

He didn't believe her, but it really didn't matter, game or no game, because he would have her when and if and for however long he wanted her. With or without her permission. "Now, there's a sweet puss," he murmured, releasing his grip, allowing her to slip downward, enjoying the exquisite ecstasy as much as she. And he matched her rhythm as she braced her hands on his shoulders and rode him. Gloried in the feel of her, in the fevered eagerness of her passion. Waited and watched and met her as she climaxed, the sound of her exultant, panting screams muffled by the solid brick walls.

Moments later, she lay replete in his arms, a sleepy novice, a lush beauty, and his, he uncharacteristically mused, captivated when he never was, charmed by her sweetness, by her gratifying propensity for sex. He kissed her cheek as she rested her head on his shoulder. "Would you like to go upstairs and sleep?" he whispered.

She moved her head in negation, the warmth and strength of his body, her sated senses, heavenly.

"A sip of wine?" Oddly, he wished to care for her, when

he was the least likely person to experience such feelings. When he'd cared only for himself since his return from India.

"Will you make love to me again?"

"Now?" He moved inside her, his arousal still in full fledge.

She shook her head and softly groaned. "Later . . ." She wanted to know she could hold him, touch him, feel what she was feeling again.

"You tell me when," he softly said, gently stroking her back.

They made love twice more before he carried her upstairs, lay her on his narrow bed, and tucked her in. She fell asleep almost instantly, fatigued by excess, unfamiliar with such sustained intensity. And he sat beside the bed, his feet up on the coverlet, a brandy in his hand, his gaze resting on her.

He should take her back to Molly's instead of gazing at her like some love-struck moonling. But he wouldn't. Draining his glass, he reached for the liquor bottle placed conveniently on the floor beside his chair and poured himself another drink, at a loss to explain his motives or her outrageous appeal. And as the bottle emptied, he debated Miss Leslie's place in his life. But no palatable answers came to mind, no easy resolution disentangled his muddled feelings.

With dawn breaking, he was no further along in solving his dilemma.

He softly swore.

He should send her back. It was as simple as that.

He inhaled deeply. If he could.

Suddenly she rolled over, opened her eyes, and catching sight of him, smiled.

And it seemed as though the sun had suddenly risen.

He didn't return Miss Leslie that morning, nor the following day. In fact, late on the afternoon of their third day together, as they rested in the marble tub amid the decorative fauna and flora, he said, "Come down to Richmond with me. I have a small home there with no neighbors."

"I'll go wherever you want."

She always surprised him with her directness. A reaction, perhaps, to all the other women he knew who never said what they meant.

"I'll have Molly pack your things. We'll leave in a closed carriage in the event your relatives are on the outlook for you."

"Tell Molly I'll thank her properly when my problems are resolved and I can travel about undisturbed. Tell her too," Isabella added with a smile, "I owe her a portion of my pleasure."

"We both do."

"And I'm learning so much," she murmured, a teasing light in her eyes.

He was as well—about unsatisfied desire and continuous rut. And in his infrequent cooler moments, he'd berate himself for his susceptibility.

Out of courtesy, he went himself to fetch Isabella's belongings. "We shouldn't be in Richmond long," he explained to

Molly. "But at the moment, I find myself unwilling to re-linquish her. So if you'd see that some of Isabella's things are packed . . ." He shrugged. "Not much, I wouldn't think."

He went on to deliver Isabella's message and an edited account of their activities as Molly began assembling a number of gowns and other necessities, his conversation desultory, fractured, the focus of his thoughts obviously elsewhere as he paced the room.

Once the two valises were ready, Molly snapped the latches shut and faced Dermott from across the bed Isabella had used. "You should bring her back instead. Clearly, you're unsettled about this, wondering, I surmise, why the customary boredom hasn't set in."

Dermott came to a standstill and offered her a tight smile. "You know me too well."

"I know what most men of your class want. Pleasure without attachment. But you shouldn't lead her on. She's going to be hurt when you decide you've had your fill."

"If I could let her go, I would." He shifted uncomfortably. "But right now that's not possible. I felt I should at least give you notice before I take her away."

Molly looked at him with displeasure. "You're being utterly selfish, of course. She already adores you, doesn't she?"

He moved back a step, as though avoiding the significance of her words.

"And the longer you keep her, the more attached she'll become." Her gaze took on a critical assessment. "What if Isabella were to become pregnant? I don't suppose you care to consider that either?"

"Lord, Molly, give me some credit. I wouldn't do that to her."

"At least you haven't lost *all* reason."

"Not quite." He raked his hand through his dark hair. "She's not at all what I expected."

"You saw her here. You knew she was innocent."

"You're wrong. That she's not."

"And your lust has found a kindred spirit?" She spoke with a nice degree of cynicism.

He gently shook his head. "If it were only that simple. Lust I understand. It's sustained me for the last few years. But she's more than carnal sport. She talks of business like a merchant banker, and her knowledge of maps—" He smiled. "We've been working on my additions to the maps of northern India. She has a sure hand and an artist's eye. And she likes many of the books I do. And of course—"

"She makes love exactly to your liking," Molly astutely affirmed. "If I didn't know you better, I'd say you're falling in love. And I mention the word with the greatest reservation, knowing you as well as I do."

"It's not love." His voice was crisp.

"But you can't let her go."

"I don't wish to yet."

"Look, Dermott, I just don't want you to leave her heartbroken. She doesn't have your experience or toughness." Her gaze was direct. "It's not an even contest."

"It's not a contest. She's enjoying herself." His mouth twitched into a faint smile. "Really."

"Ultimately, she'll lose you. And she has no one in the world to turn to, to care for her. I would if I could, but my situation would be an embarrassment to her. I can't openly offer her aid. Which means you're not allowed to deal with her in a cavalier way. I don't mean that as a warning." Her mouth set into a firm line. "Actually, I do."

"When it's over, I promise she'll be fine."

"She doesn't need your money. You're not going to be able to buy her off like all the others with an expensive piece of jewelry or a small house in Chelsea. You've thought of that, I presume."

"Of course. I've thought about every conceivable thing, dammit. Do you think I want to feel this way? I know what I'm doing isn't right, but you know," he harshly said, "she doesn't care either."

"So she says. You could do the honorable thing and marry her."

"Out of the question."

"She needs protection from her relatives."

"That I can do."

Molly glared at him. "I'm angry and I don't want to be angry with you."

"Let me make amends," he offered. "I'll see that her relatives are restrained."

"Permanently."

"Yes, of course."

Molly allowed him the smallest smile. "Thank you."

"I'm sorry, Molly, truly I am. I can't marry her. But I will at least see that she can return to her home when she wishes and live her life unmolested." He quickly glanced at the clock on Molly's desk. "I'll talk to Mathison before I leave for Richmond and have him look into these Leslies.

And once I'm back in town, I'll go to see them myself and make them fully aware of the consequences should they coerce or frighten Isabella."

"They have to be warned off before she returns to town."

"I understand. You have my word. I won't allow them to touch her."

She didn't immediately reply, vexed and saddened by the harsh realities.

"She reminds you in some ways of yourself, doesn't she?"

"Of my ill-starred past." Molly grimaced. "I suppose I can't blame you for that." She sighed. "Take care of her and give me warning when you're returning. I want to be there for her if I can."

"I'll send you notice."

"She brings you joy, doesn't she?" Molly's gaze was piercing.

"Every minute." Moving to the bed, he picked up the valises. "It might be a fortnight or so, in case you don't hear from me. Don't take alarm."

"I'll trust you to act the gentleman. You're one of the few around."

"I'll take care of her. I promise."

When the door closed on him, Molly allowed her tears to flow. She hadn't cried in years, and she wondered for a moment if she was becoming dotty. Sniffling, she moved toward her desk, intent on doing something to help Isabella herself. Long ago, she'd learned that action forestalled her moments of self-pity. Picking up her pen, she sat down to write a note to her lawyer. She would see that the Leslies were investigated by her own team of attorneys. She had plenty of money and a considerable amount of influence as well. Albeit covert. At least she'd be prepared once Isabella returned to London. Having the upper hand had always been her favorite means of doing business.

Isabella waited for Dermott in his suite of rooms, pacing at times, trying to read, unable to sit for more than a few minutes at a time. Dressed in one of his robes, she wandered the large rooms, examining the portraits and landscapes on the walls, trying to place the ancestors chronologically by dress, wondering which of them had purchased the landscapes from the past century. A traveling Ramsey, no doubt, the majority of the works depicting continental locales. In her perambulations, she was reminded of the great difference in their stations in life—regardless her mother had been a viscountess in her own right. But the Leslies were not of the first water, nor had she any contact with her mother's relatives. Although, she thought with a small smile, heiresses at least were looked upon with a degree of approval. Now, if only Dermott were a poor earl, she whimsically noted, perhaps she could contemplate something more than a brief liaison.

She'd warned herself countless times in the previous days not to wish for the stars, not to allow herself to dream the impossible. But he was so very easy to love. . . . Abruptly setting aside the book she'd been attempting to read again, she rose from her chair, needing distraction from her hopeless fantasies.

But she understood for the first time why all the millions of tomes on love and romance had been written. To remind one of the inexplicable wonder. To exalt and rejoice. To revel in the astonishing pleasure.

Hurry, hurry, hurry, she silently implored, because I need you beside me.

Standing in the middle of the immense drawing room, surrounded by miles of gilding, countless yards of turquoise damask, furniture fit for kings, she listened for the footfall that would bring her joy.

And when he opened the door almost two hours later, she turned from the windows overlooking the gardens, her eyes filled with tears.

"I thought you weren't coming back."

"How could I not." Dropping her valises, he opened his arms.

She ran to him across the great expanse of Aubusson carpet, and he felt as though he'd returned to paradise.

"I shouldn't feel this way," she sobbed as he held her close.

"I'm glad you do," he whispered, wondering how she'd completely altered his world in so short a time.

"I should be blasé and sophisticated and charming so you don't tire of me."

"I don't want that, puss." Slipping his finger under her chin, he gently lifted her face. "I like you exactly the way you are."

"You don't mind taking a crybaby to Richmond?" She sniffled and smiled and looked so utterly adorable, he forgot to be sensible.

"You're my sun and moon, Izzy," he whispered.

And her heart filled with joy.

He played lady's maid for her, which delayed their departure for some time, but eventually Isabella was properly attired in addition to being deliciously sated, and leaving Dermott's suite, she walked on air.

The servants were decorous and polite regardless the awkward status of their employer's guest. Dermott's orders had been unequivocal. And Pomeroy wished them good journey as they walked from Bathurst House into the courtyard, where a closed carriage waited. Dermott helped Isabella into the green-lacquered conveyance, and after giving instruction to the driver, climbed in, shut the door, and took his place beside her.

"You'll like Strawberry Hill," he said with a smile.

"I know I will."

11

❧

MOLLY DISPATCHED A NOTE to the Lord Moira, requesting he visit her at his earliest convenience. And when Francis Hastings was announced the following afternoon, she greeted him warmly. "Thank you for responding so promptly."

"We've been friends for enough years that I recognized a note of urgency in your request." Walking into her drawing room, he moved to the chair beside hers and sat down. "Now tell me what I can do for you."

A close friend of the Prince of Wales's and Dermott's as well, Lord Moira was a frequent patron at Molly's. And on the occasions when he'd gambled and lost more than he could afford, she'd kindly covered his losses. They both understood the specifics of patronage and the merits of giving and receiving favors.

After seeing that Lord Moira had his favorite brandy, Molly poured herself one and began relating her story. "A very strange happening occurred a short time ago. A young lady, pursued and in fear for her life, burst into my establishment one night." And she went on to briefly describe Isabella's sudden appearance and the subsequent events related to it.

Lord Moira smiled. "Dermott always manages to pluck the ripest fruit, does he not?"

Molly nodded. "He has his share of beautiful companions."

"But this young lady requires some additional aid?"

"And I'm not in a position to offer it to her. You understand."

"Of course. You're talking about—?"

"Possibly a number of things."

"Of a conventional nature, I presume."

"Yes. And that's why I need your help. There's a possibility Dermott may come up to scratch—"

"He won't." Lord Moira's words were blunt.

"I know." Molly sighed. "This young lady is wellborn on her mother's side and an heiress now that her grandfather has died. Do you know George Leslie?"

"A merchant banker?"

"The same."

"He may have supplied the Prince with some funds, if my memory serves me."

"Better yet. I shan't feel as though I'm asking for so much." She tapped the rim of her glass. "I want Isabella protected from her relatives first. Although I think I may be able to take a hand in that. But I also wish her to be launched into society, and that's where I need you."

"Does Miss Leslie have a female relative who can be useful in that regard? I could see that she receives the necessary invitations and vouchers."

"Unfortunately not."

Lord Moira pursed his lips.

"Would Mrs. Fitzherbert be willing to sponsor her? I understand she and the Prince are inseparable once again."

"Mrs. Fitzherbert's welcomed everywhere, of course, but not exactly—"

"Without the Prince. Talk to Wales, then. See what he can do."

Lord Moira smiled. "Prinny may be willing to help if for no other reason than to play a prank on Dermott. To see Bathurst squirm as this unknown paramour is thrust onto the ton might amuse Wales mightily."

"It makes no difference to me what the reason, so long as the deed is accomplished. I'll try to deal with the relatives who plague her, but if necessary, I may ask your assistance there too. They have two eligible daughters, I understand, who are angling for husbands this season."

"A banker's daughters?" Moira's brows rose in mild derision. "Would they be moving in the same circles?"

"Occasionally . . . possibly. I'm trying to consider all contingencies."

"Miss Leslie must be a very special young lady," Moira quietly said.

"Unique." Molly cast him a warning glance. "And I don't want you to charm her, Francis. She doesn't need any more ineligible suitors."

"You want her happily married to some peer of the realm, in a fairy-tale fashion."

"I'm not so naive. But I'd like her to have the opportunity to see if she wishes that world. She has background, wealth, and stunning beauty. Whomever she bestows her affection on will be a fortunate man."

"You're a manipulative darling," Moira playfully said. "I can see there's nothing for it but that I must accede to your wishes."

"You'll talk to Mrs. Fitzherbert?"

"Let me talk to the Prince first. He may have some other hostess more comme il faut who's willing to take this young lady in hand." His gaze narrowed. "Are you sure she wishes this? If she's under Dermott's spell, she may refuse."

Molly softly snorted. "He won't keep her. You know that as well as I. And once she's been discarded, as his sexual playmates invariably are, I think I may be able to convince her—to pay him back, as it were."

"A woman scorned . . ." Moira smiled. "I shudder to think of the consequences." His expression sobered. "But consider, do you want Bathurst as an opponent? Does she? He won't back down."

Molly's gaze was equally serious. "Right now I'm not concerned with Dermott. He's very capable of taking care of himself. I'm doing this exclusively for Isabella. For her future happiness."

"Very well. You have my support, of course." While Lord Moira was in debt to Molly for a variety of favors, they'd become friends as well over the years. And he genuinely liked her. He suddenly grinned. "Would you care to make a small wager on whether Dermott responds to the lady's entrance into society"—his brows flickered in sportive query—"with his usual indifference?"

"You might lose on that. Think, Francis, when has he

taken a lover to his house at Richmond, or, more to the point, to Bathurst House?"

"Not Bathurst House!" His eyes widened in astonishment. "You don't mean it."

She smiled.

"So you might have other plans as well," he murmured. "Like bringing Bathurst up to scratch another way."

"It's time, I think, that he experiences an unselfish feeling."

"You're going to reform the rake that's bedded half of London since his return from India?"

"I'm not sure Isabella requires reform so much as commitment."

Moira groaned. "Never, Molly . . . you aim too high."

"We'll see," she murmured, more aware than Moira of Dermott's response to the beautiful Miss Leslie. "In due time, Francis, perhaps all the ton will have a front row seat at the spectacle."

He laughed, his hearty guffaw a boisterous sound in the elegant rococo room. "Damn, Molly, I tell you, I wait with bated breath." He drained his brandy and set the glass down. "With such a drama in the offing, I'm in haste to set the wheels in motion. You'll hear from me soon."

"Thank you, Francis. This is important to me."

Rising, he gracefully bowed. "Then we shall see the lady launched, my dear. You can count on it."

Unmindful of the plans *en train* for their return to the city, the lovers dwelt at Richmond in an idyll of sensual delight and joy. Some days they never left their bed, the sunny springtime viewed through the open doors to the terrace, the scent of fresh air only a light wafting breeze on their heated flesh. On other days they lay in the meadow behind the ancient orchard and absorbed the sun like pagans aligned to the rhythms of nature and made love as though they were alone in the world.

They swam in the river and fished and even played croquet one night when the moon was full. They made love later in the cool grass and wondered if ever two people were so happy. Dermott had dismissed his servants, unwilling to share Isabella, and they ate haphazardly from the food left for them each morning or attempted occasionally to master the most rudimentary culinary skills. Twice they walked into the nearby village and ate at the inn, shocking the locals by hiring a private dining room and not reappearing for hours.

Then one morning Dermott seemed preoccupied, and when Isabella questioned him, he casually dismissed her queries. But he disappeared late that afternoon while she napped, and when she found him he was seated in the library, a bottle of brandy in hand.

"Have I done something?" Frightened at his odd behavior, she watched him, hoping she might read further meaning in his expression.

He looked up and seemed not to see her at first.

"I've been looking for you."

His gaze focused on her and he smiled, a distant smile without the intimacy she'd grown to expect. "I'm just having a drink." He spoke calmly, as though he did this often.

"Would you rather be alone?" Each word was fraught with anguish.

He hesitated and then answered no, when his expression said otherwise.

"I could wait for you on the terrace." The door was open, the sunshine bright even as her world was turning cold.

He softly sighed. "No, don't. I've had enough." His smile this time held some warmth. "Should we walk into the village? Are you as hungry as I?"

She agreed. She would have agreed to walk to the moon if he'd asked, stricken and fearful, feeling that her happiness was disappearing. But Dermott was charming and gracious on their excursion into the village, conversing about subjects that amused her, making her laugh as they ate and drank the local cider, restoring her good spirits.

When they returned to the house, they made love with a special tenderness that almost broke her heart. It was over, she kept thinking, not knowing how to bring him back, feeling him drifting away. And later that evening when she fell asleep, he quietly left the bed.

She found him in the library again at two o'clock in the morning. But he wasn't sitting in the chair by the window this time. He was seated before an open cabinet alight with votive candles, tears running down his face. The small shrine held a portrait of a beautiful Indian woman with a young boy in her lap. She wore luxurious native garb and fabulous jewels, and the little boy looked out from the portrait with the most beautiful eyes. Dermott's eyes.

He must have heard her, but he didn't look around. He only said, "I'd like to be alone."

It was almost midmorning when he returned to the bedroom, looking drawn, his eyes shadowed with weariness. He stood just inside the doorway, distant, remote, not the man she'd come to love. "I'm sorry," he said, his voice dispassionate, his apology politesse alone. "Perhaps it's time we return to the City."

"Who are they?" Isabella asked, needing to know, fearful of knowing, not sure he'd answer her.

She was curled up in a chair near the bed, and he gazed at her as though seeing her for the first time. As though they'd just been introduced and he was trying to recall her name.

"Tell me, Dermott, please." The sadness in her voice echoed her wretchedness. "Before you send me away, tell me that at least."

"My wife and son. They're dead."

"I'm so sorry." If she'd dared, she would have gone to him and held him in her arms.

"It's been some years now." He drew in a deep breath and seemed to come to an awareness of his surroundings. "Forgive me for involving you. I apologize. Do you need help packing? I'll send for the servants if you wish."

"There's no need. I can manage."

"Good. Say an hour? Is that too soon?"

Too soon to end the happiest days of her life? "It's fine," she calmly said, forcing a gracious smile, her heart shattering in a thousand pieces.

"I'll see you downstairs, then." And like a stranger, he turned and walked away.

She wouldn't allow herself to cry, too proud to be red-eyed with weeping when she met him downstairs. She bolstered her spirits as she packed with sensible reminders—of the ways of profligate nobles, of her understanding from the first that Bathurst wasn't offering permanence. That their arrangement had been one of expediency—a means of insuring her inheritance.

And were it not for the tormenting ache in her heart, such sensible reminders would have been adequate.

But she managed to greet Dermott before the main door with equanimity, and on their ride back to London, she even spoke with a certain casualness. It was a performance equal to the best on the Covent Garden stage, and if she'd not been crying inside, she could have appreciated the stellar quality of her dramatic talents.

Shortly before they reached Molly's, Dermott said, "I'll see that your relatives no longer bother you. My lawyer's been looking into the situation. You should be able to safely return home soon."

"Payment for my services?" Her voice was sharp. "Forgive me," she instantly apologized, understanding it wasn't his fault she'd allowed herself to daydream of more. "It's very kind of you, but not necessary. Molly's plan is sufficient."

"There's always the possibility of scandal with Molly's idea. I'd rather you let me do this for you."

"Soothing your conscience, Bathurst?" she gently inquired.

"I don't have a conscience. I thought you knew that."

"Of course, how naive of me to forget."

"I didn't intend for this to happen," he quietly said. "I'm sorry."

"No need to apologize." She managed a small smile. "I enjoyed myself." Pale words for the resplendent pleasure he'd given her, the blandest of thanks for introducing her to paradise.

"As did I." He didn't smile; he looked at her, seated across from him, with a shuttered gaze. "I'll send a message to Molly's as soon as it's safe for you to go home."

He didn't escort her into Molly's. He only helped her down from the carriage, bowed faintly, and said, "It was a pleasure, Isabella."

"Yes, very much," she answered, curtailing her tears with superhuman effort.

Mercer had a footman pick up her valises.

Dermott glanced at the man and then, turning his attention back to her, said, "Thank you again." Swinging back toward his carriage, he ordered "Bathurst House" in a clear, strong voice, and stepping up through the door held open by one of his grooms, he entered his carriage.

"This way, my lady," Mercer murmured, conscious of her stricken look.

Isabella took a deep breath and turned. How many times had he said good-bye to a ladylove, she wondered, in that cool, well-bred way. She entered Molly's through the blue door that had once offered her refuge on a wet, dark night and surveyed the resplendent marble entrance hall. She'd first seen Dermott there. It seemed like a hundred years ago. In another lifetime—when she'd not yet tasted the sweet ecstasy he dispensed with a prodigal hand, when she'd not known the agonizing torment of unrequited love. When she was an untried maid.

"Isabella!"

Molly's voice rang down the staircase, and looking up, Isabella smiled at the woman who'd given her so much.

They met midway on the stairs and hugged, and then Molly escorted her to the drawing room. "Sit down now and tell me everything." She smiled. "Or at least what you wish. Oh, dear," she added, taking note of Isabella's quivering lip as she took a seat on the brocaded settee. "He's broken your heart."

"I didn't expect he could," Isabella whispered as the tears spilled from her eyes.

"He deserves a thrashing," Molly exclaimed, moving to enfold Isabella in a comforting embrace. "I was afraid of this."

"It's not his fault."

"Of course it's his fault. I told him not to take you to Richmond."

"But I wanted to go."

"He's too wretchedly charming. As always. Dear, dear," she soothed. "Don't cry for him. He's far from worth it."

Isabella looked up, her eyes filled with tears. "Did you know of his wife and son?"

"He told you?"

"I found him this morning crying before their portrait. He has a shrine of sorts in the library."

"They died four years ago today," Molly softly said. "He's not been able to forget. And for that reason and others I implore you to not pine for him."

"I've told myself as much, but it's not quite so simple."

"With time, my dear, you'll find other pleasures."

Sitting up straight, Isabella wiped away her tears with

her shawl. "I told myself that as well," she said with a small smile.

"I have something of interest that might distract you from your melancholy."

"Not another Dermott?" A tentative teasing note colored her voice.

"Something less disastrous. You know the season is just beginning."

"You jest, surely. You know my life was of the simplest before Grandpapa died."

"It would be an opportunity to show Dermott you're capable of surviving without him."

"I doubt he'd notice or be concerned."

"Would you like him to?"

"Notice me?"

Molly shrugged. "It depends how you feel about him."

Isabella pursed her mouth. "Sad and angry both. But hardly hopeful of more. You said yourself he's not worth pining over."

"Good. What say you to perhaps finding a suitor who would return your love?"

"In the ton? I'm not sure I'd be accepted."

"If I made it possible, would you be interested in being launched this season?"

"Me?" The notion was preposterous and yet in some faint degree intriguing.

"You're beautiful, wealthy—once your relatives are thwarted—and of good birth on your mother's side. Why not you? Heiresses are much in demand, you know."

Isabella smiled. "I suppose they are. Dermott said that he'd take care my uncles were no longer a danger to me."

"I've begun inquiries as well through my lawyers. Between Dermott and me, we should be able to return you to your home with your fortune intact. Especially with our trump card." She winked. "We can always threaten to expose your indiscretion and taint all the Leslies with the scandal. And most important, I have a sponsor for you with unimpeachable credentials."

Molly smiled. "Am I supposed to ask who?"

"You are, to which I answer, the Prince of Wales."

"No!"

"As a personal favor. And as you know, the Prince of Wales's influence overcomes all obstacles."

"My heavens! Never say I didn't barge through the right door when I ran away from home."

"It would be my great pleasure to give you a season. Who knows what nobleman might offer you his heart? What do you think?"

"I'm not sure. What a startling prospect. Or daunting, perhaps, coming from my sequestered background."

"You *could* put Dermott in his place. As an added bonus. He deserves it."

"You mean he'd be opposed to seeing me in society?"

"I think he might be opposed to seeing you with other men."

"Regardless he doesn't want me himself."

"Never say love is reasonable."

"Not love surely. Not with Dermott. You use the wrong word."

"He's never had a lady at Bathurst House nor at Richmond. It says something, despite his resistance to anything smacking of attachment."

"I could make him jealous, you mean."

"If you wish, or you could find yourself another man to love. With your lack of experience, perhaps you'd do well to survey a broader field before deciding you love Dermott Ramsay."

"Do you think this is love I feel?"

"That's for you to say. I wouldn't know. But a season would give you an opportunity to decide."

"What if I fail in this bid to be launched."

Molly laughed. "Dear girl, with your looks? Even without a shilling you'd have men falling at your feet. And with your fortune you'll have to beat them off."

"Really . . . beat them off?" It was a flattering notion to any young woman.

"No doubt of that. Say yes and I'll have a dressmaker in to fit you for a suitable wardrobe."

"Here? Forgive me."

"I have a home on Grosvenor Place as well. The widow, Mrs. Peabody, don't you know," she said, grinning.

"It does sound like a very enticing prospect."

"And you could annoy Dermott in the bargain."

"If that were true, and I'm not entirely sure it is—definitely added incentive. Very well, I'll do it," she quickly said before she lost her nerve.

12

❧

AFTER STOPPING at his lawyer's office to be briefed on the Leslies, Dermott was currently on his way to Herbert Leslie's office. He was in a foul mood, although he refused to admit the actual reason for his displeasure. He told himself his resentment was directed at the family that had tried to harm a young woman without friends. He told himself his mission was one of benevolence and charity. A chivalrous gesture for a lady in distress. None of which fully accounted for his sullen rage, if he'd allowed himself to face the plain, unvarnished truth.

But he didn't. Nor had he for a very long time, intent on disallowing personal feelings—a necessary expedient for a man still dealing with loss.

The clerk in the antechamber stammered in alarm when Dermott burst through the door demanding to see Herbert Leslie.

"Never mind," Dermott growled, pushing past him, shoving the door to the inner office open with a stiff-armed push and striding in like a raging bull.

Herbert's eyes bulged with terror, and he jerked back

in his chair as though the impact of Dermott's arrival had propelled him there.

"Out," Dermott snapped to the man seated across the desk from Herbert, and without waiting for the employee to exit the room, he said in a voice so cold, the office manager told the flustered workers beginning to gather outside in the corridor that someone should call for a Bow Street Runner.

Dermott kicked aside the formerly occupied chair, and placing his palms on the desktop, leaned forward, menace in his dark gaze. "Listen carefully, Leslie," he growled. "Because I'm going to say this only once."

Herbert trembled in his chair, wondering how he'd possibly incurred the wrath of the Earl of Bathurst, who was renowned for both his temper and his skill with dueling pistols.

"I understand that you've threatened Miss Isabella Leslie with an unwanted marriage and the loss of her inheritance. Let me express this as plainly as possible so there can be no mistaking my intentions. If you, your brother, nephews, or son"—he pointedly enunciated each relationship with precision—"ever attempt to harm Miss Leslie again, I will personally call each of you out and kill you. Is that clear?"

Unable to move in his fright, Herbert opened his mouth and croaked.

"Nod your damned head if you can't talk, you bloody coward."

Gathering every ounce of energy not frozen in fear, Herbert managed to nod once.

Dermott stood upright and glared at the petrified man. "Another thing," he curtly noted. "Don't be seen within ten blocks of Isabella's house, or my same warning applies. And this isn't an idle threat. I'd take great pleasure in putting a bullet through your foul hearts."

Turning, the earl stalked from the room, scattering the huddle of employees outside like a flock of frightened birds while Herbert tried to draw enough air into his lungs to cry for help. When Leslie could finally speak again, he ordered that all the doors be locked to visitors until further notice. And it wasn't until nearly an hour later that his panic and fear subsided enough to consider the baffling question of why the Earl of Bathurst was concerned with his niece. Herbert immediately called together those members of his family included in the earl's threat, and they decided one and all, regardless the earl's interest in Isabella, that they weren't willing to face his expert marksmanship on the dueling field. Isabella's fortune wasn't worth their lives.

But by morning, greed had overruled fear and the male Leslies met again to consider possible ways to gain access to Isabella's inheritance without either the earl's or Isabella's knowledge. They discussed approaching old Lampert, although none was sure whether he actually could draw from the funds. The manager of George Leslie's bank next came under consideration. Could he be bribed or coerced to give them access to Isabella's accounts? They berated George Leslie for denying them any partnership in his businesses, conveniently forgetting he'd lent them the money to develop their own enterprises. In the course of their meeting, they scrutinized anyone close to Isabella's money in the hopes of arriving at a plan. And while they arrived at no conclusive scheme, they agreed to pursue the project. Under the deepest secrecy, however. None dared risk Bathurst's wrath.

Dermott spent the remainder of the day in his study with the shutters drawn, a brandy bottle in hand, intent on drinking himself into oblivion. And so Lord Moira found him when he stopped by on his way to Brooks's.

Dermott looked up at Moira's entrance and scowled. "I'm not in the mood for gossip or talk of Wales's latest imbroglio with his family. Or actually company at all."

"Pray tell what's put you in such a charming mood?" Hastings inquired, ignoring Dermott's churlishness and walking in.

"I dislike springtime," the earl mockingly replied.

"Ah . . . so you'll be drunk for some weeks," his friend drolly noted, taking a seat across from Dermott, lounging back and crossing his legs at the ankles.

"Don't get too comfortable, Francis. You'll find me exceedingly poor company."

"Then I'll pass on my small *on-dit* and be on my way."

Dermott cast him a moody glance from under half-lowered lashes. "I rather thought you might have a tidbit for my edification."

"It has to do with your latest paramour," Moira said with a small smile.

"And which one might that be?" Dermott drawled.

"The one you've spent the last fortnight with."

"And how the hell would you know that?" Dermott pushed himself upward from his lazy sprawl, his gaze sharp.

"Molly has Miss Leslie under her wing."

Dermott leaned back in his chair. "You're not telling me anything I don't know."

"Molly also summoned me for a boon the other day."

"I'm sure I'm not going to want to hear what that favor might be."

"She's intent on launching Miss Leslie into society."

"And your part in this?" Dermott casually inquired.

"To find her a sponsor."

Dermott refilled his glass and drained half of it before he replied. "I wish her good fortune."

"You're unconcerned?"

Dermott lifted his glass to his mouth. "Shouldn't I be?"

Moira shrugged. "I told Molly you wouldn't care."

Dermott's gaze narrowed. "Is this some form of manipulation on Molly's part?"

"Not entirely. Perhaps not at all. I think Molly genuinely wants the young lady launched. Apparently, Miss Leslie has looks and money, and if not the bluest blood, a considerable fortune that will absolve her of that unfortunate defect."

"If I know the male predators in the ton, her beauty alone will easily overcome any irregularities of birth."

"So she's fair game?"

Dermott lifted his shoulder in the faintest of shrugs. "Why ask me? I have no claim on her."

"I didn't think you had."

"I have no intention of changing my way of life. You may pass that on to Molly."

"Just so." Lord Moira uncrossed his legs. "In the event you tire of your own company, Wales is having his usual coterie to Carlton House tonight. Come and join us."

"Who's her sponsor?"

Moira's gaze took on a new alertness as he rose from his chair. "Lady Hertford."

"Prinny's newest bed partner. So he's involved in this?"

"The Prince feels he owes the girl a favor since her grandfather paid for most of his Italian art collection."

"Really. And when did Prinny acquire these philanthropic instincts?"

"Who knows what motivates him, but I doubt any of this will come to your notice anyway," Moira declared, watching Dermott intently. "It's not as though you grace the deb balls and entertainments."

Dermott softly swore, and sliding into a sullen sprawl, reached for the brandy bottle. "Nor will I, Francis," he growled. "Tell Molly that."

Later that evening, Lord Moira and Molly had a chat. After describing his visit to the earl, Francis noted that he rather thought Dermott might make an appearance at an occasional party this season. Or at least some of those attended by Miss Leslie.

"Tell me again, everything he said," Molly demanded, exceptionally pleased with Moira's account. "And exactly how he looked."

* * *

The next morning, Molly informed Isabella that she'd received a note from Dermott explaining he'd warned off the Leslies.

"I'm free to go home, then." Isabella felt both relief and sadness. Much as she wished to be liberated from her relatives' schemes, Molly and, of course, Dermott meant much to her.

"I'm hoping I may coax you into staying with me at Grosvenor Place while we're planning your entrance into society," Molly remarked. "Although I understand you have to see to your personal affairs. Might I suggest we move to my town home and from there you make the necessary excursions to your house and business. Or better yet, if you don't think me too cautious, why not have your superior servants and business managers come to Grosvenor Place. I don't trust your relatives regardless Dermott's warning to them. Perhaps I've lived too long in a disreputable world. But such evil people don't turn virtuous overnight."

"You may coax me, with pleasure. In truth, I enjoy your company enormously. As for my business affairs, between Lampert and Grandpapa's chief steward, Morgan, I may take a banker's holiday during the season without concern. It's not as though I have the opportunity to mix with such superior people every day." She lightly laughed. "Don't worry, Molly, I'm not likely to have my head turned by the haut monde."

"They're all quite ordinary people, if truth be known."

"But it will be fun for at least a brief time to observe

the social whirl firsthand. Now then," Isabella remarked in a businesslike tone that brought Molly's gaze up. "I'll send a message to Lampert and Morgan and my housekeeper. Would tomorrow morning suit for a meeting with them?"

"Consider my house yours. You decide."

"Very well. Tomorrow at nine."

And despite Molly's doubt that her houseguest would be about that early, she was surprised to hear that Isabella had been dressed and ready for her retainers shortly before nine. Such an hour was much too early for Molly's constitution. She preferred the first light of day to be approaching noon. And in that regard, she matched the tastes of the ton.

Over coffee and a light breakfast, Isabella conferred with her assistants, offering them an edited account of her activities the past month and thanking them for handling her affairs in her absence. For the next hour they discussed all that had transpired of importance during her absence. She asked questions and took notes, promising to confer with them again the following week. Should they have any questions for her before that time, they were free to come to Grosvenor Place and see her. After they'd all agreed on their instructions, and when the activities related to the house, bank, and shipping business had all been dealt with, Isabella said, "I think you all deserve a bonus for carrying on so well during very difficult circumstances. I think twenty percent would be fair. Will you see to that, Morgan? And something for the employees and household servants as well. Whatever you think adequate."

"You're very generous, Miss Isabella," Morgan replied, his expression pleased.

"And the best of luck, darling," her housekeeper, Mrs. Homer, said, beaming. "To think our little Izzy is going to make a splash in the ton. Your grandpapa would be so proud."

"It's not a splash, Homie, but only a little ripple, I fear."

"Not if they've eyes in their head," she remonstrated. "You'll outshine them all."

"Our very best, Miss Isabella," Mr. Lampert offered. "We'll be watching the society columns for news of you."

Isabella laughed. "You'll be wasting your time, but thank you for the compliment. I *am* looking forward to the experience."

"All good wishes from the employees at the bank and docks, Miss Isabella. It's a proud moment for us all."

Once Isabella was alone again, she smiled at their notions of her consequence. In their small world she may be looked upon as singular, but in the dazzling world of the ton, she doubted she'd garner much notice.

In the following days, Molly concerned herself almost exclusively with the details of Isabella's wardrobe. Since she and Isabella had moved into her home in Grosvenor Place, each morning brought another visit from the dressmakers. By the end of the week, the armoires were beginning to fill with magnificent gowns of every color and fabric, along with all the accompanying fripperies, a sufficient number that Isabella could be set up in the latest fashion. The time had arrived for a call on Lady Hertford.

Lord Moira came to fetch Isabella in his carriage, and

on the way to their meeting with the marchioness he calmed her nerves with his grace and charm.

"The Marchioness of Hertford is the Prince's lover and in that capacity is sure to have his ear. With Barbara as sponsor, everyone will understand that you are in effect sponsored by the Prince of Wales. But she's very easy to talk to, not pretentious in the least. And most important, she's more than willing to do this favor for the Prince."[6]

"I'm on pins and needles nonetheless. You can't imagine what a tremendous change this will be from my life with Grandpapa."

"You'll be a great success, Miss Leslie. Rest assured, you'll have every man in the ton begging for your attention."

For the briefest moment, Isabella thought that she would willingly relinquish all that adulation for the favors of a single man. But as quickly, she chided herself for such foolishness, and when she turned her smile on Lord Moira, she was once again in command of her feelings. "I can't thank you enough for all your help in this endeavor, Lord Moira. I'm deeply in your debt."

"Nonsense, my dear. I'm pleased to be of service. You'll be a most beautiful addition to society."

And when Isabella met the marchioness, she was all that Moira had described—gracious, without affectation, delighted to be of service to her prince. And over tea and sherry that afternoon, Isabella listened while she was apprised of the astonishing array of entertainments she would attend. Breakfast routs, tea parties, musicales, garden parties and balls, the opera and theater.

"When does one sleep?" she playfully inquired, astonished at the number of events scheduled each day.

"One sleeps very little, my dear." Lady Hertford smiled. "But it's all such a great deal of fun, you scarcely miss your bed. And with your dazzling beauty, you're going to be much in demand. I suggest," she teasingly noted, "that you sleep as much as you can this week, for after that it all begins."

Molly and Isabella sat up after dinner that night, making lists of all that still required attention.

Isabella was taut with excitement.

Molly took pleasure in that excitement, pleased to offer the young woman she'd come to love entree into the *grande monde*.

"I'm going to have to practice all the various curtsies and graceful phrases and the dance steps too. I'm not sure I'm ready," Isabella nervously said.

"Nonsense. You're very accomplished and quite up to the mark."

"Tell me again, what I should do if I chance to meet my relatives at any of these functions?"

"Follow Moira's advice. Cut them cold. Dermott sent a note telling me they'd been warned off, as you know. I expect that will be sufficient to protect you from any unwanted overtures."

"And if I see Dermott?"

"Do as you wish, of course. But if I were you, I'd make sure he saw that you were enjoying yourself."

"Might he become jealous?"

There was such a wistfulness in her voice, Molly didn't have the heart to disavow that possibility. Although after the account of Moira's meeting she felt there was a chance Dermott's feelings might be involved. Nevertheless, she warned, "Dermott's plagued by demons you and I can't understand. It's difficult to determine what he feels."

"When Grandpapa died, I felt such loneliness. I can't imagine how one would survive the loss of a wife and child."

"He's haunted by the memory; it affects his whole life. But consider, dear," she coaxed. "There are a number of other handsome, charming men in the ton without Dermott's afflictions. Perhaps you'll find one you fancy."

"Perhaps . . ." But Isabella's dreams continued to be of Dermott, and in her bluest moods she wondered how long it took to fall out of love.

"Let's decide what jewelry you'll wear with your lavender gown," Molly declared, intent on distracting her protégée from melancholy thoughts.

Isabella smiled. "My mother's amethysts, of course."

"With that new pearl tiara."

"And the bracelet you found with the flower clasp."

"Perfect. We should have a portrait painted of you in that magnificent gown. You look as grand as a princess."

Isabella laughed. "If only Grandpapa could see me now. He would tell everyone at the bank and everyone who came into the bank, and all the sailors and workers at our warehouses and docks. 'Look at Izzy,' he'd say. 'She's taken on the ton.' "

"And so you shall," Molly cheerfully replied. "Beginning next week."

13

❦

THE EARL OF MOIRA had given Isabella's schedule to him out of roguish sport, Dermott didn't doubt. But he wasn't about to rise to the bait.

In fact, he made a point of having plans the night of her coming-out ball. But in the course of Lord Falworth's revel that evening, he was more aware than he would have wished of the special event transpiring at Hertford House. At midnight, with the bacchanalia in full swing, Dermott looked up from the chaise where he lay with a beautiful cyprian—one of several Falworth had brought in for the occasion—and glanced at the clock chiming the hour.

The lovely woman lying beneath him regained his attention in a particularly arousing way, bringing his perceptions back to amorous play, and he renewed his gratifying rhythm. The private room in the tavern was furnished with a number of chaises—all occupied by young lords and their fair companions, and the consumption of liquor had had its effect on the guests. The level of dissipation had reached an unbridled state of orgy.

From which Dermott felt oddly detached.

Not that the lady beneath him had any reason for complaint. He operated automatically after so many years, instinct and skill taking over when his attention was otherwise engaged. Although, after bringing her to climax once again, he disengaged himself with well-bred courtesy—the phrases second nature to a man who never stayed long—excused himself and rose from the chaise.

Prompted by rash impulse, he swiftly dressed, making himself presentable with an adeptness acquired from countless hasty departures. And after leaving his companion a sizable purse and a gracious smile, he exited the debauch.

With a pronounced feeling of relief.

Twenty minutes later, he was mounting the stairs to Hertford House.

Standing on the threshold of the ballroom a few moments later, he was announced by the marchioness's august majordomo. A great number of guests turned their heads to stare. Not that he was overlate, for balls rarely began before eleven.

But, rather, that he was there at all.

And, they noted, in a state of mild dishevelment.

Even from a distance it was evident he'd not just come from his valet. Although the earl had a certain cachet that drew the eye regardless of the state of his dress. He wore a black swallowtail coat, an elegant waistcoat of embroidered silk, and knee breeches, the required dress for balls. And while his neckcloth might be a shade wrinkled, the beauty of his face and form eclipsed even that most reprehensible of sins. He ran his hand through his hair in a casual gesture as he stood in the doorway, the cynosure of so many eyes, and surveyed the guests with a raking gaze.

His appearances were rare at society functions, although he was known to make the exception when he was intent on making a new conquest or charming a current one.

It had to be a woman.

Who was she? everyone wondered.

And then his gaze came to rest on Lady Hertford's honored guest, and the conjecture ceased.

The earl strolled forward.

Isabella had seen Dermott the minute he'd stepped through the doorway, before he'd been announced, before he'd seen her, and her heart was racing.

His progress across the large room engaged everyone's attention, although he seemed not to notice. And when the men surrounding Isabella moved aside enough to allow him access to her and he saw her fully, his mouth curved into a smile.

An intimate smile that suggested he and Miss Leslie were well acquainted.

That made it clear to those who knew him best.

"Miss Leslie, I understand," he said, his voice deep and low, his salutation careful not to openly acknowledge their prior friendship. "Lord Bathurst at your service." He bowed with exceptional grace.

And while protocol demanded he wait to be presented to her, no one was surprised at his audacity.

She should take offense at his insolence, but he looked so beautiful, she could scarcely breathe.

But then she smelled the heavy fragrance—a woman's

scent that rose from his hair and clothes—and an inexpressible rage filled her senses.

"How dare you," she murmured, aware of the attention his appearance had evoked but unable to suppress her anger.

"I didn't realize you were such a stickler for convention, Miss Leslie. Should I find someone to introduce us?"

"Don't let me keep you, my lord. You perhaps wish to return to your lady friend."

"Not in the least. I apologize for my unkempt state. It was unavoidable."

"As is my next engagement. Excuse me, gentlemen. I've promised Lady Hertford a moment of my time." She made to walk away.

Dermott stepped in her path, his half-smile offering challenge. "Barbara won't mind waiting. Dance with me, Miss Leslie."

All eyes were on their exchange, and even those on the opposite side of the ballroom recognized a contretemps.

Isabella smiled tightly. "The musicians aren't playing, my lord. Perhaps some other time."

"An oversight, I'm sure." Gripping her hand, he stepped out onto the floor enough so the resting musicians saw him, and signaled for them to begin. They were separated from the other guests by a small distance now, their words not as likely to be heard.

"You're annoying me," Isabella snapped.

"Strangely, I feel the same way."

"Then I'll thank you to unhand me."

"I don't care to. Are you willing to make a scene at your coming-out party?" he softly jibed, drawing her into his arms as the strains of a *danse à deux* began. "Think of what you have to lose. All those potential suitors. A position as reigning belle. You're dazzling in that lavender gown, darling," he murmured. "I'm sure you know that." Pulling her closer, he gazed down at her with a cheeky grin.

"How kind of you to notice, my lord," she replied sarcastically, trying to ease backward.

"Kindness has nothing to do with it." His grip tightened as he smoothly moved them into a turn. "Your breasts are quite magnificent mounded in plump display above that very risqué neckline."

"Low décolletage is the fashion, my lord. As you well know, I'm sure, considering your major source of interest."

"As I recall, it was yours as well."

"People change. Although I see you're still in form. Who was your lover tonight? She uses perfume liberally."

"Actually, I forget."

He didn't even have the decency to deny it, she hotly reflected. "But then, you make a point of forgetting your light o'loves, don't you."

"Not always. I'm here tonight."

"Am I supposed to be flattered?" How beautifully he danced, damn him, effortlessly.

"You should be."

"You arrogant bastard!" she hissed, his cool nonchalance galling. "Is this where I'm supposed to fall into your arms and offer myself to you?"

He smiled. "You're already in my arms." With a cordial nod he acknowledged an acquaintance dancing by. "Although I'm getting the distinct impression you won't be offering yourself in the next few minutes," he murmured, his attention returned to her.

"How astute. It must come from your vast experience with women. For your information, I won't be offering myself at all."

"Really."

Another nod, a smile. He seemed to know everyone. "Yes, really," she said in a pettish tone that took issue with both the public display of adulation directed at him and his casual acceptance of it. "You're too assured, my lord. You've had your way too long."

"And you haven't?"

"Not with such selfish abandon." Most pertinently, she refused to be number two hundred and ten or one thousand fifty or whatever the sum of his conquests. The female fragrance on him tonight forcefully reminded her of his reputation for inconstancy.

"Do you wish to be courted? Is that what you want?"

"What I want, my lord, isn't within your power to give."

"You never complained before—about my giving," he dryly murmured.

Her cheeks turned red. "I have some pride, Dermott. Consider—how long would you keep me if I returned? A week, two weeks? When would you tire of the game? Because it's only a game with you. And I no longer care to play."

"Are you angling for a husband?" His voice had taken on an edge. "Is that what this is all about? This season and your newly found virtue?"

"What difference does it make."

"Tell me," he brusquely ordered, no longer nonchalant, the thought of her married to someone else insupportable.

"Unless you're thinking of proposing, I don't see how it can possibly matter what my plans are."

"So you *are* on the market." His grip on her hand hardened.

"Whether I am or not has nothing to do with you."

"I could take you away. You couldn't stop me. No one could."

"To what purpose?" Her brows rose infinitesimally.

He didn't answer.

"You see," she whispered. "Back to square one. Now, if you would stop acting like some spoiled young boy, I'd be grateful if you'd return me to Lady Hertford."

"Fine," he curtly said. Twirling them in grim-mouthed silence and flawless pirouettes through the numerous dancing couples, he came to rest directly before Lady Hertford.

"It was a pleasure, Miss Leslie," Dermott pronounced in silken accents. "I wish you a pleasant evening."

"And you as well, my lord," she murmured, as capable as he of feigned civility.

"Your party is a great success, Barbara," the earl remarked, smiling at their hostess. "Everyone of consequence is here."

"So nice of you to come, Dermott. I'm sure Miss Leslie is appreciative."

"Bathurst!" The Prince of Wales appeared in the doorway of the card room and waved as he approached. "I see you've been introduced to Miss Leslie," he said with a sly smile as he came to rest beside the marchioness.

And introduced into Miss Leslie as well—as he would be again, Dermott firmly resolved. "She granted me the privilege of a dance, Your Highness," he replied, honey-tongued and insolent. "I'm overcome with gratitude."

"And so you should be, Bathurst. Miss Leslie is a jewel of the first water, a rare beauty we're all grateful to have in our midst. Is that not true, Barbara, my dear?"

"Without a doubt, Your Highness. Why not join us for supper, Dermott. I'm sure Miss Leslie would enjoy your company."

"Thank you. I will." The smirk he turned on Isabella was one of brazen-faced impudence.

"We still have plenty of time before supper to test our competence in the card room," the Prince of Wales cheerfully declared. "Come, Bathurst. You always bring me luck."

In the interim before supper, Isabella danced with any number of the horde of men intent on claiming her company. She gaily accepted their compliments and requests to visit on the morrow, hoping to diminish the impact of Dermott's appearance tonight by welcoming their attentions, thinking she could forget his rudeness in the arms of other men.

Adoring men.

Flattering men.

Men who wanted her for more than sex.

She smiled and laughed and flirted outrageously,

wanting to pretend Dermott didn't matter, wanting to obliterate the image of his smug smile, thinking if she played at amour as shamelessly as he, she might feel a spark of interest in one of the many men who wooed her.

But no matter how handsome or charming the men, no matter their dancing skills, regardless of their title or flowery blandishments, her feelings remained sadly untouched.

She might have been made of stone.

But she steeled herself against the counterfeit joy that Dermott offered, reminding herself that all was only transient pleasure with him and the sense of loss at his leaving was too unbearable to repeat. If she were sensible—and prior to meeting Dermott she'd prided herself on her reason—she'd take advantage of her miraculous entree into society and concentrate on the amusements of a London season with single-minded purpose.

Not an easy task with Dermott so much on her mind. But the sheer number of entertainments together with her numerous gallant and enthusiastic admirers should keep her busy from morning to night. And in her present peevish mood she welcomed distraction above all else.

Gazing up into the handsome face of the Marquis of Lonsdale, she said with feigned warmth, "I'd very much like to take the ribbons of your high-perch phaeton. Say early next week? Monday?"

"Delighted, Miss Leslie," the young lord suavely replied.

"Perhaps four o'clock?"

"Four o'clock it is." His smile had charmed from a very young age. "I consider myself most fortunate, Miss Leslie."

"*Au contraire,* Lord Lonsdale. The pleasure is mine."

* * *

Dermott won at the gaming tables, of course, which didn't help her annoyance. Did he ever fail at anything? The Prince had won as well, and both men were in good spirits when they escorted the ladies into supper.

"Do you gamble, Miss Leslie?" Dermott inquired, his eyes asking something else entirely as he sat down beside her.

"I did once, to my chagrin," she pointedly replied.

"A shame. Perhaps it's like being thrown from a horse. It's best to simply try again."

"In this case, my lord, I doubt the horse has learned any better manners."

"How would you know without riding him again?"

The double entendre brought a flush to her cheeks, but her voice, when she spoke, was chill. "Some rogue horses can't be broken of their bad habits."

"What horses?" the Prince of Wales inquired in a jovial tone. "Did you buy yourself some new prime horseflesh, Dermott?"

"Miss Leslie and I were speaking metaphorically, Your Highness."

"Oh, ho! Poetry already, Bathurst. You don't waste any time. I'll drink to that, eh, Barbara, my dear. To love and romance, hear, hear!"

And there was nothing for it, but that they must join him in his toast.

Isabella tried to ignore Dermott as they were served their food by a phalanx of footmen, the menu gargantuan—like the Prince of Wales's appetite. But Dermott insinuated himself into the proceedings, indicating to the flunkies what to serve her, having her wineglass refilled as she emptied it, watching her eat each course with approval as though he had a proprietary right, touching her hand on occasion and her leg under the table with great frequency.

She tried to distance herself, but there was little room to physically move with the other guests at the table and the eyes of the Prince and Lady Hertford often trained on them. She didn't dare make a scene on her first night in society.

And Dermott knew it.

When the purgatory of supper was finally over, Dermott took her hand in his and drew her from her chair. "Miss Leslie has asked me to dance again." His smile to the table at large was sunny. "How can I refuse?"

And after the courtesies of taking their leave were complete, she was led away.

"You missed your calling," Isabella snapped, finally able to speak her mind. "You should have been on the stage."

"While you could have played the part of a sulky miss," he sportively replied. "How do you hope to bring a suitor up to scratch if you don't put yourself forward in a more flattering way?"

She cast him a steely glance. "Are you a suitor?"

"Acquit me, darling. I was speaking in an advisory capacity."

"Advice from you on courtship, my lord? I would think advice on seduction more your style."

"You don't need any advice on that, puss. You seduce in the most blatant way."

"I'll take that as a compliment, coming from a man of your repute."

"I'd rather have you take something else from me."

"Acquit me, darling," she mocked, repeating his phrase. "I've given up making love to faithless rakes."

"You knew what I was when you agreed to dispense with your virginity, so don't take on the airs of an affronted maid," he said with disagreeable calm. "I never promised you anything."

"Of course. How stupid of me to have overlooked the facts of our"—her brows rose—"agreement. Forgive me."

"Happily." Content with the lady's clearer understanding, his soft murmur turned indulgent. "Now, tell me, darling, how I can make you happy?"

It was the most tempting of questions but not one she cared to answer honestly. "If only you could," she sweetly drawled, abruptly coming to a halt just short of the ballroom, resisting the tugging of his hand. "Unfortunately, I have no intention of changing my mind."

He looked at her from under drawn brows, his gaze highly charged, examining. And when he spoke, his voice was unutterably soft. "You're sure?"

"Very."

Releasing her hand, he stepped away. "Then there's no point in wasting our time. Good evening, Miss Leslie," he murmured with the ceremonial courtesy of a stranger. And he walked away without a backward glance.

The earl danced the rest of the evening with women of every description, dispensing his charm with democratic conviviality, flirting shamelessly with the crowd of ladies that hovered around him between dances, ignoring Isabella. And when the guests were beginning to take their leave, he followed suit, coming to pay his respects to his hostess with a lovely raven-haired woman on his arm.

Lady Hertford and her guest of honor were seated with several others, indulging in champagne ices after a lively mazurka. The ladies were fanning themselves, the men wiping their brows with their handkerchiefs, and at Dermott's approach conversation trailed off. He and his companion were a stunning couple, both dark, tall, the stylish woman sumptuously provocative. She was dressed in a revealing magenta tulle gown that showed off her pale skin and black hair to perfection, and the manner in which she clung to Dermott flaunted their intimacy. Every man there envied him his night of entertainment. Mrs. Compton's beautiful mouth was reputedly one of her greatest assets.

On reaching the seated group, Dermott smiled and bowed to his hostess. "You've outdone yourself again, Barbara. The party was a veritable crush." He winked at her. "Your usual triumph."

"Thank you, darling. So nice of you to come." Her glance was amused. "You always add a bit of drama to any assembly."

"I live to entertain you, marchioness," he lazily drawled, a teasing gleam in his eye.

"And a good many others as well, you sweet man."

Ignoring her drollery, Dermott turned to Isabella. "Much success in your season, Miss Leslie." He bowed faintly. "I wish you every happiness."

With the lady on his arm fairly melting into his side, Isabella found it difficult to subdue her jealousy, and she kept her voice steady only with effort. "Thank you, my lord."

Dermott's gaze turned from her and swept the group. "We'll say our adieus, then. I'm sure we'll all see one another again—at some other crush." He turned to his companion. "Are you ready, darling?"

The resplendent beauty answered with a breathy, soft response that brought a smile to every man's lips and a disapproving severity to each woman's mouth. Isabella felt as though she were suffocating.

As the couple walked away, Lady Blandford sniffed. "How fortunate for her, Mr. Compton prefers his little bit of fluff in Half Moon Street."

"For access to the Prince of Wales's circle, Compton is more than willing to allow his wife her freedom," one of the men remarked. "That connection has nicely profited his financial firm."

"She's a bit fast even for the Prince of Wales's set," a young matron chided. "And I hardly think her dress suitable for a ball."

"More suitable to the boudoir," another woman taunted, "with her bosom so blatantly exposed."

"Come, come, Caro, your son has had his fill of her now," a gentleman noted.

"And the lady must feather her nest while she may. Her dark, sultry looks will soon fade."

"Mrs. Count'em has feathered her nest quite well, rumor has it." The sobriquet distinguished Mrs. Compton's habit of extracting expensive gifts from her lovers. "Bathurst has given more than his share to her. Recently, a necklace of pigeon-egg pearls, I hear."

"They're friends of long standing, are they not?" a man observed.

"Because they suit each other," an elderly lady calmly said, having seen enough of the world to be inured to its peccadillos. "Bathurst wishes no attachments. And Mrs. Compton likes his money."

"Enough of this tittle-tattle," Lady Hertford interposed, cognizant of Isabella's discomfort. "And if we don't all find our beds, we won't be up in time for Cecilia's Venetian breakfast tomorrow."

A small groan arose at the reminder of the morning's event.

"I for one am for my bed," Lady Hertford declared, rising from her chair.

Molly was waiting up when Isabella returned, eager for news of the evening. "Did you enjoy yourself?" she asked as Isabella entered her bedchamber.

"It was very grand, Molly. And yes, I enjoyed myself immensely."

"He was there, wasn't he?" Molly said, the reserve in Isabella's tone obvious.

Isabella smiled ruefully. "In all his glory."

"And?"

"After his very public pursuit, I told him I wasn't interested in renewing our relationship. After which he danced with virtually every woman in the room and then left with a Mrs. Compton, who was very beautiful and seductive and apparently one of his many lovers."

"He's going to be visible during the season," Molly gently noted. "Will you manage?"

Isabella kicked off her slippers and sank into a chair near Molly's. "Yes, Molly," she quietly replied. "I shall manage. In fact, I've accepted an invitation to drive Lord Lonsdale's phaeton next week when my schedule is less busy. And several other men have expressed their intentions to call."

"I'll warn Mrs. Homer of possible visitors, but you sleep as late as you may." Isabella's housekeeper had been brought to Grosvenor Place in the role of a country aunt to Isabella. A suitable chaperone was a requirement for an unmarried young lady. And Homie was capable of presenting an image of respectability.

"The Holland breakfast is scheduled for noon."

"Do you wish to attend? After so little sleep?"

Isabella smiled. "Of course, Molly. I intend to divert myself with each and every entertainment offered to me this season."

"Good for you. I wouldn't wish for you to pine over something—"

"Unattainable?"

"I was going to say something too problematical. Dermott hasn't come to terms with his life or himself since his return." She didn't admit to her bit of matchmaking after the fiasco of Richmond. "He's not ready to admit to love again. And any woman who thinks to change or reform him is bound for disappointment."

"So I've come to realize. So I shall enjoy myself in the exhilarating pace of activities. And not expect anything more than amusement."

"Exactly. Do you want a warm drink to help you sleep?"

Isabella laughed. "The moment my head hits the pillow I shall be sleeping. And thank you, Molly . . . from the bottom of my heart. For all you've given me."

But once Molly left and Isabella was in bed, she found sleep elusive. What was Dermott doing right now? she jealously reflected. Was the lovely Mrs. Compton giving him pleasure? Was she making him smile? Was she making him happy? How easy it was to mouth the words—to declare her indifference to him and express her intentions to enjoy the season. But to achieve that level of stoicism was much more difficult. He was in her every waking thought and his image haunted her dreams. Would it be possible to find pleasure with other men? Could she even seriously contemplate such an event? Or did loving Dermott Ramsay spoil one forever?

Jealousy ate at her, ruined her sleep, peopled her dreams, made her toss and turn until nearly morning. She finally fell asleep near dawn, exhausted, and when she was wakened at eleven for the hairdresser, she groggily opened her eyes and wondered how she could possibly smile today.

14

❦

DERMOTT WOKE to find Emma Compton in his arms and silently groaned. Easing her head from his shoulder, he slowly slid away, hoping he could escape her bed without a scene. While Emma may have been tempting last night when he'd drunk enough to put most men under the table and wished retaliation against Isabella, in the cold light of day he cursed his stupidity.

"Ummmm . . ." She reached for him in her sleep.

He lay utterly still until she quieted again, then carefully rose from the bed and tiptoed away. After gathering his clothing scattered about the floor, he quickly dressed save for his shoes, which seemed to have disappeared. Surveying the overgilded room, he searched the boudoir without success.

Perhaps he'd go home in his stockings, he thought, his need to flee urgent. He didn't want to talk to Emma; he didn't want to be reminded of all they'd done the night before. He particularly didn't want her to ask when they'd meet again.

The activities of the previous night had left a sour taste in his mouth. Despite Emma's agility and ready talents, he'd not enjoyed himself. He felt as though he'd reached some distasteful level of surfeit. Tired of women or sex, perhaps only of Emma, he stood in the middle of her pink-and-white boudoir, shoeless and empty of feeling.

Then he softly swore, because he realized the true reason for his discontent.

And he had no intention of acting on that knowledge.

In the end, Emma woke up because he accidentally kicked over a bottle left on the floor, and it required a delicate politesse along with a promise to buy her a brooch she wanted to placate her demands for more of his time. The jewelry was a small enough concession in his current mood; he would have offered anything to make his escape. He finally discovered his shoes under the puddle of magenta tulle, and with an evasive promise to call on her soon, he left her perfumed boudoir.

A few moments later, he stood on the pavement outside, feeling like a man just let out of prison.

Dressed, coiffed, standing in the doorway to the drawing room, Isabella viewed the scores of bouquets with amazement.

"They began arriving at eight this morning," Mrs. Homer declared. "I think we'll have to move some of them to the other reception rooms, for each knock on the door brings more. You're the belle of the ball, my dear," she added with a smile. "And the billets-doux. I counted twenty-two already."

"Oh, dear." Isabella's soft exclamation was composed

of both astonishment and dismay. While it was gratifying to be the recipient of so much attention, she wondered how she was going to politely elude her suitors' regard. None of the men attracted her in the least. In fact, she felt a poseur, for she couldn't possibly return any of their affection.

A strong inclination to bolt and run overcame her as she surveyed the vast array of flowers.

Although she couldn't, she knew.

Not after all Molly had done to see that she had a season. Not after having witnessed Dermott's shameless behavior with all the ladies at Lady Hertford's. *Particularly* not after her sleepless night, where unwanted images of the voluptuous Mrs. Compton smiled at her from beneath Dermott. Damn his unbridled philandering! Clenching her fists, she lifted her chin and prepared to face the day.

Dermott would see she could enjoy herself as well as he.

And to that purpose Isabella conscientiously read each enclosure sent with the flowers, each billet-doux. Should she meet any of her admirers at the Venetian breakfast, it would be necessary to properly thank them. She had every intention of taking part in the full gamut of society's pleasures with as much gusto as Dermott.

The Earl of Bathurst was absent from the Holland breakfast, for which she was grateful, she told herself. Although she periodically searched the crush of people—in some inner recess of her soul, hopeful of seeing him. But on the surface she performed well, accepting the role of belle as though she'd been born to the part. And perhaps she had, with a mother known for her flamboyant personality and a grandfather who had indulged her like a princess.

In the course of the festivities she found herself diverted at least, conversing with countless people, accepting flattery with grace and charm, amusing and entertaining with an easy fluency. Her unusual education allowed her to discuss feminine pursuits or business affairs with equal competence; she also understood the world of bluestocking women and was sensitive to the erudite issues they espoused. While her ready sense of humor amused without malice.

"You've introduced a most charming young lady into society," the Duchess of Kendale remarked to Lady Hertford as they surveyed the milling scene from comfortable chairs in a small flower-filled alcove.

"She's a darling, is she not?" Barbara smiled. "And quite in love with Dermott, I surmise."

The duchess lifted one brow. "A rather useless endeavor, from all accounts."

The marchioness shrugged faintly. "That remains to be seen. He was wooing her most assiduously last night until she gave him his congé."

"Is she so clever as to make him beg?"

"Apparently there is some discord in their relationship. But not so long ago, I understand, it was quite—shall we say . . . cozy."

"She's not a young gel, is she?"

"No. But an heiress of vast fortune."

"So she can afford to offer challenge."

"Or perhaps she's as prideful as he."

"Either way, their courtship should offer an interesting piece of drama."

Lady Hertford shook her head. "Surely not a courtship with Bathurst. Although, I admit, I find it amusing that at last he's found a lady who refuses to succumb to his enormous charm."

"Perhaps it's time. He's been untroubled by female rejection his entire life."

"And Isabella may decide to favor one of her many suitors instead. Who knows how practical her motives."

"A practical woman would never waste time on Dermott."

Barbara flicked her fan open with a snap of her wrist. "And he's not likely to change."

"A rake rarely reforms," the duchess pronounced softly.

Barbara sniffed. "Really, Clarissa, be sensible. They *never* do."

"Mama!" Caroline Leslie cried, her plump cheeks quivering with the intensity of her feelings. "It's the most ghastly thing ever! Her name is in almost every paragraph of the society columns! I can't bear it!"

Seated with her daughters at the breakfast table, Abigail Leslie clutched a copy of another news sheet, her thin lips tightly pursed, twin spots of red coloring her sharp cheekbones. "Somehow Isabella has managed to show herself to advantage," she grimly murmured.

"The Prince of Wales, Mama!" Amelia wailed. "How vexatious and provoking! The little bitch knows the *Prince of Wales!*"

"Mind your tongue, my dear. I doesn't suit a young lady of fashion."

"As if we even are, Mama," Amelia crossly replied. "The only parties we're invited to are ones given by mushrooms or arrivistes. There hasn't been one viscount or baron or even a knight at any of them. And that *little bitch,*" she furiously added, looking daggers at her mother as if daring she reprove her, "is not only invited to a party given by the Prince of Wales's mistress but is the belle of the ball! Papa must do something about it, Mama! He must!" She reached for a piece of plum cake, her fourth.

"You know very well, your papa has been warned off by the Earl of Bathurst. Would you wish him killed in a duel?"

Both daughters stared at their mother without speaking, their selfishness curtailing an immediate reply. And then Caroline begrudgingly said, "I suppose not."

"Why does Bathurst have a say in our lives anyway?" Amelia petulantly inquired. "Can't Papa just tell him to mind his own business?"

"Would he really, actually, shoot Papa?" Caroline queried, a hopeful note in her voice.

"I don't think your papa cares to find out whether he will or not," Abigail snapped.

"We're never going to get husbands," Amelia cried. "And next season we'll be old goods. It's not fair, Mama!"

"What if stupid Isabella fell down the stairs? That would end her season." Caroline had pushed her governess down the stairs years before and the lady had directly left the household in fear for her life.

"I won't have you even thinking of such a thing," her mother warned. "You would never receive another invitation should you be so unwise." It had taken a considerable sum to still the governess's gossiping tongue those years earlier, and Abigail didn't wish to have any old stories revived should Isabella meet with an accident on the stairs.

"She'd be out of our way though," Amelia murmured, directing a sly smile at her sister. "And we could go to more parties."

"That's enough!" Abigail chided. "I forbid you to talk of such things as pushing anyone down the stairs."

"We could poison her," Caroline suggested, her mother's warnings always lacking penalties. "That's what happened to the heroine in *Lady Blair*."

"If you recall, the hero saved her," her sister pointed out. "And stupid Isabella has any number of suitors, according to the gossip column, so she would be saved anyway."

"I can't imagine where you girls get such preposterous notions. No one will be poisoning anyone. Do you understand?" Abigail cast them a pointed look.

"And we'll just mold away at all the rubbishy parties while Isabella dances with the Prince and probably marries a duke." On which sour note Caroline stuffed an entire muffin into her mouth.

"And we'll be forced to live with Mama and Papa for the rest of our lives," Amelia said with a dramatic sigh cut short by a forkful of glazed ham.

*   *   *

After breakfast, impelled by motherly impulse and the ridicule of her friends if she couldn't marry off her daughters with ten thousand apiece, Abigail sought out her husband in his study. "I don't suppose you saw the society columns this morning," she curtly pronounced as she entered the room, displeasure in every syllable of her statement.

Herbert looked up from his desk. "Now, why would I look at the society columns?"

"To see if your daughters might be in them?"

"Not likely that." He was realistic about his daughters' prospects, understanding they would find themselves husbands only because of the generous dowries he provided.

"Well," Abigail pithily said, plunking herself down in a chair near the desk, her brows drawn together in a black scowl, "if you had, you would have seen that Miss Isabella Leslie has flown very high indeed."

His wife had his attention. "Meaning?"

"None other than Lady Hertford sponsored Isabella at a ball last evening. Which really means the Prince of Wales is her sponsor, as you well know. Our daughters are beside themselves with grief and rage."

"Don't look at me like that. I could no more get them an invitation to Lady Hertford's than I could jump over the moon." Isabella had indeed landed on her feet, he thought, Bathurst's interest in her suddenly personalized, the tidbits of gossip apparently true. His close relationship with the Prince of Wales was well known.

"You will do something, Herbert." Abigail's thin shoulders were rigid with anger. "Need I remind you what the influence of my father's firm meant when you were first gaining clients?"

"No, you need not remind me," he grumbled, "since I've heard it anytime you were vexed these last twenty years. But you didn't see Bathurst when he threatened me. He was serious."

"Surely a man of his ilk rarely appears at the deb balls. The girls wish to meet the aristocracy, not the sons of City merchants."

"Unfortunately, we don't know when he may appear, and I have no intention of meeting him on the dueling field."

"I understand, Herbert." She offered him a thin smile. "But surely there's some way around it. A means of offering the girls entree into some of the fashionable balls. Bathurst's defense of Isabella certainly can't be of much moment. He's known for the fickleness of his interests."

"Let's hope you're right. I don't relish his anger. Nor do any of our male relatives."

"You must find out when and where he will be and simply avoid those entertainments. There will be plenty enough parties left over. With the girls' dowries we can reach high, Herbert, and don't tell me you wouldn't wish a quartering or two added to our family name."

"You ask a good deal, Abigail."

"But not the impossible when every night sees a dozen balls."

"Very well. I'll see what I can do."

"That's all I want."

* * *

By one of those fortuitous freaks of fortune that occur from time to time, Herbert Leslie found himself meeting with the Marquis of Lonsdale the following day. It seemed the marquis had lost rather heavily at White's the night before, and he needed funds to pay his gambling debts. Since Herbert already held a number of the marquis's notes, he was just about to ask a favor of him in regard to invitations for his daughters, when Lonsdale asked, "Is the beautiful Miss Isabella Leslie any relation to you? She's quite charmed the ton."

It was a moment of pure opportunity.

Invitations be damned.

Since George Leslie's death, the Leslie males had been trying to find a way to separate Isabella from her fortune, and now Lonsdale had suddenly appeared in his office as though by the hand of God. Not that Herbert had a Christian bone in his body, but he recognized a miracle when he saw one.

"As a matter of fact, she is. She's my niece."

"And very wealthy, I hear." After dissipating his inheritance in five short years, the marquis was on the lookout for a profitable marriage. "She's agreed to go driving with me next week."

"Has she now?"

At Herbert's tone, the marquis looked at his banker with a speculative gaze. "She has," he softly said.

"How much do you owe me?" Herbert asked.

One of the marquis's brows rose in contemptuous regard. "How should I know. Do I look like a grubby clerk?"

"Fifty thousand."

The marquis smiled. "And you want something from me for this new loan?"

"How would you like to marry my niece?"

"I and a hundred other bucks. Do you have a suggestion on how I might accomplish that feat?"

"Possibly. But if I do, I want my fifty thousand and the running of her businesses."

"Where you'd steal me blind." It was a time when women had few rights to their fortunes after marriage. The marquis's interest in Isabella's wealth was as keen as his interest in her.

"There's more than enough for everyone," Herbert calmly said. "And need I remind you, you're near bankrupt. So a percentage of Isabella's fortune is more than you have or could possibly contemplate. You're not a great catch, Lonsdale, with your estates in ruin."

The marquis scowled at him for a moment and then said, "What do you want me to do?"

"Take her driving as planned."

"And?"

"Drive her to your little hideaway in Chelsea, where you can see that she's thoroughly compromised. We will see that there are witnesses and a minister waiting." This time Herbert planned on taking no chances. He'd see that Isabella was married to the marquis. Bathurst would be less likely to threaten one of his own kind. And should he, Lonsdale's skill with a pistol was formidable.

"Tempting." The marquis leaned back in his chair and contemplated some distant view outside the windows.

"You'd be very rich."

Lonsdale refocused his gaze on Herbert. "I could take her away to the Continent." He smiled. "For a honeymoon."

"Until the scandal dies down."

"Until I see that she's with child. Insurance, as it were."

"Very wise."

The marquis abruptly came to his feet. "I'm going to need contracts for my lawyers to review. Soon. I take her driving Monday."

"I'll have them delivered to your home."

"Send them to Jackson Hewlett. I'll stop by to see him now and give him a brief overview."

"Only of our terms."

"Of course."

"The matter of Isabella will remain private."

"Naturally."

"I'll see that your debts at White's are taken care of."

Lonsdale dipped his head. "And I'll see that Miss Leslie enjoys her drive."

15

DERMOTT HAD GONE into hermitage with Helene Kristos, a young mother who lived with her son in Chelsea. They were friends and lovers, as were many of the women Dermott fancied. But he particularly liked Helene's company, and after leaving Emma Compton's, he'd knocked on her door, claiming he'd given up women for good.

Helene had only smiled and said, "Do come in, Dermott. You look like you haven't slept." And over the breakfast she made for him, she heard of his unsuccessful wooing of Isabella at the ball as well as a highly edited account of his unsatisfying night with Mrs. Compton.

She commiserated with him, and when her two-year-old son woke, Dermott played with the young boy and forgot for a time about ladyloves and unrequited passion. Tommy was a great favorite of Dermott's, reminding him of his own son, of happier times, and he always felt a level of comfort at Helene's.

He fell into a lazy domesticity the next few days, going with Helene to the market in the morning, accompanying her to the park with Tommy in the afternoon, helping her rehearse her new part for the play scheduled to open in

Covent Garden. He didn't make love to her and she didn't question his mood, aware of his feelings for the woman who'd spurned him at Lady Hertford's ball—even if he wouldn't admit to them.

Dermott didn't drink in the evenings, when in the past he'd always emptied at least two bottles a night. He read instead, which unusual pastime piqued Helene's curiosity about the young lady he'd taken to Richmond. What had this Miss Leslie done to so powerfully change Dermott's profligate ways?

In the meantime, Isabella's schedule continued apace, and she moved from one entertainment to another with willful determination, falling into bed exhausted after dancing all night, invariably dreaming of Dermott, waking up each day to the frustration of finding herself alone in bed. While the men who wooed her with flowers and flattery didn't ignite even the smallest spark of interest.

By the end of the week, she was wishing she could change her mind and chuck it all.

And if it weren't for Molly, she would have.

But Molly was living vicariously in a world she'd seen only from the fringes, and Isabella couldn't think of denying her the pleasure.

Isabella ordered coffee with her breakfast chocolate that morning, intent on recharging her sense of purpose and vanquishing her fatigue. For she faced another grueling day of social activities, beginning with yet another breakfast party, followed by an afternoon musicale with Italian singers at the Duchess of Kendale's.

* * *

Late that afternoon, when Dermott walked into the duchess's music room, heads turned and a flurry of whispers spread across the room like a cresting wave. Even the soprano performing a solo paused infinitesimally in the midst of a soaring high note, at which point anyone not aware of his presence immediately turned to look.

He stood at the back of the room, framed by a rococo panel depicting the Shower of Danaë, and more than one guest considered the background highly appropriate for a man of his wealth and profligacy. Isabella found the juxtaposition irritating—as if she needed any reminders of his infamy. But even as she resented his reputation, she experienced a small, wistful yearning that he might have come for her. A feeling she forcibly brushed aside a moment later, reminding herself instead that Dermott Ramsay had no interest in her other than sex. And even that was of the most transient nature.

Forcing herself to concentrate on the splendid voice of the soprano, she focused her gaze on the performers arrayed before a magnificent display of lilies.

Dermott had seen her immediately he'd entered the room, the gold of Isabella's hair instantly recognizable even in a crowd. And for a brief second he debated walking out again, not sure why he'd come, more unsure of what he intended to do now that he was there. Was he like some callow youth, content to view her from afar? Did he intend to make a scene? Would she rebuff him if he approached her? How much did he care if she did? He seriously felt like a brandy; he'd not imbibed for almost a week now. Glancing about the sumptuous room filled with sunlight, he took in the colorfully gowned women, the occasional male escort, and then he spied the liquor table.

But before he'd decided whether he'd actually succumb to his urge, the aria came to a close and a number of women suddenly surrounded him—Emma Compton in the lead. Slipping her arm through his, she leaned into him and purred, "Now that you're here, darling, the tedium has suddenly lifted. I've missed you."

"We all have," the Countess of Goodemont murmured, smiling up at him. "You've been avoiding society, you inconsiderate rogue."

"Come sit with us, Ram," a recently married marchioness coaxed, her husband too old to enjoy anything but his money. "My sister and I still remember the holiday at Larchly."

"Fishing is so much fun with you," her sister interposed in a low, suggestive tone. Taking his free hand, she gently squeezed it. "We're sitting up front."

"I should give my compliments to Mariana. Her voice is superb, as usual." As though he'd come for the music and not Isabella—her schedule etched in his brain. Dermott eased his fingers free, slipped from Emma's grasp as well with skillful grace. "I haven't heard Mariana sing since Milan. If you'll excuse me, ladies." His bow was well mannered, his smile polite, and he strode away, leaving discontent in his wake.

Isabella had tried not to take notice of the swarm of admirers that descended on Dermott. She'd turned to her companion and discussed with seeming interest the particulars of the musical program. But she saw him in her peripheral vision, was aware of Mrs. Compton's closeness, couldn't help but recognize the expressions of longing on all the ladies' faces.

How was she going to deal with her hurt and anger when she couldn't even be in the same room as he without being filled with resentment?

And when Dermott approached the beautiful Italian soprano a few moments later and she enfolded him in a warm, intimate embrace, Isabella felt her teeth clench in indignation. Apparently, he wasn't content with making love to all the women in England; his amorous exploits included the Continent as well. Abruptly excusing herself, she apologized to the ladies seated on her either side for taking such hasty leave. She'd just remembered a previous commitment, she mendaciously explained, and brushing past the row of guests, she escaped the room.

Her driver was waiting down the street, sixth in line before the duchess's residence. The sun was warm and bright, the spring day balmy, scented with blooming flowers—in a word, perfect, if not for the galling presence of one man. Her heels made a brisk tattoo down the pavement as she hurried to her carriage.

"You're early, miss," her groom said as he held the landau door open for her.

"I'm tired, Sam. And more than ready to go home."

"You been rushing around, miss. Anyone'd be tired," he commiserated as he handed her into the open carriage. "We'll be home in no time." Giving directions to the driver, he jumped onto his back perch and the carriage moved away from the curb.

The vehicle gained the street, the matched team just

beginning to canter, when Dermott appeared on the duchess's porch.

"Faster!" Isabella ordered.

Dermott leaped down the short bank of stairs and ran in pursuit.

"Hurry!" Averting her gaze, she stared straight ahead.

For only brief moments more.

And then Dermott jumped onto the carriage step, swung over the low-slung side of the landau, and dropped into the seat opposite her. "Were you bored with Mariana's singing?" he lazily inquired as though his sudden appearance didn't warrant comment.

"Get out." Her voice was unutterably chill.

"Not likely." He spoke without a scintilla of ire.

"I'll have you thrown out."

He glanced at the young groom and old driver. "Not by them," he calmly replied, making himself comfortable. "So tell me, what have you been doing?"

"Forgetting you," she rudely said.

"A shame," he murmured, "when I recall our friendship with the greatest of pleasure."

"That's because your friendships, as you call them, are always suited to your particular interest and schedule."

He smiled. "I could endeavor to be more accommodating if you wish."

"I *don't* wish, Bathurst."

"Might I persuade you to change your mind?" Mocking insinuation warmed his eyes.

"Tired of Mrs. Compton, are we?"

"Have you been enjoying your various suitors?" he blandly inquired.

"You seemed very friendly with the duchess's soprano," she countered.

"I hear Lonsdale's about to propose."

"Then you know more than I," she crisply remarked. "I haven't seen Lord Lonsdale for days."

"Perhaps he's rehearsing his proposal to make it suitably sincere when he asks for your hand and fortune."

"While you have no need of money? Is that what you're not so subtly implying?"

"What I need from you, Miss Leslie," he murmured, "is without price."

"And also not available to you."

"We'll see."

His smile was gratingly assured. "No, we won't," she ascerbically noted. "And I'd thank you to leave me in peace."

"Do I disturb you?" he asked with unctuous good humor.

"Not in the least. I'm busy, that's all." She leaned forward to speak to her driver. "John, Bond Street, please." She had no intention of going home if he was to follow her in. Better a public venue.

"Ah, a lady's major entertainment. Shopping."

"Unlike yours, my lord." She settled back in her seat, her raking gaze as insolent as his. "You prefer more personal amusements."

"I wouldn't discount the personal nature of some ladies' shopping experiences," he drawled.

She blushed, recalling the illustrations in Molly's book. "I'm sure I don't know what you're alluding to."

"I could show you if you like," he silkily offered.

"No, thank you."

"Why don't I tag along anyway." His grin was cheeky. "In the event you change your mind."

"You may disabuse yourself of that notion. Under no circumstances will I change my mind." Her voice, intended to be sharp, wavered minutely at the end when Dermott recrossed his legs, and for a fraction of a second his arousal was evident.

An irrepressible heat flared inside her, a flutter rippled through her vagina as though her body automatically responded to the sight of his erection. Clasping her hands tightly together in her lap, she steeled herself against the sudden turbulent desire.

A few moments later, when the carriage came to rest midway down Bond Street, ignoring her protests Dermott helped her descend, the warmth of his hand, the firmness of his grip, heightening her agitation.

Fully aware of her response, practiced at gauging female arousal, he tucked her hand under his arm, and holding it securely, began strolling with her down the busy street.

In desperation, she entered the first shop they passed, needing to separate herself from his searing closeness, distance herself from the familiarity of his powerful body and all it provoked in terms of heated memory. Once inside, however, she found herself disastrously in a shop awash with lingerie. Every conceivable style of chemise and petticoat, nightgown and robe, was displayed, the silken garments, the intimate implications of the apparel, bringing a blush to her cheeks.

"May I help you?"

She looked up into the handsome face of a young, virile man, and recall of Molly's erotic book came shockingly to life. "I'm . . . that is—I'm just . . . looking at the moment." Were there no female employees in the shop? Quickly glancing around, she found none and turned to leave.

Dermott's grip tightened. "Show us some petticoats. Lace ones," he said with a quiet authority. Turning to Isabella, he pleasantly smiled, as though he weren't holding her captive. "White lace becomes you."

Under the clerk's regard, Isabella curtailed her impulse to scream at him. "Perhaps we could do this some other time," she replied coolly.

"No time like the present, darling." Dermott's grasp was unyielding.

"But, *darling*," she returned, oversweet and pointed, "we don't have time with Auntie's party at five."

"You know I'm her favorite." His grin held a distinct impudence. "She'll overlook our late arrival. That one, I think," he added, indicating with a nod to the clerk a frothy confection of chantilly lace. "And the pink one over there."

Disregarding her resistance, he drew her toward a bank of curtained alcoves. "You can try them on in here." Apparently familiar with the layout of the store, he pulled back an elegant drapery and stepped aside so the clerk could set the two garments on a small table. "This shouldn't take long." Directing a nod at the young man, he pulled Isabella inside and closed the curtain.

"How dare you!" she heatedly whispered, jerking her hand away from his relaxed hold, wondering if she dared run.

"I wouldn't suggest it," he murmured as though he could read her mind. "You wouldn't make it to the door."

"The clerk is an accomplice?" she hissed, her gaze hot with resentment.

"Let's just say he knows how best to earn his living."[7]

"From you?"

He shrugged. "Try on a petticoat," he suggested as though she weren't bristling with umbrage. Dropping onto a convenient chaise, he offered her a sweet smile. "I'll buy them for you; I'll buy out the store for you."

"You can't mean to go through with this!" Her voice was deliberately muted, but her rage was unmistakable.

"With what?" His expression was innocent.

"I'm not in the mood for your games, damn you!"

"What are you in the mood for? *Honestly.*"

She drew in a steadying breath, his query uncomfortably relevant. "You just have to appear and I'm supposed to immediately succumb to your charm?"

"I don't think either one of us is much interested in charm right now." He lounged in a lazy sprawl, his erection blatant even in the subdued light. "Are we?"

She wondered if he could hear the powerful throbbing between her legs.

"You're flushed," he said, his voice exquisitely mild.

He knew. "What do you have in mind?" she snapped. "Five minutes and then we'll be on our way?"

"I doubt you'll be satisfied with five minutes," he gently said. "As I recall, you always wanted more . . . and more"—he smiled—"and more."

"And you're available," she gibed, trying not to look at the tempting dimensions of his erection.

"Always for you," he said.

"This is all for me?"

His mouth quirked in a faint smile. "I wish I were so unselfish."

"And then what? I mean—what exactly happens after this interesting encounter?"

"Do you want a signed contract?" he sardonically asked.

"Would I get one if I wished?" Equally sarcastic, she gazed at him.

"We both want the same thing. I don't understand your equivocation."

"Surely a man of your finesse knows better than to so bluntly propose intercourse."

"I'm sorry." He grimaced. "I find myself unable to deal with you casually."

"And if you could, I'd be better wooed?"

He pushed himself upright and his gaze was suddenly stripped bare of indolence. "If I didn't want you so," he gruffly said, "I could say anything you wished to hear."

"And if I didn't want you so," she countered, as hindered and buffeted as he, "I wouldn't care what you said."

He sighed and sprawled back again. "I'm at a complete loss. Nothing glib comes to mind."

"You might try 'I missed you.' "

A low growl escaped him. And then another sigh. "I did."

The two words were so reluctantly uttered, Isabella found herself smiling. "Then I might indulge you after all."

His gaze slowly came up and met hers. A moment passed, two, the hush of indecision palpable. And then without speaking, he opened his arms.

Standing in the middle of the room, she understood and didn't understand and at base, perhaps, was as selfish as he because she wanted what he wanted. "I suppose I should take off my bonnet," she said because the words were safe and innocuous and the truth would never do.

"Let me," he softly replied, coming to his feet.

They made love that afternoon with a suppressed desperation, as though they both knew their fleeting moments together might be all they had, that the world and the past and their uncompromising sensibilities precluded a perfect future. They were at once selfish and generous, indulgent and self-indulgent, caught up in a frantic sense of wonder and fevered exaltation. And when at last Isabella took note of the time, or the clerk did, or she'd just imagined the knock on the woodwork, Dermott reluctantly kissed her adieu.

But later, dressed once again, standing outside the shop, neither knew what to say.

He offered her his thanks and a number of graceful phrases of leave-taking. Although even as he spoke, he was assailed with an uncustomary sadness.

"I understand," she said, capable of pretext as well, when nothing made sense at the moment, when it felt as though she were falling off the edge of the world into nothingness.

He nodded, words failing him, his emotions in chaos.

And then he walked away.

Isabella returned home and canceled the rest of her engagements for the day. Self-pity overwhelmed her, and even Molly knew better than to interfere after talking to Sam and John. Retiring to her room, Isabella locked her door, lay on her bed, stared at the ceiling, and tried to bring her feelings into some semblance of order. She loved Dermott—an appalling, wretched fact. Like a dozen other women, no doubt—or hundreds. And there wasn't a hope in the world that he would reciprocate her feelings. That he was even capable of loving someone again.

So the question was—how best to overcome her unrequited love and get on with her life? Ever practical, she understood the pathetic liabilities in loving him. And in the course of her hermitage that evening, she considered a great number of options, none of which, unfortunately, soothed her current misery. Although there was comfort in knowing Dermott cared for her at some level other than sex. Of that she was certain. It was small recompense for her sadness, but a degree of solace, however minute, that she desperately needed.

It was a shame he had so many demons in his past, she reflected at least a thousand times that night.

In a more perfect world, she might have met him sooner.

In a more perfect world, neither would have suffered loss.

In a more perfect world, he would have returned her love.

And unalloyed bliss could have been theirs.

By morning, Isabella had reconciled fact and fantasy and had sensibly put what had passed between herself and

Dermott into perspective. He wasn't about to change his life—nor should she. There was no purpose in wishful dreams. When dealing with Dermott Ramsay, cold practicality was not only critical but essential.

For her part, considering the circumstances in which she found herself, she'd decided diversion would best serve her purposes.

And so she conducted herself that weekend as though frivolous society offered her the greatest delight, as though flirtation were her raison d'être and there weren't enough hours in the day to satisfy her penchant for pleasure.

16

ON MONDAY, under Molly's watchful eye and with the help of her maid, Isabella dressed for her drive with the Marquis of Lonsdale. She wore a simple muslin gown, tucked and pleated with green ribands, a short riding jacket of bottle-green wool completing the ensemble. Calling for her driving gloves, she set a small turban of striped silk on the back of her head while her maid went to fetch the gloves. Turning to Molly, she lightly asked, "Will this do? For one must show well, mustn't one?"

"You'll show very well indeed. Everyone in the park will take note."

"Which is the point, is it not—to see and be seen," Isabella observed. "In yet another gown, on the arm of yet another man."

Isabella was deluged with suitors and callers, the drawing room thronged with hopeful men whenever she was at home. "Are you becoming weary of the scene?" Molly gently asked, hearing the discontent in Isabella's voice. "You need but say it and we'll fold up our tent."

Isabella looked at her friend and smiled. "I'd be faint-hearted to cry off so soon."

"Perhaps you should be more selective. Accept only a few invitations."

Isabella made a small moue. "At the moment, I feel a great need for distraction"—her smile was brittle—"and amusement."

"Perhaps not with the marquis, however. He's a bit of a rogue," Molly warned, "and deep in debt. I should have said something before. I almost wish you might cry off today."

"And so I might if I'd not agreed to this in order to spite Dermott." The marquis for all his lack of money was a great favorite of the ladies. "Not that Dermott will take note anyway. He's probably entertaining some lady, as usual." And who better than she to understand his allure?

"Not Mrs. Compton in any event, Mercer reports."

"And how would Mercer know?"

"Because I told him to keep watch on Dermott for me."

"Then, tell me, where has he disappeared?" With the exception of the duchess's musicale, he'd been absent from society since her ball.

"Are you sure you want to know?"

Isabella grimaced. "Another woman, I suppose."

"Dermott doesn't like to be alone."

"A convenient excuse. Who is it this time?" Even as she asked, she didn't know if she really wished to hear.

"Helene Kristos. An actress at Covent Garden."

"He's been with her all this time?" How it hurt to think of him with someone else.

"So I've been told. That will be all, Hannah," she added as the maid handed Isabella her green pigskin gloves. Molly waited until the maid left the room and then said, "They're friends of sorts. Dermott helped Helene when her husband died two years ago. Her child was only a month old, and to all accounts she nearly went mad from grief."

"How did Dermott know her?"

"How does any young rake know the actresses at the Garden?"

"Is their relationship platonic, then?"

Molly hesitated.

"Never mind. How naive of me to even ask."

"It was at first, but . . ."

"Of course. How could she resist? How could he resist when he never does."

"Dermott was faithful to his wife. That I know. But before and after his marriage, well . . ." She shrugged. "He's always been pursued; it would be rare for a man to refuse everyone."

"And there's so many."

"I'm sorry," Molly quietly said. "I know how painful this is, but the truth often is . . . and—what purpose would be served to deceive oneself?"

"I understand." Isabella adjusted the gloves on her fingers.

"I wish I could sugarcoat the facts. He seemed to look on you very differently, and I confess I was hoping . . ."

Isabella smiled ruefully. "So you have impractical dreams too. It's reassuring. I thought, perhaps, only I wished for the moon."

There was a rap on the bedroom door.

"I think my chariot awaits," Isabella said with a forced élan.

"Don't go if you don't wish to. I'll have Homie give your excuses."

"Nonsense," Isabella briskly said. "I feel the need for some fresh air. It might help to blow away the gossamer dreams from my brain."

"Take care with Lonsdale. He has a private side to him that isn't very savory."

"Are you warning me off? He's accepted at all the best functions."

"He's a marquis after all. And regardless the state of his finances and his bachelor vices, he has a title and looks. But he does need to marry for money."

"As do a great number of my admirers. I'm not so innocent that I think my allure is strictly the shape of my ankle or the color of my eyes."

Molly smiled. "You have a good head on your shoulders."

"I well understand the point of the season. The men are looking for wealth to marry as much as the women are. And if a title goes with the bargain, so much the better. But I have no intention of marrying anyone. In the foreseeable future—perhaps never. I dislike the notion of being married for my money."

"In that case, Lonsdale will be disappointed."

Isabella grinned. "Better him than me." And with a wave she left the room and descended the staircase to see Lonsdale's smart phaeton and team.

He was waiting in the drawing room, standing at the window, facing the street. He turned when she entered the room. "You look very fine today—as usual, I should add." The marquis's smile was charming as he walked toward her.

"Thank you. It looks as though the weather is cooperating for our drive."

"I ordered the sun to shine particularly for you." He offered his arm to her.

"How pleasant." Isabella placed her hand on his arm and smiled up at him. "A man of authority."

"Do you like men of authority?" His drawl matched his quirked grin as they moved toward the door to the entrance hall.

"Only when they're ordering the weather for me."

"Not in other things?" His gaze was amused.

He was very handsome, Isabella thought, in an ordinary way, very fair, like a young Apollo, with a well-formed athletic body and superb blue eyes. "Never in other things," she softly affirmed. "I fear I'm sadly self-indulgent."

The doors opened as if by unseen hands, and they moved into the entrance hall.

"Aren't we all," he agreed. "And to that purpose, I thought you might like to see a bit of the country today."

"That sounds very refreshing. Although my aunt expects me back in good time to dress for my evening engagement."

"I'll see that you don't miss your evening's pleasures," he quietly said.

The marquis helped her up onto the high-perched seat of his phaeton and then jumped up beside her. After releasing his grip on the horses, the groom leaped into place on the back of the vehicle and with a crack of the whip, they were off.

The weather was indeed fine, sunny and warm, with a

light breeze that caressed their faces as they bowled through the streets of the City.

"I'll drive out and you can drive back," the marquis offered, weaving through traffic like a top hand.

"After the hectic pace of the past week, I'm content to simply sit and enjoy the scenery." Isabella clung to the seat, swaying with the speed of the carriage and the rhythm of the horses. Lonsdale's team were coal black and gleaming, brushed to a glossy shine, the matched pair prime and fleet of foot. Before long, they were well along Kings Road on their way south. The City gave way to pasture and field and an occasional cluster of buildings. Until they reached the village of Chelsea, no longer so much on the outskirts as it once had been. With the City spreading in every direction, what had been a country village not so long ago was now a retreat for those needing rustication or a bit of bucolic repose.

The marquis drove up to an inn, brought his horses to a stop, and tossed his reins to his groom. "I thought we'd take some refreshment here—a lemonade or tea if you wish. The parlor is quite clean, I'm told, and the proprietress makes a caramel shortbread that's worth the drive from the City."

"I was tempted by the lemonade, but caramel shortbread too. How can I refuse?"

In moments she'd been helped down from the phaeton and was being escorted inside the Grey Goose. But rather than entering the front parlor, where several patrons sat, the marquis continued through the center hallway to the back of the inn, where he turned to insert a key into a door.

"What is this?" Isabella looked around at the well-kept

garden out back, at the quiet hallway through which they'd walked, the sound of customers in the public rooms only faintly heard.

"I bespoke a private parlor." Turning the key, he opened the door, and before he could turn back to her, Isabella caught a glimpse of not a private parlor, but an apartment. A well-decorated room quite out of place in the rustic inn. With two top hats on an elegant console table.

That shouldn't be there.

She glanced back to the inn entrance but saw no one. And when she swiveled around again, Lonsdale was reaching for her.

Isabella screamed, and he lunged at her, but she'd already pivoted and begun to run. As she raced down the hall, Molly's warning rang through her brain: *He has a private side . . . a private side . . .*

She could hear his footsteps pounding behind her, and grateful for her low-heeled slippers, and propelled by terror, she flew down the corridor, her scream rising to the low-hung ceiling and ricocheting back, the fearful sound filling the narrow corridor.

If he thought to capture her, she wasn't going to make it easy, she decided, raising her voice in a shrieking crescendo.

Isabella had no illusions about men like Lonsdale, who needed money to survive. She just hadn't thought he'd be so precipitous or blunt in his offensive. Naive her. And then she heard her uncle's voice shouting behind her, and a chill stabbed through her heart.

"Catch the strumpet! She stole my purse! The trollop stole my purse!"

The outside door was only feet away, and if ever she needed incentive to save herself, her uncle's voice served that purpose. Lifting up her skirts, she sprinted through the door, veered to the right, and flew down the street, crying for help.

This wasn't the time for politesse or manners. She quickly scanned the shocked faces of the people past whom she raced, debating whether any would help her, trying to gauge those most likely to lend her aid.

But her pursuers were calling her thief in loud accents as they chased her down the street, and she wasn't sure she'd have time to explain her situation to any passerby before Lonsdale and her uncle carted her off.

And with her uncle involved, she understood the nature of her fate.

Spying a village church in the distance, she sheered to the left and leaped out onto the street, wanting to make herself as visible as possible in the center of the road, hoping to gain the sanctuary of the church. Not that any ethical considerations would deter either Lonsdale or her uncle, but with luck the minister might be inside.

Surely a man of God would take time to listen to her.

She was midway to her destination, her throat parched from screaming, her breath coming in great gasps, her lungs burning, when a yellow phaeton came racing down the road.

She frantically waved her arms, but the vehicle didn't slow and, terror-stricken, she watched it hurtle toward her. Thinking her life was surely over, she jumped to one side just as the galloping horses were pulled up in a rearing, plunging stop. A cloud of dust rose up around her, the squeal of horses, male curses, a woman's voice, a child's, resounding through the haze.

And as she stood quaking from her near-death experience, a tall, shadowy outline of a man loomed through the dusky murk, the figure emerging with full clarity a second later.

"What the hell do you think you're—" Dermott's words died away.

"It's my uncle," Isabella blurted out, relief pouring over her. "They're right behind me."

"Get in the carriage," Dermott ordered, and raced away.

The dust had begun to settle enough for Isabella to distinguish the outlines of the phaeton. When she reached the side of the vehicle, she found a woman and young boy gazing down at her.

"I'm so pleased you're not hurt," the woman said with feeling.

"Dermott . . . that is—he said I should . . . join you." Embarrassed at the situation, nonetheless, Isabella needed Dermott's protection.

"Of course. Tommy, come sit on my lap." The woman helped her son onto her lap as she moved over. And once Isabella was seated, she introduced herself. "I'm Helene Kristos, and this is my son, Tommy. Say hello to the lady, dear."

"We almost wun wight over you!" the young boy exclaimed, his dark eyes bright with excitement.

"I know. Thank heaven the horses stopped in time."

The dark-haired young boy who bore a disturbing likeness to Dermott grinned. "Dermott holler loud."

"I shouldn't have been in the middle of the road,

but—" Isabella didn't care to elaborate on the complicated story. "By the way, I'm Isabella Leslie," she added, smiling at the mother and child, thinking how beautiful Dermott's lover was, small, exquisite with enormous dark eyes, Gypsy eyes. A rush of sadness overwhelmed her.

"You're Dermott's friend," Helene noted, smiling back. "He's talked of you."

"He has?" Even while she understood how unrealistic her expectations, her heart leaped with hope.

"Incessantly. Tell her, Tommy. Who has Dermott been talking about?"

"Hith horthes."

"And what lady?"

"Bad wady."

Helene laughed. "No, no, not her. The one who has hair of gold and a smile like—"

"A pwinthess?"

"That's the one."

"Is-bella." He stumbled over the pronunciation.

"Really?" Suddenly Lonsdale and her uncle, her recent terror, pragmatic considerations, dropped away before the joyful onslaught.

"They're gone. Lonsdale's phaeton's gone." Dermott's voice was gruff as he strode toward the carriage. "Not a sign of the bastards anywhere." Swinging up into the driver's seat, he glared at Isabella. "What the hell did you think you were doing, coming this far with *bloody* Lonsdale."

"Dermott," Helene chided.

"Forgive me, Helene," he said with a strained courtesy. "But this isn't any of your business. Answer me, dammit." He gazed at Isabella with fury in his eyes.

"I thought we were going for a ride in the country. I thought we were stopping for a lemonade. And while I thank you profusely for saving me, I don't think that gives you any right to become a tyrant."

"Lonsdale's a blackguard."

"He's accepted everywhere in society."

"I'm not arguing about this. You shouldn't have gone out with him."

"I appreciate your advice," Isabella tersely replied.

"Damn right you'd better."

Even little Tommy recognized the anger in Dermott's tone, and he stared at him wide-eyed; he'd never heard Dermott speak in such a voice.

"I'll drive you back to the City." It wasn't a statement; it was an order, curt and chill, uncompromising.

"Thank you very much," Isabella tautly said. She had no choice, and they both knew it.

The drive to Helene's cottage passed in silence, even Tommy's normal loquaciousness curtailed by the look on Dermott's face. After he helped Helene and Tommy down and spoke briefly to them, Dermott returned to the carriage and without comment snapped the reins. The horses jumped off.

Grim-faced on their journey back to London, he didn't speak.

After several tense miles, Isabella finally said, "I do thank you, Dermott. Very much. You must know how grateful I am."

"When I think of what Lonsdale might have done," he murmured, his jaw clenching in anger, the tick evident as she gazed up at him.

"Helene is very lovely. And Tommy is darling." They both had their jealousies.

"Don't change the subject."

"You're old friends, I understand."

He turned to her, a modicum of shock in his gaze. "What the hell is that supposed to mean?"

"It means I understand how you feel about Lonsdale."

"How can you possibly know how I feel about Lonsdale?"

"Because you've been berating me since you first saw me."

"You did a stupid thing."

"I don't see how it concerns you."

"You don't?"

"No. Tell me."

He chewed on his lip for a moment and then turned his attention to the road.

She wanted him to say he cared; she wanted him to admit to jealousy. She wanted what she couldn't have, she quickly realized, for when he looked back at her, his gaze was shuttered. "I wouldn't suggest you take long drives with anyone. Lonsdale is one of the less scrupulous, but any of your admirers might be interested in compromising you. For your money. Just a word of advice."

"Thank you. I'll keep it in mind. Now tell me about Helene."

"There's nothing to tell. When her husband died, she needed help and I helped her. I like Tommy, so I spend some time with them occasionally."

"You're not lovers?"

"I don't see that it's any of your business."

"You *are* lovers."

"Does it matter?"

"Not on any practical level."

"Good."

He was silent for the rest of the journey, and she didn't have the heart to talk. Not after such a deliberate indication of his feelings on independence. It was clear he wasn't interested in a relationship other than on his terms. Which meant a casual sexual liaison without strings or attachment.

And she'd die of sadness, sharing him with a host of other women.

He escorted her into the house and spoke to Molly as though she weren't present, as though she were a young child who needed a strong hand and stronger discipline. And when he left, he barely took leave of Isabella. He only nodded.

"I'm so sorry you had to be terrorized by Lonsdale," Molly commiserated, helping Isabella off with her jacket. "I blame myself for letting you go."

"No one's to blame but Lonsdale and my relatives. Damn them all." Isabella paced to the windows of the small back parlor where Molly had been eating an early supper. "They won't give up."

"Could you have them arrested?"

"Not likely." Isabella gazed out on the pristine green of the small lawn. "It's my word against theirs, and I'm considerably outnumbered."

"Then, I'm going to insist you have a bodyguard. If you had taken one with you today, none of this would have happened."

Isabella turned back to her friend. "I didn't think I'd ever say this, but you're right. Regardless of the lack of privacy, I don't dare be out alone."

"I know the perfect man. Joe Thurlow has given up the fight game. His best friend was killed in a match last year, and he lost all interest in the sport. He works for me from time to time. I know he's available."

Isabella came to sit down at the table with Molly. "Another thing." A small frown creased her brow. "Would you mind terribly," she slowly said, conscious she might be causing hurt, "that is—would it matter to you if I decided to retreat from society?"

Molly scrutinized her. "Because of Lonsdale?"

"No." Isabella traced a pattern on the tablecloth with her finger. "Because I don't wish to see Dermott." She looked up. "It's cowardly, I know, but seeing him today with that pretty actress and her child was awful." She slowly inhaled, as though a calming breath would help ease the pain. "And he told me in no uncertain terms on the ride back to the City that he had no wish to change the pattern of his life."

"I'm sorry," Molly murmured. "I don't know how to offer you comfort. If it's any excuse, the death of his wife and son was so deep a blow, I'm not sure he'll ever recover from it. He feels a terrible guilt for taking them along on campaign. I never told you the whole story, but his family was massacred when their camp was overrun by enemies while he and a troop were out on a scouting mission. He found his wife and son on his return; they were dreadfully mutilated."

Isabella's face had gone pale. "How awful," she whispered.

"He shouldn't have given in to his wife's pleas to accompany him, he shouldn't have left them, he says. He blames himself entirely. He couldn't bear to stay in India; the reminders were too stark, so he came home to England. But he couldn't escape his memories, and his dissipation serves to drug his senses, obliterate his nightmares." She softly sighed. "I though you were different. He treated you with a normalcy that gave me hope. He kept you beyond his usual boredom limits, took you to Richmond." She shrugged. "I thought he might have forgotten."

"I think he did for a time."

"He loved his wife and son deeply."

"So it seems," Isabella quietly murmured. "I'm going to leave the City." Her voice was suddenly brisk. "I should be safe enough on my country estate with a bodyguard. I need to retreat from my memories too."

"I hate to see you go, but I understand. Although, it might be wise to have Joe bring along his brother. They could spell each other in the course of the day."

"The way I feel right now, so recently saved from my uncle's clutches, you may hire a troop of bodyguards for me if you wish. Tomorrow, I intend to go to the bank and see to my affairs, and perhaps the next day check the warehouses and docks. After that, I'll retreat to Tavora House and begin forgetting Dermott."

"How strange life is," Molly observed. "Under normal

circumstances, we would have never met. Under normal circumstances, you and Dermott would have never crossed paths. And now we're caught up in a tangled net of impossible hopes and evil deeds while the ton whirls around us, inured to all but their frantic search for pleasure."

"I for one am about to extricate myself from the net, from the ton, from any frantic search for anything. I have a life to return to, a business to run, simple pleasures that once offered me happiness."

"I'll send Lord Moira a note of explanation. Just in case you should ever wish to resume the social whirl." Molly smiled. "He's an old friend; he'll understand."

"How optimistic you are." Isabella found it possible to smile back, and pleased with her lightening mood as she contemplated a return to her familiar environs, she added, "Who knows, maybe Dermott will give up his profligate life, be transformed into a white knight, ride up to my country house, and carry me away."

Molly laughed. "Send me a message directly that occurs. I very much want to believe in miracles."

"In the meantime," Isabella noted, "I shall busy myself with more mundane activities. Like seeing to my money."

"See to anything you wish now that you have protection from your relatives. I'll summon Joe and you may discuss your needs with him."

Dermott had his own activities to see to. After leaving Molly's, he proceeded to find his friend Lord Devon, who agreed to be his second. Protocol required the challenge for a duel be given by the seconds, so the two men went together to search out Lonsdale. They began with his home, although Dermott hardly expected to find him there. The marquis was more likely to be found at his gambling clubs or vice-ridden haunts. Since Dermott knew them all, they drove from one to the other, making inquiries, asking questions, bribing retainers where necessary, scouring the City to find the man and exact revenge.

They finally tracked him down at a Covent Garden coffee house that also served as a tavern and brothel. Lonsdale was in the back room, gambling with a table of rogues and rakes, all the men well into their cups.

"Can you stand, Lonsdale?" Dermott growled, filling the doorway like an avenging angel.

The marquis's gaze languidly came up, raking Dermott with a drunken glance. "Don't know, Bathurst." He shrugged. "Probably not, come to think of it."

"Make sure you can by tomorrow morning."

"Will you accept a challenge from Lord Bathurst?" Devon asked, playing his part.

"This is about the Leslie piece?" Lonsdale drawled, his heavy-lidded gaze insolent.

"Mention her name again, and I'll kill you where you sit."

"Not armed, Bathurst. Shame."

"Maybe I don't give a damn."

"Bad form, Bathurst." The marquis winked at him. "Think of your fine reputation for honor on the dueling field."

"Fuck you, Lonsdale."

"You must want her more than I do." The marquis

surveyed his companions with a smirk. "Wouldn't think a cunt was worth dying for."

Dermott gritted his teeth, tempted to shoot him where he sat but not capable of such cold-blooded murder. "I'll see that you're at Morgan's field at six tomorrow morning," he grimly said, "and you'll find out if it is or not." His glance swept the group at the table. "One of you should be sober enough to remember. Remind him. Six tomorrow, and if he doesn't appear, I'll come and kill him wherever he is."

"She must be damned good in bed," Lonsdale murmured.

"I'll shut your vulgar mouth tomorrow," Dermott growled, and turning abruptly, he walked away, Devon beside him.

"It must be love," one of the men mocked, "for Bathurst to fight over a woman."

"I'd say she's a hot piece he doesn't want to share."

"She's a hot, *rich* piece," Lonsdale murmured. "Incentive to kill the bastard tomorrow. I could use her money *and* cunt."

17

❧

WORD OF THE DUEL spread though the ton like wildfire. Molly heard of it through Mercer, and she debated whether to keep silent or tell Isabella. But the decision was taken out of her hands when Lady Hertford sent Isabella a note, understanding how she felt about Dermott, warning her of the event. Lonsdale was not to be trifled with, she noted, suggesting Isabella might wish to talk Dermott out of risking his life.

"He can't do this," Isabella protested, showing the note to Molly. "I have to stop him."

"It's not likely you can. Once he's challenged Lonsdale, he can't back down. Nor would he wish to, I suspect."

"If this is about me, I forbid it. Does he think I want him to risk his life over someone as base as Lonsdale?"

"Men have grievances and a sense of honor that takes precedence over reason. This isn't the first time Dermott has faced someone across the dueling field."

"Good God, does he have a death wish?"

"A temper, without doubt, and perhaps a death wish as well."

"I'm going to see him."

Molly glanced at the clock. "I'll doubt you'll find him at home."

"Then I'll find him somewhere else."

Molly sighed. "You might not wish to see where he is."

"You know."

"No. But at nine at night, he's not in church, you can be sure."

Isabella took a deep breath, steeling herself against the possible embarrassment and pain. "I don't care. I wish to talk to him."

"Very well. I'll have Joe find him and come back for you."

Shortly after eleven, a large, burly man entered Molly's drawing room, and Isabella met Joe Thurlow. He was massive, his shoulders as broad as an ox, his neck a pure column of muscle, his arms and thighs bulging. His hazel eyes remarkably kind, his smile boyish and charming.

Once introductions were complete, he said, "I found Bathurst at the Green Abbey."

"Is it far?" Isabella had been watching the clock, and she was concerned it might soon be too late to stop Dermott. The site of the duel was secret, as was usual, so the authorities wouldn't interfere. While duels often occurred, they were illegal.

"About a half hour from here."

Isabella turned to Molly. "Thank you again. I'm continually in your debt."

"Just be careful. Don't let her out of your sight, Joe," she ordered.

He nodded. "Not a chance, Molly."

Near midnight, shrouded in a black hooded cape, Isabella was escorted from her carriage up a short bank of stairs into a house bordering Green Park. The small entrance hall was deserted, although it was well lit with a crystal chandelier in the Venetian style. Joe indicated she follow him up the carpeted staircase to the main floor, where he turned to the left and preceded her down a long corridor illuminated with wall sconces. Opening a door at the end of the hallway, he ushered her into a room that looked as though it served as an office. "Wait here," he said, and left, shutting the door behind him.

Isabella quickly surveyed the small room illuminated only by a low fire. An elegant desk, a richness of Turkey carpets on the floor, a number of Chippendale chairs, two bookcases. It was obviously a workplace, but an opulent one. Her assessment of the office didn't long curtail the overwhelming anxiety plaguing her, and she soon began pacing, moving between the desk and the fireplace in short circuits, unconsciously wringing her gloved hands. She was nervous about interrupting Dermott in his night's amusements. This house was more than a gambling club, she suspected. He would think her interfering. She dreaded the thought of his coldness. But if she didn't at least try to stop this fearful duel, she'd forever regret her cowardice.

The door opened and she turned from the fire with a start, her cape billowing out at her sudden movement. Her heart was pounding in her chest.

Dermott stood in the doorway, framed by the light from the hallway, his ruffled hair limned by candleglow, his face in half shadow, his white neckcloth a pale accent in the darkness of his evening clothes. "You shouldn't be here," he gruffly said, annoyance in his tone and rigid posture, in the small impatient gesture he made with his hand.

"I need to talk to you." She tried to hide her apprehension, but her voice trembled at the end.

"I don't want to talk to you."

"Please?" It was the merest whisper, unutterably pitiful.

He shot a glance at Joe standing behind him. "Is your bodyguard for me or you?"

"For me. After the events today, Molly insisted."

"Good for her." Dermott seemed to relax.

"If you'd just give me a moment of your time," Isabella quickly said, taking advantage of what she perceived as a small forbearance. "I won't keep you from—"

"My amusements?" The faintest smile flashed for a second, and then, taking a step forward, he crossed the threshold, pushed the door shut, and leaned back against it. "I'm glad you have a bodyguard."

"I am too." She felt some of her tension ease. He hadn't walked away.

"You could have been seriously hurt this afternoon."

"I know. The events in Chelsea made me realize some kind of protection was necessary. Molly's insistence only reinforced my feelings. And I've decided to forgo the season as well," she added, "so that should diminish my public visibility. Although I certainly appreciate everything that Molly"—her voice suddenly sounded loud in the quiet of the room—"did for me," she finished, unnerved by his detachment.

A small silence fell.

Dermott hadn't moved from the door.

"I don't know how to begin," Isabella finally said.

He didn't answer.

"You're not helping."

"I didn't want to talk to you, if you recall."

"You're making this very difficult."

He shrugged.

"I heard about your duel," she blurted out.

That painful silence.

"I came to try to dissuade you from such foolishness."

"Thank you for coming. I'll bid you good night." Pushing away from the door, he bowed faintly and turned to leave.

"Dermott, wait!" Isabella cried, running toward him.

He stood with his back to her, the tension in his shoulders visible even in the dim light, his hand arrested on the door handle.

"Don't go."

She stood only inches from him; he could smell her perfume, she could feel the warmth from his body, potent memory brutalizing their senses.

"I can't bear the thought of you dying. . . ." She reached out and touched his arm.

For a breath-held moment with the feel of her hand

bombarding his brain, he tried to review all the reasons for leaving, all the pragmatic, sane, rational ones.

"Please, Dermott, hold me. . . ."

Her soft voice drifted around him, caressed him. He fought against his desires, knowing he'd only hurt her again, knowing he couldn't give her what she wanted, and then he felt her arms slide around his waist. For a second more he controlled his impulses, and then his hand slipped away from the door handle.

Gently unclasping her arms, he turned to face her.

"I'm so sorry," she whispered. "I shouldn't beg. You must be so tired of women doing that to—"

"I can't just hold you," he interrupted. "You know that, don't you?"

"I don't care."

He briefly shut his eyes against the intensity of his feelings, and when his lashes lifted, he said, "I won't be able to stay long."

"I don't care about that either."

"You might later." He drew in a shallow breath because he seemed to be suffocating. "I'm trying to be— honest. . . ."

"I understand."

"And this won't change my mind about the duel, if that's what you're thinking."

"Fine," she conceded.

"Bloody hell . . ." His voice was gruff, heated, an undertone of resentment in the expletive. And then he suddenly gripped her shoulders, his fingers biting into her flesh. "We shouldn't be doing this. We shouldn't even be talking about—"

"I'll take responsibility."

"For everything?" His dark gaze was turbulent, fierce. "I don't have protection here. This isn't a room for assignations." He was baiting her, capable of controlling his ejaculations, but restive, angry, he wished to give her no quarter.

"It doesn't matter."

"Don't say that." His voice was hot with temper, with carnal lust and craving.

"I mean it."

"You'd risk having my child?"

"I wouldn't consider it a risk."

"Jesus, Izzy . . ." Releasing his grip, he stepped back, only to come up against the barricade of the door.

She followed him that small distance, slid her gloved palms up over the lapels of his jacket while he stood rigid, motionless. Raising herself on tiptoe, she slipped her hands around his neck. "What are we going to do about this?"

It wasn't a question a man like Dermott could ignore, his sexual response honed to a fine pitch over the years, his erection hard between them. "I thought maybe I'd send you home," he brusquely muttered, restless, touchy, struggling against his base impulses.

"Send me home in an hour," she murmured, melting against him, her urges as ravenous, as outrageous. Terror-driven as well. She might never see him again. He might be dead tomorrow. And suddenly nothing mattered but feeling him one last time. "You can spare me an hour, can't you?" Her voice was liquid heat as she slid her fingers through his dark hair and tugged his head down.

Her kiss was sweet and warm, all promise and glowing welcome.

He might never again feel the sweetness of her mouth on his, he thought, understanding the odds against him. And the warmth of her body, the soft pressure of her breasts, her hips, her thighs, burned through the fabric of his evening clothes, reminding him of all the pleasures they'd shared. Of the ecstasy he felt in her arms.

"Make love to me, please . . . please," she whispered, her breath warm on his mouth.

"We shouldn't." Only sheer will kept his hands at his sides.

"But I want to feel you inside me. . . ."

Suddenly his hands came up, and gripping her face, he engulfed the delicacy of her mouth with a hard, possessive kiss that burned away his few remaining scruples. Fueled by the pent-up frustration of their separation and his rare abstinence, he no longer thought of right or wrong, impropriety or principle, but invaded her mouth as he intended to invade her body—fiercely, urgently.

Isabella had been celibate except for Bond Street, and she answered his fevered impatience with her own blazing passion, forgetting why she'd come, why they'd last parted, all the sadness and pain of his leaving. She welcomed him with a thrilling, reckless happiness, wanting his strength and virility, wanting the unadulterated bliss of making love with him, wishing she might keep him forever.

There was no tomorrow, no yesterdays, only the haphazard present, and heedless of all but hot desire and the stark brevity of their time together, Isabella slipped her hands downward to the buttons of his trousers.

"I'll do that," he muttered, quickly sliding his hands under her legs and lifting her into his arms. Striding to the desk, he swept aside the objects in his way; papers, books, pens, ledgers, flew to the floor, their impact deadened by the carpet. Although in his current frame of mind he would have been indifferent to the sound of breaking glass.

No one dared bother them anyway, not at Green Abbey. And Joe wouldn't interfere unless he thought Isabella in danger. And while she might be in a measure of danger, he thought, carefully placing her on the gleaming mahogany, she wasn't likely to want Joe's help.

Following her down, driven by lust, he kissed her with an unrestrained ferocity—briefly. "I always forget how fucking hot you are," he whispered against her mouth, swiftly untying her cloak, needing more than kisses.

"While you're still as good as ever."

"You don't know that yet." His grin was wicked as he stood up and began unbuttoning his trousers.

"I expect I will soon enough," she purred, pulling off her gloves and hitching up her skirts.

"You're never bashful."

"You taught me well."

Her words sent a rush of blood to his erection, all the heated memories of their time together flooding his senses. That was enough unbuttoning, he decided, suddenly interested in speed, and moving forward, he pushed her skirts up to her waist and spread her thighs wider with a firm brush of his hands. "Let's see how much you remember."

"More than enough." A coquettish response, so sensual and insinuating it added new dimension to his erection.

Had she'd lain with other men since they'd parted? he wondered, suddenly remembering bits of gossip from his friends, how the luscious Miss Leslie seemed bent on flirtation this weekend. Damn her, she looked like a wanton lying there with her pale thighs spread. "Have you been practicing with other men?" he gruffly asked.

"Are we comparing our schedules since Bond Street?"

He scowled. "I'm not in a humorous mood."

"I noticed."

"Answer me." How available had she been, how willing?

"If you supply me with the same information."

He retreated a step. "Maybe I won't fuck you after all."

"I think you probably will," she softly said, lifting her feet up on the desk so his view was markedly improved.

"Trollop," he murmured, his tone not so much rebuff as a caress.

"In fact, if I were a gambling woman," she said with a half-smile, "I'd bet on having sex with you. So why don't you tell me what I want to know and then I'll tell you."

"It doesn't matter for men."

"It does to me." Her brows rose, and she began opening the closures on her bodice.

"Hussy." That same velvety tone.

"Tell me," she whispered, wanting to know for a thousand jealous reasons that defied sanity. "And then put that wonderful cock inside me."

All considerations save fornication were wiped from his mind at her breathy statement. Suddenly he was past games and titillation, past conversation and courtesies. Advancing closer, he slid his hands under her hips, hauled her bottom to the edge of the desk, and moved between her legs.

She twisted away. "Tell me first."

He forced her back, his hands hard on her hips. Drawing in a frustrated breath, he met her heated gaze. "None. Your turn."

She smiled, blissfully content because now she knew his time with Helene had been platonic. "None," she cheerfully declared.

The word echoed in his ears like angel song, when it shouldn't matter, when he'd always thought women deserved their freedoms. But for some reason, he didn't want her to be free—in that sense, and as he leaned closer and adjusted himself between her thighs, he softly murmured, "Then this is just for me. . . ."

"Yours alone, my lord," she whispered, wrapping her legs around his waist. "I'll expect a suitable reward for my celibacy."

He chuckled, oddly pleased, his moodiness gone. "Instead of a dozen times, why not a score?"

"That must be why I prefer you best."

"And I you," he whispered.

They both lost count in the heated bliss of consummation, although Dermott never so forgot himself as to climax inside Isabella. It was pure torture to curtail his impulses, and at those times when she was begging him to come in her, it was very nearly impossible.

But were he killed in the morning, he didn't want to leave her with a fatherless child.

While she desperately wanted his child for that reason and a thousand more.

In that contest of wills, however, the earl prevailed.

And when the stars began to fade, he gently kissed her as they lay by the fire.

"You have to go," she whispered.

He nodded. "I have to."

"You won't change your mind?"

"This isn't something you renege on."

"I hate you for doing this," she sadly said.

He gently touched her cheek. "I'm sorry."

"I'm not worth your life."

He placed his finger on her mouth. "Hush."

"Come back to me."

He was so quiet, she frantically wished she could snatch back her words.

"I can't give you what you deserve." His distress was plain.

"I didn't mean . . ." Her eyes filled with tears because she did mean it, and she might lose him to Lonsdale's marksmanship and if not, she'd lose him anyway. Sadness filled her so completely, she felt as though she were choking on her tears.

"I wish I could." He brushed a kiss on her temple, but she could feel the constraint in his body.

"Be careful this morning," she murmured, kissing him lightly on the cheek, moving from his embrace and sitting up, separating herself before she burst into tears.

A man like Dermott must have suffered countless

weeping women in his life; she didn't wish to become another commonplace statistic. "Let me know that you're safe—once it's over," she said, forcing a calmness to her tone, reaching for her chemise. "Send Molly a note." She wished to be adult about this, not clinging or demanding, not asking for more than he could give. She'd understood from the very beginning that there would be an end to their relationship. Tonight had been a brief reprieve—no more.

He'd made that clear.

"I'll see that Molly knows," he said, rising to his feet, the perfection of his tall form gilded by firelight.

Would she ever see him again? Would she ever feel his kiss or taste his smile? His hair was tousled from their lovemaking, and she ached to smooth it with her fingers.

He smiled. "Thank you for coming here tonight." As though she'd favored him. "You've brought me luck."

"I give you all my luck. I wish I could give you the world's good fortune." Give you the sun and moon and everything, she wistfully thought. "I probably shouldn't have kept you up all night," she said, instead, in a conversational tone that made no demands.

"I wasn't planning on sleeping."

Of course, he wouldn't. And if she'd not come to Green Abbey, some other woman would have taken her place. Her expression must have mirrored her sudden thoughts, because he said, "I was drinking with friends. That's all."

A concession, a kindness, maybe even the truth, she hoped, so in love, she wasn't capable of feeling anything but the pain of his leaving.

He'd begun dressing as well, gauging the time against

the distance he still had to travel to reach Morgan's field. "I'll be sure to send Molly a note."

"Thank you." She forced herself to think of Molly, of the coming afternoon, when this would all be over. When Dermott would be safe and the trivialities of the world could go on once again.

"Do you need help with your gown?"

It was a politesse. He'd always before just helped her. "No, I'm fine," she said, when her heart was breaking.

They dressed in an awkward silence when only moments earlier they were bound by an intimacy so intense, the beauty of it still lingered in their senses.

But Dermott had gone through leave-takings often enough; he didn't expect the feeling—however unprecedented—to last. And he carried the weight of the conversation until they were dressed.

"You're very wrinkled." Isabella smiled faintly, his rumpled look so out of character. "Your valet would be mortified."

"Lonsdale won't mind."

All her fears returned in a rush. "Promise you'll not be reckless."

"Caution is my byword," he teased.

"Don't tease," she protested, "when you're risking your life, when Lonsdale doesn't deserve a chance to hurt you."

"I don't plan on giving him one." Dermott held out his hand. "I'll take every precaution," he promised. "Now, I've some way to go myself. Let me escort you to your carriage."

Joe was waiting in the corridor outside, his face impassive as they emerged from the room. And he kept a polite distance as he followed them downstairs to the carriage.

"Take care now," Dermott softly said as they stood on the flags outside in the mist of predawn, the carriage door held open by a groom.

"I insist even more that you do."

"I will." Leaning forward, he lightly kissed her mouth and then, straightening, stepped away. "Good-bye." His voice was low.

"Godspeed," she whispered, and then turned and entered the carriage before her tears spilled over.

18

DERMOTT STOPPED by Bathurst House to collect Shelby, his valet, Charles, and his dueling pistols. There wasn't time to change. He'd stayed with Isabella much longer than he should have. After a few brief orders for Pomeroy, he discussed his time constraints with his driver and then rested on the steps of Bathurst House until Charles and Shelby appeared. Quickly rising, he exchanged greetings with his servants before they entered the carriage.

"The doctor will meet us at Morgan's field," Shelby noted as the closed carriage raced through the predawn streets of London.[8] "Lord Devon left ahead of us. He stopped by Bathurst House, but since you weren't there at the appointed time, he thought you may have already gone to Morgan's field. Of course, I knew better. I knew you'd see to your pistols yourself, but one doesn't argue with Lord Devon."

Dermott smiled. George Harley was blustery, always sure of himself regardless whether he was right or not. But more important, he was an old friend and a crack shot.

"He won't be far ahead. I told Jem to make all speed and Devon doesn't like to press his grays. Charles, did you bring the brandy?"

"Yes, sir. And a clean shirt, if you wish."

Dermott laughed. "Do you think I need one?" His valet always saw to his linen with a particularly discerning eye.

"That would be for you to say, my lord, but you *will* have your coat off."

"Lonsdale will probably hie himself from some stew."

"While you, sir, will have on clean linen."

Dermott began shrugging out of his coat at such pointed comment. Although he said "I'll keep that" when Charles was about to take his discarded shirt from him. He shoved the wrinkled garment into a corner of his seat, not wishing to relinquish it when it smelled of Isabella's perfume. In short order he was dressed in a fresh shirt and well-tied neckcloth. Charles had also brought water so Dermott could wash his face and hands, although the earl hesitated briefly before washing his hands. The scent of Isabella still lingered on his fingers.

But in the end his regret didn't prevail over Charles's sense of good grooming. And once he was offered his cologne after washing, that fragrance soon pervaded the interior of the carriage.

When the earl alighted from the carriage at Morgan's field, he was as well turned out as his valet could manage under rough conditions. A faint fog swirled over the open field, the sun not yet risen to burn it away. And Dermott's boot struck spongy turf when he stepped to the ground.

The other carriages were waiting. Devon sat in the

open door of his town coach, talking to the doctor. A group of men stood together near one of the other carriages, Lonsdale's blond head visible in their midst.

Morgan's field was advantageously located near the City but not so near that unwanted spectators were likely to appear. The grassy field, surrounded by a heavy stand of sturdy English oaks, afforded the necessary seclusion. The trees also served to muffle the sound of gunshots, while Lamb's Inn was conveniently at hand just past the line of oaks, should any injured party require a bed or makeshift operating table.

Everyone's gaze turned to Dermott as he strolled toward Lord Devon, Shelby following with his case of dueling pistols, Charles last, carrying his brandy flask.

Dermott breathed deeply of the cool morning air, wanting to clear his head of the previous night, of memory and morbid musing, of any distraction that would interfere with his concentration.

Devon was in a cheerful mood as he greeted Dermott. With his friend celebrated for his skills on the dueling field, Lord Devon didn't expect any problems. The men shook hands; Dermott spoke briefly with the doctor and then turned to Charles for his brandy. He drank deeply out of habit before turning his attention to Lonsdale, who was already in his shirt-sleeves, loading his pistols.

It seemed to be time.

Neither he nor Lonsdale were novices. They'd both been here before.

The seconds met, agreed on the rules of engagement, and returned to their respective sides.

"Lonsdale's half drunk, Ram," Devon offered. "But still

dangerous, I imagine, or perhaps more dangerous. They wanted two shots at six paces; we agreed on two shots at twelve. Six paces is too damned close. And Lonsdale's not to be trusted."

Dermott handed his coat to Charles. "I already know that. I'm here today to put an end to his untrustworthy soul."

George Harley hadn't heard that icy tone before. "You're serious about this?"

"I'm always serious when I put my life at risk." Dermott began rolling up his shirt-sleeves.

"You're going to kill him?" First blood was often enough for satisfaction.

Dermott signaled for his pistols. "That's my intent, as I'm sure it's his."

"No doubt," Lord Devon said with a sigh, understanding there was more to this than a lady's reputation. "Well, bloody good luck, Ram, although you're not apt to need it. Do you want me to load your pistols?"

Dermott smiled. "No thanks. I prefer doing it myself."

His revolving-cylinder firearm design had been perfected by the best English gunsmiths over the last decades, and the two-shot pistols he and Lonsdale had were popular on the dueling field. After checking the loaded cylinders one last time, he handed one weapon to Devon, and taking the other, lifted his hand casually in adieu and walked to the middle of the field.

He and Lonsdale were supposed to exchange courtesies, but neither man was capable of such deceit, and with a nod to each other they took their positions back-to-back and waited for the signal to advance.

It was nearly light now, the mist had begun to fade, the color of the turf altering from gray to green as the sun crept over the horizon.

Twelve paces, Dermott silently rehearsed, lifting his hand slightly to test the weight of his pistol. He had a hair-trigger Manton weapon, and his finger rested on the trigger with great delicacy. Walk, turn, shoot. He ran the sequence through his mind. His nerves were sharp, clear, untroubled by anxiety. Emotion had no place on the dueling field.

The protagonists were given a verbal signal to advance, and both men moved forward. One of the surgeons counted the paces in a loud voice, Dermott silently echoing the words. Eight, nine, ten . . . He began lifting his pistol, ready to turn on twelve.

The first shot slammed into his back, the second shattered his ribs as he spun around, the impact of shot and powder at such close range dropping him to his knees. Through an agonizing roar of pain, Dermott caught a glimpse of Lonsdale's smiling face.

Astonishment and fury flared through his brain. Fucking coward shot early! A spasm of crushing pain jolted through his side, almost doubling him over, and he hung there, panting, trying to focus his senses and sight. He could hear a tumult of sound—shouts, commands, angry oaths drifting in and out of his consciousness. And suddenly through the racking anguish and distant noise, Devon's face appeared only inches away. He looked frightened. Dermott tried to reconcile that oddity in the confusion of pain and curious liquid warmth seeping through his shirt. And his knees were getting wet from the damp ground, he incongruously thought. Charles was sure to object to the stains.

"We have to get you away," Devon grunted, trying to lift Dermott.

Devon's hands on him brought him to full attention. "Not done yet," Dermott fiercely whispered, blinking to clear his vision. "Give me a hand." He gritted his teeth. "And then stand back." With Devon's help he struggled to his feet, calling on his last reserves of energy, blood gushing from his wounds. He wavered unsteadily for a moment and then with superhuman effort braced his legs wide.

Lonsdale's triumphant expression had turned to horror as Dermott came to his feet. His pistol was empty and Bathurst still had two unfired shots. He fell to his knees, faced with certain death, terror stricken, and raising his hands in entreaty, he pleaded, "Don't shoot me in cold blood. Bathurst . . . please—I beg of you—be merciful. My pistol misfired. I swear! It wasn't intentional—as God is my witness!"

It wasn't immediately apparent whether Dermott had heard, whether he was even capable of understanding anymore, until everyone watched him turn his head very slightly toward Devon. "Give him a pistol," he ordered, his voice audible only because of the horrified silence.

"Don't, Ram," Devon cried, appalled at the amount of blood pouring from Dermott's wounds, wanting to take him from the field. "He didn't give you a chance. Shoot him!"

"Hurry," Dermott whispered, hanging on to consciousness by sheer will, commanding himself to remain upright a few minutes more.

A hush had fallen over the field.

Devon ran to Lonsdale's second, ripped the pistol from his hand, raced back to the marquis, and handed it to him with an oath.

Instantly a predator again now that he was armed, Lonsdale leaped to his feet, whipped the pistol up, sighted in on his wounded opponent, and fired.

Two shots rang out.

And both men fell to the ground.

Dermott's party ran to him. Dropping to his knees, the doctor quickly checked for a pulse and then crisply gave orders. As Dermott was carried to his carriage, his eyes came open. "Lonsdale?" he croaked.

"A bullet through his heart. He deserved a slower death," Devon gruffly added.

"Send a note to Molly." Dermott's voice was a wisp of sound. "Tell her I'm fine."

Shelby had tears in his eyes as he penned the note at Lamb's Inn, where Dermott had been taken. The surgeon was operating now, the parlor having been put into service as an operating room. The doctor was trying to remove the ball and shot from Dermott's wounds before he bled to death. The pistol ball in his back had taken some of the shirting with it, and the bits of fabric were causing trouble. The metal shot in the ribs had proved impossible to locate. Not a hopeful sign when they were in a race against time.

Following orders, Shelby wrote the lie to Molly. The

earl had killed Lonsdale and he was unscathed. Shelby knew for whom the note was intended, and had he dared, he would have sent for Miss Leslie so she might see Bathurst before he died. But Shelby was loyal in all things to his master, and even if this turned out to be the earl's last request, he would honor it.

Once his task was completed and the note dispatched, Shelby returned to the parlor where Dermott lay.

He stood frozen in the doorway, shocked at the gruesome sight. The parlor had become a charnel house, blood puddling on the floor as it dripped from the dining table where Dermott lay on his stomach, motionless as a corpse. Panicked at the appalling sight, Shelby wondered how the earl could possibly survive such a loss of blood. His powerful body was mangled, torn apart, and so utterly still, the secretary debated whether he should send for another surgeon. Was there time? Or would Bathurst die before another doctor could arrive?

But Dermott had particularly chosen Dr. McTavert, Shelby reminded himself. If the earl had faith in him, so must he. Gingerly stepping around the bloody footprints leading from the door, he entered the room.

Somehow Dermott's strong heart continued to beat through the long ordeal, until at last the surgeon picked the final bits of linen and metal from the back wound with a soft prayer of gratitude. The shattered ribs posed greater problems over and above the damaged bones, for the ball hadn't been found and he didn't dare probe any deeper for fear of touching Dermott's heart. Wherever that piece of metal had disappeared, so must it remain. And pray God it didn't fester. Gunshot wounds were highly susceptible to infection.

"Is there anyone we should call?" he asked at the end when the wounds had been bandaged and Dermott had been moved into a bed.

"Only his mother, and she's indisposed," Shelby replied. "Will Lord Bathurst live?"

The surgeon didn't answer for so long, Shelby was sorry he'd asked.

"Under normal circumstances a man wouldn't. But the earl's still alive when I hadn't thought he'd survive this long." The doctor surveyed Dermott's small party, devoid of Devon, who had been sent to London to confer with Dermott's lawyers in the event of his death. "I'll stay with him as long as you wish," Dr. McTavert added. "But the earl shouldn't be moved."

"We'll all stay," Shelby declared. "Charles, see that the surgeon has a room and dinner. I'll remain with the earl. And thank you, sir, for your great skill." The earl had always called McTavert one of London's best, not the most fashionable, but the most competent, and today he'd lived up to his reputation.

The tall, sandy-haired Scotsman acknowledged the praise by saying, "I'd best wait a few days before accepting your thanks, Shelby. We've a way to go yet. I'll be back to check on Bathurst as soon as I clean up."

"Very good, sir. And if you need any messages sent to London, give Charles their direction."

And once the doctor left, Shelby began writing a carefully worded letter to the earl's mother.

* * *

Isabella had returned to Molly's from Green Abbey, and the two women had been sitting together in the blue saloon since then, nervously awaiting news.

"If he said he'd send a note, he will," Molly declared, as she had countless times already.

"How can he if he's dead?"

"Please, dear, you mustn't think the worst," Molly pacified, as she'd done since Isabella had returned. "Dermott is an excellent shot. He's been involved in duels before. No one can outshoot him."

It was a recurring conversation, for Isabella's anxieties continued despite Molly's attempts to console her. But as the morning progressed and they'd had no word, Molly, too, was becoming concerned. Although she took care to conceal her worry from Isabella, who was already white with fear.

"Maybe I should go to Bathurst House and inquire," Isabella suggested as the hour neared ten.

"Not this early. They may not be back in town yet. If we don't hear anything by early afternoon though, I'll send a servant."

"I couldn't stop him, Molly," Isabella murmured, a feverish desperation in her tone. "I wish I knew . . . why do men do such foolish things? My reputation isn't worth his *life*."

"Who knows why men do what they do? I've never understood their misplaced sense of honor," Molly said with a sigh. "Come, let's try to eat some breakfast. You haven't had a bite since yesterday."

Isabella grimaced. "I couldn't eat a thing."

"Have a cup of tea. I want company, so you must oblige me." Molly rarely spoke so severely to Isabella, nor was she hungry herself, but she needed to distract Isabella—however briefly—from her despair.

Shelby's note was delivered to them in the breakfast room, and after quickly perusing it, Molly handed it to Isabella with a broad smile. "All our fears were for naught. Dermott is fine, as always. Dear boy."

Snatching the page from Molly's hand, Isabella quickly scanned it as though needing confirmation for Molly's words. And then with a grand sigh, she settled back in her chair and felt as though life was worth living again. "Thank God," she softly said. "Thank, thank, thank God . . ."

The first rumors reached the City early but didn't arrive in Grosvenor Place until evening. It was then that Joe heard the news of Bathurst's wounds from his brother, who had heard them from Devon's valet. Aware of all that transpired in the household, Joe knew the contents of Dermott's note to Molly and the probable reason that the truth had been withheld.

After informing Molly of his brother's report, they debated telling Isabella. Obviously, the earl hadn't wanted her to know. So the question was—did they do a disservice by telling her?

"How badly is Dermott hurt?" Molly asked. "The degree of his wounds would make a difference."

"He's not expected to live." Joe's voice was hushed.

Molly, who had seen so much misery and thought herself immune, turned pale. "Poor dear," she whispered. But only seconds later, she pinned Joe with a challenging gaze. "There has to be an explanation. Dermott's never wounded; he's the best shot in England."

"Lonsdale fired early."

"Damned cur. I hope he died a slow, painful death." Her voice was pitiless.

"Apparently not, but you can be sure he's burning in hell."

"Exactly the fate he deserves for what he's done! Lonsdale should burn in hell a thousand times over!"

"Why should Lonsdale burn in hell?" Isabella had just entered the room. "Besides the obvious reasons, of course." But the look of panic on Molly's face at her question struck her with terror. Lonsdale's death should have been a triumph for Dermott. Why had they gone silent? Why were they staring at her with such apprehension? "What's going on?" she asked, scrutinizing Molly's pale face. Seized by dread at Molly's hesitation, tears sprang to Isabella's eyes. Furiously, she turned on Joe. "Dammit, *you* tell me the truth!"

Joe looked to Molly for guidance, and Isabella felt as though the world were collapsing around her.

"Joe heard a rumor that Dermott is wounded," Molly reluctantly offered, trying to speak with calm. "Don't immediately jump to conclusions. All gossip isn't true; most gossip isn't true, as you well know."

"But you're ashen and Joe is afraid to talk to me, so please don't tell me everything is all right when it clearly isn't." Isabella stood trembling with fear, her hands clenched at her sides to still the tremors, her gaze swiveling from one to the other as though she might be able to decipher their thoughts. "I want to know where he is," she whispered, her voice tight with horror. "And don't tell me you don't know."

"He was at Lamb's Inn," Molly replied.

"Was?"

"Lord Devon drove back to the inn with Dermott's lawyers, and he was gone. Against his doctor's orders, the inn owner said."

"Where did he go?"

"Apparently no one knows, or if they do, they're not talking. That's all we've been able to find out."

"Is that the whole truth?" Isabella searched the faces of her companions, looking for any indications of subterfuge. "I'm not a child," she reminded them. "I'm aware of what Dermott wants and doesn't want. You're not going to break my heart any more than it's already broken if you're honest with me. I fully realize he doesn't want to be with me, that he doesn't love me. But I'd like to know how badly he's hurt. For God's sake, tell me. I *need* to know."

"They don't expect him to live," Molly whispered.

Isabella sank to the floor, her legs suddenly gone weak. "Oh, my God . . ." Looking up at Molly, tears streamed down her cheeks. "It's all my fault. . . ."

"Don't even think that, darling." Rushing to comfort her, Molly dropped to the floor and took Isabella in her arms. "It's not your fault," she soothed. "Don't for a minute blame yourself. Everyone knows Dermott and Lonsdale have long been enemies, since their public school days at least. And Dermott pleases no one but himself. Tell her, Joe, she mustn't take responsibility for this."

"He's met more than one man on the dueling field, Miss Isabella. This weren't the first time by a long shot."

"You see," Molly insisted. "You're as guiltless now as with any of the others."

"I won't even be able to see him before—" Convulsed with a sob, Isabella couldn't conceive of so strong and vital a man facing the awful finality of death. Perhaps he was already dead. . . . Whimpering, she clung to Molly, terrified of so fearful a thought.

"Come, darling," Molly cajoled. "Come sit and have a glass of wine to ease your nerves. We'll see if we can find out more." Rising, she tugged on Isabella's hands.

Numb with grief, Isabella allowed herself to be helped to her feet and led to a chair, where Molly wiped the tears from her face. When she was handed a glass shortly after, she drank the wine, though it was tasteless in her mouth. Like dust.

She answered when spoken to, but she neither heard nor cared what was being discussed. All she could see was Dermott's cold body laid out in death. All she could think about was how sad and dreadful and devastating beyond belief the waste of his life.

And she couldn't go to him because she didn't know where he was.

Because he didn't want her to know.

"I can't stay here," Isabella abruptly declared, interrupting the murmured conversation, feeling a desperate, inexplicable need to flee. "I'm going to the country."

Molly looked at Joe and then at Isabella. "I'm glad."

Isabella came to her feet, her spine rigid, her shoulders stiff as a soldier on parade, shield against the collapse of her soul. "I'm going right now."

"Wouldn't you rather—" Molly's words died away at the look of anguish on Isabella's face. "I'll have the maids pack your clothes."

"Don't," she brusquely retorted, a kind of defensive anger in her voice. "I'm not taking anything." She didn't want to be reminded of Dermott, how he'd looked the day she'd been trying on the black lace gown at Molly's, or the way he'd stripped the white dress from her at Bathurst House and made her love him, or the scent of his hair and cologne that still lingered in the silk of her clothes. "Joe, please call for my carriage." Her voice was sharp and crisp. If she could pretend she'd never known Dermott, if she could obliterate any memory of the last unbelievable weeks, if she could physically separate herself from the people and places that reminded her of his beauty and tenderness, his playfulness and essential goodness, maybe with time she could learn to bear the unbearable pain.

Or if she couldn't, at least she could hide her misery from the world.

Dermott, traveling south, was undergoing his own unbearable torment, each revolution of the wheels an agonizing shock to his ravaged body, each bump in the road racking torture. Despite the doctor's protests, despite Shelby's pleadings, despite the horror in Charles's eyes, he'd insisted on leaving once he'd regained consciousness. He'd wanted to find a solitary cave where he could lick his wounds, a hermitage and refuge away from the world, away from prying eyes and gossip, away from help he didn't want and decisions he couldn't make. And if he were to die—he'd heard the doctor through the shifting levels of his consciousness—he'd take that final journey alone.

He didn't wish his mother alarmed. She was to be told only that he was recuperating at the seashore.

And so he meant to. His spirit willing.

He was unconscious more than he was conscious on the road to the south coast. A blessing, the doctor declared, seeing that Dermott swallowed another dose of laudanum each time he woke. And on that painful journey to the Isle of Wight, when those with him never knew if his next breath might be his last, Dermott's opium dreams were peopled with familiar images of his wife and son, the sweet visions bringing a smile to his lips. But another face intruded in the habitual, well-known fantasies—a beauty with golden hair and gentian eyes and the strength to draw him away. Sometimes he fought against her lure, and other times he willingly followed her. But their path always took them to the very edge of a high, rocky precipice shrouded in fog, and he found himself unwilling to follow her when she took that last fatal step. Invariably, he'd wake with a start, only to be met with a more brutal kind of pain, a clawing, fiendish pain that mercilessly ripped through his body and brought him panting, begging for oblivion.

* * *

The same evening Isabella was on her way to Suffolk, her uncle's family was dining at home, gloating over the events of the day.

"Herbert, tell us again when you first heard of Bathurst's mortal wounds," his wife cheerfully said, glancing at her two beaming daughters.

"And tell us, Papa, when we may attend the more refined society entertainments now that Bathurst is no longer your nemesis."

Their father cast them a lowering look. "He's not dead yet."

"But he's as near dead as ever may be, Papa!" Caroline exclaimed with considerable glee. "I heard it from Harold's valet, who heard it from any number of his friends. It's quite certain."

"So he can't hurt you now, Papa," Amelia declared. "It's so exciting! Just think, we can mix with the very best of the ton now."

"Don't set your sights too high, my dear," her doting papa remarked, more sensible than the females in his family of their station in life.

"But, Papa, you're ever so rich and you know that means we'll have our pick of a number of eligible parties. Now that we aren't obliged to go to those dreadful routs in the City."

"And have to talk to mushrooms without titles."

"Abigail," he sternly noted, "I suggest you set your daughters on a more realistic path. The world of the ton doesn't offer many titles to bankers' daughters."

"Oh, pooh on you, Papa. Just think of Evelina Drucker, who married a viscount only last year."

"A very poor and old viscount."

"Well, who would give a fig how old or poor they might be if one could wear a coronet," Caroline maintained.

"And you know the aristocracy never even talk to each other," her sister chimed in. "They live in separate parts of their great mansions and see one another only at ceremonies."

"So you girls know it all."

"Enough, Papa, to know that the only thing that matters is your money. And now that Bathurst is almost dead, we will be allowed to dance at the very best balls."

"Isabella is gone as well, Herbert. You said it yourself. Your watchers told you. So surely there are no further impediments to our daughters' season."

"Where did she go?" Harold had just come down from his chambers, his dandified attire having taken considerable time to adjust on his porcine body.

"You've missed the first course, Harold," his mother admonished him.

"Save your reproach for Steeves," he protested, sitting down across from his sisters. "He ruined a dozen of my neckcloths before managing to make me presentable. So where did she go?"

"To Tavora House. Are you going to woo her now that Bathurst is dead?" Amelia teased, knowing of her brother's tendre for their cousin.

"She's not worth my time now that she's used goods," he said in an affected manner, Isabella's relationship with

Bathurst the stuff of gossip. "But I may pay a visit on her—and give her the benefit of my advice."

"Used goods, indeed," Abigal sniffed. "She was out and out Bathurst's whore."

"But Lady Jersey slept with the Prince of Wales for years and now Lady Hertford does and the Duke of Devonshire has a mistress living in his house along with his wife and any number of nobles do—"

"For heaven's sake," Abigail exclaimed, directing a blistering glance at her younger daughter. "How in the world would you know such scandal?"

"From Maude, of course. You know how informed she is, Mama, and that's the reason you keep her. And if I'm going to be married soon, I should understand how the world goes along."

"Herbert! I would wish you to inform our daughters that immorality is wrong regardless of rank."

It took a moment for Herbert Leslie to gather the proper severe expression when he knew very well how the beau monde conducted itself. Fornication and flirtation had long been the amusements of the leisured class. "Listen to your mama, girls. She knows best."

"A little more sincerity, if you please, Herbert."

"Cut bait, Abigail," he brusquely retorted. "As if you don't know how the ton play at life and the world be damned."

The girls snickered and Harold smiled, but none dared confront their mother openly. She managed the household with an iron fist, and even Herbert rarely interfered in his wife's domain.

"We'll have no more talk of disreputable people at this

table." Abigail scanned the faces of her family with a penetrating gaze. "Now then," she said in her most proper tone, "what if we all attended Mrs. Bambridge's tea tomorrow—as a family."

"I have to work, as you well know, Abigail."

"And I'm bound for the races, Mama."

Abigail frowned at her husband and son. "It wouldn't hurt you to show yourselves at some of the girls' parties."

"Not old lady Bambridge's tea though, Mama. There's no one of consequence there."

"Mrs. Bambridge has hired an opera singer. And she has hopes that Baroness Tellmache may appear, for she likes Madame Dolcini's voice above all things."

"Mama, don't bother. Harold would lief walk to his races before he'd listen to an opera singer. And Lucinda and Emilie will be there, which is quite enough for us to have fun."

"Lucinda's maid knows the dresser for Lady Jersey, so she always has the most divine gossip about the royal family," Amelia added, grinning at her sister.

"There you go, Abby, the girls will have a great good time without us men to bother with. And as a little compensation for my busy schedule at the bank, why don't you girls go shopping for new gowns and bonnets."

"Oh, Papa!" his daughters both squealed, indifferent to their father's company but charmed by his purse.

"You're the greatest papa in the world!" Amelia cried. "I know exactly what I want. Remember, Mama, that darling primrose gown that you wouldn't let me buy because it was too dear. Is that all right now, Papa?" she cajoled.

"Of course, poppet." For all Herbert's grasp on reality,

he had hopes that his girls would make good matches—
maybe even titled gentlemen if ones could be found who
were necessitous enough. "Abby, you see that our daughters look up to snuff, now." He winked. "And I'll see that
the bills are paid."

The rest of the dinner conversation was taken over by a
discussion of various gowns and milliners, while the men
enjoyed their roasts and wine without further interrup-
tions. And once the women had gone from the table and
father and son were left to their port, Herbert said, "I'd
like a word with you about your cousin."

"I thought I might call on her after the races. Tavora
House is only a few miles from Newmarket."

"I've sent some men to follow her there. With Lonsdale
out of the picture, and very luckily, since Bathurst is near
dead, I thought you might like to consider marrying Isabella."

"Mother won't allow it. Her reputation after
Bathurst—" He shrugged at the impossibility.

"Just leave your mother to me. We're talking eighty
thousand a year, my boy. I'll see that she understands one
way or another. Isabella could be kept in the country until
the season is over, I was thinking. No one need know
you're married."

"I *might* consider it, then."

"Don't put on airs with me, son. I know how you feel
about Isabella. And now with the threat of Bathurst over,
we can return to our original plans. The money should be
kept in the family anyway, by Jove," he gruffly noted. "And
if George hadn't had his head turned by your cousin's

sweet ways, he would have done the right thing. Call on her, by all means, when you go to Newmarket."

"Is her bodyguard still in place?"

Herbert lifted his brows. "There's two of 'em now. But you needn't make more than a social call. See how she seems. Whether she's friendlier. Reconnoiter, as it were."

"Until such a time as we find a means to carry her off?"

His father nodded. "Exactly."

"If Bathurst kept her," Harold slyly murmured, "she's bound to be well trained."

"And capable of giving you a go for it in bed, eh, my boy?" his father replied with a soft chuckle. "Nothing wrong with that."

"A man wouldn't dare give her much freedom—if she's such a hot little piece."

"No need to give her freedom, son. She'll be your wife. You can keep her locked away in the country or in the mews behind the house if you like. And if I didn't trust your mama's sterling reputation, I'd do the same." It was bluster, of course. Abigail would have his hide if he dared cross her. Or her brothers would, and they were more powerful and influential bankers than he. "Fortunately, Isabella is without family to come to her aid," Herbert said in a musing tone. "We can be grateful for that."

"Lonsdale proved very convenient, didn't he—killing Bathurst like he did."

"And he had the decency to die as well," Herbert observed, lifting his glass to his son with a smile. "To the noble art of dueling."

Harold raised his glass. "May they both rest in peace."

"Not likely with Lonsdale—or Bathurst, for that matter. Hell's likely waiting. Now, just a word to the wise on the issue of honor. Such sublime principles may be well and good for the aristocracy, but don't let me ever hear of you involved in anything so dangerous. We can hire men to fight our battles, as anyone with half a brain does."

"Don't worry, Papa. I know better than to risk my life."

"You're a sensible young man." He smiled. "As my son should be. I never brought you up to foolishly spill your blood on the dueling field."

"I prefer the pleasures of life, Papa. Like this very good port." He held the rich ruby liquor up to the light.

"Shipped in from the Douro despite that damnable Peninsular War that's bleeding England dry. If they'd let the bankers run this country, we wouldn't be fighting to keep some damned king on his throne. Making money for England and ourselves. That's what counts."

"And I'll do my best to bring Uncle George's money back into the family," Harold said with a grin.

"Hear, hear." Herbert saluted his son, and lifting his glass to his mouth, drained it in one gulp.

19

FOR THE FIRST FEW DAYS at Dermott's manor house on the island, his survival remained questionable. Dr. Mc-Tavert kept the earl heavily sedated to alleviate as much of his suffering as possible, but despite the powerful narcotics, Dermott was still in agony. He tossed and turned, trying to escape the pain, his agitated movements causing his wounds to break open, the renewed bleeding further weakening him. The doctor tried having him tied down, but the restraints only worsened his restlessness, so the small staff kept at the house were pressed into service, everyone taking turns holding the earl as still as possible.

Dermott had hardly eaten anything since the duel, and the amount of liquid he'd drunk was so limited, the doctor was becoming fearful of dehydration. The earl's weight was dropping precipitously. In order to keep him from wasting away, the doctor ordered he be fed at least a few spoonfuls of broth every half hour. But the procedure was laborious and not always successful. Despite Dermott's weakened condition, he was still a strong man, and even sedated, occasionally he'd strike out at the annoyance and the soup and spoon would go flying.

One afternoon, in a rare moment of rest, Shelby and the doctor stood on the terrace, breathing in the fresh sea air.

"He's better—don't you think?" Shelby had been diligent in his duties, scarcely leaving the earl's side since the duel.

"He's not worse." The doctor was cautious, particularly with such severe wounds.

"Not worse is good news in itself."

McTavert nodded. "It's an indication of the earl's general good health. He's been able to fight off the infection I feared. At least, so far."

"It could still appear?"

"It could, but it's not as likely after this much time. I'm more concerned that his wounds won't heal if he continues to be so unsettled."

"I'll take care of that," a soft voice affirmed.

The men turned to find the dowager Countess of Bathurst standing in the doorway. "I've already been to see Dermott. He's much too thin, of course, but he seemed to know my voice, and I was able to quiet him."

"How did you know we were here?" Shelby was astonished. The earl had particularly wished his mother to be spared any anxiety.

"I believe you mentioned the seashore in your note, Shelby, and there is only one seashore for Dermott. He's always loved this place. I came as soon as I received your note and could get my maid to pack." She smiled. "Betty is not easily persuaded to travel."

"Countess, may I introduce Dr. McTavert." With a small gesture Shelby indicated the doctor. "He saved Lord Bathurst's life."

"Pleased to meet you, ma'am. Although I've been cautioning Shelby about being too optimistic. Not that your son is in any immediate danger," he quickly added.

"But we must get some food into him," the countess asserted, her mind crystal clear when it came to her son. "If someone would bring me a cup of tea and make up some barley soup for Dermott, I'll go to sit with him."

"I'll see that a room is prepared for you," Shelby said.

"Betty is already unpacking in my usual room, Shelby. And if someone would see that she has a wee bit of brandy, she will prove much more amenable. She likes it with warm water," the countess added with a sweet smile. "Come, Doctor. I wish for an expert opinion on my son. And I warn you, I listen only to good news."

While the doctor was explaining the nature of Dermott's gunshot wounds, Isabella was aiming a small pistol at a target Joe had set up in the orchard. They'd been practicing for several days now, and as a pupil, she was showing great promise.

"Sometimes I wonder why I let you talk me into this exercise." Isabella squinted down the barrel of the firearm.

"Because we saw those strange men loitering in the village and again, not half a day later, near your stables. And they weren't lookin' for work, even if they pretended they were." And you needed to get out of your room, he thought, and stop crying. "Squeeze that trigger nice and slow now."

Isabella exerted deliberate pressure on the trigger, held her breath, and fired.

"Right through the head!" Joe gleefully exclaimed. "You have talent, damned if you don't."

Joe had drawn a human form on the target, against Isabella's better judgment. Which is why they were well away from the house. She found it mildly disconcerting to be learning to shoot another human being.

"Thanks to your teaching, Joe." But she was smiling, pleased she was capable of learning to shoot straight. There was a certain satisfaction in taking charge of one's safety, and she had Joe to thank for her increasing expertise. "Now, if only I could learn to reload faster."

"That just takes practice, Miss Isabella. But an eye, now, that's another thing. Some people have it and some don't, and your aim is tops."

"So you think I might actually have to shoot one of my uncle's henchmen?" Still not completely reconciled to the possibility, she carefully took aim with the second round in the chamber.

"I'd say you'd better be prepared. I hope I'm here to guard you, but you never can tell. They know Mike and me are here, and any attackers are bound to try to deal with us first."

"If I don't want to spend the rest of my life hidden in my room, waiting for a possible attack, I suppose I'd better learn to protect myself."

"Now you're talkin', Miss Isabella. I'm glad you're comin' around."

His arguments had fallen on deaf ears at first, Isabella refusing to believe her life was still in danger. But Bathurst was gone, Joe had reminded her, and with him the only real threat her relatives respected. And the two strangers with their dubious story had finally convinced her. They hadn't had the look of day laborers or farmhands.

A small explosion of gunpowder left a puff of smoke in the air, and her second ball took out the target's eye.

"Remind me to keep on your good side," Joe teased.

"And now I have to reload," Isabella grumbled, the procedure lengthy.

"I'll do it for you this time." Joe took her weapon from her and bent to the task.

Dropping onto the grass, Isabella leaned back on her arms and gazed up at the sun-filled sky. "It seems so peaceful out here, it's hard to fathom my uncles' malevolence."

Joe looked up from his task. "It's just about money, miss. You have it and they want it."

"It's hard for me to fathom such greed when they have enormous wealth of their own."

"People like them don't never have enough. I'd suggest you think of their fat, evil faces when you're aiming—"

She quickly shook her head. "I couldn't, Joe. Not ever . . . even this target is disturbing for me, though I understand your reasoning. But I don't want to think of them at all if I can help it." She briefly shut her eyes, as though she could erase the memory of her relatives with so simple a gesture. "Let's not talk about anything distressing," she suggested. "Especially on such a lovely day."

It warmed Joe's heart to see her able to enjoy the fine weather, when she'd been so wretched their first week at Tavora House. Part of the reason he'd suggested teaching her to shoot was to deliver her from the prison of her room. She'd not stepped outside her apartments the first week in the country; she'd barely eaten, and whenever he'd spoken to her concerning some matter of guarding the estate, her eyes had been red from crying. He'd almost welcomed the Leslie spies, for it gave him the opportunity to lure her outside and attempt to distract her from her melancholy. The lessons had served to focus on something other than her loss of Dermott. And her constant fear that he was dead.

As an added advantage, the shooting practice gave Joe another opportunity to be near her.

That night after Joe and his brother had patrolled the grounds before trading shifts outside Isabella's door, the two men stood in the kitchen garden and smoked their evening cigars.

"It wouldn't do for you to fall in love with our employer." Mike's tone was mild. "Just a cautionary word."

Joe didn't immediately answer.

"I see how you look at her."

Joe blew out a cloud of smoke. "It doesn't hurt to look."

"It will eventually. You can't have her."

Joe half smiled at his younger brother. "Allow me my pleasures."

"She's very trusting."

"She's been protected all her life. And I intend to see that she continues to be. Fat Leslie isn't going to have her."

Mike chuckled. "At least she'd have a wide target if he shows up."

Joe's brows rose faintly. "Or I would."

* * *

In the following days, Isabella made a conscious effort to keep busy, filling her time with numerous activities that would enhance her tenants' lives. She began planning a new schoolhouse for her tenants' children as well as an addition to the small lying-in hospital on the estate. She oversaw the enlargement of the south gardens and agreed to judge the yearly flower show in the village. She met with her steward and listened to his reports on the state of the crops. She even invited the neighbor ladies over for tea—an experience that required a feigned rendition of cheerfulness that would have done any actress proud.

But when evening came, her tenants returned to their hearths, neighbors went home, stewards must be allowed rest from their duties, and an immense loneliness stretched like an interminable void. She slept poorly if she slept at all, her melancholy crushing in the quiet of night, and she despaired of enduring a life without Dermott. She still yearned for him every minute, every second, with such a raw, aching sadness, she'd long before run out of tears.

She'd often lie awake at night, praying he lived—praying to any god who'd listen—to spare his life. And each morning she'd impatiently wait for the mail, hoping for word from Molly—for the blessed message that he'd survived.

But days passed and then weeks, and no one heard a whisper.

The afternoon Harold Leslie was announced, Isabella glanced at Joe, lounging on a chair in her office.

"You're not home," he said, coming to his feet in one lithe movement. "I'll tell him."

"No, wait." She held up her hand and pushed away her account book. "He might know something of Dermott. Surely the Leslies are concerned with his whereabouts more than anyone."

"Regardless, I'm not sure it's safe."

"Is my cousin alone?" Isabella's gaze turned to the footman who waited in the doorway for her instructions.

"Yes, miss."

She set down her pen. "Is anyone outside in his carriage?"

"He rode up on a bit of new horseflesh he bought at Newmarket." The young flunky grinned. "And he couldn't control that high-spirited animal. He were sweating mightily, miss."

"Perhaps he's looking for a ride back to Newmarket in one of my carriages." Isabella couldn't help but smile at the thought of Harold's corpulent body astride a temperamental steed. "Show him into the Chinese saloon and bring tea."

"You're not going in there alone," Joe declared.

"Heavens no. I wouldn't think of it. You have tea with us."

"I'd rather throw his fat ass back up on that horse and whip him down the drive."

"He's here for a reason though." Stacking the papers on her desk into a neat pile, she rose from her chair. "Let's go and see what Harold wants."

"We know what he wants," Joe muttered.

"But he might have news we want as well." Isabella

moved toward the door. "And don't be surprised at what I might say. I intend to make it clear, he needn't call again."

"I could do that."

She smiled faintly. "I believe I can do it without bloodshed, however."

Harold was scrutinizing the stylish Chinese wallpaper, the hand-painted designs portraying colorful vignettes of Canton.

"Do you like the scenes, cousin?" Isabella inquired as she entered the room, keeping her voice intentionally bland. "Grandpapa preferred this room above all the others. He said it reminded him of his youth in the China trade."

Harold spun around and immediately frowned at Joe, who stood directly behind Isabella. "I'd prefer a private audience, cousin."

"I'm so sorry," she said with artificial sweetness. "I've become attached to Joe."

Harold's face flushed a vivid crimson. "In what way— er—that is . . . I say, cousin, don't know that's all the thing—with an employee—"

"Oh, dear. You misunderstand. I meant Joe is the ideal bodyguard. He never leaves my side. I confess," she murmured, "it makes me feel delightfully safe." Let Harold take that titillating bit of misleading information back to his father. They might think twice about any base plans. "Could we interest you in a cup of tea," she pleasantly added. "Joe particularly likes Grandpapa's special blend, don't you, Joe." She smiled at him over her shoulder.

If Joe weren't a head taller and solid muscle, Harold would have answered differently. As it was, he consoled himself with shooting the ex-pugilist a black look and answering Isabella with as much politesse as he could muster. "I'd be pleased to stay for tea."

"Isn't that nice. Joe, isn't that nice?" She touched Joe's hand lightly, intent on giving Harold every impression that she and her bodyguard were very close. "Do sit down, cousin. And if you'd ring for Henderson, Joe, we'll all sit and chat. Tell him to add a little brandy for you men with the tea," she added, smiling at her bodyguard. "What brings you to Suffolk, Harold?" She turned back to her guest.

"Came for the Newmarket races." As he sat, the points of his shirt collar pushed up into his heavy jowls, his lofty neckcloth crushed between his tightly waistcoated stomach and his chin. His plump thighs stretched the fabric of his fawn-colored pantaloons, his weight tested the strength of the fine Sheraton chair, his red-faced corpulence an anomaly in the saloon's refined decor.

"You must give us the news from London. We're sadly behind in the latest gossip here. Has the Prince of Wales tired of Lady Hertford or has her husband tired of the Prince?"

"Neither, apparently—according to the news sheets."

"And does the Princess still languish at Blackheath?"

"I believe so."

Isabella asked several more frivolous questions concerning the ton before casually saying, "And is my Lord Bathurst back in town after his misfortune? Or did we miss his funeral?"

Harold's mouth tightened into a grim line, his jealousy of Bathurst's claim on Isabella intense. "There's been no word," he muttered.

Isabella felt such relief, she unconsciously offered Harold a warm smile. "Did you enjoy your ride from Newmarket? It's such a lovely day." More so now that there was no news of Dermott's burial. She almost felt sorry for poor Harold, who was quite out of his depth on this mission for his family.

"My new mount's a bit high-spirited—frisky . . . got him from the racecourse—needs some training, I don't doubt."

"Would you like Joe to take you back in my phaeton?"

So the damned guard was driving her phaeton. Not suitable at all. Harold's flush deepened at the injustice. "Wouldn't mind a hand at that phaeton myself," he bluntly said. "Might just take you up on your offer."

"Joe knows my team so well though, cousin. I'm afraid the horses might balk at your handling. They're too temperamental, I'm afraid. Didn't you just say that to me the other day, Joe?" She glanced at him walking back from conferring with Henderson, and smiling, patted the settee, indicating he sit beside her. "I'm afraid Joe does most of the driving here," she murmured, fluttering her lashes in a parody of female submission.

Joe kept from laughing only with supreme effort, Isabella's driving skills the equal of any Corinthian whip.

"I say . . . I say, Isabella," her cousin stammered, his expression one of dismay. "Can't think it's altogether proper—I mean—"

"Oh, there you are, Henderson." Her majordomo was

carrying a salver with two brandies. "We don't worry about propriety so far out in the country. We're quite informal. Aren't we, Henderson?" she cheerfully maintained as he waved in a footman carrying the tea tray.

"Yes, miss, very informal," her majordomo replied, humoring her when he ran her establishment of two hundred servants and laborers, putting the fact that Joe was sitting much closer than usual to his mistress to the unwanted presence of Harold Leslie. Bets below stairs were that Joe would throw Cousin Harold out within the half hour. Personally, he'd placed his money on twenty minutes, but his face was expressionless as he set a brandy before each gentleman.

"I do adore those pink cakes. Thank Mrs. Parker for me, Henderson." Isabella picked up the teapot from the tray that had been placed before her and began pouring tea. "Milk or lemon, cousin?"

With Joe a bulwark at her side, Isabella took a measure of revenge for the indignities she'd suffered at her Leslie relatives' hands. Flaunting her simulated relationship with Joe, she would glance at him as they conversed or smile affectionately at something he said, while he played his role of stalwart companion with aplomb. He spoke little, but when he did, Isabella always listened and agreed.

Increasingly ill-tempered and petulant, Harold couldn't long suffer the insolence and presumption of a man of Joe Thurlow's station behaving toward his cousin with such disgusting familiarity. Faced with the limited options of challenging Joe or departing, he chose the more prudent. Abruptly coming to his feet, he took his leave with a stiff bow and a tight smile.

"I wish you good-day, cousin," he said with constraint, ignoring Joe.

"It was so nice of you to visit us. We get so little company. You must come again, mustn't he, Joe?"

Joe had risen when Harold did, and his towering height required Isabella look up a great distance.

"It's a mighty long way from Newmarket. I doubt Leslie will care to ride so far again."

"Oh, pooh, Joe, when Cousin Harold has that wonderful new mount? He won't mind riding to see us at all, will you, cousin?"

"I won't be long in Newmarket," Harold curtly said, thinking Isabella was going to require a very strong hand once they were married.

Isabella made a small moue. "Dear, what a shame. And when I was so hoping you might come for tea again. I fear we weren't good enough company." Her smile was dazzling. "Would you like Joe to see you out, cousin?"

"No need, no need," Harold quickly replied, not inclined to be alone with Joe Thurlow, whose dislike was patent despite his quiet forbearance.

"Well, we wish you good journey, cousin," Isabella cheerfully declared. "And give our regards to your family."

"Isabella said 'our regards' about *Joe Thurlow,* damn her wantonness. And Bathurst not even cold in his grave." Harold Leslie pursed his fleshy lips, his eyes snapping with indignation. "I tell you, Thurlow was sitting so close to her, you couldn't have slipped a piece of paper between them."

"Interesting," his father murmured. "She seems to have found her calling. Who would think Uncle George's sweet granddaughter, the apple of his eye, would turn out to be a trollop?"

"Like mother like daughter," Abigail tartly observed. "That Frenchy mother of hers walked out of that convent school and took off around the world. Blue blood or not, that's a hussy. As is Isabella with her latest paramour. If your father insists you marry her, and I'm on the record as opposed—"

"But not opposed to having her money," Herbert interjected.

Abigail sighed dramatically. "A shame the lawyers seem to think George's will is incontestible."

"But since it is," Herbert smoothly noted, "we must consider our options now that Thurlow is in such proximity to her. We'll need more men."

"Harold, I want you to promise to keep that woman locked up somewhere once you're married," his mother insisted. "I don't want her contaminating your sisters. She is completely without morals. And while I understand men's beastly natures and perhaps your interest in her, I don't want any of her licentious ways to taint the girls. Is that clear? Herbert, you tell him I'm quite resolute on that point."

Her husband looked at their son. "You heard your mother."

"Yes, Papa. She can stay at Tavora House. There's no need for her to come into the City."

"And it goes without saying, you'll want some brats off her, to insure the inheritance."

"Herbert, really!" Abigail affected a shocked look.

"Hush, Abby. You know as well as I that we need heirs to keep the fortune, should she die."

"This is all so revolting," his wife murmured.

"But not her millions," her husband pithily noted. "We'll have to put a larger team of men together, Harold." His mouth set in a grim line. "One capable of handling the Thurlow brothers."

20

THE DOWAGER'S PRESENCE at the house by the sea had a calming effect on her son, and shortly after her arrival, Dermott opened his eyes and for the first time surveyed the room with an unclouded gaze. Recognizing his mother seated in a chair beside the bed, he managed a small smile.

"I'm here, darling," she murmured, leaning over him and kissing his cheek. "And I insist you get better."

His chuckle turned into a groan as the slight movement jarred his afflicted body. And when he found his breath again, he whispered, "I'm hungry."

"You have your choice this morning, dear. Betty and the cook have been busy since dawn."

His gaze flickered around the room again. "My shirt."

The countess looked to Shelby, unsure what her son wanted.

"I have it, sir."

"Go and fetch it, Shelby," his mother ordered, intent on giving her son whatever he wished.

When Shelby returned with a wrinkled shirt in his

hands, she raised her brows in surprise, but she kept her peace, and when Dermott tried to lift his hand to take it from Shelby, she saw that it was slipped into his grasp. The scent of perfume clung to it, the fragrance sweet on the air. And she came to her own conclusions.

Dermott's recuperation from that point was a slow but steady progression, his every whim seen to by his mother, her capacity for managing a household a surprise to Shelby, who had perceived her as a woman sequestered and unbalanced by the events of her marriage. She was neither, but capable, cheerful, and fully in charge of her son's recovery.

She and Dermott sat on the terrace one evening a fortnight later, enjoying the last vestiges of the sunset as the violet twilight crept in. Dermott lounged on a chaise, his awful gauntness having been relieved by a steady diet of his favorite foods, beefsteak a mainstay once he was strong enough to sit up again. The countess rocked in a chair she'd brought to the island as a girl when her father had owned the manor house. She was slender and fair, her hair untouched with gray, her beauty so well preserved, Shelby had once asked her whether she'd married as a child.

"I like the perfume on that shirt you keep." She'd not mentioned it before, but Dermott seemed in considerable good spirits. "Although it's none of my business, I'm sure," she added, smiling.

He softly laughed. "I was wondering when you'd ask."

"The lady must mean something to you."

He didn't answer for some time, and when he did, his words were hesitant. "I think she does."

"Why are you saving the shirt if you don't know?" she gently prodded, his mood veiled and somber in the weeks of his convalescence.

"Good question."

The sound of shore gulls filled the ensuing silence.

He recrossed his ankles, restlessly looked out to sea again, straightened the cuff of his robe, and when he finally spoke, his voice was unusually quiet. "Do you remember me telling you I'd been married?"

His mother's brow creased in concentration for a moment. "I don't. How strange that I'd forget something so important. Did I know the girl?"

He shook his head. "I married in India."

"You were in India?"

"For five years," he murmured.

She shut her eyes briefly, and when she looked at him again, she said, "I feel so wretched I can't remember."

"It doesn't matter, *Maman*," he gently replied. "You never met my wife and son. They died in India."

"Darling, how terrible." She reached over to touch his hand. "I wish I'd known. How impossibly hard for you— how you must have grieved. . . ."

It took him a very long time to respond, a rush of painful memories flooding his mind, all the what-ifs and should-haves that had haunted him for years fresh and raw. "I haven't been able to forget."

His dark eyes held a sorrow she'd never seen. "You should have told me." She fluttered her hands as though to erase her words. "Darling, I'm dreadfully sorry I was so self-absorbed when you needed me most."

"It's not your fault, *Maman*."

"I should have recognized your sadness."

"I didn't want you to." He'd wanted to protect his mother from further pain; his father had caused her enough for a lifetime.

"I'm not going to need coddling anymore though." She smiled. "Now it's your turn to be coddled. Having you so near death made me deeply aware of all I truly have, how lucky I am to have you. And from now on I intend to see to your happiness."

He gazed at the sunset hovering on the horizon. "After so long, I'm not sure I'd recognize happiness. Although," he softly added, "I can look at a sunset now and actually see its beauty." His mouth curved into a faint grin. "That's definitely progress."

"Your brush with death has helped us both appreciate the simple joy of living. I think we've *both* dwelt in the past far too long."

"I can't ever forget though." His eyes filled with tears.

"You won't," his mother whispered. "No one would wish you to. Tell me about your family," she gently added. "I want to know everything. What was your wife like? How did you meet her? Did my grandson look like you? Did he have your smile?"

As the sun set and evening fell, Dermott spoke openly of his family for the first time since his return. He laid bare his suffering and heartache, disclosed his agonizing guilt, voiced the depth of his love for his wife and son, revealed a small measure of his intemperance in the aftermath of their death. That confession not without guilt as well.

And when he'd finished, his mother said, "How

fortunate you were to have experienced such love. I know, because I love you very deeply too." She lifted her hand, the slight movement a gesture toward the expanse of starlit sky twinkling above them. "We can't always control what happens to us in this boundless world." She offered him a rueful smile. "Although I certainly wasted a great deal of my life trying. Don't waste your life too, darling. Please."

Dermott smiled faintly. "I'm going to like having you back, *Maman*. I won't feel so alone. And maybe the past—"

"Will be a memory you'll always carry in your heart." Her gaze was tender. "How few of us even have such loving memories."

He knew she didn't, and his heart ached for her.

She straightened her shoulders as though meeting an attack; he remembered that gesture from his childhood— seen whenever his father came into a room. "But consider, darling," she said with a kind of bracing resolve that matched her posture, "if we're going to try to live in the present, do you think perhaps it's due time to admit to your feelings for the woman whose perfume is on that shirt you saved? She's been in your thoughts, I know."

"I don't know if it would be fair to admit my feelings to her. I bring so much ruin in my wake."

"She might prefer making that decision herself rather than having you decide what's best for her. And if you don't think me interfering, I'd really like to meet her."

After being without his mother for so long, her interference was welcome. But he gave her warning. "I'm not sure Isabella will come."

"If you and I can forget, maybe she can as well. Ask her."

Dermott grinned, the thought of having Isabella in his life suddenly warming his soul. "Even if she agrees, I have to forewarn you, *Maman*—I don't know if she rides."

"If she doesn't, then we'll just have to teach her."

"She may not want to learn. She has a mind of her own," he added with fondness.

"Good for her. She'll be able to keep you in your place. Now, what do you think about my blue diamond for an engagement ring?" she briskly asked. "Just in case," she interjected quickly. "It was your grandmother's and very lucky for her and, oh, dear, I'm being dreadfully pushy. Although I feel as though I've wakened after a ten-year sleep and have to make up for lost time."

"You're allowed to be pushy, *Maman*." He took enormous pleasure in her excited interest, recalling his youth, when they would go off on wonderful play adventures. She made him feel alive again, although he cautioned himself against Isabella welcoming him with open arms. "Why don't I let her choose a ring—if she'll have me," he circumspectly noted. "I've not treated her well."

"I expect, darling, you're capable of persuading a woman to love you. You could always tell her of your wonderful collection of bird feathers."

Dermott chuckled. "You haven't thrown those away?"

"Of course not. You worked on that collection until you were twelve."

"Well, if all else fails, I'll use the bird feathers as a last bargaining chip."

"Then, of course you'll succeed. How can she refuse?"

* * *

But the dowager countess didn't rely alone on her son's persuasive charm. She wrote a letter to Isabella as well. It was easy enough to discover her full name and direction from Shelby, and justifying her interference as a mother's prerogative, she told Isabella about Dermott's feelings for her.

A week later Dermott walked into Molly's parlor in St. James's Place.

"Rumor had it you were dead," she said, her expression reserved.

"And so I nearly was, Shelby tells me."

"But with no black crepe on Bathurst House," she coolly remarked, "I began to suspect you'd survived." She didn't offer him a chair.

He took note and remained near the door. "I know you're angry about Isabella."

Her gaze narrowed faintly. "Very perceptive for a man who's considered only himself these last many years."

"I've come to make amends."

"To me?" Her brows lifted. "Don't bother."

"To both of you. But I can't find Isabella. She's not at home and no one will tell me where she went."

"Maybe you should consider that a clue."

"I know what I did was wrong," he quietly said. "But almost dying makes one consider one's life from a new perspective. Please, Molly, if you know where she is, tell me."

"And why should I after the way you treated her?"

"Because I'm not the same," he softly said. "I feel as though I'm capable of having a future now. I *want* a future. I want Isabella to share my life, Molly, if she'll have me."

"I doubt she will." Molly couldn't so easily forget how much he'd hurt Isabella, how callous and cruel, how selfish he'd been. "She took nothing that would remind her of you when she left, not a gown, not a book or scarf. Nothing."

"Let me talk to her at least. I'm a changed person, Molly. My mother will tell you, Shelby will tell you—hell, Charles is concerned for my consequence because I've given up all my vices."

Her reserve melted marginally. He seemed sincere, not charming or glib. "She's not alone. Joe and Mike Thurlow are with her. So don't expect to just walk in and seduce her again."

"I understand. Seduction isn't my intent."

"You'll have to convince Joe, not me." Her mouth curled in distaste. "She's not rid of the Leslies either. Her cousin Harold called on Isabella. Mercer keeps me informed."

"Then her relatives are still a danger to her."

"Of course. Your disappearance from the scene left them free to pursue their nefarious aims. So tell me," she briskly said, "are you serious this time or just missing your amusements?"

"I'm utterly and completely serious. I brought my grandmother's diamond ring to offer Isabella along with my heart. You may see it if you question my sincerity. The ring was my mother's idea."

"The dowager countess knows, then."

"She knows—and approves and is waiting for me to bring Isabella home to Alworth to meet her."

"Hmmm."

"Don't look at me like that. I'll willingly pay penance for all my sins. You can make up a list while I'm gone. But give me Isabella's location so I can plead my case in person."

"What if she's forgotten you?"

"Then I'll do my best to refresh her memory."

"She may want you to beg," Molly tartly submitted. "And I wouldn't blame her."

His dark gaze was unambiguous. "Then I'll beg. I'm dead serious, Molly."

She smiled for the first time since he'd entered the room. "The thought of you on your knees, pleading, almost makes one wish to post to Higham and see for oneself."

"She's at Tavora House?"

"Since the day of your duel."

"With Joe," he murmured, suddenly thinking Isabella and her bodyguard had been together a very long time. He and Joe had met occasionally at debauches, the heavyweight champion welcomed into the male preserves of the beau monde.

"And Mike is there as well," Molly reminded him. "You may have to convince them both of your sincerity."

"Really." One brow rose faintly. "Are they her duennas?"

"At the moment, yes, and Joe's resentful of your cavalier treatment of Isabella. She cried for weeks after they reached Tavora House, he said."

The earl inhaled softly. "I see."

"Just a word of warning."

"You don't think I can take on the heavyweight champion?" he dryly noted.

"Not in your present condition. How much weight have you lost?" Dermott was noticeably lean.

He smiled. "Not as much as Lonsdale."

"Point taken, but I wouldn't suggest you irritate Joe."

"It sounds as though he has a tendre for my wife-to-be."

"*Perhaps* she's your wife-to-be."

"You don't think I can prevail?"

"I wouldn't lay any bets on it."

His smile was the familiar, warm smile she'd missed.

"Fifty guineas says I win this one," Dermott playfully challenged.

"I'm not sure I care to bet."

"Don't want to lose your money?"

She glared at him for a moment. "Probably not," she relented with a sigh. "You damnable rogue."

"I'm not a rogue anymore, darling."

"Humpf," she snorted, clearly skeptical.

"My bride and I will come and call on you when we return to the City."

"And how long will the honeymoon last, I'm wondering."

"So cynical, Molly, when I'm in love."

He'd never uttered those words since his return from

India, and that simple phrase did more than a thousand arguments to change her mind. "Say it again," she ordered.

"I love her," he quietly repeated.

Her smile this time was affectionate. "Then you might just manage to get your way."

"No might about it, Molly." Walking over to where she sat, he bent down, kissed her cheek, and whispered, "Thank you for bringing her to me."

21

JOE AND ISABELLA WERE WATCHING the new foals in the pasture. Standing next to each other, leaning against the high wooden fence that surrounded the pasture, they were talking in a desultory way about the gamboling frolics of the young Thoroughbreds, the beauty of the day, their trip to Higham the next morning. The occasion was no different from countless others during their sojourn in the country.

Until Joe reached out, cupped the back of her head in the palm of his hand, and bending close, gently kissed her.

How long had it been since she'd been kissed? She thought. How long had it been since she'd felt the warmth of a man's body close to hers? But she couldn't offer Joe what he wanted, no more than she could make herself happy again, and a moment later she gently pushed him away.

He acquiesced when a man of his size wouldn't have had to.

"I'm sorry," she whispered.

He brushed his hand through his fair hair, a quick, nervous gesture like that of a young boy. "I shouldn't have taken liberties." His voice was low, apologetic. "If you fire me, I'll understand."

Such a huge, strong man capable of such sweet earnestness brought tears to her eyes.

"And now I've made you cry with my stupidity," he muttered in self-reproach.

"No, you haven't made me cry because of that. I'm just touched." She gazed up at him, overcome with melancholy. "And if I could ever love anyone again, dear Joe, it would be you. But—"

"You still love Bathurst." Taking out his handkerchief, he carefully held it out to her when he wished he could wipe away her tears himself.

"I don't know if I do or not, but I can't forget him." Even while she understood all the liabilities in loving Dermott. Her eyes held Joe's over the crushed linen of his handkerchief. "And you're not fired. What would I do without you?"

It was scant comfort for a wounded heart, but he said with good grace, "I'm glad, because I wouldn't want to leave."

She handed his handkerchief back. "So we shall muddle on here at Tavora as best we can."

He smiled. "Fair enough."

"And I liked your kiss very much," she softly said.

"Then, that makes two of us."

She laughed. "Good God, life is complicated."

"No one ever promised it would be easy."

"How selfish of me to whine about every little thing when you've literally fought your way to all your successes."

"I was lucky to have survived. Tony Marshall didn't."

"Your friend. Molly told me about it."

He nodded. "So you see, we're both lucky to be here enjoying the sunny day and looking forward to more."

"We are, aren't we? And you're going to take me to Higham and I'm going to buy a great number of bonnets because new bonnets always put me in a good mood."

"You're damned easy to please," Joe said with a chuckle.

"Someone else once said that to me," she murmured.

He could hear the poignancy in her voice. "Probably not just like that."

"No."

"Bathurst might not be dead," he offered, trying to console her. "There's been no announcement in the papers. While Lonsdale's obituary and will were both published."

"That lack of information does make me hopeful."

"Do you want me to try and discover what happened to him?"

She shook her head. "No. It doesn't matter, because he didn't want me in his life."

"The man's a fool."

She smiled. "I agree."

The dowager countess's letter arrived a short time later, having been delayed by the necessary rerouting from Isabella's London house.

Isabella was in her boudoir, selecting a bonnet for a drive with Joe, when her lady's maid answered a knock on the door, took the letter from a footman, and carried it to her. One glance at the name of the sender and Isabella felt a moment of unsteadiness. Forcing her voice to a calmness she didn't feel, she instructed her maid to tell Joe she'd be down in five minutes, shut the door on her maid's back, and sank into a chair before her legs gave way.

Visibly shaking, she held the letter for a few moments, terrified of its contents, fearful it was news of Dermott's death, not sure it wasn't easier not knowing. But she had to read it, she knew, so offering up a prayer of hope, she eased the seal apart, spread the sheet of paper open, and swiftly perused the brief sentences for the word "death."

None.

Inhaling with relief, she then began to read from the beginning.

Dear Miss Leslie,

Forgive me for speaking so plainly, but I wanted to inform you of my son's feelings for you. As you may know, he's been severely wounded [Isabella's heart caught for a moment before the next phrase came into focus] *but is now recovering at our home on the Isle of Wight. He feels you may harbor ill will toward him, and I'm very much hoping you don't. He's a good boy who's suffered a great sadness in his past. If you didn't know of this suffering, I was hoping that knowledge might excuse some of his conduct. He tells me his behavior has been less than chivalrous. Do come and see us. I'd very much like to meet the woman Dermott loves.*

She'd signed her Christian name as though they were already friends.

Isabella gently traced the word *love* with her fingertip,

happiness flooding her senses. He was alive! And blissfully, he *loved* her!

Every tear she'd shed in the past weeks was suddenly irrelevant, all her misgivings and uncertainties, her anger and resentment, wiped away by a single word. Paradise was hers, the entire world was hers, never had the sun shone so gloriously, nor the air felt so pure. Carefully folding the precious letter and placing it in her reticule, she ran from her suite and raced down the stairs, screaming for Joe.

Waiting with her phaeton in the drive, he accepted her joyful news with good grace, careful to mask his feelings, well aware of where her heart lay. And when Isabella said "I want to leave immediately," he only asked where.

"To the Isle of Wight. We'll have a change of clothes packed for us. I'd like to leave in ten minutes," she added, intent on departing with all haste.

Joe only insisted that Mike accompany them, and within the allotted time they were on the road south, carrying only light baggage. And early the next morning, after a long, grueling night on the road, just as the sun began to rise, they came to the ferry that would take them to the island.

They found Dermott's house closed except for a small staff of retainers, and Isabella's spirits, sustained at soaring levels during their journey south, abruptly plummeted.

"I'm sorry, miss, but his lordship went up to London and the countess be at Alworth," the housekeeper informed her, taking in the dust-covered state of the visitors' clothing. "If you'd care to clean up, miss, you're most welcome, considering the countess called you here."

"I must have misunderstood," Isabella said, flushed with embarrassment, thinking herself the world's biggest fool for hying south on the merest insinuation Dermott might care. "And thank you, but we have rooms on the mainland," she fabricated, not about to leave herself open to further embarrassment. What if Dermott were to return and find her there? Whatever his mother's motives, apparently he hadn't been informed. And if he were in London, no doubt his health was sufficiently restored that he was back in his old haunts. Having renewed hopes after the countess's letter that her love was returned, the pain of rejection was now doubly hurtful. And Isabella suppressed her tears only with supreme effort.

Joe and Mike were politely silent as they returned to the ferry, but they knew she felt as jilted as though she'd been left at the altar.

Dermott had spent the night in Higham at the King's Arms, having arrived in the area too late to make a social call. He'd barely slept, and by four, he'd given up even trying. Rising, he dressed himself, not wishing to wake Charles so early, and descending to the public rooms downstairs, he surprised the scullery maids who were just lighting the kitchen fires. Asking for coffee, he sat down in the kitchen and waited, making them extremely nervous. Although, as it turned out, he made the coffee himself. Neither of the young girls was familiar with more than her menial chores, while he'd made many a pot of coffee while out on campaign.

He was just pouring himself a steaming cup of fresh brew, when the cook came bustling out of her parlor, having quickly dressed when one of the maids came to warn her that a fine lord was making coffee in her kitchen.

"Good morning, sir," she said, sweeping a hand over her disordered hair. "Would you like something more with your coffee?"

"If it's not too much bother." Dermott couldn't possibly call at Tavora House at four-thirty in the morning, so he might as well eat. A bit of fortification for the coming ordeal probably wouldn't be out of order.

"Are you here for the races?" the cook inquired as she set about her cooking.

"Actually, no. I'm visiting."

"You have friends in the neighborhood?"

"Yes."

"Where might that be?" Mrs. Notkins wasn't known as the most knowledgeable gossip in Higham without reason. She stood looking at him in expectation of an answer.

Amused at her catechism, he debated briefly whether his visit required secrecy. And deciding it didn't, he said, "Tavora House."

"Ah. The beautiful Miss Leslie. Such a shame about her poor dear grandfather, but she seems to have company now in her sorrow. A bodyguard," she reported in a confidential whisper. "Some says it's her relatives she fears. You're not one of them, are you?" Mouth pursed, she studied him and then shook her head. "You don't favor them Leslie men at all. Fat, every one of them, and no one can accuse you o' that."

"She's often with her bodyguard?" The hair on the back of his neck had risen like hackles.

"Of course. Why wouldn't she be? He's there to guard her, and that he does, right and tight. It's her money, you know," she added in the same conspiratorial whisper. "Them Leslies want it."

And by the time his breakfast had been prepared, he was completely informed of the activities at Tavora House during Miss Leslie's residence. Mrs. Notkins had a number of relatives on the staff there. Her extended family, native to the area since before the Conquest, she proudly explained, also included several local tradesmen, who added considerably to her knowledge of Miss Leslie's activities in Higham. In fact, her niece, who owned the milliner's shop on High Street, was expecting Miss Leslie later that morning for a bonnet fitting.

"So you might as well wait until she comes into town. That way you won't meet her on the road. Both herself and that there bodyguard of hers drive at a right fine clip—dangerous, some say. Wouldn't want you to have no accident coming around a curve on that narrow road."

Whether it was the coffee or the information dispensed, by the time he'd finished breakfast, Dermott found himself thoroughly discomposed and agitated. Leaving the King's Arms, he followed Mrs. Notkins's directions and walked down High Street to Miss Armistead's millinery shop. Staring into the window at the bonnets covered with muslin for the night, he wondered what Isabella was doing just then.

Was she just waking up beside Joe? Was it possible? Had he come so far both in terms of understanding and distance, only to find that Isabella had forgotten him and moved on to another man? Had he waited too long to recognize his heart? He turned from the shrouded display, from the shop, and walked away, plagued by jealousy and doubts.

Lost in his disconcerting thoughts, he walked the town with unseeing eyes, trying to reconcile the events described to him by the cook at the King's Arms with his own hopes and dreams. Wandering from street to street, he reflected on the possibilities open to him, on the course he should pursue in the wake of the new information he'd received.

Not least was concern for his mother. How would she deal with his return should he be unsuccessful in his suit? Would such a setback to her wishes harm the new equilibrium of her life?

He was personally capable of managing emotional pain. Hadn't he perfected the art in recent years? But he couldn't but be aware of the irony of his present situation, after having refused so many females. Perhaps Isabella would take pleasure in rejecting him. Would she even talk to him? he wondered. Or was she so involved with Joe Thurlow, she couldn't be bothered seeing him?

In time he became aware of the bustle of businesses opening their doors and shutters and setting up for another day of commerce. Checking his watch, he retraced his steps to the millinery shop on High Street, took up a vantage post across the street, and waited.

By ten, when she'd not arrived, he questioned the proprietress and was assured Isabella was expected.

By eleven, Miss Armistead thought perhaps Miss Leslie had had a change in plans.

By twelve, Dermott agreed and drove out to Tavora House to find her.

Miss Leslie had left that morning with Joe and Mike, he was told. But Henderson would reveal little else to the man who called himself Lord Bathurst. Whether it was because the entire household knew of the lordship's ill treatment of Isabella or whether Henderson questioned Dermott's identity after Joe's orders to treat all strangers with suspicion, no further information was forthcoming from Tavora House.

Frustrated, Dermott returned to Higham and offered Mrs. Notkins a substantial sum to discover Isabella's whereabouts. At first the cook feigned offense, but she could no more resist the lure of so much money than she could resist the delicious gossip she might uncover. The high-and-mighty London nobleman was used to getting his way. And Miss Leslie wasn't known for her submissiveness. There was the possibility of high drama in the offing.

But her inquiries revealed only that Isabella had traveled south. Even the staff at Tavora House knew little else. "They left in a great hurry, you see," she explained to Dermott later that afternoon. "Miss Leslie and her bodyguards took only a change of clothes. Right strange, isn't it," she murmured, watching the lordship's face. And after Dermott's departure, when she was relating her story to her friends, she said, "And he didn't look a speck happy with the fact Miss Leslie left with both them men. His nostrils flared considerably, they did, and the tick over his right fine cheekbones were a sight to see. But he paid me like a true gentleman regardless my news weren't to his liking. Mark my words, when he finds Miss Leslie, none o' us want to be in her shoes. Not for all the tea in China," she added dramatically.

There was no point in fruitlessly searching England for Isabella, Dermott decided, testy and bad tempered at the thought of Isabella with Joe. Particularly after all Mrs. Notkins's gossip. What was the point?

He was too late. She'd found someone new. And considering her ready passions, he couldn't honestly say he was surprised. Isabella was hardly the kind of woman to go through life celibate.

Perhaps she'd gone to London. The simple luggage they'd taken suggested a short journey. He could find her there if he wished. But after hearing all he'd heard in Higham, he wasn't inclined to proclaim his love to a woman who'd already transferred her affections to someone else, a man she'd been with for weeks. A man he well knew could satisfy her needs.

He stood outside the King's Arms, immune to the bustle of the village, to the passersby who looked at him with the curiosity his fine London tailoring and fashionable air attracted. He felt deflated, irritable, out of temper. The sun was already low in the sky, but despite the late hour, he wasn't about to spend another night in Higham. And in his current mood he didn't relish returning to London, the thought of any sort of company distasteful. Only the Isle of Wight offered him the seclusion he sought—his remote home distant from any memories of faithless women.

Although his mother must be told—which necessitated a detour to Alworth. He fervently hoped his explanation wouldn't compromise her renewed pleasure in life.

Dermott rode through the night, hardly taking notice of the rain when it began, oblivious of the physical world, completely absorbed in his discontent. With each unwanted reflection of Isabella and her new beau, his moodiness increased, a chafing resentment overlooking the critical part he played in their ruined relationship.

His Thoroughbred set his own pace, as though understanding his master's travail, and only at first light did the black turn his head and whinny—reminding Dermott of the need for rest. When they reached St. Albans shortly after, Dermott made his way to the White Hart, where an ostler led his Thoroughbred away to be dried and fed. After dismounting, Dermott suddenly realized he was soaked through, hungry, and so exhausted, he felt as though he could fall asleep on his feet. Perhaps, he decided, he'd do well to rest a few hours before setting out again. Threading his way through the congestion of vehicles and passengers in the courtyard, he made his way to the inn entrance, his sodden clothes cold on his skin.

Just short of the veranda that fronted the inn, he came to an abrupt stop, his gaze on a familiar figure lifting two leather satchels from the boot of a mud-stained phaeton.

Brushing his hand over his eyes, his first thought was

that he must be mistaken. It couldn't be Joe Thurlow. He was tired, fatigue was obscuring his vision. Joe wouldn't be so far south.

But when the man turned from the phaeton with the satchels, Dermott went rigid. His pulse rate spiked as Joe strode toward him, a host of hotspur questions convulsing his brain, an explosive bitterness and jealousy inundating his senses.

A second later the two men came face-to-face in the light mist.

"I don't suppose you're traveling alone?" Dermott growled.

"Are you?" Joe's voice was cold. "You always have a woman close by, if I recall."

"Let's not fucking play games. Is she with you?"

"If she is," Joe curtly said, "I don't see that it's any business of yours."

"What if I make it my business." Challenge rang in every word.

"Haven't you hurt her enough, Bathurst? I recommend you leave her alone"—Joe smiled tightly—"and get out of my way."

"So you can have her for yourself? In Higham, it's said you two are damned friendly. Why don't we discuss that?" Dermott silkily murmured.

"Lonsdale nearly killed you, I hear. You wouldn't go your usual ten rounds from the looks of things. I'd suggest you walk away while you can."

"I'm going to see her, Thurlow, bloodied or not." Even at his peak, Dermott couldn't have lasted more than a few

rounds with Joe Thurlow, who had taken on all contenders for eight years. "Either way, makes no difference
to me."

Something unusual in his tone struck Joe's consciousness. A low-pitched humility, or was it the fact that the
depths of Dermott's eyes held a weariness of spirit he'd
never seen before. Or was it simply the recognition that he
faced an adversary who would fight to the last extremity?
"After the merry chase you led us, I doubt she'll talk to
you, you bastard. She's been crying since Wight."

Astonishment flared in Dermott's eyes. "What was she
doing there?"

"Looking for you," Joe spat out. "More fool her."

"My mother," Dermott breathed.

"And you must have changed your mind," Joe said in
disgust. "Not that I believed it anyway."

"I swear, I didn't know." Dermott's anger evaporated;
she had gone to see him. "We can argue about my character later." His tone was more reasonable now. "But I
haven't slept for three days"—he surveyed Joe's mud-
stained clothes—"and you don't look as though you spent
last night in a clean bed either. Could we sheath our
swords and let Isabella decide? Or is that a problem for
you?" The earl glowered faintly, his jealousy still not completely appeased.

"Do you love her?" Joe bluntly asked, watching Dermott's face as though the truth might be revealed in some
fleeting expression.

"Do you?"

"I asked first."

Both men were tall, the width of their shoulders identical, and had the earl been less recently on his deathbed, they might have been more nearly matched in strength. But their eyes held equal challenge, the air was charged.

"No offense, Bathurst, but your answer matters more than mine."

"Why, when you've been with her every day for weeks."

"Because she loves you."

Had Mrs. Notkins been less informative, Dermott might have been able to speak without cynicism. "What else do you know about Isabella, Thurlow, when you know such personal things as who she loves?"

"What the hell are you implying?"

"I'm implying you're a lot closer to her than I am."

"Christ, Bathurst," Joe resentfully muttered. "Do you think I'd bother talking to you if I thought I had a chance with her? I'd knock you flat, step over you, and forget I'd ever seen you. So answer me. Do you love her?"

"Until recently, I was under that assumption," Dermott growled.

"I'm going to need more than that." Joe's tone was brusque.

"Are you her vetting agent?"

"I am." Two words backed up by eight years of heavy-weight championships. "Are your intentions honorable?"

"A bold question, unless you're her guardian."

"At the moment I am, and I require a suitable answer if you wish to see her with your pretty face in one piece."

Dermott brows rose. "So we *are* rivals."

Joe's eyes held Dermott's for a tense moment, and then he shook his head. "She turned me down, Bathurst—for you, so believe me, I don't have any friendly feelings toward you. But I care about her and I won't have you play fast and loose with her again. She's been miserable since you left, more miserable after this morning on the island."

Where Dermott may not have completely believed him before, Joe's words about Wight were so unusual, his sincerity couldn't be questioned. "I don't know anything about your trip to the island, but I assure you, I'm here with the most honorable intentions." His voice was as grave as his expression. "I have a ring for Isabella, along with the offer of my hand and heart. Will that do?"

"It's enough for me. I can't speak for her." Joe suddenly smiled. "She may prefer your heart on a skewer."

Dermott returned Joe's smile with a tentative one of his own. "I'm not unaware of her possible outrage. If she throws me out, will you throw me back in? I intend to persist in this suit."

"I'd be pleased to throw you anywhere at all, Bathurst." Joe grinned. "But, unfortunately, she wants you, not me, so—that's what I want too."

"She's very easy to love, isn't she?"

"Damn right she is. You don't know how much I envy you. Now, don't fuck up again." His voice was brusque.

Dermott's mouth quirked into a grin. "Would you like to come along and advise me?"

"I think you can handle the charming of a woman with the best of them, Bathurst. You don't need any advice from me."

His gaze turned serious. "Thank you for taking care of her."

"I didn't do it for you."

"I know." Nervous, Dermott touched the ring in his

pocket, uncertain of his reception despite Joe's assurances, not at all sure he wasn't too late. He drew in a deep breath, then slowly exhaled. "Wish me luck."

"I suppose if someone has to have her, I'm glad it's you," Joe replied. He winked. "Although, looking like you do, you're going to need some luck."

22

❧

SECOND DOOR AT THE TOP of the stairs, Joe had said.

He'd also said Isabella loved him. Hopefully, he was right.

Dermott rapped twice, then winced. A little overzealous, he thought, shaking his stinging fingers.

But she called out, "Come in, Joe!" and he forgot his pain and jealously decided she sounded much too friendly. Why was she letting Joe into her bedroom anyway? He looked more grim than he intended when he entered the room.

Although, as it turned out, Isabella didn't notice because she was nowhere in sight. He surveyed the small bedchamber.

"Just leave my bag anywhere, Joe!" Isabella's voice came from behind a screen set before the fireplace, as did the sudden sound of splashing water.

What if he *had* been Joe? Dermott moodily thought. What if Joe weren't so damned polite and honorable? What if he'd taken advantage of the fact she was obviously taking a bath . . . *or*—green demons whispered—maybe Joe *had* already taken advantage.

With a loud thud Dermott dropped the satchel Joe had given him.

"Thank you!"

He didn't respond, and a moment later she hesitantly said, "Joe?"

"It's not Joe."

He heard her gasp, heard the slap of water hitting the floor, a spreading puddle appearing soon after under the linen screen.

"What do you want?"

No words of love in the harsh question, although he was realistic. Instead, the sound of wet feet striking the floor and brisk toweling-off reached his ears—an activity that momentarily stopped when he said, "I'd like to talk to you."

She didn't answer for so long, he found himself holding his breath.

He was alive! An unguarded happiness transiently disregarded her saner judgment—those more lucid thoughts surfacing seconds later, the ones that reminded her of all he was and all he'd done to her or not done to her. And all the conscious resentments that she thought she'd consigned to the past came flooding back.

She walked from behind the screen, her coarse robe obviously borrowed, a too-small robe. "I'll give you two minutes." Her voice was cool. "Where's Joe?" Dermott had to have come through him.

Her hair was dripping water onto the floor, and he was reminded of the first time he'd seen her at Molly's. But his brief nostalgia was almost instantly supplanted by umbrage at her concern for Joe. "He can take care of himself. Are you worried?"

"Of course I'm worried. You're not very trustworthy—among other things," she pointedly added.

"How *much* are you worried?"

She surveyed him, her chin slightly lifted. "I don't think that's any concern of yours. Actually, nothing about me is any concern of yours. You made that quite plain. Why are you here?"

She was angry, although he'd expected as much. What he'd not expected was his inability to control his jealousy. His voice was mild only with effort. "Joe tells me you were at the Isle of Wight."

She colored furiously.

"Did my mother write to you?"

"It doesn't matter if she did."

"I didn't know. I'm sorry I wasn't there."

"I'm sorry I went," she crisply noted, humiliated afresh at the memory.

A hush descended on the room.

"I owe you a great number of apologies," he finally said.

"Yes, you do."

He took a small breath because he wasn't in the habit of apologizing. "One of the reasons I'm here," he added, "is to offer atonement for everything and anything I may have done to hurt you. There's no excuse, but I want you to know I'm deeply sorry."

"And?"

Another small breath. "You're not making this easy."

"Like our meeting at Green Abbey. As I recall, you didn't respond at all to *my* pleas."

"I did to some of them."

Her smile was tight. "But then, that's automatic with you, isn't it—the sex. I'm talking about the part that requires empathy for another human being, I'm talking about you leaving me on the curb that morning with a casual good-bye. I'm talking about you not contacting me, not letting me know if you were alive, letting weeks go by without a word." Her voice sharpened. "You didn't care that I suffered for weeks . . . thinking the worst, thinking you were dead. But then, you never did care, did you?" she tartly declared. "So, you see, I'm not really in the mood to make anything easy for you. In fact, I'd take pleasure in having you—"

"Do you have something else you could put on?" His voice was constrained.

She snorted, disbelief flaring in her eyes. "You can't be serious." Her gaze raked him. "I'm raising holy hell, taking wrathful issue with your behavior and my frustrations, and you're getting a hard-on?"

"I'm sorry," he muttered. "But, Christ, you're practically naked in that damp, undersized robe—and looking incredible, as usual."

"And you've forgotten what you intended to say because your brains are in your cock."

He hadn't, of course, the ring burning into his rib cage. He'd only hoped to put her into a better mood first.

Obviously—that was a failure.

"I went to Higham to ask you to marry me," he brusquely said, because his unnatural, conciliatory pose had collapsed at her tart comment about the position of his brains. "And when I discovered you'd taken off with your bodyguards, one of whom the village of Higham considers your *very special* beau," he jibed, "I figured fuck it and fuck you and fuck all women in general. I was on my way back to Wight when I saw your sweetheart, Joe, outside."

"He's not my sweetheart." The phrase *marry me* was ringing in her ears, the loud reverberation capable of drowning out a devil's chorus of resentments.

"It's damned hard to tell." He was sulky, aroused and sulky, or sulky because he was roused to no damned purpose.

"Well, now you know," she calmly said, "and there's a better robe in that satchel if you want to throw it to me."

He looked at her. Her tone had changed, and she was regarding him with a faint smile.

"Why don't you come and get it," he murmured, instinctively recognizing female goodwill.

"The robe?"

"The robe . . . and the ring . . . and me and my thousand apologies." He paused and smiled. "And all my love too."

"You're sure now."

He nodded. "I don't know what my mother wrote, but it's all true."

"A lady might like to have such a message personalized." Her gaze slowly drifted down his body and then up again, coming to rest on his eyes. "You look like you're old enough to speak for yourself."

"I'm very wet." An unconscious evasion perhaps, after so many years of avoiding the words. Nervously rocking on the balls of his feet, his boots squished.

"Does that affect your voice?"

Motionless now, he chuckled. "No . . . and not my cock either."

She smiled. "How fortunate on both counts."

"Will you marry me?"

She cupped her ear, tipped her head slightly forward. "Isn't there usually some flowery preface to a proposal?" she queried. "Something poetic that has to do with mountains and rivers and endless time?"

"I love you like a fast river running through a mountain valley forever."

She laughed. "I'm sorry I asked."

"I really do love you, Izzy," he softly returned, "and I will as long as mountains exist and rivers run. Every day seemed endless without you, every night empty without you, every breath I took useless without you. Marry me— please?"

"Only if you promise to never fight another duel." Her voice went very quiet. "I couldn't live through that again."

He blew out a breath and gazed at her. "Ask something else. There's always going to be some young Turk wanting to test his luck. I can't promise you that."

"Then we'll have to stay in the country, far away from all the young Turks."

"A pleasant solution." His brows rose. "Are you saying yes?"

She nodded.

"Isn't there usually some flowery response to a marriage proposal?" he teasingly mocked. "Something having to do with gratitude and devotion?"

"I know you're grateful I'm willing to marry you and you'll be eternally devoted to me."

He chuckled. "That's it."

"How nice that we agree."

"How nice to look forward to living again," he whispered. "And I *am* sorry for everything."

"I know." She moved toward him, leaving wet footprints on the floor, and when he took her in his arms, he softly said, "I'm going to make you happy."

"I know . . ." she repeated, twining her arms around his neck. "And speaking of happiness," she murmured . . .

EPILOGUE

THE LOVERS WERE MARRIED a week later in the Tavora House chapel so Isabella's grandpapa could see her married—in spirit at least. And the dowager Countess of Bathurst joined Molly—Mrs. Peabody that day—Isabella's employees, and a select number of the ton in celebrating the joyful nuptials.

The Leslie relatives found themselves thwarted in their plans, not only by the marriage but by the birth nine months later of a son and heir to the earl and his countess—followed in quick succession by two additional children. And during the course of their marriage, the earl faithfully kept his promise to make his bride happy and in the process found the blessed joy and contentment that had so long eluded him.

NOTES

1. See page 51. It wasn't unusual for well-known courtesans to write their memoirs in their retirement years as an added source of income. Names of lovers could be omitted from the publications for a suitable sum of money, although Lord Chesterfield and/or the Duke of Wellington (sources vary on the attribution) weren't alone in their famous remark: "Publish and be damned." Because of the intimate nature of these memoirs, the accounts are fascinating glimpses into the temperaments and personalities of these noble lords. Harriet Wilson's early-nineteenth-century memoirs are some of the most interesting, for her friendships included many of England's most powerful and influential men. And contrary to popular belief, the life of a courtesan wasn't necessarily that of degradation and ruin. Many beautiful young ladies found prosperous, loving husbands in the course of their careers. Harriet Wilson's youngest sister, Sophia, was a case in point. With her older sisters in the business, she'd determined from a young age to parlay her youth and beauty into the ultimate triumph. And she succeeded. She charmed and married Lord Berwick, immediately became conscious of her new dignity, and cut herself off from her sisters and former acquaintances.

2. See page 67. Mrs. Fitzherbert, twice widowed and childless, first attracted the attention of the Prince of Wales in March 1784. He was twenty-two and she was twenty-eight. With the

Prince already notorious for his drinking and womanizing, she shrewdly resisted his persistent passionate advances, refusing to become his mistress until December 15, 1785, when he agreed to marry her in a secret ceremony. While the marriage wouldn't be legal under the Royal Marriages Act, in the eyes of the church it would be a marriage and that was sufficient for Mrs. Fitzherbert. One child, possibly two, were a result of their union (take your choice of inferences and evidence), but like so many of the Prince's relationships, it was threatened by his dissolute lifestyle and disreputable friends. By the winter of 1793, the love affair was over and Lady Jersey became the Prince's favorite. In addition, his mounting debts required he marry legally, which would increase his income by at least 100,000 pounds a year. A bride was found for him—his current lover, Lady Jersey, having a hand in her selection—and not by coincidence his cousin, Princess Caroline of Brunswick, proved to be unremarkable and plain. His remark on first meeting her is legendary: "I need a brandy." The marriage, which took place April 8, 1795, was disastrous, lasting only two weeks. Completely alienated from his wife and tired of his mistress Lady Jersey, in the summer of 1798 the Prince sought to win back Mrs. Fitzherbert. By midsummer 1799, she at last relented. Their reconciliation was now official. "A Gentleman of high rank and Mrs. Fitzherbert are once more 'Inseparables,' " announced The Times on July 4, 1799. "Where one is invited, a card to the other is a matter of course."

The next eight years were the happiest of their connection, although the Prince still spent a great deal of his time with his cronies.

3. See page 67. Princess Caroline was treated abominably by both the Prince of Wales and his family. As mentioned above, she was spurned almost immediately after the wedding and once her daughter, Charlotte—conceived in the brief two weeks of their conjugal union—was born, she was deliberately kept from her child. Miserable in the royal apartments,

she was allowed to rent a house at Blackheath in the summer of 1797, where she continued to live for many years. She was rumored to have a sizable sexual appetite, and stories circulated concerning her various lovers. Gossip had it she delivered a child in 1802, but no definitive proof survives. Until she was allowed to leave England in 1814, she lived apart from the court with only a few retainers in attendance.

Her stay on the continent fueled more scandal, and a commission was funded by the government to investigate the allegations of adultery for the purpose of a divorce action. The then Prince Regent was eager to divorce his wife. His only child, Charlotte, had died in childbirth, leaving the English throne without an heir, since all the royal dukes had morganatic marriages. Charlotte's death created a rush for the royal dukes to marry and provide an heir to the throne. The Prince Regent brought divorce proceedings against his wife in 1820 but failed in his attempt. Caroline died on August 7, 1821, and by her will wished to be buried in Brunswick with the simple epitaph: Here lies Caroline of Brunswick, the injured Queen of England.

4. See page 67. Beau Brummell was a favorite of the Prince of Wales's from 1794 until 1813. His reputation was founded upon his preoccupation with dress and his wit. The cut of his clothes, the fit of his gloves, and the shine of his boots were exquisite. The secret of good grooming, he said, was "no perfumes, but very fine linen, plenty of it and country washing." His major influence in male fashion was the introduction of two innovations: starched neckcloths and Hessian boots. With the Hessians came pantaloons—tight-fitting leggings—and before long, trousers were replacing knee breeches. Brummell had managed to discourage the excess of silk and satin, gold lace and multicolored embroidery so beloved of the Prince of Wales and his friends. The Prince and Brummell may have shared the same tailors— Schweitzer and Davison, Weston and Meyer—but only one of them was setting the fashion—Brummell. The Beau was

also responsible for introducing the left-hand-only style of opening a snuffbox.

Although the Prince and Brummell had been drifting apart for some time, July 1813 saw the final breach between them. Brummell and three of his dandy friends gave a ball at the Argyle Rooms and deliberately omitted the Prince Regent from their guest list. But when the Regent wrote to announce he would attend, they were forced to send him an invitation.

On the evening of the ball, the Regent was met at the door by the four hosts. Bowing to Pierrepoint on one side, the Prince turned to the next host, saw Brummell, and ignored him. The shocked silence was broken by Brummell's casual drawl: "Ah, Alvanley, who is your fat friend?"

Brummell and the Regent never spoke again.

In 1815, Brummell was forced to flee his debtors in England. He died at Calais in 1840.

5. See page 147. I'm always fascinated by the ingenious plumbing incorporated into some of the grand residences, at a time when indoor plumbing wasn't universally available. But water provision was in the hands of numerous private companies and had been as early as 1581, when waterwheels were pumping Thames water to parts of the City. At the end of the seventeenth century, the use of steam for power was made effective by Thomas Savery. In 1712, a pump worked by a Savery engine was installed at Campden House in Kensington. It could raise three thousand gallons an hour up fifty-eight feet to a cistern at the top of the house. In 1723, the Chelsea Waterworks Company was incorporated "for the better supplying in the City and Liberties of Westminister and parts adjacent with water." The company was responsible for introducing the first iron main in London in 1746, and by 1767, with the widespread use of steam pumps, 1,750 tons of water were pumped daily. By the time Celia Fiennes was touring England in the late seventeenth and early eighteenth century, water was being supplied for indoor fountains, baths, and water closets.

6. See page 187. Isabella, Marchioness of Hertford, was an ambitious woman. Born two years before the Prince of Wales, the daughter of the ninth Viscount Irvine, she became the marquess's second wife when she was just sixteen. Eighteen years her husband's junior, she was tall, handsome, and elegant—though a little portly. I've dated their relationship earlier for the purposes of the story, but she and the Prince didn't become involved until 1807. So why did the Prince replace one aged companion (Mrs. Fitzherbert was now fifty-one) with another almost as old (Lady Hertford was forty-seven)? Lady Bessborough's suspicion that the Prince was suffering from boredom—"alas! No cure—the disease is fatal" was probably correct. Lady Hertford was intelligent and worldly enough to both stimulate him mentally and satisfy him emotionally. Their liaison lasted ten years.

7. See page 228. I'm always intrigued when I come upon some rare note on female sexual amusements. While thousands of volumes have been written on male sexual diversions, women have not been as well documented—although certainly there is historical evidence of female sexual assertiveness (i.e., to cite only a few—Cleopatra, Empress Theodora, Heloise, Diane de Poitiers, and my all-time favorite, Catherine the Great of Russia). So in the interests of scholarship, the handsome young male shop assistants of Bond Street can be added as further proof that females have always found pleasant ways to entertain themselves. According to Malcolm (*Anecdotes of the Manners and Customs of London During the Eighteenth Century,* 1810), "as early as 1765 came the demand for strong, good-looking young men to serve in the ladies' fashion shops, who would create a market through the impression made by their personalities on the world of prominent ladies, and many scandals arose even in those days from this custom." At the end of the century Boettiger (*London and Paris,* 1799) says: "As the female population of this town is not devoid of feeling for a handsome male form and fresh red cheeks, the cunning Bondstreeters look out for well-built, personable

and promising shop assistants with whom a lascivious lady might very well care to exchange a couple of dozen more words than is warranted by her business."

8. See page 266. Since dueling was illegal, a closed carriage was often used to drive to the dueling rendezvous so the occupants wouldn't be recognized.

9. See page 269. The dire consequences of an error in loading a pistol is emphasized by Abraham Bosquett in this grim warning from *The Duel* by Robert Baldick:

"It has been known, that by injudiciously overloading, the Principal has been killed by his own pistol bursting, a part of the barrel having entered the temple; and it has frequently happened, through the same cause, that the pistol-hand has been shattered to pieces. I was present on an occasion when the Principal shot his own Second through the cheek, knocking in one of his double teeth, not by the ball, but by a part of the pistol barrel, that was blown out near the muzzle. I was also on the ground when a Principal shot himself through his foot, at the instep, which nearly cost him his life, but put an end to farther proceedings at the moment; his Second had given him his pistol at full cock, with a hair trigger, which he held dangling at his side, before the word was given, and in that position it went off. On another occasion the Second had charged his friend's pistol so carelessly, that the ball and powder had fallen out before he presented; when, but not till after receiving the opposite fire, snapping, and burning prime (the matter being then accommodated), he discovered, on making several attempts to discharge his pistol in the air, that it was unloaded."

ABOUT THE AUTHOR

SUSAN JOHNSON, award-winning author of nationally bestselling novels, lives in the country near North Branch, Minnesota. A former art historian, she considers the life of a writer the best of all possible worlds.

Researching her novels takes her to past and distant places, and bringing characters to life allows her imagination full rein, while the creative process offers occasional fascinating glimpses into the complicated machinery of the mind.

But perhaps most important . . . writing stories is fun.

Look for Susan Johnson's next thrilling
historical romance, available fall 2001
from Bantam Books

Turn the page for a sneak preview.

AN IMPOSING BUTLER ushered them into Frederic Leighton's studio, despite the inconvenient hour and the artist's custom of receiving by appointment only, and despite the fact that the artist was working frantically because he was fast losing the sun. Although perhaps a man like Leighton was never actually frantic, his sensibilities opposed to such plebeian feelings. Ever conscious of his wealth and position, particularly now that he'd been knighted, he cultivated friendships in the aristocracy, as his butler well knew.

The room was enormous, with rich cornices, piers, friezes of gold, marble, enamel, and mosaics, all color and movement, opulence and luxury. Elaborate bookshelves lined one wall, two huge Moorish arches soared overhead, stained-glass windows of an oriental design were set into the eastern wall, but the north windows under which the artist worked were tall, iron-framed, utilitarian.

Leighton turned from his easel as they entered and greeted them with a smooth urbanity, casting aside his frenzied air with ease, recognizing George Howard with a personal comment and his two male companions with a cultivated grace.

Lord Ranelagh hardly took notice of their host, for his

gaze was fixed on Leighton's current work—a female nude in a provocative pose, her diaphanous robe lifted over her head. "Very nice, Sir Frederick," he said with a faint nod in the direction of the easel. "The lady's coloring is particularly fine."

"As is the lady. I'm fortunate she dabbles in the arts."

"She lives in London?"

"Some of the time. I could introduce you if you like."

"No, you may not, Frederick. I'm here incognito for this scandalous painting." A lady's amused voice came from the right, and a moment later Alexandra Ionides emerged from behind a tapestry screen. She was dressed in dark blue silk that set off her pale skin to perfection; the front of the gown was partially open, but her silken flesh quickly disappeared from sight as she closed three sparkling gemstone clasps.

"It's you," Ranelagh softly exclaimed.

Her eyes were huge, the deepest purple, and her surprise was genuine. "I beg your pardon?"

"Alex, allow me to introduce Viscount Ranelagh," Leighton said. "My lord, Alexandra Ionides, the Dowager Countess of St. Albans and Mrs. Coutts."

"*Mrs.* Coutts?"

"I'm a widow. Both my husbands died." She always enjoyed saying that—for the reaction it caused, for the pleasure it gave her to watch people's faces.

"May I ask how they died?" the viscount inquired, speaking to her with a quiet intensity, as though they were alone in the cavernous room.

"Not in their beds, if that's what you're thinking." She knew of Ranelagh, of his reputation, and thought his question either flippant or cheeky.

"I meant . . . how difficult it must have been, how distressing. I'm a widower."

"I know." But she doubted he was distressed. The flighty,

promiscuous Lady Ranelagh had died in a riding accident—and very opportunely, it was said; her husband was about to either kill her or divorce her.

"Would you men like to stay for drinks? Alex and I were just about to sit down for a champagne." Leighton gestured toward an alcove decorated with various colorful divans. "I reward myself at the end of a workday," he added with a small deprecating smile.

A bottle of champagne was already on ice atop a Moroccan-style table, and if Alexandra might have wished to refuse, Leighton had made it impossible. Ranelagh was more than willing, Eddie had never turned down a drink in his adult life, and George Howard, like so many men of his class, had considerable leisure time.

Ranelagh seated himself beside Alex, a fact she took note of with mild disdain. She disliked men of his stamp, who only amused themselves in ladies' beds. It seemed a gross self-indulgence when life offered so much outside the conventional world of aristocratic vice.

He said, "Meeting you this afternoon almost makes me believe in fate. I came here to discover the identity of the exquisite model in Leighton's Academy painting, and here you are."

"While I don't believe in fate at all, Lord Ranelagh, for I came here today with privacy in mind, and here you all are."

He smiled. "And you'd rather us all to Hades."

"How astute, my lord."

He'd never been offered his congé by a woman before and rather than take offense, he was intrigued. Willing females he knew by the score. But one such as this . . . "Maybe if you came to know us better. Or me better," he added in a low murmur.

Their conversation was apart from the others, their divan offset slightly from the other bright-hued sofas, and the three men opposite them were deep in a heated discussion of the best routes through the Atlas Mountains.

"Let me make this clear, Lord Ranelagh, and I hope tactful as well. I've been married twice; I'm not a novice in the ways of the world. I take my independence very seriously and I'm averse, to put it in the most temperate terms, to men like you, my lord, who find amusement their raison d'être. So I won't be getting to know you better. But thank you for the offer."

Her hair was the most glorious deep auburn, piled atop her head in heavy, silken waves, and he wished nothing more at the moment than to free the ruby pins holding it in place and watch it tumble onto her shoulders. "Perhaps some other time." He thought he'd never seen such luscious peaches-and-cream skin, nor eyes, like hers.

"There won't be another time, my lord."

"If I were a betting man—"

"But you are." Equal to his reputation as a libertine was his penchant for high-stakes betting. It was the talk of London at the moment, for he'd won fifty thousand on the first race at Ascot yesterday.

He smiled. "It was merely an expression. Do I call you Mrs. Coutts or the Dowager Countess?"

"I prefer my maiden name."

"Then, Miss Ionides, what I was about to say was that if I were a betting man, I'd lay odds we are about to become good friends."

"You're too arrogant, Ranelagh. I'm not eighteen and easily infatuated by a handsome man, even one of your remarkable good looks."

"While I'm not only fascinated by a woman of your dazzling beauty but intrigued with your unconventional attitude toward female nudity."

"Because I pose nude, you think me available?"

"So blunt, Miss Ionides."

"You weren't interested in taking me to tea, I presume."

"We'll do whatever you like," he replied, the suggestion in his voice so subtle, his virtuosity couldn't be faulted. And that, of course, was the problem.

"You've more than enough ladies in your train, Ranelagh. You won't miss me."

"You're sure?"

"Absolutely sure."

"A shame."

"Speak for yourself. I have a full and gratifying life. If you'll excuse me, Frederick," she said, addressing her host as she rose to her feet. "I have an appointment elsewhere."

The viscount had risen to his feet. "May I offer you a ride to your appointment?"

She slowly surveyed him from head to toe, her gaze coming to rest after due deliberation on his amused countenance. "No, you may not."

"I'm crushed," he said, grinning.

"But not for long, I'm sure," she crisply replied, and waving at Leighton and the other men, she walked away.

Everyone followed her progress across the large room and only when she'd disappeared through the high Moorish arch did conversation resume.

"She's astonishingly beautiful," George Howard said. "I can see why you have her pose for you."

"She *deigns* to pose for me," Leighton corrected. "I'm only grateful."

"I'm surprised a woman of her magnificence hasn't married again."

"She prefers her freedom," Leighton offered. "Or so she says."

"From that tone of voice, I'm surmising you've propositioned her," Eddie observed. "And been refused."

Leighton dipped his handsome leonine head in acknowledgment. "At least I'm in good company, rumor has it. She's turned down most everyone."

"Most?" Ranelagh regarded the artist from beneath his long lashes, his lazy sprawl the picture of indolence.

"She has an occasional affair, I'm told."

"By whom?" Ranelagh's voice was very soft. "With whom?"

"My butler seems to know. I believe Kemp's acquainted with Alex's lady's maid."

"With whom is she currently entertaining herself then, pray tell?" The viscount moved from his lounging pose, his gaze suddenly intent.

"No one I know. A young art student for a time." He shrugged. "A banker she knew through her husband. A priest, someone said." He shook his head. "Only gossip, you understand. Alex keeps her private life private."

"And yet she's willing to pose nude—a blatantly public act."

"She's an artist in her own right. She accepts the nude form as separate from societal attitudes."

"Toward women," the viscount proposed.

Leighton shrugged again. "I wouldn't venture a guess on Alex's cultural politics."

"You're wasting your time, Sammy, my boy," Eddie told Ranelagh, waving his champagne glass toward the door through which Alex had exited. "She's not going to give you a tumble."

The viscount's dark brows rose faintly. "We'll see."

"That tone of voice always makes me nervous. The last time you said *We'll see*, I ended up in a Turkish jail, from which we were freed only because the ambassador was a personal friend of the sultan's minister. And why you thought you could get through the phalanx of guards surrounding that harem, I'll never know."

"We almost made it."

"Nearly cost us our lives."

"You worry too much."

"While you don't worry at all."

"Of course I do. I was worried Lady Duffin's husband was going to break down the door before we were finished last week."

"So that's why Charles won't speak to you anymore."

The viscount shrugged. "He never did anyway."

Alexandra didn't have another appointment, but feeling the need to talk to someone, she had her driver take her to Lady Ormand's. This time of day, she'd have to sit through the tedium of tea, but not for long, since Rosalind's guests would have to leave soon to dress for dinner.

She felt strangely agitated and annoyed that she was agitated and further annoyed that the reason for her troublesome feelings was Viscount Ranelagh.

He was just another man, she firmly told herself, intent on repressing her astonishing reaction to him. She was no longer a missah young girl whose head could be turned by seductive dark eyes and a handsome face. Nor was she some tart who could be bluntly propositioned, as though he had but to nod his perfect head and she would fall into bed with him.

But something remarkable *had* happened when they met, and try as she might to deny his startling sexual magnetism, she was impossibly drawn to him.

Unfortunately, that seductive power was his hallmark; he was known for the carnal eagerness he inspired in females. And she refused to succumb.

Having spent most of her adult life struggling against conformity, trying to find a role outside the societal norms for women of her class, *needing* the independence denied so many females, surely she was strong enough to resist a libertine, no matter how sinfully handsome or celebrated his sexual expertise. Regardless, she'd not slept with anyone since her disastrous affair with Leon.

Reason, perhaps, for her injudicious impulses now.

But after Leon, she'd vowed to be more prudent in her choices.

And Ranelagh would be not only imprudent but—if his conduct at Leighton's was any evidence—impudent as well.

Inexhaustible in bed, however, if rumor was true, a devilish voice in her head reminded her.

She clasped her hands tightly in her lap, as though she might restrain her carnal urges with so slight a gesture. Impossible of course, so she considered spending a few hours with young Harry, who was always so grateful for her company. But gratitude didn't have much appeal when images of Ranelagh's heated gaze filled her brain. Nor did young Harry's sweetness prevail over the shamelessly bold look in Ranelagh's eyes.

"No!" she exclaimed, the sound of her voice shocking in the confined space, as was the flagrant extent of her desire.

She desperately needed to speak with Rosalind.

Her friend was always the voice of reason . . . or at least one of caution to her rash impulses.

But when the last teatime guest had finally departed and the tale of her introduction to Ranelagh was complete, Rosalind said, "You have to admit, he's the most heavenly man in London." She shrugged her dainty shoulders. "Or England or the world, for that matter."

Alex offered her friend a sardonic glance. "Thank you for the discouragement."

"Forgive me, dear, but he *is* lovely."

"And he knows it and I don't wish to become an afternoon of amusement for him."

"Would you like it better if it were more than an afternoon?"

"No. I would prefer not thinking of him at all. He's arrogant and brazenly self-assured and no doubt has never been turned down by a woman in his life."

"So you're the first."

"I meant it facetiously."

"And you've come here to have me bolster your good judgment and caution you to reason."

"Exactly."

"And will that wise counsel suffice?"

Alex softly exhaled. "Maybe if you're with me day and night."

Rosalind's pale brows rose. "He's said to have that effect on women."

"And it annoys me immeasurably that I'm as beguiled as all the mindless women he amuses himself with."

"You wish your intellect to be in control of your desires."

"I insist on it."

"Is it working?"

Alex shoved her teaspoon around on the embroidered linen cloth for a lengthy time before she looked up. "No."

"So the question becomes—what are you going to do?"

"I absolutely refuse to fall into his arms." She glared at her friend. "Do you understand? I won't."

"Fine. Are there matters of degree then?"

"About what?"

"About falling into his arms. Would you, say, after a certain duration, or never in a million years?"

Alex shifted uncomfortably in her chair, tapped her fingers

on the gilded chair arm, inhaled, exhaled, and was silent for several moments more. "I'm not sure about the million years," she finally said.

"You're boring the hell out of me," Eddie grumbled, reaching for the brandy bottle at his elbow.

Sam looked up from his putt. "Go to the Marlborough Club yourself."

"I might." Refilling his glass, Eddie lifted it in salute. "As soon as I finish this bottle."

"After you finish that bottle, you'll be passed out on my couch," Sam murmured, watching the ball roll into the cup on the putting green he'd had installed in his conservatory.

"You don't miss a night out as a rule," Eddie remonstrated. "Did the merry widow's refusal incapacitate you?"

"Au contraire," Sam murmured, positioning another ball with his golf club. "I'm feeling first-rate. And I expect she's in high mettle as well."

"She turned you down, Sam."

"But she didn't want to." He softly swung his club, striking the ball with exquisite restraint.

"And you can tell."

The viscount half smiled. "I could feel it."

"So sure . . ."

"Yes."

"And you're saving yourself for her now?"

"Jesus, Eddie, if you want to go, go. I don't feel like fucking anyone right now and I drank enough last night to last me a week."

"Since when haven't you felt like fucking someone?" his friend asked, his gaze measured.

"What the hell are you insinuating?"

"That you fancy the voluptuous Miss Ionides with more than your usual casual disregard."

"After meeting her for ten minutes?" Sam snorted. "You're drunk."

"And you're putting golf balls at eight o'clock when you're never even home at eight."

Sam tossed his club aside. "Let's go."

"Are you going out like that?"

The viscount offered his friend a narrowed glance. "None of the girls at Hattie's will care."

"True," Eddie muttered, heaving himself up from the leather-covered couch. "But don't do that to me again. It scares the hell out of me."

Sam was shrugging into his jacket. "Do what?"

"Change the pattern of our dissolute lives. If you can be touched by Cupid's arrow, then no man's safe. And that's bloody frightening."

"Rest assured that after Penelope, I'm forever immune to Cupid's arrow," Sam drawled. "Marriage don't suit me. As for love, I haven't a clue."

"I'll drink to that," Eddie murmured, snatching up the brandy bottle as Sam moved toward the door.

But much later, as the first light of day fringed the horizon, Lord Ranelagh walked away from Hattie Martin's luxurious brothel pervaded by a deep sense of dissatisfaction. What had previously passed for pleasure seemed wearisome now; a jaded sense of sameness enervated his soul, and sullen and moody, he found no pleasure even in the glorious sunrise.

Walking home through the quiet city streets, he was plagued by thoughts of the bewitching Miss Ionides, wondering where she'd slept or, like him, not slept. The rankling thought further lowered his spirits. By the time he reached his town house, he'd run through a mental list of any number of men who might be her lovers, the image of her voluptuous body in the arms of another man inexplicably disagreeable.

It shouldn't be. He should be immune to the nature of her liaisons. He had met the damned woman only a day ago and there was no earthly reason why he should care who the hell she slept with.

He snapped at the hall porter when he entered his house, immediately apologized, and after making some banal excuse, pressed ten guineas into the servant's hand. When he walked into his bedroom a few moments later, he waved a restraining hand at his valet, who came awake with a start and jumped to his feet. "Go back to sleep, Rory. I can undress myself. In fact, take the day off. I won't be needing you."

His young manservant immediately evinced concern. The viscount was accustomed to being waited on, his family's fortune having insulated him from the mundane details of living.

Recognizing his valet's hesitation, Sam said, "I'll be fine."

"You're sure?"

"Why not take Molly for a walk in the park," the viscount suggested, knowing Rory's affection for the downstairs maid. "She may have the day off as well."

"Thank you, sir!"

"Go, now." Sam waved him off. "All I want to do is sleep."

In a more perfect world, he might have slept, considering he'd been up for twenty-four hours; but Miss Ionides was putting an end to the perfection of his world *and* to his peace of mind. He tossed and turned for more than an hour before throwing aside the blanket and stalking over to a small table holding two decanters of liquor. Pouring himself a considerable amount of cognac, he dropped into an upholstered chair, and sliding into a sprawl, contemplated the injustice of Miss Ionides's being so damned desirable.

Half a bottle of cognac later, he decided he'd simply have to have her and put an end to his lust and her damnable allure. He further decided his powerful craving was just the result of his not having what he wanted—her. And once he'd made love to the delectable Miss Ionides, that craving would be assuaged. Familiarity breeding contempt, as they say, had been the common pattern of his sexual amusements. In his experience, one woman was very much like another once the game was over.

But this particular game of seduction was just beginning, and glancing out the window, he took note of the position of the sun in the sky. The races would be starting soon at Ascot, the entire week scheduled with prestigious races, the Season bringing all of society to the track.

Including Miss Ionides, if he didn't miss his guess.

Rising from his chair, he walked to the bellpull and rang for a servant. He needed a bath.